TRACKING TERROR

HOWARD GIORDANO

Barringer Publishing, Naples, Florida
www.barringerpublishing.com
Cover, graphics, layout design by Lisa Camp
Editing by Carole Greene

ISBN: 978-0-9839050-1-1

Library of Congress Cataloging-in-Publication Data
Tracking Terror / Howard Giordano

Printed in U.S.A.

This is a work of fiction. All characters, organizations,
and events portrayed in this novel are either products of the
author's imagination or are used fictitiously.

The hero is commonly the simplest and obscurest of men.

Henry David Thoreau

TRACKING TERROR

FIVE DAYS AGO

Thursday, May 22

Roaches scrambled in every direction across the graffiti-covered walls on both sides of the tenement hallway. They looked as if they were trying to avoid a conflict that was none of their business. The squalid surroundings assaulted his senses: the urine smell overwhelmed him; the greasy film on everything he touched made him nauseous. The sooner this is over, the better, Pete Fanning thought.

"Police," he shouted. "Open up!"

He tilted his head and listened. No response.

Fanning balled a fist and hammered the paint-flaked door. He nodded to his partner, Detective Walsh, who had gripped his weapon with both hands and squatted low to one side. Four more narcotics detectives hung back in the hallway, ready to provide backup. Behind them, coming from another doorway, the sound of a crying baby broke the silence.

Fanning stepped away from the door. He brought his right knee up to his chest, held it there for a beat, and with the full force of his 175 pounds, slammed his heel into the door, meeting it just to the left of the knob. The dried wood splintered easily around the cheap, worn out lock. The door banged open, bouncing off the wall and back into his waiting hand. He pushed it back and thrust his 9mm Glock into the lighted, open space. An uneasy silence met him.

Walsh entered first, darting to the right in a semi-crouched position. Fanning followed to the left. The sparsely furnished, dingy living room smelled of the hallway filth. He motioned toward the kitchen. Walsh moved in that direction. Fanning stepped to the closed bedroom door. His back flat against the wall on one side, he twisted the knob with his free hand. When the door swung open, he saw the drug dealer standing at the raised window, prepared to climb out onto the fire escape.

"Freeze, Ramirez!"

The dealer turned. He pointed his 25-caliber automatic at Fanning and squeezed off a shot. The gun misfired.

Fanning heard the weapon click. A rush of adrenalin pumped through him. Death had taken his measure, and he wasn't waiting around to give it a second opportunity. He returned fire. Two of his four shots hit their mark, one in the drug dealer's head and the second smashing into his neck. The dealer's body whirled from the impact before going down. Ramirez hit the floor, and Fanning watched, squeezing the air out of his lungs. The baby in the next apartment stopped crying.

Blood from the severed carotid artery saturated the floor of the bedroom. Pieces of skull dotted the wall next to the window. The paramedics arriving on the scene told him Ramirez died instantly.

That's what Pete Fanning was thinking of on Monday, five days later, when he rear-ended Teddy's SUV.

CHAPTER 1

Monday, May 27

"Jesus, Pete, where the hell was your head? Didn't you see the damn car?" These were the questions he knew his wife, Anne, would fire at him. The only thing he'd be able to say would be, "Well, yeah, I guess I did, but what the hell, how often do you shoot and kill someone? I mean, as much as I was trying to put thoughts of that nightmare behind me, that's where my mind was, not on my driving, where it should have been."

Fanning had been tailgating an SUV down the on-ramp to the Grand Central Parkway. He neared the end and tossed a quick look over his shoulder to check the oncoming traffic. The approaching right lane was clear. He hit the gas pedal hard, thinking the SUV had moved out. The impact seemed disconnected, like watching a movie. He heard the sounds of crunching metal and breaking glass, but off in the distance. Fanning sat dazed for several seconds before he realized his car had stopped. When he refocused, he saw a hulking figure coming toward him, bent over like an NFL running back breaking toward a hole opening in the line. Instead of a football, he held a two-foot long metal pipe.

For the second time within five days, Fanning went for his duty weapon. This time it was not in his shoulder holster strapped under his arm. It was beneath his tan windbreaker on the seat next to him. He reached for it, stepped out and shoved the barrel of his 9mm Glock into the face of his road-rage attacker. "Police. Don't move!"

The man raised the pipe. Now he was the quarterback with a wide receiver in his sights. He saw the gun pointed at his head and froze. Wide-set eyes stared out over a flat nose, not in fear but in frustration. He was a boiling pot ready to explode. Fanning had locked a lid over him.

The man's dark complexion made Fanning think he might be a Latino, or maybe from the Middle East. Not certain he understood English, Fanning mouthed his words with a slow exaggeration. "Slowly lower your arm. Do it now!" The arm stayed suspended. "You understand what I'm saying?" No answer. Instead, the hulk rolled his eyes as Fanning's teenage son, Luke, did when his mother caught him sneaking out the back door after dinner without finishing the dishes. The big arm came down.

"Place the pipe on the ground. Do it now!"

He obeyed immediately, laying it on the pitched roadway. It tumbled to the curb.

"Now step back five feet." The man hesitated but when Fanning shouted, "Now!" he responded.

The man was big, easily two-thirty, maybe two-forty, with a broad neck, tree trunks for arms and a huge head of black curly hair that crept down over his wide brow like a sprig of ivy. He wore athletic sneakers, faded jeans and a clean, white tee shirt with Mickey Mouse painted across his expansive chest like a mural on a small wall. Weight lifter, Fanning guessed.

The parkway traffic motored noisily past, ignoring them. Fanning wondered if he could control the guy until he got a squad car there. At age forty and 175 pounds, he was still in fit condition, his five-foot, eleven-inch compact body kept in shape by regular workouts at the local YMCA. Yet, he doubted he would have a shot against the moose in front of him, who was nearly half again his weight.

"Step over to the curb and sit down," Fanning commanded. The hulk inched backward toward the curb, sat on the grass and folded his arms around his legs. Fanning punched in 9-1-1 on his cell phone and waited, his golf shirt sticky with perspiration. "Hey, yeah, this is Detective Sergeant Pete Fanning from Queens Narcotics...."

He completed his call and said to his attacker, "Unless you want me to cuff you, you'll sit there quietly." The man nodded and lowered his forehead to his knees.

Fanning strapped on his holster, keeping the flap unhooked. He picked up the pipe, surprised by its cool, smooth texture. The polished finish said it was new. He laid it on the back seat of his car and slipped into his windbreaker. Examining the two vehicles, he was amazed to see how little damage he had done to the man's mid-sized SUV. The left front headlight unit of his Ford Taurus was a jagged mass of chrome and glass. The fender, crushed against the tire, could be pulled free with a little well-placed leverage. He had drifted to the right just before he whacked the well-protected rear bumper of the SUV.

Fanning looked back at the hunched-over figure. "Hey, looks like I got the worst of it."

"Shoulda let you shoot me." The sound came from between the man's knees.

"How's that?" Fanning took several steps toward him and stopped when he looked up.

"I said...aah, the hell with it. Never mind." The big man lowered his head again.

Fanning waited while an American Airline jet from nearby La Guardia Airport roared upward, climbing into a bank of low-hanging clouds. It passed over them, so close he could smell the jet fuel. When he could hear himself again, he said, "No, tell me. You say I should have shot you?"

"Yeah, that's what I said," the hulk mumbled from between his knees. "Thought you were somebody else. Just forget it." His voice was weak, but he had no language problem.

"Shoot you? Why, man? You that determined to die?" He moved closer and picked up a musky scent of aftershave. "Why would you want to die?" Fanning asked again.

The hulk raised his head, reached behind and started to push up. Fanning's hand went to his holstered weapon under his windbreaker. "Don't move! Stay right there."

Sliding back down, the man wrapped his arms around his knees and lowered his head. Fanning had moved to his weapon to show he was not playing games. He considered what might have happened if it hadn't worked. Any attempt to take down that huge body down by physical force would be laughable.

When the man looked up, his eyes were watery. He tried speaking, but his heavy breathing choked back his words. He stopped, swallowed hard and started again.

"What do I have to live for? Since 9/11, my life has been a disaster. Lost my job, my two kids have been going through all sorts of hell at school, my wife's been called everything from a whore to God knows what, and by people we've known for years."

"Hey, you an Afghan?" It came out sounding as if he had asked him if he was a wizard.

"No way, man. I'm Indian. My family's from Delhi. Been here since '58. So's my wife's family. We both grew up in Brooklyn. Went to Brooklyn Tech."

Fanning remembered Tech was a high school well known for its powerhouse football program in the New York City area. He eyed his size again. "You play football there?" He noticed his breathing had slowed.

"Yeah. Made All-City, too, like anyone gives diddly-shit these days."

Fanning thought of his friend, Mike Allen, who, as an outstanding linebacker on their high school football team, had also made All-City. "What's your name?"

"Teddy. Teddy Vijay."

Fanning looked at him with a puzzled expression. "How'd you get that name? Teddy's not an Indian name, is it?"

"No. My given name is Teji Mahmud, after an Indian squash champion my folks liked. I changed it in high school to Teddy."

"Good move, man. Teji Mahmud doesn't sound like someone who could rip a person's head off on a football field." Fanning laughed then shot a look at Teddy. He was smiling. That's when he figured the potential for more trouble had eased. Still, he wished someone from the One-ten Precinct would show up soon.

"You a New Yorker?" Teddy asked.

The question surprised him. Once someone heard him speak, he could not imagine anyone taking him for anything but a New Yorker.

"Yeah, of course."

"Well, so am I. Born here," Teddy shot back. Then he asked, "How long you been a cop?"

It began to sound like an interview. Fanning had his fill of questions recently, from Internal Affairs after shooting the drug dealer, and now from Teddy. However, continuing a dialogue with the man just might keep things cool for a while.

Fanning ran his fingers through his prematurely iron-grey hair. "Fifteen years, Teddy, but if my life doesn't stop being threatened like it has been this past week, I might not get to retirement."

"Your life threatened? By who?"

"You mean, besides you? Some dirt-bag drug dealer up in the Bronx last week tried to take me out. First time in fifteen years on The Job, I had to shoot someone."

"The first time?"

"Yeah. Oh, I'd fired my weapon before, never at anyone. Gave me one hell of a scare…you know…seeing his gun pointing at me. I was lucky to get my shot off first."

"How'd you feel about taking someone's life?"

Fanning didn't have to think long. The image of bullets smashing into the drug dealer's head and neck, shattering his skull and severing the carotid artery, haunted him. The EMS technician told him Ramirez died instantly, but that provided little relief.

"Not too hot. I decided to take these next two weeks off to get through the trauma." He looked around at their two vehicles. "This is a hell of a way to start my vacation."

"Killing him was justified, wasn't it? It was you or him."

"The guy was garbage. Kind of what they got trashing the streets of Baghdad these days. No one's gonna miss him. Still, it's not easy taking someone's life."

"But that's part of being a cop, isn't it?"

"Right, but it's the one part I struggle with. I happen to believe life is precious, but if someone can't respect yours, he doesn't deserve to keep his."

He noticed Teddy winced. Was he going to say something? Maybe apologize for attacking him today. He just said, "I wasn't going to kill you."

"Yeah? Well, you could have fooled me."

"No, honestly, I just wanted to hurt you."

"So trying to do that, you were willing to be charged with assaulting a police officer with a deadly weapon?"

"I didn't know you were a cop."

Fanning grinned. "What's the difference? It's still assault with a deadly weapon."

"I lost it. You rammed me. All I could think was you did it intentionally …another guy using me as a scapegoat…again. I exploded. I decided no more crap from anyone."

"And that's why you came at me with the pipe? A little over the top, wasn't it?"

Teddy shrugged. His enormous shoulders touched the bottom of his earlobes. "Yeah, I know. The fall-out from 9/11…it's driven me nuts…destroying my life, my family. I can't handle it."

"How come you lost your job?"

"Same bullshit. Several big contracts cancelled because of the Iraq war. Said they couldn't afford to keep on two computer programmers. One troubleshooter had to go. I was it. I know it was more about me being a Muslim."

"That's rough," Fanning said. "You're not the only one hurting from the fall-out. There's the families of the three-thousand-plus who lost their lives. That includes my kid brother."

"He was in the World Trade Center?"

"A firefighter trying to save lives until the south tower folded on him."

"I'm sorry. How old was he?"

"Twenty-six. On The Job four years."

Damn! Fanning thought. This bozo just tried to take my head off. Now he has me talking about my brother. Gerry called that *taking the air out of the fire.* His life was all about fire fighting. "Jeez, Pete, I'm sorry," Gerry had said after passing the NYFD test. "I feel guilty not following you, but you know me and fire fighting." Fanning was relieved. No need for both of them putting their asses on the line every day. One ass in the family was enough. Yeah, sure.

Teddy started to stand. "How about you? You blame everyone from that part of the world?"

Fanning's hand went back under his windbreaker. "Hold it there, Teddy. I told you to stay put. If you move again, I'm going to cuff you. Don't test me."

Teddy lowered his large frame. "Sorry, man. It's hard to sit still and talk about it."

Fanning understood. Thinking of his brother going down with the south tower drove him wild. When it happened, he wanted to nuke the whole Middle East. It was weeks before he could discuss it with his wife without shouting. "It's the one time," he told Anne, "I can justify the idea of seeking revenge."

Fanning studied the large man. "Well, you better get past those feelings soon, Teddy, or you'll end up in worse trouble, like killing someone. That would fix it for your wife and kids."

Teddy sat still for several seconds. He sucked in a large supply of air, and the ears of Mickey Mouse inflated. When he exhaled, he started to shake. Fanning suspected his road rage behavior was not the norm for him. Coming eyeball-to-gun barrel with his service weapon certainly woke the guy up if it didn't scare the hell out of him.

Teddy asked again, "Are you holding me responsible, like everyone else, because I'm from that part of the world?"

"Hey, man, hard not to lump all you towel-heads together, don't you think?"

The towel-head crack slipped out before he could check himself. He was losing patience with Teddy's whining. Teddy showed no sign he had heard it so Fanning continued. "Those terrorists flying the planes…aren't they from a lot of different countries?"

"Yes...I mean, no...that is, they aren't sure where they came from." Teddy shook his head, beginning to become more animated. "Some had stolen Saudi ID's. You know that? Later the real Saudis, whose ID's they stole, turned up."

"Yeah, but don't forget, the al-Qaeda are Arabs, Pakistanis, Iraqis and Kuwaitis. They're from all of those countries, not just from Afghanistan. And some of those captured in Afghanistan turned out to be from Bangladesh, Tajikistan, Uzbekistan and a few of those other stan-countries that seem to have an axe to grind with the US."

"Correct. However, no one from India. You get my point?"

He was right. Fanning remembered the NYPD profiling problems with African-Americans. "Well, apparently we have a tough time telling one Mideast country from another."

"India is not a Mideast country. It's in South Asia."

When Teddy said it, Fanning realized he had indeed been lumping together all the nations of that part of the world, holding them responsible for his brother's death—not just the Egyptian, Mohammed Atta, and his band of scumbags.

"So, Teddy, aren't India and Pakistan ready to nuke each other to hell and back with their own disputes? Maybe take the rest of South Asia and the Middle East with them?"

"That's not going to happen."

"You know what worries me? Maybe Nostradamus got it right. The end of the world is going to start with the crazies in the Middle East."

"Come on, man. Osama bin Laden isn't the only crazy one in that area. But remember, Islam's fanatical jihad has nothing to do with India."

"Well, you better hope their nuttiness isn't catching. Nothing justifies the use of nukes by India or Pakistan, or the use of pipes, for that matter. Now, you get my point?"

"No argument from me. I think you know how sorry I am."

His look said he meant it. Fanning could tell. Teddy wasn't some low-life dope dealer apologizing as he's being locked up for selling crack in the schoolyard. The 9/11 fallout had pushed him to the end of his patience. Rear-ending him became the ultimate insult.

"Yeah, well, what the hell were you doing with that pipe in your car, anyway? Driving around with a two-foot metal pipe...hey, that can be considered carrying a concealed weapon, you know. The way you tried to use it today qualifies as a certain nuttiness, doesn't it?"

Once again, Teddy attempted to stand. "Did you look in the back of my SUV?"

"Stay sitting, Teddy," Fanning ordered.

Teddy settled back down. "I wanted to show you the box on the back seat, that's all."

"I noticed the box before, while looking over the damage. What's in it?"

"I was coming from Forest Hills Plumbing Supplies when all this happened," he said. He motioned to the damaged vehicles. "I'm converting a walk-in-closet into a second bathroom. The box is full of pipes and sink fixtures."

"Show me," Fanning said. He decided at this point that Teddy wasn't a flight risk.

Teddy rose up and Fanning trailed behind him to the SUV. A long line of vehicles had formed along the entrance ramp. One by one, they edged past the two vehicles parked to the side, each car patiently feeding out onto the parkway.

"Watch yourself," Fanning warned as they came up to the vehicle. "Stay on this side. And don't touch the door, Teddy. I can see okay through the window."

He could see the logo of Forest Hills Plumbing Supplies, visible on the side of the long packing box that rested on the rear seat. The top flaps were open, left that way after Teddy had reached in to grab the section of pipe he brandished when he came at Fanning.

"Still think I carried the pipe to use as a weapon?"

Before Fanning could reply, the flashing dome light of the squad car cut him off. It pulled out from behind the line of crawling cars and onto the grass. Two police officers jumped out holding their weapons.

"It's okay," Fanning called out, "put 'em away. Everything's under control."

The two police officers around the same age as his brother Gerry looked at Teddy, taking in his size and ethnicity. Fanning could see the questions coming. He remembered his towel-head remark and cringed.

"You okay, Detective? We were told you'd been attacked."

"I'm fine, boys. The 9-1-1 dispatcher must have misunderstood. Nothing more than a little old fender-bender. My fault. Too quick on the gas pedal."

"Nobody hurt?"

"Nobody. In fact, we've been here shootin' the breeze the whole while. We haven't exchanged driver and insurance info yet. Give us a few minutes. After, you can make your report. Then Teddy here can help me pull my fender off the wheel so I can drive it. Right, Teddy?"

CHAPTER 2

Seamus Slattery raised his eyes to watch. At the end of the long bar, the insistent ringing noise of the pay phone demanded the attention of an old man like an annoying mosquito. The phone hung on the wall outside the men's room door not three steps away. Slattery smiled, enjoying the way the man's head swiveled with indecision.

The telephone almost never rang, at least not while the old guy was there, which Slattery knew was practically every day. The Irish pub was a second home to many dockworkers who worked the Hudson piers in the Hell's Kitchen section of Manhattan. Everyone knew one another, bought each other beers and told endless stories about their grandkids. They returned daily to occupy the same bar stool as though their names were engraved on it.

The man continued listening to the pestering sound. He threw several looks down the length of the bar filled with other regulars. No one moved. With a slow resignation, he slid down from his stool, shuffled over to the black box and snatched up the receiver.

"Milligan's, wadda ya want?" He listened for a second and looked toward the far end of the bar. "Slattery…boyo…telephone's for ya," he yelled above the ambient elements of masculine voices and rising trails of cigarette smoke.

Colin Flynn turned toward his companion. "You expecting a call, Seamus?"

"Yeah, but I thought it was gonna be on my cell. Khalid misplaced my number again…the twat." Slattery looked at his watch and shrugged. Slipping from his seat, he said, "Well, least he's callin' when he said he would." He turned and limped toward the rear of the pub and the waiting telephone.

He returned after several minutes. Climbing onto his stool, he lifted his Guinness and swallowed the remainder of the dark ruby liquid. Flynn had fixed his gaze on him as though he expected a report on the phone call. Slattery set his glass on the bar and looked at his watch again. "Gotta meet Masab in two hours. He's delivering the Arabs' contribution Khalid promised. I'll be dropping it off with Tommy on my way home."

"Jesus, Seamus, I wished we didn't—"

"I know, I know, you've beaten that tune to death, Collie. We've no choice, as I see it."

"But—"

"Colin, damn it! Listen to me. When you and your brother Tommy were soliciting funds here to support our cause back in Belfast, before that feckin' treaty, we could count on a steady flow of cash from our good people in the States. Now we're on our own. Those sources, you know, all but dried up…skittish about contributing. We can't be choosers, can we, fella?"

"If the Westies were still around. Wouldn't need the help of those damn Arabs, now would we? Be a walk in the park for the likes of Jimmy Coonan and Mickey Featherstone, them runnin' things around here."

"Well, they're not around anymore, so it's up to us," Slattery said, trying to restrain his anger with his friend's impatience and lack of understanding.

For the next few seconds, Flynn shuffled several Guinness bar coasters in front of him. He looked like a Four-Card Monte dealer. Slattery listened to the rumbling sounds from two heavy trucks making their way down Eleventh Avenue toward the Holland Tunnel. Their air brakes punctuated their noisy arrival at the red light on the corner.

Slattery blinked then shot an appraising look at Flynn. His friend's wrinkled brow gave the impression that he'd gotten a whiff of a bad smell. "What's the matter?" Slattery asked.

"I just don't trust those damned Bedouins. They'd murder their own mothers if push came to shove. Sorry, but I still see those flailing bodies on their way down from the top floors of the Trade Tower. I get the willies every time we have to meet with them in their damn mosque."

Slattery frowned. "Come on, Collie, this'll be over soon. Twelve more days. Besides, they need us as much as we need them." He gestured to the bartender and slid his glass forward. "Give 'em another too, Paddy. He could do with a bit of cooling down," he said. He let out a chortle.

"Shit!" was all Flynn could add.

Slattery continued speaking. "Understand this, Colin; you getting that maintenance job at the racetrack three months ago was like finding the key to the Arabs' vault. We'd not be able to pull this off without their financing, and it's a sure wager they couldn't get by the gate on their own. And then wouldn't bin Laden be disappointed?" Paddy returned and placed two brimming glasses of Guinness on fresh napkins in front of them. "Thanks, Paddy. Next jar's on him."

The bar man moved away, and Slattery turned toward Flynn, playfully punching him in the shoulder. "Let's not forget the hundred fifty-thousand donation they're makin' to our account. Let it be, lad."

They fell silent, taking time to sip their brews. Slattery took in the collegial surroundings of this pre-prohibition dated tavern, a landmark on

Manhattan's west side. During the IRA's heyday in Northern Ireland, he remembered that many a fugitive looking for temporary sanctuary had found his way to this establishment. Hell's Kitchen, once a bastion of poor and working-class Irish-Americans, had undergone tremendous gentrification over the past three decades because of its proximity to midtown. The patrons of Milligan's, nevertheless, had a long history of support for the cause of the IRA, despite the waning fervor among others since the treaty of 1998.

"What time you meeting him?" Flynn asked, breaking into the Irishman's reverie.

"Between 7:15 and 7:30, at the Vernon-Jackson Station." Slattery checked his watch again. "Best be on my way no later than six. Don't know how quick I'll get a cross-town bus to Times Square. They don't appear to keep to a consistent schedule."

"Khalid gonna have the chemicals together and mixed in time for Pearse to build and wire it?"

"I hope so, though I don't think Pearse will need a whole lotta time. He's such a feckin' genius at bomb makin'."

Mike Allen entered the subway at Times Square on his way home from work. He swiped his transit card across the reader and pushed his large frame through the subway turnstile. The man at the next turnstile spun through and made a sharp left, crossing into Allen's path, causing him to pull up. He scowled at the man and watched him limp toward the stairway down to the Queens-bound train platform. "Shithead," Allen grumbled. He followed him to the stairs.

Allen had gotten a good look at the man's face. He was certain he had seen this rude stranger before. But where? Nothing leaped out at him. He wondered if the queasiness in the pit of his stomach had something to do with it. Maybe he was just another commuter, someone he'd noticed in the subway during his nightly travels home. They were going in the same direction, weren't they…to Queens…taking the same train?

He watched the man hobble along the platform, darting looks back into the dark tunnel, in the direction from where the Number 7 train would be coming. He stopped mid-way, leaning out over the edge, shifting his weight from one foot to the other like an expectant father.

Allen walked to within a few yards and stopped. Well, shit, we're both waiting for the same Flushing Line train, he thought again. Yeah, that's why he looks familiar, expecting this reasoning to resolve the familiarity question and relieve his queasiness. Instead, he continued to struggle with the man's image. Suddenly, a vision came into focus. He stiffened. Good God, it couldn't be, he thought. Ten years later? Impossible! Yet….

Allen slipped out his wallet and removed the folded *New York Times* article, examining the photo of the terrorist. He turned his attention to the stranger standing a few yards away and, without hesitation, tossed out any thoughts of it being the same person in the photo. The left hand of the man on the platform lacked two fingers at the knuckles.

He was guilty again of ghostly imaginings, a habit he had fallen into since the bombing ten years ago. He felt his heartbeat slowing. He pushed the stranger out of his mind while thoughts of his wife's tragic death flooded in.

Allen studied the ten-year-old, tattered *Times* article, bringing it up to his face in the dim light of the subway platform. The small photograph of the IRA terrorist buried among the painful text caused him to wince as he absorbed the Irishman's impudent expression. The man in the photo wore his hair cropped short, military-style. A sharply carved jaw jutted forward like the prow of an old sailing ship, supporting an angry mouth that turned down at the ends. Pencil-thin eyebrows and pointy ears seemed at odds with the flat nose buttered across his face, giving the impression of a pug with a losing record. Hatred burned unchecked in the charred cavities of his eyes while a soft wool peak cap dangled arrogantly on the end of the middle finger of his left hand, a *fuck you* expression for his English enemies. He looked to be in his late thirties. The caption identified him as Seamus Slattery, an IRA soldier, the leader of the Belfast group responsible for the bombings at the railway stations in London.

Again, Allen tried to glean some sense from the senseless act. How in God's name can someone intentionally kill innocent civilians and call himself a soldier? Some day he'd like to ask that of Seamus Slattery.

He pressed his bulky frame against the graffiti-covered steel post at the edge of the platform. His forty-year-old blue eyes strained under the low-level glow of the neon fixtures above him, lights that lined the full length of the steamy subway platform. In what must have been his two hundredth reading, he had all but memorized each tormenting word.

"For the first time in more than seven years, the group has inflicted casualties among ordinary civilians in England...."

The vein in his left temple pulsed. Those God-damn sons-a-bitches! Forty wounded, six dead. For what? What the hell did it accomplish? He'd asked himself that question over and over.

"Mikey, why keep tormenting yourself?" Pete Fanning asked the last time they shared a pitcher of beer. "Throw the clipping away. All you're doing is keeping the anger alive. What for? It's not going to bring back Kathy."

Allen didn't want to hear his best friend's well-meant advice. Strangling the life out of Seamus Slattery would satisfy his need for revenge. Only then would the Atlas-like burden he carried for allowing his wife to travel to England without him, be eased—but never relieved. He continued reading.

"The bombs that rocked two central London railroad stations on Monday appear to signal a change of tactics by the Irish Republican Army...."

Allen had spent the last ten years trying to put the shattered pieces of his life back together. He struggled with it every waking hour, trying to understand why it happened.

The Number 7 train rumbled into the Times Square station, the final stop in Manhattan. He refolded the page along its well-defined creases and slipped the clipping back into his sweaty leather billfold before shoving it into the hip pocket of his black gabardine trousers. He watched the stranger side slipping back and forth, anticipating where the doors would open. Allen had no such problem. He knew from years of commuting where to stand.

The car's double doors opened in front of him. Allen moved his six-two, linebacker frame to one side, making room for the exiting passengers. A wave of coolness washed over him as he strode inside the empty air-conditioned car. He slid across a seat to the window end, curled his back into the molded form, and propped his elbow on the dusty window ledge.

The limping stranger entered the same car through the next set of doors. He stood, gripping the pole in the foyer area. Soon the train would reverse direction for the fifty-five minute trip across Manhattan, under the East River, then through the populated neighborhoods of Queens, past Shea Stadium and into the Flushing Main Street station, the end of the line. Within minutes, it would reverse its monotonous circuit back to Manhattan.

The collected perspiration beading on Allen's wide forehead evaporated fast. He removed the black clip-on bow tie he wore at his bartending job and put it in his pocket. The damp underarms of his white dress shirt, unbuttoned at the collar, made him shiver in the cooler air. During the trip across Manhattan, the empty car would take on passengers until it filled. It would remain crowded until it reached the Jackson Heights station, where he would get off, descend to the street below and walk the six blocks to his house—a routine he followed every evening.

The train pulled from the station. Allen slumped to one side, peering out the dirty window into the tunnel's murkiness. Lighted arched stanchions rhythmically whipped past, each glowing torch reflecting on the cold glass that supported his head. Why did I give in to Kathy's Celtic stubbornness, he thought, agreeing to let her go on ahead? "Can't you wait?" he had argued. "I mean, my vacation begins next week. We can fly over together then."

"But I'll miss the christening if I wait," she insisted. "Mike, it's my sister's first child. It's important that I'm there."

He thought again of Kathy's train trip from Maidenhead into London's shopping district to shop for a christening present. A birth and a death—the connection always drew pain. She had no doubt taken a moment to freshen up after the long ride. The two bombs exploded in sequence, two minutes apart. The first went off in the lost package area at Victoria Station and the other at the Paddington Station in the ladies room where they found Kathy's body. Scotland Yard assured him that her death had been instantaneous, as if he might find solace in that fact.

Allen ignored the rush for the remaining seats by those boarding at Grand Central, the last station in Manhattan. The doors closed, and the train lurched into motion, embarking on the six-minute crossing under the East River to Queens. The stranger remained standing, his head swiveling side to side.

Vernon/Jackson, the first station on the Queens side of the river, was located in a desolate industrial area. The figure waiting on the platform surprised Allen. He tried to remember the last time he saw anyone get on or off at this station.

The limping stranger let loose of the pole when the train stopped, and he plunged toward the opening doors. With his torso halfway out, he beckoned to the man on the platform who had been scanning the cars. The man spotted the waving friend and boarded the car before the doors snapped closed behind him. With little formality, he nodded and handed the stranger a brown envelope.

Both men moved toward seats across the aisle from Allen. The limping one stumbled when the train lurched into motion. His foot came down on the instep of a man in an adjacent seat. The rider jerked back his leg, his face registering anger when the offending stranger offered no apology. Turning away in disgusted resignation, the rider went back to his newspaper. The incident went unnoticed by most of the passengers.

Allen, unaware he had been staring, was surprised when a challenging voice confronted him. "And what would ya be lookin' at? Do ya think you might have a problem or somethin'?"

It was the unmistakable Irish lilt, not the words, that caught Allen's attention. "Excuse me. Are you talking to me?" His voice was calm.

"I was asking why ya staring? Ya haven't stopped since I came aboard. You know me?" The scowl and tone was hard to miss. "Do I look familiar?" The voice had grown louder and angrier. When he spoke, he flashed his yellowed, cigarette-stained teeth and fleshy gums.

The surrounding passengers sneaked looks, newspaper pages flipped noisily, and feet shuffled on the car's surface.

The Irishman waited for a reply.

Allen, alerted by the challenge, scrutinized the two men as though he was seeing them for the first time. The Irishman's disheveled appearance—his baggy, European-style slacks; Nike running shoes; dark, short-sleeve shirt unbuttoned at the neck; his narrow, soiled red tie with the knot pulled down for relief from the heat—made him ordinary and unimposing. He held the delivered brown folder on his lap, secured by a left hand with two missing fingers.

The new arrival with a swarthy complexion and dark hair wore a buttoned and pressed business suit over a white dress shirt and dark tie. The contrast of attire was glaring. Except for the antagonistic demeanor of his questioner, Allen would have paid them little attention.

He ignored the man's question, turning toward the window and closing his eyes. When he opened them, he looked out into the tunnel's darkness. The Irishman's reflection filled his window from across the aisle. He watched him bending in toward his companion, talking in a low voice, resigned to having cowered Allen into silence.

Mike Allen never backed off from a fight, but a dumb confrontation like this, he decided, was not going to provoke him into doing something foolish. The Irishman was an asshole.

The train left the Hunters Point Station. Allen continued to study the Irishman through the window's reflection until the train emerged into daylight and washed out his image. Once in the open, the train began its gradual assent to travel elevated over the crowded neighborhoods of Queens. The queasiness he had felt earlier returned.

It was a warm, late May summer evening with the sky losing light rapidly. Visibility waned and dark shadows would accompany his walk home under the arcing glow of the overhead white street lamps.

The Irishman still bothered him. Allen turned his attention to the series of large outdoor advertising billboards cruising past his window, some rising from the street below, others plastered to the sides of multi-storied commercial buildings or mounted on their rooftops.

**FLY AMERICAN—SCHICK BLADES SHAVE
CLOSER THAN EVER—DKNY IS NEW YORK
FUN-FILLED JAMAICAN HOLIDAYS.**

He read each word, eyeing their accompanying visuals with mild interest.

**CATS, THE MUSICAL TO SEE—AVIS TRIES HARDER—
THE *NEW YORK TIMES* COVERS IT ALL.**

As the *New York Times* billboard zipped past, Allen jerked his head rearward, his eyes locked onto the poster until it was out of sight. For a second time, his jogged memory exploded, except this time it had him sucking breath like a child trying to avoid discovery in a game of hide-and-seek. His hand went again to his billfold, stopping when he realized the Irishman had paused in his conversation and looked in Allen's direction.

Two passengers standing in the aisle edged sideways between the Irishman and Allen in preparation for detraining at the Queensboro Plaza Station. When they cleared out, he saw the darker man stand up and make his way toward the middle doors. The train slowed, and Allen's pulse quickened. He watched to see if the Irishman would also get up. Instead, he remained seated and head-bobbed a farewell to his departing companion.

Commuters transferring to the Flushing Line crowded the express platform. The train stopped and the doors opened. Those exiting riders switching to the Astoria Line muscled their way out of the car through the maze of impatient passengers boarding. Moments later, newcomers filled every vacated seat. Those too slow in boarding jammed the aisles, left standing to read the car-card ads above their heads. Allen could see the Irishman's legs and feet through the forest of standing riders. His face was no longer visible as the train left the station.

Allen reached for his billfold, removed the Times clipping, unfolding it to re-examine the picture of Seamus Slattery. He scrutinized the ten-year-old photo, trying to imagine how the years might have transformed the terrorist. His military haircut, now gone and replaced by a full head of tangled graying hair, was the most apparent difference. The jutting jaw and pointy ears were still in evidence. Allen pictured the man's earlier angry look when he had accused him of staring. He projected it alongside of the arrogant expression in the photo where the terrorist dangled his wool cap on the now missing tip of the middle finger of the left hand.

He was convinced of the strong resemblance, despite the absent digits. The reality of this chance encounter astonished him. How could an IRA terrorist be riding a New York City subway unchallenged? He came off as any working stiff on his way home. Allen fought back denial, wanting to believe it was Seamus Slattery. He refolded the article. What should I do? If it's him and he gets away, I'll be sorry for the rest of my life.

At the Bliss Street Station, Allen watched the half-dozen young recruits from the area's Police Academy, dressed in grey and blue student uniforms, board the car and cluster at one end. He often ran into these rookies, always picturing himself among them, imagining what his life would be like if he had been accepted fifteen years ago. He scored well, above the norm on the written exam in fact, and made a joke of the physical agility test. The slight heart murmur detected during his medical exam, however, had prevented him from joining that rookie class with his friend Pete.

Over the next several station stops, passengers exited the car with practiced speed until Allen could again see the Irishman's face through the thinning crowd. Familiar landmarks passed his window. He could see street lamps coming alive, the setting sun disappearing behind the mountain range of apartment buildings in the distance, and in the western sky, a jet airliner winking its lights turned into its final flight path toward nearby La Guardia Airport.

His chest felt heavy. He began to sweat again. Was he being rational? Was he trying to wish this bizarre chance encounter true?

The train slid into the Woodside Station, and the Irishman stood. Without looking in Allen's direction, he limped to the door in front of several other departing riders. In an instant, Allen decided. He jumped to his feet before the closing doors could shut him off from the terrorist forever, and darted out onto the platform. A small wall of slow shuffling people formed in front of him. He hung back as they headed for the down staircase and followed at a safe distance.

At the change-booth level, the Irishman turned left and went down the next flight of stairs to the street. Allen raced to the open stairs on the opposite side, careful not to lose sight of the man. At the base of the steps, he peered across the wide span of Roosevelt Avenue and watched the man stop at a newspaper stand nestled under the staircase. When the Irishman stepped away, Allen noticed the brown folder tucked under his arm was gone. A newspaper had replaced it.

The man hurried along Roosevelt Avenue and disappeared around the corner. Allen crossed the avenue, melting into the shadows on the opposite side. He followed down the tree-lined residential street, careful to use the large, full-leafed oak trees and bumper-to-bumper parked automobiles as a cover. It was not difficult keeping the Irishman in view as that hour produced little foot traffic. Most residents had already arrived home.

The quiet Woodside residential neighborhood developed into a mixture of six-story, pre-war apartment buildings and rows of red brick, two-family homes, not unlike the one he owned in Jackson Heights. A narrow driveway to a rear garage separated each home. Like sentries for the two-family homes, the tall apartment buildings framed the ends of each street.

Irish residents had populated Woodside in droves over the last twenty years, many of them recent immigrants settling with or near relatives already established in the area. Heavily Irish and heavily Catholic, he thought. A logical safe haven for a Seamus Slattery.

The headlights of an oncoming car created a flood of broken shadows among the trees, causing a brief whiteout. The car passed. He picked out the form of the man as he turned to go up the two steps to the doorway of a house. Allen stopped behind a wide oak, trying to shrink his large body. He watched as the Irishman fumbled with his door key. Lights glowed through the downstairs windows. The second floor was dark. The man went in, closed the door. Moments later, Allen saw the upstairs lights go on.

It was nearing midnight when Pete Fanning joined his wife Anne in bed. Ten minutes later the ringing phone broke through the sound of the TV, muffling the punch line of a joke Jay Leno was telling about Teddy Kennedy. He looked toward Anne, who had already curled up on her side, and then at the lighted digital clock on the nightstand, before hitting the remote's mute button.

Picking up the phone, he said in a low voice, "Hello."

"Pete, Mike. Sorry to bother you guys this late, but I need to talk to you about something."

"Sure, Mike. Anything wrong?"

"Huh, uh…no. Nothing's wrong. Just need to ask you something."

"Hold on," Fanning said, switching the phone to his other hand in order to turn away from Anne. She had pushed herself upright, plumping the pillow behind her. "Mikey, what's up?"

"I need to talk to you. Can you come by the restaurant tomorrow night after my shift?"

Fanning had become accustomed to Allen's growing seriousness over the last few years. He tended to make large the most insignificant matters. Fanning had learned not to play into it.

"Sure, pal."

"I'm off at seven, so come by a few minutes before. You're not working, are you? Didn't you tell me you were taking the next two weeks off from work?"

"Vacation…starting yesterday. But it didn't begin quite the way I expected." He started to go into the story of his fender-bender, but he saw the irritated expression on Anne's face when he turned toward her, a clear signal to cut the conversation short. He winked. "I'll tell you when I see you," he said to Allen. "Should we plan on having dinner there?"

"Yeah, if it's okay with Anne. I'd say bring her along, but I need to talk to you alone."

"Okay, Mikey, see you around seven."

CHAPTER 3

Tuesday, May 28

Pete Fanning pulled on his Yankees cap and stood watching the starting nine of Forest Hills Junior High School shagging flies and fielding grounders. He remained standing until he caught his son's eye and waved. Luke raised his glove to ear level and wiggled it, trying to be cool with his greeting, as though it was an ordinary event to have his father sitting in the stands.

Yesterday, Luke had announced at dinner the coach had decided to let him start at first base the next day, the last game of the season. As the youngest eighth grader to make the squad and used sparingly as a pinch hitter or pinch runner all season, Luke exploded with excitement.

"What do you think, Dad? Can you come? It starts at three. Can you…can you?"

His son's Opie-like innocence was pure joy to him. "Buddy boy, I'll be there. I promise."

Sitting down, he pulled up the sleeves of his sweatshirt, propped his elbows against the worn wooden step of the tier behind, tilted his face skyward toward the warm rays of the late afternoon sun and smiled. Finally, he would enjoy seeing his son play ball.

Fanning thought of the many times he'd wished his own father had felt that way. If he had, he might have witnessed his own teenage son gracefully pulling down long fly balls hit to center field, where the high-school senior covered the acreage better than any center fielder in the recent history of Bryant High School. At least that's what the coach told him when he announced that a major league scout was going to be in the stands the day of the final city championship game. The scout saw him but his father never did.

Forest Hills won. The final score was twelve to seven. Luke made one throwing error. Nerves, Fanning thought, but he was near perfect fielding his position. He batted at the bottom of the order, had a single, walked once and struck out once. One for three—not a bad day for a seven-inning game. He knew Luke would get better, his arm stronger.

They hugged after the final out and walked together to the parking lot with Luke waving to his teammates. "Good game, Frankie. Way to go, Gerry. See you tomorrow."

Fanning moved the Taurus into traffic and looked over at his son's face. It radiated with pride.

"I'm glad you came today, Dad."

"I am too. I wish I could do it more often. It's difficult right now with the assignment I got."

Fanning's thoughts drifted back to the shooting. He pictured the grizzly scene in the drug dealer's apartment. The fallout of the incident had led to this rare opportunity to see his son play ball. At least something good came of it. Thinking aloud, he said, "Tough way to earn time off."

Luke turned toward him with a quizzical look. "You mean shooting that guy?"

The question took Fanning by surprise. He forgot Anne had told Luke the story. He'd become angry with her. It was nothing he felt comfortable sharing with his thirteen-year-old son.

"That's what I mean," Fanning said. "It wasn't something I liked doing."

"But you had to do it, didn't you?"

"Sure. I might not be here if I hadn't."

They rode in silence until they reached their street. Luke spoke up. "Dad, I'm glad you did."

Turning off the engine in the driveway, Fanning reached over, and, wrapping one arm around Luke's shoulder and pulling him toward him, he kissed the top of his son's tousled head.

Anne stood at the counter chopping onions into tiny pieces as Fanning and Luke came through the kitchen door. A bowl of diced tomatoes sat next to another small bowl full of shredded cheese. "So how'd it go?" she asked without turning around.

"We won," Luke shouted.

Anne wiped her hands across her apron and held out both arms to Luke. The boy rushed into his mother's embrace. When he pulled away he asked, "What's for dinner?"

"Tacos, your father's favorite, but he's not staying for dinner."

Luke looked back at his father. "You have to go out?"

"Yeah, afraid I do. Mike asked me to meet him after work. It's something important. I couldn't say no. Your mom's punishing me by making tacos."

Luke snickered. He stepped toward the refrigerator. "Mom, okay if I have a Coke?"

"Just one," she said, turning back to her chopping. "You're going to be eating soon."

"While you're at it, bring me one too," Fanning said, taking a seat at the kitchen table.

Luke sat down opposite his father, sliding one of the cans across the table.

Anne walked to the table and put her hands on Luke's shoulders. "Why don't you go upstairs, get out of your uniform and wash up. We'll be eating in fifteen minutes." She looked across at Fanning. "You better get ready too or you'll be late."

He remained seated until Luke disappeared up the stairs. "You're not pissed, are you?"

"Pete, you go. Take care of what you have to. You always do that anyway."

"Come on, Anne, what was I supposed to do? Mikey's got something bothering him. He wouldn't have called if it wasn't important."

"You know, Pete, everything seems important to you but your own family."

"That's bullshit! How the hell can you say that?" He got to his feet.

Anne spun around to face him. "How?" she asked. "When was the last time you spent an entire day with Luke and me?"

His arms flew toward the ceiling. "It's my job. I can't help it if it's not a nine to fiver."

"Never mind," she said and turned away.

He knew if he continued the argument, it would end the same way it always did, a day of painful silence between them. He left the kitchen and took the stairs two at a time.

Dressed in a casual open-neck shirt and khakis, Fanning arrived at the theater-district restaurant five minutes early. He found Mike Allen braced against the service end of the long oak bar of Frank and Pat's Steak House, waiting for him. His large body blocked the busy wait staff, forcing them to reach around his bulk when picking up drink orders. Fanning slipped onto a vacant stool adjacent to the service bar end. The late shift bartender poured him a Dewar's without asking.

"What's up, Mikey?" Fanning stirred the ice around in the glass.

Allen's unclipped bow tie hung from his shirt collar. His face expressed real concern, not just his everyday heavy look. Fanning had not seen it for a while.

Allen nodded his head. "Let's move to the table back there."

Early diners trying to make their eight o'clock curtains filled the dining room. Pat Ryan, the efficient steak house owner, orchestrated the service from the kitchen. Fanning turned on his stool and looked to the corner where Allen had pointed, to a small, empty table, a two-seater, one of six lining the antiqued brick wall that partitioned the bar section from the dining area. Small Tiffany-style lamps suspended from the ceiling splashed each tabletop with just enough light to create an air of intimacy one would expect of a cozy two-seater.

Fanning laughed. "You know, if I didn't know any better, I'd say you were coming on to me."

Allen made off without replying. Fanning pushed a five-dollar tip across the bar and picked up his scotch. He followed his friend to the table. As soon as they sat down, Allen dropped his bomb. When he completed his narration, he looked up at Fanning for his reaction.

"Are you out of your mind? Millions of Irishmen in New York City, and you think you ran into Seamus Slattery on the goddamned Flushing Line? Jesus, Mikey, you gotta let it go."

He studied Allen's angry face. He'd seen him lose it many times in high school when a classmate pushed too far. Without warning, Allen's pent up anger could explode. He had to be careful. After ten years, Seamus Slattery was still Allen's hot button.

Their friendship went back a long way, over thirty years. They'd become tight as brothers from grade school and throughout high school, graduating and enlisting together in the Army. Both went to Fort

Benning, Georgia for Military Police training. Fanning remained for a year as an MP instructor; Allen shipped out to England, but their closeness resumed after they returned.

The big man continued to simmer, not moving. He looked like an enormous statue of a Buddha Fanning once saw during his tour in the Far East. Seconds passed before he decided it was safe to probe Allen further.

"Okay, tell me again what you did when you left the train."

Allen took a deep breath. "I went down the steps on the other side. I'm certain he never saw me. When I got to the street, I watched him stop off at the newsstand to pick up a paper."

"Probably, the *Irish Echo*." Fanning smiled at his own humor, but Allen's grim face remained.

"I don't know what it was but when he left, he didn't have that damn brown envelope he'd been carrying. At first I thought he'd set it down when he paid for the paper and forgot to pick it up. I waited because I thought he'd come back to get it."

"And he didn't?"

"No, the bastard kept walking down Roosevelt Avenue. When he turned left at the corner of Sixty-first Street, I crossed Roosevelt to the opposite side. I waited until he got fifty yards ahead. I didn't want to get too close."

"How the hell could you see him? It was dark, wasn't it?"

"Yeah, but by then the street lights were on. There was enough light. With his limp, he couldn't walk that fast. There was nobody else around...." Allen's voice trailed off when he spotted one of the Cuban busboys coming toward their table.

"*Perdóneme*, Mike, but you guys gonna eat here or you wan me set you up inside?" the young Cuban asked. The kid stood before their table like a rigid soldier awaiting his orders.

"No, *chico*, inside. But not right away, okay? I'll tell you when. And Willie, ask Bryan to bring Pete another Dewar's, will you? And me a Bud Light."

"Si, Mike, *pronto.*"

"*Gracias, amigo,*" he said and the Cuban left.

Listening to Allen addressing the young bus boy, Fanning flashed back to their high-school years, remembering that Allen had an easier time in Spanish class than he did. Allen was smart, a good student who scored in the low fifteen hundreds on his SATs. Nevertheless, Fanning knew enough Spanish words now to get his meaning across to those Hispanic drug dealers he encountered.

"Hey, and you never thought Spanish would come in handy after high school," Fanning said.

"Good thing we're not in Cuba. Castro might run me out for murdering the language."

Allen seemed to be loosening up. "So, go on," Fanning urged. "What happened when you followed him? How the hell did you keep your big body from being spotted?"

Allen pushed his chair away from the table. He stretched his long legs, careful not to get them in the way of customers heading toward the rest rooms in the back. "That neighborhood's not like Jackson Heights. It has these big, old oak trees. Between them and the parked cars and vans, I had plenty of cover."

"And you watched him go into one of the houses on Sixty-first Street?"

"Yeah. He crossed over the next avenue. The house was midway down that block."

"Well, it's easy enough to find out who lives—"

"I know that," Allen shot back. "But you don't think some shit-for-brains terrorist is going to list his name in the phone book, do you?"

Bryan arrived with their drinks, dampening Allen's rising anger. He pulled his long legs in and sat up straight to make room. Bryan set the tray down, lifted the Bud Light and Fanning's scotch and placed them on the small table.

"Thanks, Bryan," Allen said when the waiter turned to leave. "By the way, how's your audition for that new show going?"

The young man faced them, holding the empty tray at his side. One sneaker-clad foot rested on top of the other, showing off his perfect balance. His broad grin could not hide his appreciation that Allen had asked. "Third call-back tomorrow," he said, full of pride. "If I get it, I'll be able to pay my roommate for the back rent."

"You'll get it," Allen said, "and if you don't, there'll always be another show."

"Chorus line dancer?" Fanning asked when Bryan left.

"Yeah. Chasing the spotlight. Those kids have it rough." He picked up his Bud and poured half into his Pilsner glass. A foamy head bubbled to the top.

Fanning watched Allen take a large swallow. He hoped to convince his friend before the night was over to come to terms with his Seamus Slattery fixation, get him to admit that the appearance of this terrorist ghost of ten years ago was an unlikely, one-in-a-million shot.

"Look, I know it's Slattery. I mean, there must be a way to check the guy out, isn't there?"

Short of taking the ghost of Seamus into custody and running a background search on him, there was little Fanning could do to satisfy Mike. "You know, I hate to break this to you," he said, "but somewhere along the line I think I heard those bastards from the IRA were given immunity when the shooting over there stopped."

Allen's normal fair complexion turned whiter. His eyes narrowed. "That's bullshit! How could they let those bastards go after killing so many innocent people? There's gotta be something wrong with that."

"Well, I'll check it out with our rep on the JTTF."

Allen looked back at him.

"Joint Terrorism Task Force. It's part of the FBI. It's a team made up of representatives from every level of law enforcement, from local to federal. Our rep ought to know. Meanwhile, just keep cool. You know where the guy lives. If you want, I'll run a check, see who owns the house. Okay?"

Allen's wide brow looked like a football field of yard lines. "Yeah, okay."

"Good, now let's get some supper. I hope they're not out of filets."

Fanning arrived home in time to catch the eleven o'clock news with Anne, a habit she followed every night. Those nights he worked, she stayed up after the news, watching either Letterman or Leno, depending on which guest line-up appealed to her. During the early years when both were working, she fell asleep by eleven-thirty. Their schedule left no time for passion, Fanning complained. He liked to joke they had conceived their only child, Luke, in one giant gymnastic move, on the fly while moving in opposite directions. He could pinpoint that weekend morning they did it.

Since he began working in Narcotics five years ago, things got worse. His schedule, his hours, plus the risk-tightrope he walked, had not been kind to his marriage. He loved working in Narcotics, loved the excitement, but most of all he loved the idea he accomplished something good. These satisfactions, to his regret, cost him time with his family. He carried his guilt like a heavy suitcase. He knew he had to find a middle ground soon.

"You got a call after you left," Anne told him, hitting the mute button during the first commercial break. "From the guy you rear-ended. What was his name, Teddy something?"

"Vijay. Like the golfer, except Teddy is Indian, not from Fiji. He say why he called?"

He recognized, at once, that familiar expression forming on her face. It telegraphed a sarcastic reply. After fifteen years of marriage, he could finish her sentences.

"No, but he probably wants to sue your ass off. He needs to know how much you're worth."

"Boy, is he in for a surprise. He leave a number?"

"Yes, it's on the pad next to the phone in the hall."

CHAPTER 4

Wednesday, May 29

Fanning slipped a bagel into the toaster and poured a fresh cup of coffee. Luke had left for school, and Anne was still upstairs making beds. The house was quiet except for the strains of some elevator music coming from the small kitchen radio. Waiting for the bagel, Fanning thought of his promise to check out the amnesty question with the Joint Terrorism Task Force representative, Detective-Sergeant Casey Franks. He decided to go down to police headquarters. Talk with her in person.

Anne suggested a movie after dinner. "As long as it's not another tearjerker like the last one you roped me into," he told her. After last night's bitter words, he figured he owed her that much.

The bagel in the toaster popped as Anne's voice floated down from upstairs. "Pete, don't forget to call that guy. The number is by the phone."

"Soon as I eat," he yelled. He tossed the hot toasted bagel onto a plate. It stung. He licked his warmed fingers.

"Pour some OJ," she called, then added, "It's in the fridge, second shelf on the door," as though he'd never find it without her coaching.

After breakfast, he reached for his cell phone and tapped out the numbers Anne had scribbled on the pad. "Hey there, Teddy, this is Pete Fanning."

"Oh, hi ya, Sergeant. Thanks for getting back." The voice was friendly, not litigious-sounding.

"Sorry about bothering your wife last night. I lost your card with your cell number so I got your home number from information."

"No problem, Teddy. Something wrong?" Anne might be right. Teddy looked to sue.

"I was wondering," Teddy said, "ah…if…ah…have you reported the accident to your insurance company?"

"No, not yet. I haven't made up my mind if I'll get them involved…you know, risk having them jack up my insurance rates. Why do you ask?"

"Well, I was thinking, if you did, wouldn't your insurance company have to notify mine?"

Fanning could hear the tension in the question. "Probably, but you got nothing to worry about. I hit you. Besides, you didn't have more than a few scratches on your bumper. Right?"

"Yeah, but I just know once they get your company's report, they're going to drop me regardless of whether it was my fault."

"Why? You got a bad accident history?"

"No. It doesn't seem to matter when it comes to anyone with an Asian background."

Jesus, here we go again, Fanning thought. "Teddy, you're being paranoid. You won't be dropped." When he said it, he realized Teddy might be right. Insurance companies had become risk-skittish since 9/11.

"It's already happened to an uncle of mine," Teddy said. "He got into a small accident not his fault. The company dropped him. Listen, Sergeant. I was thinking, if you decide not to submit your claim, I'd be willing to go halves with you on the cost of your repair."

Fanning thought over the offer. Go for it or face a rate hike. Go for it, he decided. "Sounds like a plan, Teddy. You won't be hit hard. I have this great body shop on the west side. The owner is a buddy. He's always taken care of me. I'll call you when I know the damages."

❖

Fanning climbed the stairs to the street, squinting at the daylight. He realized he had spent more time riding the subway today than he had during the last five years. The poor Transit Police, he thought, working in that steamy, stuffy underground during those unbearable, hot summer months. Chasing drug dealers at least kept him out in the open air.

After breakfast, he dropped the car off at Bubba's Body Shop. "I'll get right on it," Bubba promised. "Have it finished tomorrow, late afternoon."

From there, Fanning jumped on the subway, riding it downtown to One Police Plaza to meet with Casey Franks. He and Casey had been in the same rookie class fifteen years ago. They hit it off from the beginning. She was attractive—not a beauty—with the athletic body of a cheerleader, short blond hair, ski-jump nose, a crooked but engaging smile and a light sprinkling of peach fuzz on her cheeks. When he looked at her, he saw a vanilla ice cream cone.

Their brief dating relationship was limited to several unfulfilled evenings of passionate groping and kissing on the front seat of his car. High-school stuff. Casey's driving ambition short-circuited their would-be affair. "I'm sorry, Pete. I like you a lot, but I don't have time to get serious. Police work is a male dominated world, so I have to push harder." The letdown was easy because Pete met Anne at about the same time Casey graduated at the top of their class.

During their rookie years on The Job, he saw little of her. She was busy completing her college studies, along with making a bunch of spectacular collars. These accomplishments, in large part, were due to having a fearless partner, someone who liked operating at the high-risk end of the spectrum. Thanks to him, she found herself in the middle of two life-threatening situations from which she narrowly escaped.

These days a shared pitcher of beer described their relationship. Now and again, they met with a few of their rookie classmates to exchange professional gossip and boast of their latest war exploits, each trying to outdo the other with tales of exaggerated heroics. During these bragging sessions, when he would lock onto Casey's face, thoughts of what might have been would smuggle back into his mind, sending him home to Anne feeling a sense of guilt.

The trip downtown took an hour. He had to change trains three times. At his meeting, Fanning learned the rumor regarding amnesty for the IRA was not a rumor.

"It's been in effect since 1998 when Senator George Mitchell helped broker the Good Friday Accord," Casey Franks told him.

"What's the Good Friday Accord?" He hated sounding like a rube about current events, but the truth was, his job in Narcotics left him little time to read *Time Magazine*.

"A landmark peace agreement between the political parties in Northern Ireland, Sinn Fein, and the British and Irish governments, signed on Good Friday in 1998." Anticipating his next question, she added, "Sinn Fein is the political representation of the IRA."

"So with that agreement, the terrorists were turned loose? That's hard to believe."

"I'm afraid so. In 1998, the British released more than 420 of those paramilitary prisoners when they signed the Accord. And in 2000, they announced that they were no longer pursuing convicted terrorists who had escaped custody and fled abroad."

"It's positively mind-blowing." He paced the length of the small office, stopped and spun around. "And so, this Irish terrorist, if that's who my friend saw, is walking around a free man, and the U.S. can't do jack shit about it." Fanning shook his head. "How the hell do I tell that to Mikey without sending him into orbit?"

"What did you say this IRA guy's name was?"

"Seamus Slattery. He's supposed to be from Belfast."

"Tell me again how your friend was able to I.D. him."

"From a ten-year-old picture in The *New York Times*…an article on the bombings. He saved it all these years. Reads it every day, honest, like he's doing penance for his sin."

Casey wrinkled her brow. "Sin?"

"He needs to be reminded how dumb he was to let his wife go to England alone."

"And he's sure it was this terrorist…this Seamus Slattery, he saw on the train?"

"Yeah, except the guy Mikey saw was missing two fingers on his left hand. And he limped."

"Tell you what. Give me time to check on something. No promises." She tapped her computer's space bar a few times. "I'll probably come up empty but it's worth a try."

Fanning arrived home late afternoon and found Anne's note on the kitchen table. *"Gone to Bloomies. Back by five. If you're hungry when you get home, I made you a sandwich. In the fridge on the shelf next to the milk. And don't forget, we're going to the movies tonight after dinner. You promised. Love you. A"*

He looked at the refrigerator door, at the calendar secured there by a magnet. He studied it with intensity, counting the days before he would go back to work. He wondered how he could take retirement from The Job if it meant nothing more exciting than going to the movies.

Admittedly, he had no real outside interests, no hobbies or anything considered an avocation. Oh yeah, he followed the New York Yankees' progress during the season in a haphazard way, despite failing his tryout with them years ago. Occasionally, he'd take in a game with Luke and Mike, but The Job was his form of entertainment, his excitement, his source of satisfaction. It gave him a real high when he made an important collar, sometimes rambling on for hours with Anne until she shouted, "Enough! I don't want to hear anymore of how you almost got yourself killed." He loved Anne's realistic approach to life. She was his connection to a sane understanding of what he did for a living. It was why he was still alive. Nevertheless, the stress on both sides took its toll on their relationship.

His cell phone ring tone, the opening bars of Dave Brubeck's *Take Five*, reached his ears. He flipped it open. "Fanning here."

The voice sounded muffled, the way it would if you cup your hand over the mouthpiece. "Sergeant Fanning, this is Teddy Vijay."

"Hey, Teddy, I just dropped the Taurus off at the body shop today."

The voice remained muffled. "That's not why I'm calling, Pete. I need to talk to you about something else, but not on the phone. Can we meet? It's important."

"Right now?"

"Yes."

Squeals of laughter filled the warm air of the early summer evening. Mothers and babysitters pushed soaring tots on swings as though they intended to launch them into space. Teddy led Fanning to a bench at the far end of the small, vest-pocket playground. Looking around, Fanning supposed Teddy chose this place because it was within walking distance from his home.

"Teddy, make it short," Fanning said when they sat down. "The wife's expecting me home for dinner in an hour. What's so damned important it couldn't wait?"

Teddy lowered his head, touching his chin to his round chest, looking like he was trying to decide where to start. He raised it, looked out at the traffic moving along the wide expanse of Queens Boulevard. "Pete, something happened the other day...I mean, uh...I overheard something...uh, well if they knew I heard...I mean, I don't know if they know, but if they do, my life, my family, we may be in danger. I'm afraid to go to the police...I mean to the authorities...that is, except you. I know I can trust you."

"Wait! Slow up, will you? You heard what? Who's threatening you? Don't tell me it's the people giving your family a hard time because you're Indian."

"Oh, no, it's nothing involving them. This happened in our new neighborhood in Astoria."

"You never mentioned you moved. When? Before the accident?"

"Yeah, two months ago. But as it turns out, I moved my family out of one bad situation in Flushing into a worse one in Astoria."

Teddy waited, craning his head, looking over one shoulder, then the other. His breathing shortened, his eyes widened. If Teddy was trying to create an atmosphere of drama and suspense, Fanning thought he was doing a damn good job.

"I'm in a section of Astoria called Astoria Park, near where the Grand Central Parkway turns into the on-ramp to the Triborough Bridge. It's heavily Pakistani, Iranian and Iraqi."

"Used to be Italian and Irish. Jesus, it's become some melting pot these days. So what's the problem? They don't like Indians either?"

Teddy's eyes flashed with worry. "There's a mosque in that neighborhood."

"Yeah, I think I know it. What about it?"

"I attend daily prayers there." Teddy bent over, turning his head toward Fanning. "I'm certain it's being used as a meeting place for an al-Qaeda cell," he said, his voice barely a whisper.

Mike Allen stared anxiously at the door ahead of him, then at the framed flower prints on the soft beige-colored walls and back to the door again. He remained alone until the patient scheduled ahead of him walked out of the inner office. He had never seen another person in the waiting room, so why the three armchairs and a sofa? Dr. Jordan saw patients one at a time for fifty minutes. Some months later, he felt comfortable enough to ask. That's when he learned the doctor also did marriage counseling.

A coffee table piled with outdated magazines and two end tables with low wattage lamps completed the furnishings of this quiet room. The surroundings, meant to have a calming effect, were not working for Allen this afternoon.

Allen glanced at his watch as the door opened. The same young woman always appeared. She would go to the small coat closet, slip into the Burberry raincoat she always wore, regardless of the weather, nod with a forced smile, and silently disappear out the front door. It was a dreamlike sequence…a Fellini movie.

Doctor Jordan appeared at the open door. "Come on in, Mike."

He was a short, trim man, neatly barbered, mid forties, but with a cherubic face that belied his age, something that bothered Allen when he first started seeing him. He wanted the doctor to be older and more fatherly. The absence of a beard, tweed jacket and pipe added to Allen's skepticism. During their earlier sessions, Jordan had dealt with these preconceptions, and the psychiatrist quickly established a level of confidence.

Allen entered the cozy, book-lined study. He sat in the chair to the right of the large oak desk. The desk backed up to a window that overlooked the greenery of Central Park seventeen floors below. The doctor moved around it to his leather chair and opened the folder in front of him. A small clock hummed in one corner of the desk.

"So…what's been going on?"

Jordan always started their sessions that way unless their last meeting ended in a cliffhanger. Then he would jump right to where they left off.

Allen had been making extraordinary progress—the doctor assured him of that the last time they met. When he finished relating his encounter with Seamus Slattery, he shook visibly, certain the doctor was revising that assessment.

Jordan had been making notes the whole time, uttering an occasional "Uh huh," but for the most part, failed to interrupt. Allen finished and Jordan looked up.

"Mike, even if the man you saw is who you thought it was, which I seriously doubt, there is little you can do now. I believe the man you saw as Seamus Slattery is a product of your intense yearning for revenge. That's something you have to put behind you. Kathy was an unfortunate victim of a war, much the way innocent civilians in Baghdad are being killed today."

Fuck the Iraqis, Mike thought. They brought on their own miserable fate when they didn't stand up to Saddam in the first place.

The doctor continued. "Ten years ago, the terrorists involved in those London bombings no doubt thought they were justified, fighting for whatever cause they felt was right. We may not agree with their politics, and we certainly don't condone their tactics, but every war in history has claimed innocent casualties."

Suddenly, Allen thought of his parents. His tone became angry. "My mom and dad were innocent casualties too when that fuckin' college student slammed into them on the Long Island Expressway. There was no war going on then."

"You were stationed in England when that happened, right?"

"Yeah. Flew home for the funeral, but after the kid hit them head-on, there wasn't much left to bury."

"I know. We've talked about this before. Nevertheless, let me ask you again. Do you feel responsible for their deaths, that somehow you could have prevented it?"

The question didn't surprise him. He had dealt with it in one form or another in past sessions, during the early years of his therapy when he was seeing Jordan twice a month. This past year, he had progressed enough for the doctor to suggest they meet on an as-needed basis.

"No, I guess not. I mean, how the hell could I? I wasn't even there."

"Exactly. Look, the timing of Kathy's trip was horrific, but you couldn't have anticipated the consequences. The bombings could have easily taken place a week later, when you were with her."

"I wish they had."

"Mike, you have to stop blaming yourself for her death. You're no more responsible for it than you were for your parents' unfortunate accident."

The small desk clock chimed softly, signaling the end of their fifty minutes that always started promptly at seven o'clock. Allen was the doctor's last patient of the day. The window behind his desk now displayed the darkened sky over the park.

"I know that, but I'd still like to strangle Seamus Slattery."

The corners of the doctor's eyes wrinkled. "Maybe he'll drop dead. That'll save you the trouble."

"What if I confronted him?" Allen asked. "Say flat out, 'Who are you?' If he is Seamus Slattery, believes amnesty is protecting him, maybe he'll own up." He paused, thinking it over, then said, "Yeah, what then? Turn him in? He'd be released in a heartbeat."

Allen exited the lobby and crossed Central Park South to the other side. He walked east along the wall of the park, toward Fifth Avenue. This latest session with Dr. Jordan had accomplished little in the way of convincing him that his Seamus Slattery of the Flushing Line was not real. The traffic light at the corner of Fifth Avenue and Sixtieth Street turned green. He sprinted across the wide avenue and darted down the steps of the subway entrance.

It was nearing eight-thirty when the train entered the Vernon/Jackson Station. He pressed his forehead against the window, scanning the platform while the train slowed to a stop. It was as though he expected to see the companion of Seamus standing there, ready to board the car.

At the Woodside Station, Allen rose up, exited and stood on the platform, looking confused. The train pulled away, abandoning him to his foggy state. Departing passengers moved around him to the stairway.

Allen followed, retracing his steps along Roosevelt Avenue. He turned down Sixty-first Street, arriving at the house he had seen Slattery enter. The area was quiet. Positioned on the opposite side, he looked up through the limbs that canopied the street, at the lights on the second floor. He pressed his shoulder against a tree, thinking how he would approach the man in a way that appeared natural, in the event he was wrong and the man wasn't Seamus Slattery.

Glancing back at the house, he saw the second floor go dark. He slipped back into the shadowed driveway between two homes. The front door across the street opened, revealing the silhouette of the Irishman. Allen tensed, quieting his breathing. He was unprepared for this confrontation opportunity.

The dilemma was resolved when the Irishman limped to the VW Jetta parked in front of the house. Allen froze, watching. Before he could react, the car pulled from the curb, speeding off in the direction of Roosevelt Avenue. He stared at the vacant parking spot, angry with himself.

Arriving home tired and thirsty, Allen made straight for the refrigerator and a bottle of Bud Light. He dropped into a chair at the kitchen table and took a long pull. The face of Seamus Slatttery was still vivid in his mind. Questions buzzed. What should I do? Should I let it go? Can I let it go? Life with Kathy was all I had. Now that's gone.

In several strides, Allen was at the door leading to the basement. He flipped on the light switch and took the narrow stairs two at a time down to the cement floor of the musty smelling understructure. He moved to the rear of the basement, ducking under the asbestos-wrapped pipes, toward the closed-in corner area, partitioned to the ceiling on two sides with a constructed wall of plywood. A hinged door, now open but always kept locked when Allen was a child, blocked the narrow entrance. An eight-inch round support column, in the middle, held up that corner.

A seven by seven storage room his father built, it held items used infrequently, or not at all, items like sleds and bikes. It became home to boxes of Christmas ornaments and a six-foot artificial tree. As a child, during the Christmas season, the room became off-limits to him. His parents hid his gifts there, locked away to ensure prying eyes did not spoil their fun on Christmas.

Allen entered through the narrow opening. He looked around at the crowded space, brushed past the stacked storage boxes, taking stock of the memorabilia left by his parents, packed after their death. Despite Kathy's urgings, he was unable to dispose of them. He had piled a similar collection of boxes containing all of Kathy's clothing next to them.

He emptied the storage room, stacking boxes and cartons at the base of the wall on one side of the basement, partially blocking the small, shoulder-high window. Satisfied, he went upstairs, changed out of his sweaty shirt, and tossing it in the laundry basket in the bathroom, he returned to the small nightstand beside the king-size bed. He opened the drawer and removed the Colt .45-caliber, semi-automatic issued to him as an MP. He checked the firing chamber and dropped it onto the bed. It was time for another beer.

❖

"That's a weird movie complex," Fanning said, trying to get his pillow to stay upright behind his head. It kept caving each time he had it plumped up.

"Why?" Anne asked from the bathroom interior. "Because they show old movies? At least they offer movies that were box-office successes."

"Whatever," he mumbled. He could see her form bent over the bathroom sink, rinsing her toothbrush. He wondered how much longer she was going to be.

"I think we were the model of democracy in action tonight," she said.

"Oh, yeah? How so?" he asked, half interested in what she had to say, hoping it wasn't going to consume any more valuable time. It was getting late.

She had flossed for over three minutes. Fanning was getting antsy waiting for her in bed. His libido ignited the moment she stepped out of the shower. He saw the naked form of his thirty-five-year-old, well-endowed wife towel drying her hair in front of the mirror. It raised his alert level.

"Well, you wanted to see *Training Day*, I wanted to see *Bridget Jones' Diary*. We compromised."

"Some compromise. *A Beautiful Mind* won an Academy Award a couple of years ago. What's to compromise?"

"It was wonderful, wasn't it? Aren't you glad we went to see it?"

"Yeah. You almost done?"

He saw the light go out, and he reached across to fluff up her pillow. Anne emerged wearing a cotton-gauze nightgown, which, as she passed the bedroom window, became translucent against the glow from the street lamp outside. He watched, mesmerized, as she undid the buttons down the front, one by one, shrugging the gown free of her arms and shoulders. It cascaded around the long line of her soft body like the unveiling of a statue, gathering in a small pool around her ankles. She posed there for him in an erotic moment of tease, her shapely form visible in the available light, smiling that familiar way she did whenever she'd become aroused. The moment, as well as her nakedness, felt perfect and natural.

"Get away from the window, for God's sake. Somebody will see you."

He heard her giggling like a high-school freshman going to experience her first copped feel.

She slid under the sheets and edged her body against his, allowing him to take her into his arms.

"You smell delicious." She always did before they made love.

"Baby powder. That's it."

His mouth found hers, and their lips locked tight for several seconds. When they separated, she asked with a note of conceit, "So, am I as beautiful as Jennifer Connelly?"

"Was that her name? She's okay. So tell me, am I as sexy as Russell Crowe?"

"More, but you're not close to being as confused as the guy he played."

"But he was better at math."

"But you're better at making love, so show me."

He did.

Later, when she rolled over on her side, he turned his body and tucked it into the contour of her spoon position. She fell asleep immediately, drifting into a light snore.

Fanning lay listening to the faint sound of the nightstand clock. He remained wide-awake, his mind running at full speed. His vision adjusted to the darkness, making friends with all the shapes in the room.

Teddy Vijay's account of an al-Qaeda cell in the Astoria Park mosque had shaken him. He worried that Teddy and his family were at risk, as were the millions of people living in New York City. He imagined the devastation of a suicide bomber's attack on New York City's subway system, plastic explosives wrapped around the waist of a radical Islamic–a nutcase all too anxious to give it up for Allah—as he entered the crowded E train at Lexington Avenue during rush hour. He pictured in his mind the unbelievable widespread lethal effect that al-Qaeda's tampering with the Big Apple's vulnerable water supply might produce. He thought of his brother Gerry, and he knew he was in for a restless night. The hum of the clock grew louder.

CHAPTER 5

Thursday, May 30

Casey Franks got up from her chair and walked to the Mr. Coffee on the counter in the corner of her office. "You want me to warm up yours?" She picked up the glass pot.

"No thanks," Fanning said. He folded both arms on the flat surface of Casey's desk, burying his head between them. "I'm wired enough over this as it is."

Casey returned to her desk and tapped her computer keyboard. "He said he overheard their conversation while taking a dump in the men's room of the Astoria Park mosque? That's the kind of cliché you'd find in a mystery novel."

"Yeah, I know, but that's what he told me." Fanning picked up his head and looked at her. "I swear. I don't know if he's making the damn thing up, or if he's on the level. Yesterday he confessed he came at me with a pipe the other day because he thought I was one of them."

"You don't know this guy very well, do you?"

"Beyond what he told me while we waited for the One-ten to show up, the guy's a total stranger." He refolded his arms and lowered his head. "Shit, I didn't sleep too hot last night." Her question bothered him. He had no justification to suspect Teddy had set him up. What purpose? What reason? "Jesus, Casey," he mumbled from between his forearms, "I'm not in the business of chasing terrorists. I'm in narcotics. My world is drug dealers. What do I know?"

"Well, it's easy enough to check him out, see if he's on anybody's watch list. I doubt it. India has spawned a few terrorists, but not enough for the U.S. to be worried. Pakistan, its neighbor, on the other hand, might be a country we should be keeping our eye on. Not India."

Fanning tried to imagine Teddy involved in a clandestine role as a terrorist. The picture did not compute with the image of the big blob sitting at the curb on the side of the Grand Central Parkway, crying genuine tears into his lap like a child. Either Teddy was for real or the best actor he'd seen off the silver screen.

Casey turned to her computer. Pulling up the JTTF web site, she asked, "How's the name spelled?"

"V-i-j-a-y."

"Is that Theodore or is Teddy his birth name?"

Fanning looked up, then stood and peered over her shoulder. "No, it's Teji. Spelled T-e-j-i. He told me he changed it to Teddy in high school. I don't know if it was a legal change or what. Anyway, that's what's on his driver's license and car registration. He's about thirty-five."

Casey completed the data entry, picked up the phone and hit three numbers. She waited. "Wanda, please bring in the active folder on the Astoria Park mosque. Thanks." She turned to face Fanning, who was standing behind her. She wore a knowing grin.

"You sneaky holdout," Fanning said, mussing her hair with both hands.

She reached up and placed her hands over his, holding them still. "But it wouldn't be any fun if we let you in on everything we know, now would it?" Her fingers raked through her short blond hair, smoothing the tangled strands. Looking up, she taunted him again with a wide grin.

Fanning realized the story Teddy had painted for him in the park now took on a new level of seriousness. He picked up a fresh coffee cup and filled it. Initially, he thought the emotion-prone hulk could have misconstrued the conversation in the mosque's bathroom, hearing bits and pieces about obtaining detonators and the delivery of chemicals. Returning to his chair, he asked, "So the Feds are on it?"

"Yep. Have been for a while now," she said. "They've been watching five members of that mosque. Did Teddy say how many he overheard, and did they know he was in the stall?"

"He's not certain. He thinks there were two. At least he heard two voices. When he realized the nature of what he was hearing, he had the good sense to raise his feet out of sight."

"And you believe his story?"

"Hey, sweetie, like I told you before, I hardly know this guy."

Wanda appeared with the folder, handed it to Casey and left without speaking.

"You think the Feds should talk to him…I mean, see if he's on the level? He could be useful in the future. No?" The idea of turning Teddy into an undercover plant was a stretch, but he had worked with less likely snitches in the narcotics business. Teddy just might be up for it.

"I'm certain they'll want to interview him once they're sure he's not in the al-Qaeda camp. But if he's not, and the bad guys know he was in that stall, he might be a dead man at this point."

Fanning's shoulders tightened. He bounced to his feet, splashing coffee on her desk. He thought again of his conversation with Teddy, reluctant to believe he had missed the call on him. He had good instincts for who was dirty and who was clean when it came to drug dealers and druggies. But terrorists? He liked Teddy. He worried for him. He knew he didn't want him killed.

"How soon you gonna know about Teddy? If he's on their side, I mean."

Casey looked at her watch. "You up for lunch? It's twelve-thirty. I'm getting hungry."

"Yeah, but I gotta pee first. This coffee goes right through me. How soon about Teddy?"

She looked at the folder on her desk, then at the computer screen. "I got it already. He's a good guy. At least, there's no book on him under that name. I'll have the Feds pay him a visit. Don't say anything until after they contact him. You don't want to spook him. You like Chinese? There's a place a few blocks from here that has a great Cantonese chef."

Casey Franks leafed through the papers in the folder on her desk and pulled out one. She could have mentioned it to Fanning at lunch, but she didn't see the need to raise a red flag. Not until the Feds could get a positive I.D. on the second guy. They knew about the first one. He was still on their radar screen. They could pick him up at any time for questioning, but it was unlikely to happen soon. At this point, they were certain of just one thing. A pair of non-Islamic men entering a Muslim mosque at eight o'clock at night was not something they ran into every day.

I'm not spending another damn hour on the subway, Fanning decided after walking Casey back to One Police Plaza. He hailed the first cruising taxi. Sliding across the seat, he directed the driver to Bubba's Body Shop on the west side. Before he could describe the route he wanted the driver to follow, the cab did a u-turn, entered a street leading onto the FDR Drive and followed it around the tip of lower Manhattan. Before the cab headed north on the West Side Drive, his heart raced, and he smelled death as the excavated site of the World Trade Center appeared on his right. Fighting back tears, he gazed out the window in the direction of his brother's resting place. Fanning and his family had attended the memorial services at the site after that horrifying day. He had listened to the reading of the names and heard the tributes by a host of dignitaries, but he never found the strength to return to the site. They never found Gerry's body, and he tried not to dwell on it as the cab darted north along the Drive.

"The Taurus looks new," Fanning told Bubba when he got behind the wheel. "You did great."

"Hey, man, thanks for the referrals," Bubba said, waving to him as he pulled out of the shop.

He headed toward Thirty-fourth Street, a big mistake. The late afternoon traffic on the wide cross-town street—clogged with buses, delivery trucks and other commercial vehicles—turned his fifteen-minute trip to reach the FDR Drive into an hour-long odyssey.

Crawling along in traffic, he thought of the problems facing both Mike Allen and Teddy Vijay. He worried about his childhood friend's state of mind, worried that the torment Allen continued to feed on would drive him over the edge. He had to find a way to coax him back from that brink, of being a danger to himself. Teddy, on the other hand, was in danger from sources outside his control. He wanted to tell him to leave, get his family the hell out of sight, but he remembered Casey Franks had cautioned not to spook him. The Feds better act before the consequences from Teddy's situation became deadly.

He arrived home and summoned Anne from the kitchen. "Come out here. Take a look at the job Bubba did," he said, standing in the driveway next to the repaired fender. He ran his hand over the newly painted area. "Feel it. You can't tell a thing. This guy's an artist."

Anne caressed the fender. "Okay, how much?"

"You're not going to believe it. Four bills. That's it. Anywhere else, twice that…maybe three times…and the work not as good. Teddy's going to be happy about Bubba's price."

"What magical hold do you have over this guy, this Bubba? You catch him selling hash, or something?"

He loved Anne's wicked sense of humor. "No, you suspicious twit. I've sent a pile of business his way…the guys on The Job. He's showing his appreciation, that's all."

"Speaking of guys on The Job," Anne said as they entered the house through the kitchen, "Casey Franks called. You didn't tell me Casey was female."

"Sure I did," he lied. "You remember, I told you about her being appointed to the Joint Terrorism Task Force a couple of years ago. I've known her fifteen years."

Anne lowered her head and looked back at him through the tops of her eyeballs.

"She was in my rookie class. Went up the ranks like a rocket, all the while getting her degree in criminal justice. A real brain."

Anne stood gripping the refrigerator handles, listening. Suddenly, she let go. "Is she the one you told me about? The one you had the hots for…at the academy? But all she had time for was a little kissy-face?" There was no humor in her tone.

Fanning bit his cheek. He remembered he had mentioned Casey Franks to Anne, or more accurately, confessed of his brief fling with a nameless female cadet while they were both attending the police academy. He revealed it soon after he and Anne were married, during a one-time boozed-up-game of *let's get stupid and bare our past love affairs to each other.*

"Yeah, she's the one. You know nothing happened. Besides, it was fifteen years ago."

"She wants you to call her tonight. What's that about? You setting up a little tryst?"

"Strictly business, my little love bug."

"So why does she need to talk with you? You're not getting involved with terrorist chasing now, are you?"

Fanning didn't know if she meant to say, *Casey chasing*, but he didn't wait for her to think of it.

"She's just checking out something for me, something I was working on before I got into it with that sleazebag drug dealer I blew away. I'll call her after dinner."

He had a firm rule never to discuss his ongoing cases with Anne. While the matter of Teddy and the mosque was not his case, he was sensitive to her low tolerance for danger. The less she knew, the less she had to worry about. Anne was a professional worrier, ever since her father, a thirty-year veteran with the NYPD, was killed in the line of duty when a metal trash can, thrown from a rooftop during a riot up in the Bronx, landed on him. She listened as he related the results of his collars, but she did not want to know the details of how he got there.

Following dinner, Fanning went to the phone in the hallway instead of using the one upstairs in the bedroom. Luke and Anne were in the kitchen, the teen performing his nightly task of loading the dishwasher while Anne assisted with the clean up. He wondered why Casey had called the house number. He took out his cell phone and had his answer. He had forgotten to put it on the charger last night before going to sleep. He recalled he and Anne had arrived home from the movie around eleven. After showering and climbing into bed to wait for Anne to slip in beside him, the phone was the last thing on his mind.

He dialed in the number. Casey Franks answered, and he said in a voice louder than necessary, "Fanning here. What's up?"

"Hey, Pete. You free in the morning? Can you come down for a meeting at Twenty-six Federal Plaza, twenty-third floor, nine-thirty?"

The familiarity of the address rang in Fanning's head as the New York Headquarters of the FBI. He'd been there once in recent years, the time he was working on a case that had a few strange national implications. "Sure, but you want to give me a head's-up? What it's about?"

"Couple of agents, Jack Fields and Tony Condon, got hold of Teddy Vijay today. They are bringing him in for an interview. Teddy asked if you could be there. Said he would feel a lot more comfortable. The boys asked me to call…invite you to their tea party. You up for it?"

Fanning was relieved to know they lost no time getting in touch with Teddy. The interview should provide insight as to Teddy's vulnerability. Yet, he was hesitant to get personally involved. He was on vacation—time to spend with Anne and Luke. No need to give Anne another reason to be pissed at him for neglecting family. Then he remembered he already mentioned to her that he had to make a quick trip to his Creedmore office in the morning.

"No problem, I'll be there. I can go to Queens Village in the afternoon."

"You back to work? I thought you were still on administrative leave."

"I was. I'm on a two-week vacation now. I need to use our resource at the office to check on the ownership of that house in Woodside." He lowered his voice. "The one my buddy, Mike, said he saw his phantom IRA guy go into. I told you that story the other day."

The line went silent until Fanning asked, "You still there?"

"I'm here. I was just thinking of something I dug up."

"About Mike?"

"Yes. I discovered the IRA is not a dead issue. I'll give you the details tomorrow after Teddy's interview."

CHAPTER 6

Friday, May 31

At exactly nine-thirty, Fanning stepped off the elevator at the twenty-third floor into the FBI reception area wearing a fresh Tommy Bahama golf shirt under his navy blazer. Agent Tony Condon greeted him.

Condon chirped, "Detective." After a polite handshake, the agent ushered him past the smiling receptionist, through rows and rows of cubicles, entering an interior conference room somewhere in the middle of the floor.

The meeting space was a fifteen by fifteen room, a perfect square, no windows or wall-decoration except for the large, round official seal of the Federal Bureau of Investigation facing the door. Fanning glanced around and suspected the decorator must have been an ex-math teacher. The conference table in the middle of the room was circular. The rectangular Parson's table against one wall and the triangular étagère near the door balanced the room like an illustration from a tenth-grade geometry textbook. The Federal Bureau of Investigation's New York City office, if nothing else, he thought, must pride itself on form and function.

Agent Jack Fields stood and stretched out his hand. "Detective Fanning, thanks for coming. You know Detective Franks," motioning to her already seated next to him, "and of course you know Mr. Vijay, who has valuable information he willingly agreed to share with us today."

Fields, the senior of the two agents, was a tall man with broad shoulders and a tapered waist. Looking him over, Fanning had the impression the agent had forgotten to remove the hanger from the dark blue, three-button suit. A white shirt set off a bright yellow tie full of sailboats. Fanning recognized a New England twang and guessed him from Maine or New Hampshire.

Condon, in similar conservative attire, had an obvious penchant for paisley. His tie and breast pocket handkerchief matched. He stood with a ramrod spine, holding his chest and his stomach like someone who had never heard the order, *At ease.* With his severe brush cut and steely eyes, Fanning had no difficulty visualizing him in the dress blues of the Marine Corps. So far, the agent had not spoken a word since greeting him at the elevator.

Nodding to Casey Franks, Fanning sat in the chair next to Teddy. The big man was dressed in khaki pants and a light blue linen sports shirt. Fanning was glad Teddy had left his Mickey Mouse tee shirt at home.

"How goes it, Teddy?"

Teddy sat with his hands folded on the table, wearing a worried expression. "Okay, I guess," he said. Then he blurted, "I'm glad you're here, Pete," and reached over to shake his hand.

Teddy's large hand was sweaty. Fanning wondered if the agents had already started questioning him. He turned toward Casey. "Did I miss anything?"

She looked first at Fields and then at Condon before answering. "Nothing you don't already know. Teddy started to explain how the encounter in the mosque bathroom went down. He was going to fill us in on the details of the conversation he overheard."

Fanning sensed the tension in her voice. The two federal agents looked uncomfortable. He assumed their sphinx-like posture was not their norm.

He placed his hands flat on the table. "Look, guys, I know my being here might be a bit unorthodox. If you feel I shouldn't be privy to certain things you need to talk about, I can leave." He heard Teddy take a deep breath. "It's your party," he continued. "I'm here at your invitation, so I hope I can be useful. But if you expect to get anything valuable out of this interview, why don't we all just sit back and relax?"

Agent Condon's upper lip began to curl, starting to form either a smile or a snarl.

"Don't worry, Detective, we're relaxed," Fields said. "Rest assured, we do appreciate you being here. Mr. Vijay expressed complete trust in you, as we do."

"Why don't we continue?" Condon suggested without waiting for Fields to take the lead. "Teddy," he said, slipping into a less formal form of address, "how long were you in the bathroom...that is, in the stall, before the two men came in?"

Teddy looked across the table. "Well, I was...I mean, I was constipated, so I guess it was a good seven or eight minutes," he answered, cutting his eyes over at Casey.

Fanning sensed his discomfort. "Don't worry, Teddy, I'm sure Detective Franks has heard details of bathroom experiences discussed before. She's a pro."

"Yeah, well, I just finished...I mean, pulling up my pants. I heard two of them come in."

"You're sure there were only two?" Fields asked. "Could you see them?"

"No...that is, I heard only two voices. One was very raspy sounding. I mean, they were down at the other end. It's a big bathroom. Gets plenty of use before evening prayers." Teddy gave up a self-conscious chuckle and looked again toward Casey. She maintained a poker face.

"They were speaking in English?" Condon asked. "Is that unusual for two Muslims talking with each other? Maybe they were American Muslims, like you."

Teddy hesitated. "They spoke English with a heavy accent, not like Muslims born here."

"Wouldn't they be using their native Arabic language, then?" Condon asked.

"They were probably from different Islamic countries," Teddy said, "where Arabic was not their first language. Like Sudan, Syria, and Pakistan. In countries like Kuwait, English is their second language. But most better educated Muslims learn a little English. It's become common."

Fanning looked into the face of the agent, searching for a *tell me something I don't know*-look, but didn't see it. He thought, perhaps Condon was playing Teddy.

Fields continued the questioning. "So you could understand everything said?" He had a yellow legal size pad in front of him, jotting notes without looking up.

"No…I mean, yes. I understood what I heard. They were so far away, I couldn't hear everything. No complete sentences…fragments sometimes, sometimes just a word or two."

"What were they?" Condon asked, pushing his elbows out onto the table.

Teddy looked over at Fanning. He rolled his shoulders, rotating them into his broad neck as if attempting to relieve the strain. Fanning gave a thumbs up, trying to convey that everything was fine.

"I heard the words *explosives* and *detonator* several times, and *bomb canister* once. I heard one guy, the one with the raspy sound, say *delivery of the sodium cyanide.* At one point, I was sure I heard the other mention Prince Faisal bin Abdullah. That's when I got up and squatted on the toilet seat, holding my breath."

Fanning waited for a follow-up question to the Saudi prince reference. None came. He assumed they were reluctant to expose details of a matter they knew about, information that was already on their scope. He'd question Casey Franks later.

"You think they knew you were in there?" Agent Condon wanted to know.

Teddy's eyeballs widened like giant white saucers. His huge frame began trembling, reminding Fanning of that day of the accident when Teddy sat on the curb of the parkway trying to control his emotions. He wanted to reach out, put his hand on Teddy's arm to calm him.

Casey Franks came to the rescue. "Easy, Teddy. It's okay. We just need to get a handle on your potential vulnerability."

Teddy looked like his thoughts were traveling in another world. Fanning could read his fear. It was for his family's safety, not his own. Teddy reminded him of Mike Allen, a bear of a man you staked your life on when things turned nasty. Allen and Teddy mirrored each other.

"If you think they know you heard them," Jack Fields said, "we will do everything possible to protect you and your family. We can relocate you out of harm's way, anyplace you choose."

Fields paused, giving Teddy a chance to respond. Teddy waited.

The agent continued. "But if you're certain they didn't know you were in there, well, then you could be extremely helpful to this government as another pair of eyes and ears in place."

Teddy cocked his head like someone startled by a strange noise. He repeated the words aloud, "*…another pair of eyes and ears in place.*" Turning to Jack Fields, he said with unmistakable anger, "Does that mean you already know about this al-Qaeda cell?"

Fanning watched Teddy twist in his chair. He wondered how much they were going to reveal.

They ignored his question. Instead, Jack Fields repeated his own. "How confident are you they didn't know you were inside that stall?"

"Damn it, I never said they didn't know. That's what's got me worried." He wrapped his large arms around his chest and hugged himself, as though to provide comfort and safety.

The door to the conference room inched open but stopped. A voice on the other side said, "Sorry." The faint sound of a police car's siren penetrated the interior space of the conference room from the street. The sound faded when the door clicked shut.

Teddy continued. "I stayed for another twenty minutes before I got down from the damn toilet seat. When I left the mosque, it was empty. I went straight to the parking lot, got into my SUV and got the hell out of there. It was dark. I kept looking for anyone following me."

"You've been back to the mosque?" Condon asked.

"For Friday prayers…sometimes on Saturday. I lost my job three months ago. I stay close to home, keeping busy working in the house." He looked at Fanning. "I'm redoing a bathroom," he said, releasing a nervous laugh. "Looks like bathrooms are a big part of my life these days."

Without waiting, Fanning described the circumstances of his rear-ending Teddy's SUV five days ago, forgetting that Casey had already covered the incident in her briefing to the Feds.

"He thought I was al-Qaeda, out to kill him," Fanning said. No one in the room laughed.

"Two days later," Teddy said, "I decided to ask Pete for help. We met and I described what happened in the mosque." He drew in a deep breath and squeezed it out.

❖

Fanning and Casey exited the Federal Plaza building, out into the brightness that reflected off the white concrete of the plaza, leaving Teddy upstairs with the two agents. Casey had her jacket tossed over her shoulder. "Let's walk a bit," she suggested. "That room was so damn stuffy."

It was a warm, humid, late-May morning, unusual weather for so early in the year. Casey was dressed for it. Her sea green pantsuit with a soft white blouse made her appear more feminine than usual. Abstaining from her normal jeans, short sleeved tee-top "one of the guys" look of One Police Plaza was a wise choice.

"Tell me something," Fanning said, as they ducked the spray from the fountain in front of the building. "That Condon fellow, did he get his training with the Gestapo? I mean, that was supposed to be an interview, not an inquisition."

"Ah, Tony's all right. His manner is a bit abrupt, but he's a good agent."

"I'll have to take your word for it. You want to head north or south for lunch?"

"Let's go north, toward Little Italy. There's nothing south except City Hall. I know an Italian deli off Broome Street where we can get a great hero and homemade minestrone soup that'll knock your socks off." She took his arm and pulled him northward past the Plaza.

"How far is it? I have to be home by six," he said, dragging his feet.

"It's a three-minute walk, for heaven's sake. Really, Pete, you have to get out of Queens once in a while." She spotted him grinning and threw a lightning backhand slap to his shoulder. "Are you ever serious about anything?"

"Yeah, about things that matter. Like with Teddy. I was surprised how quickly he agreed to work with those guys."

Casey, for all of her five-four height, dictated a rapid pace. Fanning noticed he had to lengthen his strides to keep up. Good God, he thought, this is a driven woman. He imagined her in bed and wondered if her intense drive, given the right ignition, translated into intense sexual passion.

"Well, they assured him he was in the clear as far as those two goons in the bathroom went. They didn't know he was in there. At least the Fed's undercover Muslims couldn't find any evidence to the contrary."

"I wonder how much help Teddy can be. They already have two plants on the inside. Besides, he never saw faces, so he doesn't have any idea what they look like."

They reached Canal Street, always trafficked with volumes of commercial vehicles traversing lower Manhattan and over the Manhattan Bridge to Brooklyn.

"That's why we were invited to leave," Casey said. "They kept Teddy back to brief him. Right now, they're showing him photos of the five known al-Qaeda."

A small panel truck with, TONY'S — *Fishes to Knishes*, painted on the side, cut in front, the driver coming from the outside lane to make the turn without touching his brakes. Fanning shook his head while he watched the vehicle tear down Centre Street. "Damn cowboys."

She ignored him. "All they want is for him to stay alert for anything suspicious. During daily prayers, see who these guys talk to, who they get chummy with, that kind of stuff. Six pairs of eyes are better than five, right?"

The traffic light flashed *WALK*. She took hold of Fanning's arm and dragged him into the wide thoroughfare. Her feet moved in a fast shuffle.

"Jesus, slow down." She pulled him along as if they were engaged in a tug-o-war.

"Hurry, this light is shorter than you think."

When they reached Broome and Centre, Casey said, "We go left here. Down a block and then to the right. They have a few tables set up outside on the sidewalk. We can eat out there while I bring you up-to-speed on what I have on that IRA situation."

They carried their hero sandwiches and containers of soup to one of the three vacant tables. Inside the deli's plate glass front window, logs of salami, prosciutto and pepper-hot sausage rained down. Hot and spicy, Fanning thought, looking down at his hero sandwich. Once he started on the soup, he stayed focused on the carton's contents, inhaling the lusty aroma, drifting into an epicurean trance. They exchanged no words for the next several minutes except for a few *umm-umms*.

"Didn't I tell you?" she said. Fanning was holding the container upright, draining the last bit of Neapolitan elixir. "It's an old family recipe, Guido told me. He reveals it to no one."

"Maybe, if I put a gun to his head?" he said, turning his attention to his sandwich.

"Before you get too involved with that hero, let me brief you on the status of the IRA."

He put the sandwich down, refolded the paper around it to deny access to the flies hovering in the area and looked up. "What's the story? You already told me about the '98 amnesty agreement. Something else?"

"Yeah, a couple of things."

"What's the first one?" he asked, eyeing his sandwich. The minestrone soup had whetted his appetite. "Say it quickly."

"There's a group of Irish dissidents called the Real IRA. They formed as a splinter group from the original Sinn Fein organization. They're IRA extremists that wouldn't accept the Good Friday Accord in 1998. They designated them a foreign terrorist organization. Not unlike the1923 treaty that led to both dissident factions killing one another instead of the English, they're at it again."

"Not surprising. Doing that for years. They active now?"

"They're responsible for a gang of high profile bombing attacks since

1998, both in Ireland and on the English mainland. In 2001, they numbered between a hundred and fifty and two-hundred members."

"So I guess nothing's changed."

"They've had their assets in America frozen, denied U.S. visas. Americans have been banned from giving any money or support to the organization."

Fanning reached out for his hero, forgetting for the moment, there was a second piece of information. "Can I finish this now?"

Her stern expression stopped him midway to his mouth. "I don't think you want to get caught with prosciutto, salami and gorgonzola in your throat when I tell you this."

The sandwich remained suspended in front of his face before he placed it back on the paper. "Okay, what?"

"Contacts at State and Scotland Yard have both confirmed Seamus Slattery is an active member of the Real IRA. They aren't sure if he's in this country, but nothing is off the table."

Teddy spun through the revolving doors of the FBI building. Standing before the decorative fountain in the Federal Plaza, he looked into the spewing waterfall while a slight breeze carried a welcomed spray of cool water lightly across his face. It felt good. He stretched his large arms overhead, feeling every muscle in his shoulders and back resisting the pull. As he brought them down to his sides, he huffed out a small blast of air.

He fingered the agent's business card in his breast pocket, intending to program it into his cell phone as soon as he got home. Wow, now I'm an FBI spy, he thought.

Fields cautioned against discussing the arrangement with his wife, reminding him of the need for secrecy. Five suspected al-Qaeda members were still running free. Tell Ellie? That's the last thing he'd do. He didn't need a swami to predict Ellie's reaction.

Ellie was a strong woman, proud and supportive of him. When his company laid him off, he went on unemployment, despite feeling humiliated. He decided to wait out the 9/11 backlash before sending out his resume. It made sense to him. Ellie agreed with his decision. They had enough banked to carry them for six months.

They said it was okay to talk to Pete Fanning or Casey Franks, but they preferred he work through them with any information he might have. "We'll call you on your cell phone when we need to contact you." Fields had told him. "Just go about your life normally."

Threading between the scurrying masses that crowded the sidewalks of downtown Manhattan, he became conscious of his proximity to the World Trade Center site and the destruction at the hands of the terrorists. He headed south a few blocks to the Brooklyn Bridge subway station and the Number 6 train to Grand Central. His new FBI assignment fresh on his mind, he sneaked several furtive looks over his shoulder before descending the subway steps.

CHAPTER 7

At four-thirty when Fanning arrived home, he mentioned to Anne he needed to discuss something with Mike Allen. "Hey, ask him to dinner tonight," she suggested. "I know he loves my meatloaf. Call him now."

"He's still at work."

"Leave word on his answering machine, so he won't pop in a Stouffer's when he gets home."

The answering machine failed to pick up. It was either broken or Allen forgot to turn it on. "Mikey, you cheap bastard," he had kidded him many times, "subscribe to the damn telephone company's answering service instead of that cheap answering machine of yours. At least your message wouldn't sound like you recorded it with your head sticking in a tin can." Fanning decided to call him at the restaurant.

Pat Ryan answered. "No, Pete, he hasn't been to work the last three days. Didn't you get the word? Fractured his elbow. He's taking a few days off."

"No kidding. When? He was fine when I was there having dinner three nights ago."

"Maybe when he got home that night. He called the next morning to say he was going to the doctor and expected to be out of commission for a couple of days."

"He might have gone back to the doctor today. I just called the house, but the answering machine didn't pick up. One of these days he'll break down, get a cell phone. I'll try him later on. Thanks Pat."

At five-thirty, Fanning called again. The phone rang a dozen times. He tried again at six-thirty before he gave up.

"Looks like no Mikey for dinner," he told Anne.

She came to the kitchen doorway. "What happened?"

Fanning didn't answer. He began running various possibilities through his mind. Nothing made sense. Allen's routine varied little in the ten years since Kathy's death. Any interruption came at his own instigation, like inviting himself to dinner. On occasion, Allen took Luke up to Yankee Stadium for a home game if someone in the restaurant gave him tickets. His son and Allen were die-hard Yankee fans. If the game was on TV, he knew Allen was at home in front of his set. His life was like the works of a good Swiss-made clock—steady and dependable.

"Pete?"

Her voice penetrated his musings. "Um, oh yeah, sorry. No answer again."

"You look worried. Where do you suppose he might be?"

"Sweetheart, I have no idea. How soon before dinner?"

"Twenty minutes. Why? You thinking of driving over to his house to check on him?"

"Yeah, I think I should."

"Fine," she said, "but it can wait 'til after dinner."

Mike Allen circled the block several times until he found a parking space on the same side of the street, twenty yards down from the

Irishman's doorway. He turned off the Buick's engine, pushed back and waited.

Last night he had again blended his six-two frame into the setback at the base of the stairs of the Woodside train station, the way he did on that first encounter with the Irishman. He watched him on both nights descend from the elevated platform on the opposite side between seven-thirty and eight, stop at the newsstand for a few moments and emerge with a newspaper in his hand. His pattern seemed to be consistent, or at least, he hoped it was.

Allen glanced at his watch. Six forty-five. He had given himself a fair cushion of time in the event that the man arrived earlier this night. It was too soon for streetlights. Full-leafed trees cast long, flickering shadows. To his relief, most walkers passed without notice.

At seven, precisely, before the last of the fading light disappeared, the street lamps overhead came on. Since he had carefully parked between two light stanchions, the glow from both fell short of his car, leaving him in a pocket of darkness. He tweaked the side view mirror, allowing him to see back down the sidewalk. He could spot anyone approaching from fifty yards.

Allen rehearsed again how he planned to accomplish this, running through in his mind what to say when he confronted the Irishman, trying to anticipate his reaction. The Colt .45, tucked into his belt and hidden by a loose pullover sweatshirt, felt enormous against his belly. As an MP, Allen always had it holstered on his hip. This morning he had stripped down the Colt, giving it a thorough cleaning and oiling before reassembling it. The slide cocking action worked just fine, and after triggering the firing pin several times, he was satisfied the gun was in good operating order. He loaded the chamber with one round, slipping the magazine containing seven rounds into the butt before locking the safety.

Two men walked past, busy in conversation. They ignored him. Minutes later, a single woman, both arms wrapped around two paper bags of groceries, waddled by, her short steps laboring under the weight of her load, the bags hiding her face. Fifteen minutes passed without anyone appearing in his side view mirror. Allen pressed the stem of his watch and lit the dial. It was approaching seven-thirty. His plan counted on the light traffic pattern he had observed: the later the hour, the fewer people on the street.

Just a shadowed figure at first, but as it passed under the street lamp behind him, Allen could see the limp, the unmistakable gait of the man he had been waiting for, fifty yards back. Still too far. At twenty-five yards, he reached under the dash and pulled the lever. He heard the trunk-lock pop, releasing the lid a few inches. His hand went to the door, resting there with his fingers wrapped around the handle. His right hand pulled up his sweatshirt just far enough to expose the butt end of the pistol. He opened the door and stepped out onto the sidewalk. He could feel the veins of his neck pulsing, the muscles in his shoulders beginning to knot. Slow and calm, he told himself. Nobody in sight.

Allen reached the Irishman just before he turned up the short walkway to his house. "Excuse me," he said, "I wonder if you could help me?" His arm covered the butt of the .45 in his belt.

The man stopped, taking a step back. He had a newspaper tucked under one arm. His other hand fiddled with a ring of keys. "What is it you lookin' for?" he asked.

The Irishman's face reflected tension. Allen stepped forward to within a few feet, his own face backlit, not yet recognizable. "I'm looking for a…"

He reached out and grabbed the man by the arm, yanking him around and pulling him back into a right-arm chokehold. Taken by surprise, the Irishman released a small grunting sound. His newspaper and keys went sailing in opposite directions. Allen placed the Colt .45 under the man's left ear. "Walk slow, straight ahead," he said in a whisper. "If you make a sound, I'll blow your fucking head off. You understand?"

The man's attempt to answer failed, his windpipe crushed under Allen's forearm. Allen let go of his hold, slapping a vice-like grip on the man's right arm. He kept the 45's barrel at the man's head while he propelled him forward toward the Buick.

"Hey, ya can't do—"

"Shut up and keep going."

They arrived at the Buick, and Allen pushed him to the unlocked trunk. "Lift it," he ordered.

The Irishman hesitated, beginning to turn around. "What the hell's goin'—"

Allen banged his large fist into the man's ribs. "Lift it, fuckhead!"

The Irishman doubled over, gasping. When he straightened on his shaky legs, he reached for the trunk lid, struggling to pull it up. It sprang open, revealing the dark, empty space.

"Stand still. Put your hands behind you."

Allen pulled the handcuffs from his fatigue pants pocket. With split-second-timing, he locked them onto the man's wrists. Shoving his hand into the Irishman's left pants pocket, he searched for the bulky object he had felt against his thigh when he first grabbed him. It was a cell phone. Allen removed the instrument and dropped it into his fatigue-pocket. He explored the man's other pocket and found some folding money with a few coins.

"Okay, now get into the trunk."

The Irishman planted his knees against the Buick's bumper, resisting with all his strength. "What the feck is it you're wanting of me? I've no money, 'cept the twenty dollars in my pocket."

"Get in the damn trunk or I'm going to leave your worthless dead body right here in the street. Now go!" Allen pushed the man's shoulders forward with the full force of his 220 pounds. The Irishman's head ricocheted off the edge of the trunk lid with a loud crack before his upper torso folded over into the trunk cavity like a rag doll, falling forward into the darkness. He showed no sign of movement. Allen realized he was out cold. In one sweeping motion, he lifted the unconscious man's legs, shoved them in and slammed down the trunk lid.

"Can I come with you?" Luke asked. "I finished all my homework."

"Naah, Luke, I won't be long. Besides, isn't there a game on TV tonight? I'll be back before the seventh inning stretch."

Fanning hated not giving Luke some one-on-one time, but he had a bad feeling about what he might find. If something was wrong, he didn't want his son exposed to it.

Fifteen minutes later, he picked his way through the familiar streets of Jackson Heights to Allen's house, a brick, two-story Tudor home. It was close to nine o'clock. The surrounding houses glowed with suburban family life in stark contrast to Allen's dark house.

Fanning sat looking at the Tudor, hoping that at any moment he'd see Allen pulling into the driveway. He studied the brick structure, recalling that his friend had known no other home. He was born in this quiet, middle-class neighborhood, in the house his parents purchased in 1959, the year his father, Herb Allen, was Merck's top producing sales rep on the east coast. Fanning had seen the plaque many times on the wall of their den while he and Allen watched TV.

It was a neat-as-a-pin house on a neat-as-a-pin street. Except for the years away in the Army, Allen had always lived in it, as a child growing up, and after the tragic accident took the lives of Herb and Kristin Allen, when he moved in with Kathy.

Fanning remembered how devastated Herb Allen had become when his son turned down the football scholarship offered to him by Florida State. Instead, Allen enlisted in the Army. His father stopped speaking to him for weeks.

He thought of his own family. His father, a sales rep for a clothing line, often on the road, was never a major wage earner. Until he entered the Army with Allen, Fanning and his brother had lived at home. Their three-bedroom rental apartment, four blocks from Allen's house, was on the sixth floor, high up enough to feel like they were living in the flight path of every plane destined for nearby La Guardia Airport.

He unclipped the phone and punched in Allen's number. "God-damn it!" he shouted at the constant ringing sound. He stepped from the car, climbed the two steps to the front door and noticed the collection of mail in the mailbox. Removing a few envelopes, he examined their postmarks. Allen hadn't touched them in days.

Fanning thumbed the doorbell several times before trying the door handle. He felt his worry intensify. The clockwork existence of his friend must have missed a few ticks. Searching for all possible explanations, he came up with just one that made sense: Allen's heart murmur of fifteen years ago. Did it become an enlarged threat within his bulky torso? The possibility of finding his friend's dead body in the house entered his mind. He was glad he left Luke at home.

He went to the back door. Finding it locked, he stepped to the garage and pulled out a small penlight. He pointed it through one of the two small, grimy windows on the face of the garage door. The tiny beam flitted from side to side but failed to reveal the Buick. With both Allen and the car gone, Fanning took it as a small positive. He had disappeared somewhere, still breathing, he hoped. But where the hell was he?

Mike Allen had made the short trip from Woodside to Jackson Heights in minutes, but when he neared his house, he kept driving. He circled the neighborhood, struggling to work through his thoughts, to come to terms with the gravity of his act. He had just kidnapped the man in his trunk, the man he was certain was Seamus Slattery, the IRA terrorist. Once he took the next step, he knew there would be no retreating. He needed more time to think.

He entered the eastbound entrance of the Grand Central Parkway and clocked off the miles through Queens County toward Long Island. By the time he crossed into Nassau County, he had reached his decision. He exited at the next off-ramp, crossed over and re-entered the Parkway.

It was five minutes after ten when Allen pulled to the rear of his driveway. He positioned the Buick closer to the kitchen doorway before turning off the engine. Unlocking the back door, he pushed it open and glanced around. With the Colt .45 in one hand, he unlocked the trunk lid, lifted it and saw the curled form in the dark space. There was no movement. Allen feared the Irishman had suffocated during the two-hour ride. He felt a rush of relief when the man gave out a low moan like someone waking from a deep sleep. When he rolled to one side, a splash of moonlight reached inside the trunk and highlighted the bloody gash on his forehead.

"Whu…where am I?" the Irishman asked, coming around.

Allen stuffed the pistol in his belt and reached into the trunk. He grabbed the Irishman's ankles, uncurling his legs, pulling them out and over the edge. Once he had him in a bent-over-sitting position, he took him under both arms and pulled forward, levering him out and onto the ground. The groggy man pushed erect, wrists still cuffed behind him, and rocked on his feet. Allen held both arms, providing support. When he had him stable, he started moving him.

"In that door," Allen ordered. "And don't make a sound or I'll waste you right here."

Inside the dark kitchen, moonlight filtering through the bay window over the sink lit a path to the open basement door. Allen grabbed a heavy Mag-Lite from the counter and flooded the narrow stairway with its beam. He descended with his captive in tow. At the bottom of the stairway, he led him across the basement's cement floor into the makeshift jail at the far corner.

In preparation for the man's arrival, Allen had placed a twin-bed mattress on the floor at the base of the metal column in the middle of the space. He had also locked a heavy-gauge, four-foot-long chain around it to serve as the Irishman's leash.

Allen nudged him into his new home. Shining the flashlight in his face, he asked, "Are you right handed or left?"

The man shut his eyes and turned his head away, confused by his new surroundings and puzzled by Allen's question.

"Are you a righty or a lefty?" Allen asked again.

Several seconds elapsed before the question penetrated the man's foggy consciousness. "Right," he answered after figuring it out.

"Sit down. Back against the post." He pointed the Mag-Lite at the base of the column.

The Irishman, slow to respond, fell to his knees. Allen helped him turn into a sitting position so that he could edge his body back against the support.

Kneeling down behind, Allen removed the cuff from the right wrist. With the Irishman's left wrist still secure in the other cuff, Allen hooked the open clasp of the right cuff through the end link of the chain and locked it.

"You can slide the chain up or down. That's the extent of your freedom for now. Give me any trouble and I'll shorten your freedom. You understand?"

His prisoner grunted, giving a reluctant headshake. Allen saw him turn both ways, trying to take in his limited surroundings.

For the first time in many years, Allen closed and padlocked the door to this cubicle of memories. He climbed the stairs and left the house through the kitchen door. Driving the Buick to a Chevron station three blocks away, he left the car in a space at one end. Earlier that day he had arranged with the station owner to park it for several days, telling him they were doing repairs to his house, repairs blocking access to his driveway.

Fanning hadn't mentioned anything to Anne about Allen's encounter on the train with Seamus Slattery. Until this afternoon, he was certain Allen was mistaken about his Slattery sighting. He had dismissed it as wish fulfillment by his emotionally stretched friend. Now, with the new information provided by Casey Franks, the picture came into sharper focus. It was clear Allen had met his nemesis on the Flushing Line. Serious questions remained, however. Where was Allen and what was he up to? That had Fanning very worried.

"So he wasn't home?" Anne asked as she pulled down the blanket on her side.

Fanning rolled over. "It was dark. His car wasn't in the driveway or the garage."

"Okay, Pete, what the hell is going on?" She rose up on her elbow and looked down at his face. "Something's happened, right?"

Fanning reached over to turn on the night table light. "I would have told you before, but until today, I thought Mike was just being his usual irrational self."

Anne listened without interrupting while he repeated Allen's account of seeing Seamus Slattery on the Flushing Line and of his impulsive behavior following the man home. He told her of the information Casey Franks had received concerning Slattery's involvement in the IRA and the amnesty agreement that came with the '98 Good Friday Accord.

"And just today," he said, "Casey hit me with a real blockbuster. She confirmed Seamus Slattery was an active member of the Real IRA and could be in the country. That's why Mike has me concerned. I'm afraid he's gotten himself into some pretty deep stuff."

Anne remained perched on her elbow. Worry-lines formed. "You mean you think he might have tried to confront the terrorist…by himself…that something bad happened to him?"

She became teary-eyed. He knew he had unleashed the professional worrier.

"Damn it, I hope not."

"Well, what are you going to do?" she pressed. "I mean, can't Casey Franks and her terrorist task force do something?"

"She's one person, and not a field agent. She's a detective like me, assigned to the JTTF."

Anne fell back on the pillow. He reached over and caressed her cheek. "There is something I can do. I'll get right on it in the morning, so stop worrying. Okay?"

"Just be careful, will you?"

CHAPTER 8

Saturday, June 1

The noise of iron wheels clacking overhead on steel rails of the Astoria Line smothered all other sounds for about thirty seconds. Agent Tony Condon ignored it, his eyes carefully studying the scene around him as he made his way under the elevated structure that paralleled Twenty-First Street.

The residential area's blue-collar work force would soon fill the trains that ran elevated between Queens Plaza at one end and Ditmars Boulevard at the other, despite it being a Saturday. Storefronts lining both sides of Twenty-First Street rang out intermittently with sounds of metal shutters rumbling open, their shopkeepers and merchants quickly preparing for the early rush of local residents.

A pulled down Mets baseball cap shaded Condon's face. He had chosen to wear an old pair of stonewashed jeans, a faded Grateful Dead tee shirt under a Safari jacket—long enough to cover the Glock 22 tucked into his waistband—and a ten-year-old pair of tattered Reeboks, all contributing to the innocuous, ordinary appearance he needed to assume. He left hanging in the closet at home his Bureau attire of dark suit, white shirt and tie with sailboats. He walked swiftly, with perspiration collecting on his forehead. The city was about to come to life; sunrise was minutes away from making the day official. Even at this early hour, he could tell it would be a warm one.

Condon looked at his watch. It was almost five-twenty. He would be ten minutes early, but he always made it his business to arrive at these bi-monthly meets ahead of the two FBI moles, Abdul Basit and Rashid Alghamdi. It allowed him an opportunity to scope out the surrounding area to determine if anyone was watching the store. Condon had a heightened sixth sense for picking up anything that looked suspiciously out of place. If the moles didn't find him waiting in the back room of the Pakistani food store owned by Abdul Basit's older brother, Hamed enjoying a freshly made kaak pastry bracelet covered with sesame seeds, and a mug of black tea, they understood he had split, the meet cancelled until further notice. So far, it hadn't happened.

Despite the Fed's standard operating procedure requiring the two moles to check in every Wednesday morning by phone, Condon insisted on these bi-monthly face-to-face meets. It was his way of conveying to them that the Bureau cared about them, that their value was more than merely a voice on the phone providing information.

"Morning, Hamed," Condon said, entering the empty store.

The Pakistani shopkeeper looked up from behind the counter. "Good morning. Breakfast awaits you on the table," he said. He nodded toward the rear. "Let me know if the tea is hot enough."

"Thanks," Condon replied.

He proceeded in a straight line through an aisle of shelves stocked with both Pakistani and American groceries. He opened the door to the back room and closed it behind him. The storage room was large, with space enough to accommodate a thirty-six inch round pedestal table and four cane-back chairs, positioned at the rear wall. The adjacent door of the delivery entrance would facilitate a hasty exit should Hamed sound the warning buzzer that he had installed at the top of the doorframe.

Rashid Alghamdi and Abdul Basit arrived together precisely at five-thirty, walked past Hamed and disappeared through the storage room door. Condon stood and shook hands with each man without speaking, pulling them into an embrace before letting go. Basit had been working for the Bureau for the past three years. This was Alghamdi's first assignment, having signed on as an FBI operative only six months ago. Condon had become fond of both men, admiring their dedication and effectiveness.

Basit, a typesetter for a print shop in Long Island City, was dressed in a dark cotton mock turtle and baggy khaki pants. He was forty-three years old but looked ten years younger because of his short clipped hair.

Alghamdi drove a school bus for the Queens Department of Education. He was tall and lean, sported a full head of black curly hair, and came off awkward in appearance in the same way the forties dancer/movie star Ray Bolger did. A hooknose was his most prominent facial feature. For these bi-monthly meets, his attire was always the same: a white long-sleeved shirt opened at the collar, and black pants.

Basit was a Baluch and a Sunni from western Pakistan. His Baluch ethnic group was at sharp odds with Tehran's Shia clerical regime and, like his family before him, Basit had carried out terrorism against Iran for many years. Because of this background, the FBI had recruited him.

Rashid Alghamdi, also a Baluch and a Sunni, was a cousin of Basit, and upon his cousin's arrival in the States eighteen months ago, Basit had suggested to Condon they consider Alghamdi for employment. After a thorough vetting by the Feds, they took him on for this assignment.

Once the three sat down, Condon opened a small spiral pad and studied his notes. "So, Rashid," he asked, suddenly looking up, "how goes it? Any second thoughts about this job you volunteered for?"

"No. No regrets," Alghamdi replied. He leaned back and folded his long arms across his chest. A smile formed at the corners of his mouth. "I am very proud that I can serve my new country in such an important way."

"Well, rest assured we appreciate that," Condon said. "Abdul, how's the family?"

"Everyone is fine, thank you. My son just graduated high school with good marks. Soon, we hope to find a college that will take him."

Condon made a notation on the opened pad. "That's wonderful. You should be proud."

"Oh, I am. Especially his mother."

"Okay, then. Let's get to business so we can get out of here fast before Hamed's customers start filling up the store. I have only two items that I want to cover. They're important."

Alghamdi pressed into the table, placing his large, flat hands on the surface as though he felt he needed to brace himself for what was coming. Basit's eyes opened wider, preparing to absorb and understand Condon's words.

"As of now, we have every reason to suspect arms and explosives have been smuggled into the mosque and are being stored there," Condon began. "Our problem is, until we are certain...that is, have irrefutable proof, we cannot obtain a search warrant to enter the mosque. To do so would set off an avalanche of protests from the imams and mullahs, as well as the entire Muslim community. Raiding places of worship in the U.S. is frowned upon, and these al-Qaeda jackals know that."

"I believe I know where they are hiding these weapons," Basit volunteered. "There is a large room downstairs at the rear of the mosque. Used for storing folding chairs and furniture not needed by the mosque staff. It is always being kept locked."

"You have that lock pick set I gave you a while ago, don't you?" Condon asked.

Basit nodded.

"Okay. Here's what I want you to do." Condon reached for the pen sticking out of the top pocket of his safari jacket. "Do you think you can pick the lock to that room in about thirty seconds?"

Basit raised his head and laughed. "No problem. I have practiced using the picks on many different locks…in my house, at the print shop…everywhere. I am good. Not to worry."

Handing Basit the pen, Condon said, "This is a digital high definition camera. It also writes, but that's not what I want you to use it for."

Basit took the pen and studied it. "You want photos. Yes?"

"Yes, as many as you can in as little time as possible. I want you to get in and get out quickly, but with photos that show the weapons and explosives."

"We can do it," Basit said.

"We can," echoed Alghamdi with a note of boastful eagerness in his tone.

Condon took a sip of black tea, which by this time had cooled. He put the cup down and reached into a side pocket of his jacket. Placing a Polaroid snapshot on the table in front of the two men, he said, "We have a new addition to our team."

Both Afghanis leaned in to examine the man in the photo.

"He's a member of your mosque. You may have seen him at prayer services."

The men stared at the photos without acknowledging recognition.

"Anyhow, he recently came to us after overhearing some incriminating conversation between two al-Qaeda brothers in the mosque's bathroom. He's an Indian Muslim, born and raised in New York."

"Does he have a name?" Basit asked.

"Teji Vijay. He's called Teddy."

"Why should we know about him?" Alghamdi questioned.

"We've asked him to be another pair of eyes for us. Unofficially, that is. Report anything that seems unusual or out of place."

"I understand," Basit said.

Condon continued. "I want you to know what he looks like in case you run into him during services. Do not...I repeat...do not identify yourselves. He doesn't know what you look like...only that we have operatives there working undercover. Okay?"

"Okay," both men replied together.

"Now," Condon said, "let's get out of here...one at a time. And I'll speak with you on Wednesday."

Once he had the Irishman locked away, Mike Allen closed the slats on the Venetian blinds of all of the downstairs windows, just enough so as not to look suspicious from the outside. With the car gone, his neighbors would assume he was away. He had spent five hours on the sofa in the darkened living room, listening to the chimes of the grandfather clock in the corner and staring at the ceiling. It was four o'clock before he climbed the stairs to get into bed.

He sat at the kitchen table latticed with morning daylight. After eating a few slices of dry raisin toast, he gulped down his third cup of coffee. The grandfather clock struck nine. He realized he'd had his captive locked away for more than eleven hours. He poured fresh coffee into a Styrofoam cup and carried it to the basement doorway.

At the bottom of the stairway, he heard the pinging sound of the chain-leash sliding on the metal post. Unlocking the door to the cubicle, he made out the form on the mattress, seated with his back against the post, the same position he had left him in last night.

Sunlight sifted in around the corners of the stacked cartons in front of the small shoulder-high window on the opposite wall, creating a fractured patchwork of patterns on the concrete floor. The light stretched toward the cubicle, leaving the Irishman in dark shadow.

"Brought you coffee," Allen said in a stern voice—his remembered Military Police voice.

His captive remained silent.

Allen's vision adjusted in the dark. He could see the man holding his head with both hands, like someone with a giant headache. Sweat had soiled the Irishman's rumpled blue denim shirt and khaki trousers.

"You want it?"

The man looked up, his face masked in anger, his forehead clotted with dried blood. "In the name of Jaysus, who are ya?"

"We'll get to that soon enough."

"Damn it, I've no money. You'll get nothing holding me like this. You're wasting your feckin' time and—"

"Shut your mouth. You want it or not?" Allen shouted, holding up the coffee.

"What in bloody hell am I doing here?"

Allen's patience ran out. He turned to leave the cubicle when he heard the reluctant reply. "Okay, then. I'll have it."

Allen held out the coffee. The Irishman reached up and took it with both hands, wrapping his surviving eight fingers around the cup. Allen made a note to ask him about those missing digits.

Standing to the side of the mattress, looking down at the Irishman taking large gulps of his coffee, Allen's thoughts became a mosaic of images. He pictured Kathy as the beautiful childlike bride, wearing the wedding dress that had been her mother's, walking toward him from the rear of the little parish church in her village. He visualized the amazed look on her face when he first showed her the brick vine-covered Tudor, her new home in the States, and then the tired, stoic expression she wore that morning in the hospital room after her miscarriage during their first year. The shape of her small hand waving as she passed through the boarding gate at JFK produced an ache in the pit of his stomach that brought him back to the present. He shook his head, trying to clear his mind, and spoke in a flat voice.

"You want something to eat?"

The Irishman looked up, eying Allen with suspicion. "Sure you're coddin' me now?"

"No. I'll fix you eggs, if you want."

"Yeah, but what the hell's going on? I mean, Jaysus, who are ya?"

Allen left through the cubicle door, closing it. He slipped the lock on the hasp and climbed the stairs to the kitchen. Opening the refrigerator, he realized he was hungry. The meager raisin toast he consumed earlier wasn't enough for the big man's appetite.

While he sat at the kitchen table eating bacon and eggs, the noise leaped out at him. He was confused. After several seconds of looking around, trying to identify the sound, he realized the ringing came from the living room. He jumped to his feet and headed toward the source. On the coffee table, the Irishman's cell phone demanded attention.

Allen picked it up, examining the unfamiliar instrument. He remembered he had to flip it open to activate it, as he had seen others do. He put it to his ear and listened.

The voice sounded edgy and angry. "Seamus, lad, where the feck are ya?"

Allen closed the phone and put it on the table, returning to the kitchen and his breakfast.

Twenty minutes later, he carried two Styrofoam cups down the stairs, the first stuffed with two hard-boiled eggs and the second filled with fresh coffee. The Irishman, stretched out on the mattress, pushed up into a sitting position. The arrogance that greeted Allen on the train six days ago was no longer there. His captive looked wary, like a cornered animal.

"Here," Allen said, handing the seated man the two cups. "And when you shell the eggs, don't throw them on the floor. Put them back in the cup. This is going to be your home for a while. I don't want to have to clean up after you. Got it?"

"Christ, how long ya gonna keep me here?"

"As long as I want."

Allen turned to leave but the shouting voice stopped him.

"Wait up, sham. Wait. What if…you know…what if…?"

Allen listened, losing patience.

"…if…if I need to take a piss, bad? You want me to piss right here, mess up the place?"

Remembering the small toilet in the basement, Allen looked back at the chained man. "You'll have two chances a day to use the toilet down here. Morning and at night. You gotta go now?"

"Bladder's about to bust."

"Finish the eggs. I'll be back in a minute," Allen said.

Pete Fanning found a space at the far end of the one-way street and parked the Taurus. The numbers of the houses around him were higher than the address written on the paper. He walked back in the direction of Roosevelt Avenue, thinking it had to be somewhere in the middle of the block.

All the houses on the street looked alike: two-story, two-family brick structures. The two front doorways, side-by-side, faced the street. One led to an upstairs apartment, the other to the ground floor unit. A driveway separated each building the way Allen had described the area to him that night in the restaurant.

Fanning glanced down at the address. He was getting close. Ahead, a figure emerged from the right hand doorway of a house beyond the next driveway, pausing to lock the door behind him. He failed to look in Fanning's direction. Taking the two front steps in a small jump, he started up the street, speeding away like someone with a destination in mind. He was a big, hefty fellow, square-shouldered. His scruffy hair was reddish, like his skin, and his neck bulged over the back of his collar. His triple-X shirt hung outside of his pants, covering his butt like a small tent.

Fanning held back until the man reached the end of the street. He watched him cross over and continue toward Roosevelt Avenue. Stopping in front of the fat man's house, he looked up at the white enameled numbers on each of the two doors. The man had come out of the door on the right. The door on the left was the address he was looking for. He glanced up the street again. The fat man was out of sight. For someone so large, he moved pretty fast.

Fanning turned back and caught the reflecting glint of an object in the grass at the base of the steps. A chewing gum wrapper among the blades, he thought. On closer examination, he saw it was a key ring, and he picked it up. The ring had two keys attached: an auto ignition key and a house key. The raised lettering on the ring's leather holder was the logo, VW.

Fanning moved to the curb. Parked cars lined both sides of the street. There he spotted a green VW Jetta twenty feet away. Looking around, he noticed a rolled up newspaper peeking out from under the automobile in front of him. He reached down for it, at once recognizing the banner of the *Daily Racing Form*.

It took a few seconds before the significance of the newspaper roared in his head like a clap of thunder. "Holy shit, that's it!" Slattery had stopped for a newspaper the night Allen followed him home. It wasn't The *Irish Echo*, as he had joked, but the Irishman's daily copy of the *Racing Form*. Slattery was a punter, a follower of the ponies.

Fanning could visualize how the keys and the *Form* ended up where he found them. On the surface, the loss of both items appeared to be random, but he sensed it was not accidental. He looked toward the door of the upstairs apartment and then back to the parked Jetta. "And what do you wanna bet both keys fit," he said aloud.

Back in the Taurus, Fanning opened his cell and called Casey Franks. "Wanda, this is Pete Fanning. Is she in?" Seconds later, she picked up. "Hey Sherlock," he said, "did you run down that name I gave you yesterday, the guy who owns the house Mike saw Seamus go into?"

"Rory McCauley? I sure did."

"And ..."

"Clean."

"Damn."

"But his brother isn't, and right now that's who lives in the downstairs apartment."

He pictured the fat man lumbering up the street like a bull in search of a heifer.

"Pearse McCauley. IRA. He escaped London's Brixton prison in 1991 while awaiting trial for charges linked to a murder campaign in England."

"Nice guy."

"A real sweetheart."

Fanning's jaw tightened. "The damned Peace Accords. So you can't touch him now? Even though he's a murderer?"

"Even though. He was in the U.S. when the pardons were handed out, living with Rory. Two years ago, Rory moved out to Long Island's south shore. He left the house to Pearse. My guess is he didn't like his brother's IRA associations. Who knows?"

Looks like Pearse is now using it as a safe house for Irish terrorists in this country, Fanning thought. He was going to suggest it to Casey, but she was already there.

"Pete, I'm beginning to think the guy your buddy saw is Seamus Slattery. We have to get the boys at Federal Plaza involved."

"Not yet, Casey. Not until I resolve a little mystery."

"What mystery, Pete? You're not taking on anything by yourself, are you?"

"Well…something's developed."

"What?"

"It's something involving Mike Allen."

"And the Irishman?"

The woman's a bulldog, he thought "Uh…yeah."

"Pete, what's going down? Where are you? You had better not do anything stupid or the next call I make will be to Jack Fields. Remember, this is a federal matter."

"Okay, okay, I'll tell you. But you gotta promise you'll give me time to do some checking."

"All right, just 'til this afternoon. Now tell me what you're up to."

Fanning kept her on the phone for twenty minutes.

On his walk back to the house, he stopped to try the key in the Jetta's door. No surprise, it popped the lock. He relocked it and continued toward the house. The street was quiet except for the occasional passing car. At the top of the steps, he glanced around before inserting the house key. The lock turned, and he pushed open the door.

Once inside, he twisted the locking tab on the door and found himself standing in a small foyer, looking up the long flight of uncarpeted stairs. He had left his service weapon in the glove compartment of the Taurus in the event something went wrong. That way, they couldn't charge him with armed robbery—only breaking and entering. Now he wondered if leaving it was smart.

He eased up the stairs, stopping halfway. No sound reached him. Find evidence that Slattery lives here, he thought, and get the hell out fast. Then figure out where that lunatic, Allen, took the Irishman. He was certain that's how it went down.

He finished the climb, inching into the apartment. His eyes scanned the room, alert for any movement. The sparsely furnished living room reminded him of the tenement apartment where the drug dealer, Ramirez, came within a hair of taking him out. Missing were the roaches and scents of filth. This one smelled too, but of beer and cigarettes.

Fanning entered the kitchen and poked around. The trash was stacked with empty beer bottles. A laptop computer sat open on the kitchen table with several floppy discs scattered about. He thought of scooping them up, taking them and the laptop with him, but dismissed the idea. He was in the apartment unlawfully; therefore, nothing he took could be admissible evidence. He spotted a six-pack of unopened Harps left on the counter next to the sink and laughed. The occupant was definitely Irish.

Fanning reentered the living room and spied a soft, faux-leather case tossed on the coffee table, filled with papers and lists of names and addresses. One list contained nothing but Irish sounding names and their addresses in the New York metro area. In addition to the lists, he found a rubber-banded wad of laminated driver licenses tucked away into one corner of the case. This place is a treasure trove of incriminating evidence, he thought.

An interest in Thoroughbred racing appeared to be the remaining identifying characteristic of the person living there—besides the Harps. A collection of *Daily Racing Forms* shoved under the coffee table had dates going back several weeks. Why keep out-dated issues around? Fanning wondered. Then he remembered the agents down at Queens Narcotics who played the horses had become real students of the game. They'd follow a horse's past performances leading up to a race. The source of this handicapping data was their *Daily Racing Forms*.

He checked the two bedrooms, both furnished with twin beds. One room showed signs of occupancy, the other didn't. A raincoat, a pair of khaki pants and two lightweight jackets hung in the closet. The drawers of the bureau were empty, except one. There he found a small cluster of shorts, socks and shirts, tossed in haphazardly. Whoever lived there traveled light.

A small framed photo sat on top of the bureau—a posed shot of a man and a woman. They appeared to be in their late twenties, formally dressed, with the woman holding an arrangement of flowers in the crook of her arm. Wedding picture, Fanning guessed. He went to the window to examine it in the light. Allen had shown him the picture of Seamus Slattery in the saved *New York Times* article several times. He tried to remember that image as he looked at the faces of the happy couple. Until he examined both pictures side by side, he couldn't be certain, but if someone offered him odds against it being the same man, he'd have to take the bet. It might be his second winner of the day.

Fanning slipped the frame down the front of his pants, covering it with his shirt, and looked at his wristwatch. He had been in the apartment twelve minutes. Long enough, he decided.

It was nine-fifty when he returned to his car. He found what he was looking for. In fact, he found a lot more. It was time to get the boys, Fields and Condon, there for an authorized visit. The problem was blowing that whistle without incriminating himself. He was sure Casey would figure something out. The important thing was to get the Feds involved before the fat man came back and cleared out the place.

He telephoned Casey.

"I think they'll want you to come downtown...confirm everything in person," she told him. "I'll call you back in a few minutes...let you know where."

Fanning drove south toward Roosevelt Avenue. He had mentioned to

Casey the stack of Daily Racing Forms he found in the apartment. It reminded him he needed to check out the newsstand under the Woodside station platform. Allen's observations that first night might have been distorted by his excitement of seeing Seamus Slattery, but if not, the large brown envelope Slattery dropped off was a curious loose end.

Fanning double-parked at the corner, stepped out of the car and walked over to the stand. A tall, middle-aged man with blondish hair stood behind the stack of newspapers, racks of magazines and large display of candy. Fanning heard the unmistakable Irish accent when he answered, "Yes, sir, the *New York Post,* right away."

Before the man finished counting out change from the five-dollar bill, Fanning noticed the pile of *Daily Racing Forms.* "Hey, while you're at it, throw in a *Form* too," he said, and removed the top copy from the stack.

The news dealer recounted the change.

"Thanks. Maybe you can tell me, what's the quickest way into Manhattan from here?"

The man's agreeable face turned thoughtful as he considered the question. "I'd be thinkin' Skillman Avenue is better than following Roosevelt Avenue this time a day. Go two blocks, make a right. That street leads to Skillman. When you reach it, go left and straight."

"Thanks, my friend. Much obliged."

Sliding back under the steering wheel, he tossed the newspapers on the seat next to him just as *Take Five's* notes grabbed his attention. He flipped open the phone. "Fanning."

"Pete, the boys are already in this neighborhood, so come to my office."

The Flushing Line Express rumbled overhead, blurring her voice. "You said your office?" he shouted.

"Right. They'll be here in twenty minutes."

"I'm on my way," he said and snapped the phone shut.

CHAPTER 9

The closed door to the small windowless toilet allowed the Irishman privacy while he relieved himself. Allen stood outside holding the Colt .45, listening and waiting. When he heard the flushing sound, he pushed back the door and stepped away.

The Irishman emerged, greeted by the barrel of Allen's weapon pointing at his head. He stopped short. "Whoa, fella, hold on there. No need for that."

Allen motioned with the gun toward the cubicle. "Back in there," he said, taking the man by the shoulder and shoving him toward the cubicle. Once he had him secured, he backed out of the door.

"Okay, let's talk," Allen said, taking the kitchen chair he'd brought down earlier and sliding it up to the cubicle opening. He straddled the chair, the .45 tucked into his waistband.

The man pressed back against the post and looked up. Allen noticed three Styrofoam cups stacked at the end of the mattress. The top one contained the eggshells, as he had directed.

"Damned good idea" the Irishman said. "Might ya begin tellin' me what's this about? Why I'm here?"

His calm, unthreatening manner was a surprise. The change in demeanor worried Allen. The notion of mistaken identity re-entered his mind. Then he recalled the phone call, the caller's angry use of the Irishman's name, demanding to know where he was.

"Let's begin with an easy question. What's your name?"

The Irishman shifted his position on the mattress. Settled, he said, "Hey, sham, before we start, I could use a *fag*. What do ya say?"

Allen felt a flash of anger. He hadn't heard the term fag used in years, not since he returned from England with Kathy. He remembered her father always referred to cigarettes that way.

"No!" he shot back. "I don't smoke."

"Oh? Too bad."

"What's your name?" Allen asked again.

"Gerard Hoey. I'm an electrician from Cork, Ireland, and I've no bloody idea what you'd be wantin' with me."

Allen gripped the back of the chair. He focused on the man's blackened right eye and dried blood on his forehead, the signs of his forceful abduction. "Okay. We both know that's bullshit, so let's start over. What's your name?"

"Gerard Hoe—"

"That's not your name," Allen shouted. "It's Seamus." He rested the .45 on top of the chair back. "If you don't level with me, this is going to turn out to be a very short conversation."

The Irishman's head recoiled as if it had taken a punch. Hearing his name had no doubt surprised him. Allen waited, certain he could read the Irishman's thoughts. *Was it just a wild guess or does he know me?*

"Right. My name is Seamus," he spoke with the sound of surrender.

"That's Seamus Slattery," Allen added, tucking the .45 back into his waistband. "IRA terrorist from Belfast."

Slattery took a breath. "Former IRA," he corrected. "We received amnesty in '98, ya know. Been a peace lovin' man since."

"That's a crock of shit!"

"Came over last year. Work as an electrician for a company in Long Island City."

Slattery looked into Mike Allen's eyes. The Irishman began showing tension, waiting for an acknowledgement to his statement. When none came, he continued.

"The Good Friday Peace Accord. Ya heard of it, have ya?"

Allen stiffened. The reference stung.

"Read the newspapers, do ya?"

The smugness of Slattery's question ignited an explosion. Allen leaped to his feet, tipping the chair forward. The .45 semi-automatic was out of his belt and in his hand. In one motion, he launched his large frame into the cubicle like a linebacker, landing knees first on the chest of the Irishman. The weight of his body caused Slattery to flatten out on the mattress and release a gust of air that sounded like a squeezed accordion.

Allen pressed the gun against the man's temple. "If you so much as try to smart ass me again, I'll spill your God-damn brains out on this floor. You got that?"

Slattery nodded.

"Fuck your peace accord. I never granted you amnesty, and that's what this is about."

Allen got to his feet and picked up the toppled chair. Slattery remained prone on the mattress, trying to regain his breathing, rubbing his chest plate where Allen's knees had landed. With difficulty, he rolled to one side, then pushed up into a sitting position.

"I...what? I don't understand," Slattery mumbled. "What call would ya be havin' with me? You're not even from Ireland, are ya?" He inched back against the post.

"No, I'm not."

"Are ya English, then?"

"No, but my wife was."

Slattery went mute, thinking, trying to process Allen's reply. Seconds later, the use of the past tense penetrated. "Was?"

"Was," Allen parroted. "Gone. Like dead."

"Sorry 'bout that."

Allen said nothing, letting the Irishman give it more thought.

"Ya think I had something to do with it?"

Allen tightened his grip and took a deep breath. "You had everything to do with it."

"I did? Where? Where did it happen?"

He thought of the article in his wallet. There was no need to produce it. He had the date and circumstances scored in his brain.

"Ten years ago…in London."

Slattery made a face as if trying to clear his confusion. "I could be wrong, but I don't think I was anywhere near London ten years ago. Never left Belfast 'til I came here."

"How about the two bombings on that day…the simultaneous bombings at Victoria and Paddington Stations? They bring back any memories?"

Slattery shook his head, ready to question any accountability for these events.

"Still doesn't ring a bell?" Allen shouted. He reached for his wallet. "Tell you what. I'll save you the effort of racking your memory."

Having placed the Mag-lite on one of the packing boxes at the wall, he grabbed for it. When he sat back down, he unfolded the article and held the flashlight beam on the page. He began reading from memory, keeping watch on Slattery, glancing down at the paper like a speaker using his notes. When he finished, he held out the clipping. Slattery made no effort to take it. His expression said it was unnecessary.

"She was there, was she?" Slattery asked, his tone subdued like a concerned family member. "Bleedin' bad luck, I'd say."

Allen tilted forward in the chair, almost tipping it again as he started to stand. Catching himself, he sat back down and locked his fingers around the spindles of the back support. His eyes narrowed but stayed riveted on the Irishman's face as he machine-gunned his words at him.

"Bad luck? You fuckin' murdered her and five other innocent people in cold blood. Bad luck my ass! Bad luck is when you step off a curb into the path of an out-of-control car. She died because you took aim at her. Luck didn't have a God-damn thing to do with it." His voice had become shrill. Slattery hadn't moved a muscle. His steel eyes stared back. Allen sucked in a deep breath before continuing his assault.

"Fuck ya think you were accomplishing, killing innocent people? Did you really believe the English would become more sympathetic to your cause…carry your banner to the English parliament…make your case for home rule? Jesus, if that's what you thought, you're fuckin' deluded."

Slattery remained silent. His expressionless face showed no reaction to the fierceness of Allen's verbal attack. He looked comfortable sitting with his head pressed back against the post as if at any moment he would close his eyes and drift off to sleep.

"You hear what I'm saying?" Allen shouted. "You don't give a shit, do you?"

The Irishman's mouth twitched. He raised his three-fingered left hand to his face and scratched the side of his flat, wide nose.

Allen continued. "The people you killed, the lives you destroyed, nothing more than faceless, meaningless collateral damage. Is that how you viewed them?"

Slattery lowered his voice. "Fella, what can I say? I only wish your bride was somewhere else at the time. But she wasn't. 'Tis a shame, and for that I'm sad for both of ya."

His tone was conciliatory, not defensive, but Allen heard it as patronizing.

Slattery went on. "We did what we thought we needed to do to bring a halt to the Prods abusing our people and holding us down. The bloody English, ya understand, did nothing but encourage the Prods for years."

"And terrorism was your answer?" Allen countered. "No other recourse but blowing up your enemies along with innocent people like my wife?"

Slattery opened his mouth to begin a response but caught himself before any words came out. Allen sensed the man was being cautious with his answers. Slattery spent the next several seconds gazing at his lap. He concentrated with intensity.

Allen had more questions to ask, but he drew a blank. He stared back at Slattery sitting with his chin on his chest. He decided to go upstairs, leave the Irishman to his thoughts, but he remembered a question for Seamus Slattery, the one he'd waited ten years to ask.

"What I can't figure," Allen began, "is the IRA considered itself an armed force, opposing an illegal foreign occupation of its country. Isn't that right?"

Slattery looked up and bobbed his head once.

"And your jailed members call themselves political prisoners?"

"That's right," Slattery mumbled.

"And your army of terrorists referred to themselves as soldiers?"

Slattery again lowered his head.

"Soldier is an honorable term," Allen said. Wouldn't you agree?"

Slattery nodded, showing impatience.

"Well then, how the hell does killing innocent civilians by soldiers become an honorable act? How can you consider yourself a soldier?"

Allen's voice had become reedy again, but the wait was over. He had asked the question.

Slattery's back became rigid, and when the Irishman looked up, Allen thought he saw a trace of confidence returning.

"As soldiers, we all make mistakes," he said. "Yours was in Viet Nam at Mai Lai, wasn't it?"

Allen got to his feet again, this time without charging into the Irishman's space. Instead, he remained standing. He had lots more questions he wanted answered. I'll have plenty of time to kill the son of bitch, he thought.

"Yeah, it was," Allen shot back. "But we crucified the bastard responsible for those atrocities, didn't we? Who, in your so-called army, crucified you for yours? No one." Allen looked over to the stacked boxes of Kathy's personal effects. "That is, until now."

The earlier trace of confidence drained from the Irishman's face.

Teddy had positioned the last ceramic tile along the base of the bathtub when his cell phone rang. He looked at the caller-ID display and didn't recognize the number.

"Hello."

"Teddy Vijay?"

The voice sounded familiar.

"Teddy, this is Jack Fields."

Hearing his name, Teddy remembered he had yet to program the agent's number into his cell. "Oh yeah, Jack. How are you?"

"I'm great, Teddy. Get you at a bad time?"

He looked down at the line of tiles. Adhesive oozed out around the edges of the squares. "No, no. It's fine. What's up?"

"You plan to go to prayer service tonight at the mosque?"

"Yes I am. Around eight-thirty. At least I think that's the time. My daily prayer schedule is in another room."

"I'm pretty sure it's eight-twenty-four tonight." Fields corrected. "In any event, we'd like you to pay particular attention to who's there tonight."

"Why?"

"See if you spot anyone who appears out of place. I mean, like anyone obviously not a Muslim, not Middle Eastern. Maybe he's just waiting around to meet with someone after prayer service. You understand what I'm asking?"

"Certainly. Any idea what he looks like…height, hair color…you know, things like that?"

"We do but we prefer not to prompt you. We think there are two non-Muslims working together with this al-Qaeda cell. We haven't been able to identify the second one yet. See if one of them shows up tonight, the same guy we have on our radar or the unidentified second guy."

"I can do that."

"Good. When we get your description, we'll know which one it is. If it's the second man, we'll be able to get a fix on him in our data base."

"I guess I better get a close look if you want me to be that accurate."

"Teddy, no. Listen to me. Do not…I repeat…do not approach the man. Do nothing obvious. If you're too far away tonight, let it go. There'll be other nights."

"Right. When should I get back to you?"

"I'll call you tomorrow morning. Bye, Teddy."

"Bye, Jack."

Teddy turned to see Ellie standing in the doorway, her hands on her hips. A floral-embroidered apron, tied around her waist, covered the front of her slacks.

"Who was that?"

"Jack Fields, the FBI agent I met with yesterday."

Sensitive to her already high state of alarm regarding the mosque incident, he had to be careful. When he arrived home yesterday, he told her they needed a first hand account of what he heard in the mosque. She knew of his meeting with Pete Fanning in the park, but Fields had cautioned him not to tell her anything more.

"What did he want now?" The question was full of suspicion.

"Nothing important. Just to say thanks."

Ellie stared at him, arms folded, eyebrows raised, dishtowel tossed over her shoulder. She had the look of a schoolteacher who had just caught a child misbehaving in the coatroom.

"Really? That's all?"

"Yeah. You know, for meeting with them yesterday, giving them a heads-up and all that."

She unfolded her arms. "I thought you said they already knew about those men."

"That's right. They do. I merely confirmed what they already knew."

"Teddy, why did you have to call that detective in the first place? We should have minded our own business. Now the FBI is involved. I'm worried about what could happen to us."

Teddy put his arms around her. "Nothing's going to happen. I promise."

"How do you know there aren't more than two of them…more of the al-Qaeda?"

"There aren't," he said. He hated lying, but Fields had cautioned him not to say anything to her. It isn't as though I'm in any danger, he told himself, so there's no need to worry. I didn't agree to become an undercover agent or anything like that.

Teddy knelt down with a sponge and cloth and began wiping the excess adhesive around the base of the tub. He hoped Ellie would cut the subject short, that she would not force him to invent more answers.

"The card on the dresser, is that his…with the one that detective gave you?"

"Oh. That's where it is. I looked for it earlier. I need to program his number into my cell phone address book."

"Whatever for? They don't need you anymore, do they?" Without waiting for his reply, she pounced. "Teddy, don't get in any deeper. You hear me?"

"Ellie, damn it, I'm not getting involved, so stop worrying."

She glared at him before turning away. She was a schoolteacher again. "Lunch is ready."

"Okay, I'll finish up here later. I just need to grout the tile, mount the fixtures and shower rod and it'll be ready for use by Monday."

He was sure she never heard him.

CHAPTER 10

Jack Fields and Tony Condon sat across from each other at one end of the large conference table at One Police Plaza. Pete Fanning sat alongside Condon while Casey Franks took the seat next to Fields.

"Pete, you still have the keys on you?" Jack Fields asked.

Pete shoved them across the table followed by a scrap of paper with the license number written on it.

"The ignition key is to a 1997 green VW Jetta, New York tags. When you run a check on the plates, I'd be interested knowing who it's registered to. If it's in Seamus Slattery's name, I'm gonna burn somebody's ass down at the DMV."

"I doubt it," Casey said. "It's probably in Rory's name."

Fields looked down at his notes, then up at Fanning. "Let me read you this," he said, sliding his hand over his necktie and tucking it back under his jacket. This time it was a tie of antique autos. "I want to be sure everything jibes before we ask for a search warrant."

Fanning grew anxious. They were taking too much time. He knew once Pearse McCauley realized Seamus Slattery was gone, the terrorist would have stripped the apartment of every piece of incriminating evidence.

The two agents appeared in no hurry. At this point, Fanning wondered how much success they had in the past catching bad guys.

Fields started to read from his yellow pad.

"Mike Allen, a bartender friend of yours, encountered a man on the subway—"

"Flushing Line," Fanning corrected. "Runs elevated in Queens...other side of the East River."

Fields crossed out the word and wrote over it. The agent continued reading. "...the Flushing Line, who he believed to be a former IRA terrorist, a man involved in two London bombings ten years ago that killed his wife. He followed him to a house in Woodside, Queens, which we subsequently learned was owned by one Rory McCauley...."

Fields droned on, covering all the details Casey had reported to him earlier, until he got to the part where Fanning found the keys and the *Daily Racing Form* in front of the house.

"At this point, you called Detective-Sergeant Franks to report what you found, including the sighting of the man exiting the house from the downstairs unit. You know it is not Seamus Slattery because you have seen a ten-year-old photo of him, shown to you several times by Mike Allen. The description of the man coming out of the downstairs apartment fits a man we have on record, that of a pardoned IRA terrorist known as Pearse McCauley. Correct, so far?"

"So far."

"Because of where you found the keys, you believe your friend, Mike Allen, might have physically confronted the man, Seamus Slattery, in front of the house. And at this juncture, we do not know what has happened to either Mike Allen or the supposed terrorist, Seamus Slattery."

"That's right." Now, he thought, comes the touchy part.

"Okay, I believe we've got enough probable cause for a search warrant,"

Fields said.

Fanning looked at Casey Franks. She looked back, puckering her cheeks, forcing a grin. Jack Fields never mentioned my unauthorized entry, he thought. On top of it, he claims to have enough for probable cause. I'm blown away. At Creedmore, with so little evidence, I couldn't get a warrant to look up Seamus Slattery's nose.

"How long to get the warrant?" Fanning asked. He eyed his watch. It was just after one o'clock.

Fields turned around in his chair. "Where's a phone?"

Casey pointed to a corner of the room. "Over there on that table."

Fields moved to it. "We'll swing by Federal Plaza on our way…pick it up."

"Jesus, that soon? You're joking, aren't you?"

Tony Condon spoke. "Nope. Thanks to the Patriot Act." Smiling uncharacteristically, he rubbed the top of his brushy skull as if it was part of a good luck ritual. "It expanded the Foreign Intelligence Surveillance Act to include this type of search where international terrorism is involved."

Fanning looked toward Casey again. She grinned and two large dimples appeared in her peach-blossom cheeks.

"You guys ready?" Fields said after hanging up the phone.

"That include me?"

Fields laughed. It was the first time Fanning had seen him show anything broader than a grin.

"Yeah, you too. We need to be sure we're at the right house, don't we?"

"You want to follow me?"

"No, you go ahead. We have to pick up the search warrant first. Casey, why don't you ride with Detective Fanning? We'll meet you in front of the house."

❖

Casey Franks and Pete Fanning came out the door, leaving Fields and Condon still up in the apartment. Pearse McCauley left little behind after he cleaned out the place: a bit of clothing plus the pile of *Daily Racing Forms*. Pete wondered if they were also going to inventory the six-pack of Harps.

Fields said they needed another warrant to enter Pearse McCauley's apartment downstairs. He intended to return with it, but it was unlikely anything of importance would turn up. If Pearse cleaned out the upstairs apartment, it was certain he left nothing incriminating in his own.

"You want to wait for Frick and Frack or ride back with me?" Fanning asked her.

"I think I'll go with you. Give me a second. Let me tell them we're leaving."

When Casey returned, she was giggling.

"What's so funny?"

"They asked if you wanted to come back with them later when they searched Pearse's apartment. I told them you had to get back. "

"Were they serious?"

"Yes, that's what I find so funny."

Fanning steered the Taurus in the direction of Skillman Avenue and the Queensboro Bridge to Manhattan. At the bridge's mid-span, he spoke up. "What a pair of assholes."

Casey showed no reaction except to say, "Well, they are deliberate and thorough."

"I should have grabbed all that stuff while I was there earlier instead of waiting for their search warrant. We could have claimed we found it after we went in with the warrant. What's Seamus gonna do, argue with that?"

"They don't work that way. Besides, then you'd have to explain your illegal entry."

"You already told them, didn't you, you fink? They're just playing dumb."

"Lucky you," she said, grinning.

At the end of the bridge, they circled the local streets to enter the FDR Drive, downtown. The traffic was still light with most of the heavier flow coming uptown from lower Manhattan.

"I know for sure Seamus Slattery was using that apartment," he said.

"How? Nothing there had his name on it."

"Open the glove compartment."

Casey pressed open the lid and looked in. "What am I looking for?"

"Right there, on top of the owner's manual…the picture frame."

Casey took it out and held it up. "Who is it?"

"Seamus Slattery's wedding picture. I copped it when I was up in the apartment. I'm positive it's him. Mike showed me the picture in the article a couple of times."

She held up the photo to the window, examining it. "Cute couple."

"Yeah, I can see him cradling the frame, pining for his wife while he blows away some English soldier on the streets of Belfast."

"Well, he doesn't match the description of the white guy the Feds have seen going in and out of the Astoria Park mosque."

Fanning whipped his head around. "Is that right? You're holding out on me?"

"I didn't mention it because they haven't a clue who this guy is. Just a description. Tall, blond or red hair, mid-forties. Drives a white panel truck."

An image of the news dealer emerged. "Any pictures?"

"Yeah, from far away. The enlargements are fuzzy."

They were passing the Twenty-third Street heliport when a whirlybird, rising over the river, caught Fanning's attention. He looked up. "Delivering some corporate big shot to his South Hampton getaway for the weekend," he said, thinking aloud.

"What is?"

"The chopper…just took off from the heliport. Didn't you see it?"

"No. I was still looking at this photo."

"That reminds me. Do you know where Pearse's brother, Rory, moved to on Long Island?"

"Yeah. I'm sure we have it on record. I seem to remember he opened another pub somewhere on the south shore. Bay Shore, I think. Why?"

"I want to pay him a visit tomorrow. Want to come with me?"

"You think he might be willing to talk? Maybe give us information on his brother?"

"Yeah. I have a feeling Rory decided to wash his hands of Pearce's IRA shenanigans. That's why he moved out. Worth a shot. Bring your bathing suit. If it turns out to be a bust, we can always check into a motel. Go for a swim at one of the beaches out there."

She laughed. "You'd like that."

Teddy left the men's room having washed his hands, mouth, nose, face, arms and feet as prescribed by Islamic practice, and took his place near the back of the mosque's meeting room.

Tonight, it would be silent prayer, standing, bowing and in a prostrate position, but no sermon. That was reserved for Fridays, when the whole congregation met.

Hatred and violence were often keynotes preached openly by the firebrand imams at the more radical mosques in New York. Teddy had not heard that level of rhetoric from the imams of the Astoria Park mosque. Not until three Fridays ago. That night he heard a harsher tone injected into the sermon by the younger of the two prayer leaders, the lightly bearded Sheik Omar, a Sunni. More evidence of it appeared in his sermon a week later.

He looked around and recognized a few of the attendees, devout bearded Muslims he had seen in the past at the Friday noon sermon. Their presence always tweaked his conscience, reminding him of his own half-hearted practice of the faith into which he was born.

They began taking their positions on the floor for the start of the eight-twenty-four prayer service. He scanned the faces of the men surrounding him. He found nothing but Islamic characteristics in their features and dress. Nobody among them looked anything like the photos of the five-suspected al-Qaeda Jack Fields had shown him. Teddy had a clear view of the door that led to the outside corridor of the mosque. Throughout the fifteen-minute prayer service, he kept watch. No one came through or passed by.

At the conclusion of the service, he filed out with the others but chose to make a fast bathroom stop before going to his SUV. He entered the bathroom. To his relief, it was empty.

He arrived at his automobile in time to see a white panel truck pull into the lighted parking lot and stop at the rear door of the mosque. Teddy peered over his SUV's hood before climbing up behind the wheel. The panel truck had markings on the door. The letters, framed within an oval outline, were too far away to read them. The exiting driver was a tall man with light hair color, definitely not Middle Eastern. Teddy thought he should drive past to get a closer look, but he remembered Jack Field's warning.

"You have a problem?"

The familiar raspy voice came from behind. Teddy whirled, startled by the intrusion. From a black pick-up truck parked nearby, a short but well built, dark haired Muslim man, clean-shaven with a trimmed mustache, closed in on him. He wore a loose fitting long sleeve shirt that reached above the knees of his black trousers. His English had a heavy Middle Eastern inflection.

"Oh, no. No. I was just going though all my pockets looking for my car keys. I thought I had dropped them during prayers this evening. I found them. Here," he said holding them up. "I usually keep them in my pants, but I guess I put them in my jacket pocket by mistake."

The man fixed his gaze on him. "I see. You okay then?"

"Yes, yes, thanks very much."

The man nodded and started in the direction of the mosque. Teddy climbed into his vehicle, driving off in the opposite direction toward the parking lot's exit. He watched though his rear view mirror as the man disappeared into the mosque's back door. He remembered he had mentioned to Jack Fields that one of the voices he'd heard in the mosque's bathroom that day had a raspy sound to it. He wondered if it had registered with the agent.

❖

"You're going where?" Anne asked as she slipped into bed beside him. She smelled of baby powder and toothpaste.

"Bay Shore," Fanning said. "On the south shore. It's where the ferry leaves for Fire Island. I need to talk to a guy who might help in locating Mike."

"Jesus, Pete. It's Sunday. All you've been doing is finding excuse after excuse for being somewhere else. This whole week, you haven't spent an entire day at home."

"What am I supposed to do? Mike's gone missing. I can't just forget that."

Please don't ask if I'm going alone, he thought. Admitting Casey Franks was going with him would set her off, for sure. He felt the heavy grip of guilt take him by the throat.

"I'll be back late afternoon," he said, whining out the words. "We can go to a movie after dinner, if you like." He stole closer and kissed her neck "You in the mood?"

"No," she snapped, rolling away from him.

CHAPTER 11

Sunday, June 2

Pete Fanning steered the Taurus into the small parking area behind the weatherworn building and pulled to the rear entrance of The Lobster Shack. The clean aroma of salt air filled their nostrils as soon as he and Casey Franks stepped out of the car.

"God, that smells good, doesn't it?" she said. "Salty."

"Yeah. You can almost hear the ocean surf, and we're still a block away. Bring your suit?"

She shook her head, smiling.

"Me neither. Maybe after we finish here, we go find the nude beach, do a little skinny-dipping. I understand there's one out on Fire Island."

This time she laughed.

"Let's go in the front," he said. "We don't want to scare him coming in through the kitchen."

They rounded the corner of the sun-bleached clapboard structure, traversed the white pebbled ground cover, arriving at the entrance as the wind picked up. It peppered their faces with a soft, salty breeze.

"Aaah, feel that," she said, pausing at the door.

Round tables sporting a rainbow of multi-colored umbrellas, but few patrons, filled a raised, open deck to the ocean side of the restaurant. Still early, Fanning thought, checking his watch.

They inquired at the bar for Rory McCauley. The bartender phoned the back office, and Fanning slid from his bar stool when he saw the proprietor approaching.

Fanning had caught a glimpse of Pearce McCauley's face the other day as the bull-like Irishman dashed out his front door and down the two steps. The stronger image of the fat man etched in Fanning's memory was from the rear—of the big frame rumbling up the street. Still, looking at Rory McCauley now coming toward him, there could be no doubt they were brothers.

"Hi Rory," he said, extending his hand. "I'm Detective Pete Fanning, and this is Detective Casey Franks. We're with the NYPD," he said, displaying his gold shield. "We'd like to ask you a few questions. Did we catch you at a bad time?"

McCauley eyed Fanning with caution. The man was large, but not fat like his brother, and older by ten years. He had on a short sleeved mock turtle that fit him like someone who had tried to keep his body in good shape without much success.

"Is there a problem?" McCauley asked. "What's this about?"

"We'd like to ask you some questions…about your brother," Fanning said. "Can you give us a couple of minutes?"

McCauley looked toward the black-shirted bartender washing glasses at the sink nearby. "Yes, sure. Let's go out on the deck. Can I offer you something to drink?"

Casey spoke up. "Iced tea, if it's not any trouble."

"How 'bout you, Detective? A beer or something?"

"Nothing for me, thanks. On second thought, a cup of black coffee would be great."

"Lew?" McCauley said, looking at the bartender.

"Right away, Rory."

They followed him through the open French doors leading out to the deck, to a table at the back corner. McCauley dropped into a chair, folded his arms across his broad chest and shook his head. He closed his eyes, spitting out his brother's name like a swear word. "Pearse."

They waited.

"Glory to God," he said, "what in hell is he up to now?"

Fanning's eyes landed on Casey with a look that said, *I told you, no sympathy here*, and sat down.

"That's what we were hoping you'd be able to tell us," she said.

The muscles of McCauley's face tightened.

"The 1998 amnesty agreement covered his past activity with the IRA," she continued. However, it appears he's now playing house with a Seamus Slattery, a member of a dissident group called the Real IRA. The group is banned from this country and support of any kind is prohibited."

"Slattery? Jaysus! The man's a feckin' psycho." His eyes darted to her face. "Sorry, ma'am."

"Nothing I haven't heard before, although I think I prefer the way the Irish say it."

"You know him, I take it?" Fanning asked.

"Him and his whole bleedin' family. They were all nuts. Half of them killed in Londonderry during the Bloody Sunday riots in '72."

"But a great many Irish Catholic family members, active in the IRA, were killed in that fighting. Isn't that true?" Casey asked.

"Absolutely. In 1913, on the day it was established, Slattery's grandfather and mine joined the IRA. My grandfather stood with Michael Collins in the Dublin General Post Office during the Easter Rising in 1916. He was one of the sixteen leaders executed by the

British." A noticeable tone of pride accompanied the short recitation of his grandfather's fate.

McCauley was a large, raw-boned man, round-shouldered, with thinning red hair and a pronounced bulbous nose showing a roadwork of fine purple veins. He had soft eyes, and when he spoke, the timbre of his voice had the soothing effect of an old fashioned storyteller.

McCauley continued. "I have a framed reproduction of the 1916 Proclamation of the Irish Republic hanging in my living room. It's the one read at the GPO by Padraig Pearse before that bloody morning turned bloody."

"I remember covering that in one of my history courses," she said. "It was the defining event in the history of Irish republicanism. You must be proud of him?"

McCauley's gaze drifted. When he spoke, his voice had a tremble in it. "By God, I am. My *da* named my brother after Padraig Pearse. Those were the real heroes of the Irish cause. A couple a hundred brave Irish patriots took over important government buildings…held off a heavily armed British force—over eight thousand—for a week."

"Was Seamus's grandfather killed in the fighting?" Fanning asked.

"No. Killed later, ambushed by the Black and Tans in the late thirties. In '43, his son, Eamon, signed on. Later, he brought Seamus and his two brothers aboard when they were old enough."

"Sounds like a long patriotic history," she said.

"Naaah. They were off their nut, willing to kill anyone that got in their way, Irish Catholics included. I'm ashamed to say, that's when Pearse threw in with them."

Lew arrived with the ice tea and coffee. The bartender set them on the table and went back inside.

"I gather then, you didn't join up with the IRA," Fanning asked.

"Oh no, you're wrong. I was a member. As active as anyone in Belfast, until my group firebombed the La Mon House Hotel in '78, killing twelve innocent people. That's when I packed it in, came to America. Ten years later I became a U.S. citizen."

"Why did you sell your pub in Woodside and move out here?"

McCauley's face saddened as he looked back. He spoke, lowering his eyes, his head bent. "My wife of twenty years died of ovarian cancer four years ago. A little over a year ago, Pearse showed up looking for a place to live. I took him in until he could get on his feet."

"What happened when he moved in?" Casey asked, squeezing a wedge of lemon into her tea.

"He got a job with a company in Long Island City rebuilding electric motors, or so I thought. Owned by an Arab family, he told me. My upstairs tenants moved out, so Pearse moved up there. Next thing I know he's using the apartment to put up fugitives still wanted back in Ireland."

Fanning rested his coffee cup on the table. "You couldn't stop him?" he asked.

"No. He was out of control. I had a good notion what they were about. I didn't want any part of it. I needed to get the hell away, so I sold my restaurant in Woodside, came out here."

"Do you remember the name of the company he worked for?" She asked. "And where in Long Island City it was located?"

Several gulls swooped overhead, circling the deck, landing on the eave of the roof behind them. McCauley watched for a moment. "No, I don't. However, it couldn't have been far from the Vernon/Jackson train station in Long Island City. Pearse always took the train at Roosevelt Avenue. That's where he got off."

The station's name clicked. Fanning remembered Mike Allen's initial encounter with Seamus Slattery. Someone boarding the train at that station joined the Irishman. Allen described him as a swarthy, well-dressed man. He could be one of the family owners of this electric motor company. A picture started to form.

"You said before, you had a good idea what he was up to," Casey said. "Can you elaborate?"

"Jaysus, I shudder when I think what it might be."

"And that would be…?"

McCauley drew in and blew out a large breath, inflating further the rounded paunch that spilled over his belt line. He shook his head and looked off with a pain-filled expression. Fanning surmised the internal fight between feelings of family allegiance and a citizen's duty tore at him.

"Well, I've no real proof of anything," McCauley said after the long pause, "but both Pearce and Seamus, you understand, were electricians by trade."

He hesitated. The few lunch-hour patrons drifting into the restaurant remained inside, away from the heat. After scanning the empty tables around them, he continued.

"Pearce was what you'd call in this country, a master electrician. He was…Jaysus, I hate to say it…a genius at bomb making. His skill at building and detonating them was the bane of the English soldiers in Belfast for years. Seamus was good too, but he was better with the planning end of things. His weapon of choice was the gun, and the bastard loved to use it. He was a shooter, a crack shot."

"So you think they might be plotting something…in New York City specifically?"

The restaurateur reached out to tap the arm of a passing waitress. She pulled up like a reined-in filly. "What can I get you, Rory?"

"Bring me an Irish coffee, will ya darlin'? No hurry." He turned back to Fanning. "Sorry. You were saying?"

"I was asking if you think they might be plotting something here in the States?"

"Mother of God, I hope not. I can't think of any reason why they would do something that foolish. They'd surely alienate what little support the

Real IRA may have in this country. As I said, Seamus is a total psycho. There's no tellin' what would push him in that direction."

"Speaking of support," Casey said, "where do you suppose they get their financial backing? Before the amnesty agreement, we know there were tons of Irish-Americans giving money to support the IRA cause. Does this splinter group engender the same level of backing?"

"I've no idea," McCauley answered. "Not from any of the Irish I knew back in Woodside." He fell silent, thinking for a moment before adding, "Or no one I've come to know out here during this past year. I suppose there are still those fanatics living in this country who hold on to the dream of Irish home rule…see the British the hell out."

While McCauley spoke, Fanning remembered the Arab family business in Long Island City. Was there an al-Qaeda connection with the business? Was al-Qaeda financing Seamus Slattery and Pearce McCauley and their purpose for being in the U.S.? If so, were the Irishmen working for the Arabs in exchange for something? These were questions for the Feds.

He thought of another question for McCauley. It had bothered him since the day he found the *Daily Racing Forms* in the apartment. "I realize you haven't seen him in over twenty years, but before you left Ireland, did you ever see Seamus show an interest in the Sport of Kings?"

For a moment, McCauley looked puzzled by the question until he burst out laughing. "Oh, you mean horse racing, do you? Seamus was too low class for anything that elite. Believe me, any outside interest he might have would need to involve a blood sport."

"Just a hunch," Fanning said, taking a last swallow of coffee.

"You've been most cooperative," she said, motioning to Fanning that it was time to leave. "I think we'll let you get back to business, and we'll be on our way."

"Yeah, thanks, Rory. You've been a great help. We need to piece together the info you've provided into the puzzle, see where it leads."

McCauley pushed his chair back and stood. "My brother's his own worst enemy, he is. I just hope he's not up to anything as stupid as you suspect."

"We do too," Casey said.

McCauley placed his large hand on Fanning's shoulder. "If you got time, stay for lunch. Our menu is the best in Bay Shore."

Fanning looked over at Casey. She looked at her watch. "I guess I could do with a quick bite before heading out," adding, "provided we're allowed to pay the tab. Okay, Pete?"

McCauley protested. "You mean I can't treat you guys to lunch?"

"Next time. When we come back off the clock," Fanning said. "The lobster looks great."

The Taurus rolled along the bumpy surface of the Sagtikos Parkway, heading toward the Long Island Expressway. Casey sat in silence as they covered the five-mile stretch to the interchange. The car radio, tuned into a local all-jazz station, filled the void.

Fanning tossed around in his mind the information Rory McCauley had provided while Casey examined the passing arid terrain of Long Island's south shore. He circled the cloverleaf onto the L.I.E. and looked over. "So, how were the steamers?"

"Outstanding. How was the lobster and shrimp sandwich? It looked yummy."

"Fantastic. Gotta find an excuse to come back out soon. Try the lobster dinner."

"Rory seemed like a straight-shooter," she said.

"I got the feeling he wasn't his brother's biggest fan."

"Pearse doesn't sound too stable."

"Still, they're brothers. Whatever Rory said has to be considered in that light."

"I didn't think he was being protective of him. Did you?"

"I don't know. He did show a little brotherly worry at the end. That's natural, I suppose. Do you think if he knew anything, he'd throw him to the wolves?"

"Well, he showed no fondness for Seamus," she said. "That much was obvious."

Exits whizzed by as they sped along the six-lane highway. Fanning lowered the radio volume. "Why don't we go over what we have? See how it fits together with what we already know."

"For starters," she began, "Rory seems to have washed his hands of the IRA."

"So, can we assume he's not involved in whatever his brother and Seamus are up to?"

"That's my guess," she said. "Over twenty years of clean living without a trace of activity in anything IRA. Pretty solid evidence he's distanced himself from his former life."

"Okay, what else do we know?" he asked.

"Pearce is a master electrician and an expert bomb maker."

Fanning glanced down at his speedometer. "Hey, I better slow down. Last time I was on the L.I.E., a state trooper in aviator sunglasses stopped me for going ten miles over the limit. He gave me a pass after I flashed him my badge, but I can't be sure *Trooper Good-guy* would be that forgiving a second time."

Casey chuckled.

"Okay, so they worked for a company in Long Island City that repairs electric motors."

"Well, at least Pearce did," she said. "We're not sure about Seamus."

"Rory said it was a company owned by Arabs…Mike's account of the man he saw on the train with Seamus…remember? He described him as a well-dressed Arab. Could be the owner."

"Sounds like it."

"Think you could run it down tomorrow when you get to the office? See how many Arab-owned electric motor-repair companies there are in that area. Not many, I suspect."

"And if I find one or two, do I fill in the Feds or keep it to ourselves?"

"Fill 'em in, of course. It's their caper. I hope they'll know what to do with the information and move off their asses in a timely way."

"Christ, Pete, you're pretty tough on them. The Feds are always slower than the local police when it concerns terrorism. Picking up one or two known suspects isn't as effective as grabbing a whole cell at one time."

"Yeah, but I worry ole Frick and Frack move like snails."

"Don't sweat it. They know what they're doing."

They covered the next few miles in thought until a lipstick-red Mustang convertible flew by. The driver, her rumpled blond hair streaming in the wind, was doing well over eighty.

"Damn, where's that state trooper now?"

Casey snickered before falling back into silence.

"You know what bugs me?" Fanning asked several minutes later.

"What's that?"

"Rory couldn't say if the Real IRA received financial contributions in the US. Then why the lists of Irish names and numbers I found in the apartment? It pisses me off that these misfits are getting money from Americans to support their activities in Ireland."

"We don't know they are."

Fanning shook his head. "Well, if not from Irish sympathizers, who?"

"Maybe the Arabs."

"That's possible. But why would they get involved helping the IRA cause?"

"You mean, what's the *quid pro quo?*"

"Exactly."

"Maybe a common enemy...a common target. The boys' bomb-making expertise is a commodity that might be useful to them. You know, putting it together and planting it."

Fanning thought a moment. "And a terrorist with a brogue? Not apt to attract attention like someone with a Muslim appearance. Right?"

"You got it."

He reached over, raising the palm of his hand in the air. When Casey returned the high-five, he chuckled. "Sweetheart, that's why you get the big bucks."

"I'd take the credit, but it's a theory the Feds have been working on for a while. They've been watching the two non-Muslims going in and out of the mosque with that in mind."

"Wow! I'm impressed. I have a feeling we find their connection, we find their plot."

Fanning slowed as they came to the Queens-Midtown Tunnel tollbooths. Once inside the westbound mile-and-a-quarter-long tube to Manhattan, Casey said, "I'm curious, why did you ask Rory if Seamus was into horse racing?"

"Why? Have you forgotten the stack of *Daily Racing Forms* I found in the apartment?"

"You think he was a bettor?"

"No. If he had them there for handicapping, the racing charts would have all sorts of notations on them. There were none on any of the copies I examined."

"What's your feeling? Why were they there?"

"I'm not certain," Fanning admitted. "Several were left open, folded to articles on the up-coming Belmont Stakes. I didn't read them. I had to get the hell out of there as soon as possible."

"I'll pass that onto Fields and Condon. See what they think."

"I hope they haven't tossed them out with the six-pack of Harps."

CHAPTER 12

Mike Allen slipped his thumb and forefinger between two slats of the blinds in the living room picture window. He spread them just enough to see the black metal box at the side of the door filled with mail. He thought of stepping out, grabbing the envelopes, but changed his mind. He remembered the overflowing box was further visual evidence no one was home.

He moved back into the kitchen to check on the Stouffer's in the microwave. The freezer had another week's supply of frozen dinners. When they were gone, he would have to consider re-stocking—that is, if he intended to keep Seamus Slattery locked up much longer.

He hadn't made up his mind. Killing him was the most appealing option. But was it? Could he commit cold-blooded murder? It was a decision with so many consequences, consequences that, in the quiet of his recent sleepless nights, he anguished over. Was he ready to embrace the inevitable outcome of such an extreme act in the name of revenge? He imagined how Kathy would respond—a foolish exercise because he knew the answer.

The fury he nurtured these ten years had begun to temper each time he vented on his captive like a slow letting of air from an inflated balloon. While he knew he hadn't expelled the complete measure of his anger, he had a good idea where less heated, more rational thoughts would eventually lead.

Still hungry, he finished the Stouffer's dinner. It surprised him. His usual large, man-sized appetite during the past three days had all but disappeared, until today. Returning to the pantry, he opened a four-serving can of Progresso Tomato Soup, intending to feed Slattery half its contents along with dry toast.

Descending to the basement, Allen placed the Colt .45 on the chair outside the cubicle and unlocked the door. He lowered the cup and toast to the floor within reach of the Irishman.

Slattery looked up from his prone position on the mattress. He had his head propped on one elbow like a sunbather on a beach. He sat up and reached for the cup of soup with his right hand, bringing in his three-fingered left hand to lend additional support.

Allen slipped the .45 into his belt and straddled the chair, facing into the cubicle. "What happened to your hand?" he asked, uncertain that Slattery would answer honestly.

The Irishman lowered the cup from his mouth. "Had a bit of nitro explode accidentally," he said, surprising Allen with his candid response.

"And your limp? A birth defect?"

"No, to be sure."

"So, what happened?"

Slattery bit off a corner of dry toast, chewed and washed it down with a gulp of tomato soup. After swallowing, he said, "Took a round in that hip during a skirmish in Belfast with the Prods. Six-and-a-half years ago."

"A shoot-out?"

"Ambush. Never saw them coming from behind."

"That's the part I can't get my mind around, the idea of Irishmen killing Irishmen. You share the same country…for the last couple of centuries, the same heritage. I read that 3,200 on both sides, Protestant and Catholic, have died since what you call the *Troubles* began in '69."

"And how's that different from your own civil war? Lots more people died for that cause."

The ringing sound of the telephone drifted down from the open kitchen door. Allen ignored it. "You're right, I'm afraid. The difference is our insanity lasted four years. Yours has been going on for four centuries."

Slattery put the cup down next to him. "Fella," he began softly, "ya don't understand Ireland if ya think we're of the same heritage as the Prods. They came from England. Took away our homes, our land, our self-respect. We're just fightin' to get back what's rightfully ours."

Allen sat up straight. "I don't know what they teach in your schools, how all this shit between Protestant and Catholics came to be."

"And how would ya know? You're not Irish." His faced pinched as he shouted at Allen. "You're not even English."

"Man, I read every historic source I could get my hands on these past ten years, trying to understand why my wife had to die in a fight she had nothing to do with."

"Well then, can ya now appreciate why we hate the English?"

"No I can't. Here's why. Your Gaelic kings…all of them…they rolled over for the English when England invaded Ireland in the twelfth century. Those provincial kings …they spread their knees for Henry the Second and pleaded, 'Oh please don't take my kingdom. I'll pay you rent, obey your mandates. Just let me keep my lands.' They could have banded together, stood their ground. Instead, they became a self-serving, greedy lot.

"Next two centuries when any of these Gaelic kings died off, the English replaced them with their own aristocracy. You know what happened then?" Allen paused, waiting for his question to sink in. "Intermarriage. That's what. And presto! Up popped a large Anglo-Irish population. Ireland became their country. Like it was to your Gaelic ancestors."

Slattery glared, digesting what he heard. "Yeah, but they were all Prods."

"Not all of them. Some of them were Catholic."

"The majority were Prods beholden to the kings of England. Those bastards spent the next six centuries keeping Catholics down."

"Because you let them."

"And what would ya have us do? We tried politics. That never worked. Them representing the Irish never got anywhere with the British Parliament. Even today, that feckin' toe-rag, Trevor McNeill…supposed to be fightin' for Irish interests as the spokesman for Northern Ireland. Turns out he's useless as a lighthouse on a bog. Shines up to anyone in Parliament can do him personal good."

"Those are the ones I'm talking about. Your politicians throughout history…a bunch of scumbags out for themselves, like your kings. Few were honest men."

Slattery seemed to be absorbing his words. Allen continued.

"You guys should have stopped listening to the clergy."

Slattery jerked up his chin.

"That's right. The lords controlled the clergy from early times, in both the Gaelic and Anglo-Irish churches. Jesus, your priests and bishops were their clients. Your clergy, your poets, your writers…they all romanticized the Irish cause. It fueled your anger. Kept you looking for a solution through violence."

"There was no other way," Slattery protested. His voice had become shrill. "Ireland was fightin' for its existence. If we gave in, there'd be no Ireland today. England was a powerful country."

"It certainly was. Like it or not, the English brought Ireland out of the dark ages. Every time you fought back with violence, you lost. They confiscated more and more of your land. You never seemed to get the message."

"And how would ya have us done it different?" Slattery challenged.

"To start, recognize you guys were too culturally backward, too weak economically and militarily to resist the might of the British Empire. Then fight them by trying to assimilate."

"What's that mean?"

"That means learn to speak proper English, self-educate, elect honest politicians to the Irish Parliament. Don't you know Ireland could have broken England's colonial hold a century ago just by becoming their equal? You'd already proven yourselves in commerce, in letters, intellectually many times over. Instead, you went for the gun."

The telephone on the kitchen wall rang again, breaking the mood. Allen stood, slipping the chair out from under him. Time to end it, he decided. The air was out of the balloon. He didn't have the will to execute the Irishman. He knew that now. The question was what to do with Slattery. He had kidnapped him, and for that he was liable. Slattery could bring charges or, in a moment of understanding, let it go as a bad experience.

The Irishman's voice broke through his distraction. "Ya think I can have a piss now?"

"Huh, oh yeah."

Allen followed him to the small bathroom in the corner of the basement and waited while Slattery entered and closed the door. Facing the stairs with the .45 in his hand, he thought of what to tell Pete. He knew his friend would explode when he learned of his insane act.

After several minutes, the bathroom door crept open. With a swift sideways glance, Allen caught sight of the porcelain top of the toilet tank sailing toward him. Too late to move out of the way, he ducked his head, and the tank cover crashed into the back of his skull, sending him down to his knees, sprawling face down across the concrete floor.

The .45 semi-automatic flew from Mike Allen's hand, landing a few yards from his prone body. Seamus Slattery darted for it. Wheeling around, he aimed the barrel at his jailor's head. The big man lay frozen on the floor. Slattery wasn't sure if he had knocked him unconscious or just stunned him. He could see the right side of his face as he lay on the concrete floor. He steadied the weapon and continued to point it at Allen's head until he was satisfied his abductor was not conscious. With deliberation, he lowered the gun barrel slightly, moved it an inch to his right and pulled the trigger. The bullet smashed into Allen's back, just above the right shoulder blade, splattering blood from underneath and across his face.

Slattery whirled, taking the stairs two at a time, reaching the top step before the echo from the gunshot faded. Realizing he had no way to hide the weapon, he raced into the living room in search of a coat closet. He found one in the foyer at the front door. The windbreaker he pulled off the hanger was huge, but he slipped it on anyway, zippered it to cover the pistol, and turned back to the kitchen. Passing through the living room, he spotted his cell phone lying on the coffee table. He shoved it into his pocket and dashed out the kitchen door.

When Fanning dropped off Casey at her apartment in Murray Hill, the gas gauge in the Taurus showed he had a quarter of a tank left. He decided to head home by way of Jackson Heights, fill up there, and at the same time, check Mike's house again. He pulled into Tony's Chevron on Northern Boulevard and spotted his friend's Buick parked to one side.

"Hey, Tony, how are you?" he yelled to the man in the open bay, under the car on the lift.

Tony looked over. "Damn, if it ain't Pete Fanning. How goes it, Sarge?" The mechanic walked toward him, wiping his hands with the rag he took from the back pocket of his coveralls. "How's the new neighborhood? Forest Hills, isn't it?"

"You got it, pal, but it's not new any more. Unfortunately, there's no friendly Tony's in the area. I miss your smiling face."

Tony chuckled. "The blarney's still flowing, I see."

"Hey, Tony, that's Mikey's Buick over there, isn't it?"

"Yeah. Funny thing. He asked if he could leave it for a few days while they did work on the side of his house. That was four days ago. I haven't seen him since."

"Strange," Fanning said as he finished filling the tank. "I'll tell him you're gonna charge rent. That'll get him to move it."

Fanning made a left turn into Allen's one-way street lined with parked cars. A limping man coming from Allen's driveway and wearing an oversized windbreaker caught his eye. The man, hobbling with great effort, made his way toward Northern Boulevard.

Twenty yards past the strange figure, Fanning grasped the situation. "Son of a bitch, that's Seamus Slattery." He hit his brakes and began to back up, when a car turning into the street appeared in his rear view mirror. "I'm screwed," he moaned and threw the Taurus into drive.

He sped to the corner, took the next two right turns without stopping, and reached the intersection at Northern Boulevard. There was no sign of the Irishman in either direction. He noticed a local transit bus off in the distance heading west toward the city. He thought of chasing it to its next stop, but he remembered Mike Allen. Instead, he made two right turns.

The Taurus flew into the driveway and screeched to a stop at the back of the house. Fanning leaped out with his service weapon in his hand. He entered through the kitchen door, left wide open by the fleeing Slattery, and shouted for Allen from the middle of the kitchen. He heard the echo of his own voice and felt a chill.

Spotting the open door to the basement, he moved to it and stopped at the top step. His fingers tightened around the grip of his Glock before he raised it to a ready position. He could see the hanging bulb at the base of the stairs splashing a faint glow of light across the cement floor.

"Mikey," he called, whispering the name. An ominous silence came back. He remained locked in position until a rush of adrenalin propelled him forward.

Fanning took the steps slowly, both hands on his weapon. His ears strained for any sound. He reached bottom, slid around to the rear of the open staircase and crouched on one knee. His eyes and the 9mm Glock scanned the semi-lit space before he saw his friend sprawled on the floor.

He waited, listening, checking all the shadowy corners of the basement. It was deadly silent. He edged along the wall to the cubicle's open door, took a low position and pushed the Glock into the empty space. Satisfied the basement held no hidden danger, he scrambled to Allen's side.

Fanning drew a breath, feeling his own heart pounding as he put his fingers to Allen's carotid artery. The pulse was strong. Thank God! This is one tough son of a bitch, he reminded himself, enjoying a brief moment of relief.

The bullet had torn Allen's shirt where it hit. Blood was evident at the point of entry under his shoulder and at the side of his face. He prayed the bullet didn't hit a vital organ or a main artery. He had to act fast. Allen could bleed out in a short time. He dialed 9-1-1.

After identifying himself, he gave his badge number and command to the dispatcher. The voice requested his location and condition of the victim. Fanning complied. "Can you give me a description of the suspect and his last known location?" the dispatcher asked. It tested his patience.

He spit out the information, and before the voice could ask another, he exploded.

"Now get EMS here, fast," he screamed, just before he ended the call.

He flipped the phone open again and speed-dialed Jack Fields, giving him a rapid-fire account of the situation. "I lost him when I got to Northern Boulevard."

"You have no idea which way he went?" Fields asked.

"It's a good bet he's headed for the Woodside house. After he sees we emptied it out, he won't stay long. He's gonna know his safe-house cover's been blown."

"He was on foot, you say? We'll catch up to him there."

"Got anybody staking out that house? Because you'll never get there in time from downtown."

"We'll handle it," Fields replied.

Shit! Back to square one, Fanning thought.

He called Anne next. "Sorry, babe, but dinner and the movie will have to wait. I found Mikey, and it's not good."

He related what happened and heard her sobbing. "The good news is his pulse is strong. I'll call you when the paramedics get here. I'm going to follow them to the hospital, of course."

"Pete, I'm going too. I'll meet you there."

Slattery hobbled the sidewalk along Northern Boulevard, looking back over his shoulder every twenty yards. The butt of the .45 semi-automatic tucked into his waistband and hidden under the billowing, oversized windbreaker, stabbed at his rib cage with every step. Perspiration rolled off his brow and down his checks, burning his eyes. He reached the overpass of the Brooklyn/Queens Expressway, turned the corner and stopped to catch his breath. Pressing his back against the stone abutment, he wiped the sweat from the corners of his eyes and took in deep swallows of air, trying to calm himself. Jaysus, he thought, I'm not fit for this shit anymore. He choked out a guttural sound meant to be a laugh.

Traffic overhead rumbled as he peeked around the corner of the abutment, back in the direction of Allen's house. Satisfied no one followed him, he continued up the street in the direction of Woodside and his own flat. He reached the small, tree-lined park at the intersection of Broadway, stopped, looked around, and seeing no one in the park, took a seat on a bench. He fumbled for his cell phone and punched in Pearse McCauley's number.

"Seamus, ya arse-hole, where the feck ya been?" the voice screamed into his ear.

"On a three-day nightmare listening to a lot of blather, that's where."

"On a what?"

"Later."

"Where are ya?"

Slattery looked up at the street sign behind him. "Sixty-ninth Street and Broadway. I'm heading to the house."

"No, don't go there. It's being watched."

"What?"

"They got into the house. Searched it."

"Who?"

"Don't know, the Feds, probably."

"Holy shit! What about my lap top, my papers?"

"I got them. I grabbed everything."

Slattery thought back to his abductor, wondering if there might be a connection. Nothing said between them during his confinement gave any clue that the man knew why he was in the states. Or that he was on the FBI's watch list. Still…

He heard the fat man wheezing at the other end. "How'd ya know they got in?"

"I don't know for sure. I do know they're watching it. Had Tommy walk past the last two nights after he closed up the newsstand. He saw him. Same guy both nights."

"When did ya empty the flat?"

"Ya didn't get back Friday night so I called your cell Saturday morning. Someone answered. Didn't say anything. That's when I figured they'd grabbed ya. Went upstairs, packed up your lap top and brief case and beat it the hell out of there."

"Where'd ya go?"

"To the shop. I'm there now."

"My car, where is it?"

"At the house...on the street."

For a moment, Slattery considered trying to reach it, but he remembered he no longer had his keys. Besides, he guessed they were watching the car. "Is the pick-up there at the shop?" he asked.

"Yeah. Ya want me to come get ya?"

"I think so. Can't risk walking to Roosevelt Avenue...taking the train. There's a pub down the street. I can see it from here. Seaweed Tavern. Pick me up there."

CHAPTER 13

After Teddy's two-hour battle trying to get the shower curtain tension-rod to stay in place, he told Ellie, "If you insist on using both a rubberized curtain with the plastic liner, this type of rod is never going to work. It's too much weight."

"It works in our other bathroom," she said.

"The other rod sits on screw-in type brackets. It's not a tension rod. Besides, we don't need both curtains. The rubberized one is all we need."

"I like the way it looks," Ellie insisted, "with the inside and outside curtains."

Teddy found two screw-type brackets in his hardware catchall box in the closet and immediately went to work drilling holes in the tiles at both ends of the tub. When he completed that project, he called to Ellie.

"Where do you want me to mount the towel rack?" He knew where it should go, but he didn't want to be Monday-morning-quarterbacked again. The only thing he had completed that afternoon without being second-guessed was the installation of the sink spout and the hot and cold-water knobs. She had chosen the hardware, and thankfully, he thought, there wasn't much flexibility in where they went.

She appeared at the doorway, looked around in the manner that a construction project superintendent might, and said, "Right there, behind the door. Where else could it go?"

As Teddy drilled holes in the tile wall for the towel brackets, he wondered why he had not heard from Jack Fields today. He might have tried calling him after his encounter with the man in the parking lot last night, but Jack had made a point of saying, "Don't call me, I'll call you."

He finished mounting the towel rack and began feeling anxious. He knew what was bothering him. Grabbing his cell phone, he walked to the front door. "Ellie," he yelled, "I'm going out to pick up a *Sunday Times*. Be back in fifteen minutes." He didn't wait, bounding out of the house before she could respond.

Teddy turned up Twenty-third Avenue, heading toward the small 7-Eleven three blocks away. He looked at his watch. He knew if he took longer than he said, he'd be inviting Ellie's interrogation when he returned. The kids were at the public pool in Astoria Park. When the teens weren't around to distract Ellie, he became the focus of her unrelenting need to control.

He came out of the 7-Eleven with the *Sunday Times* cradled in his arms, flat against his broad chest. He stopped at the corner, took a seat on the bench adjacent to the kiosk of the Green Line bus stop, set the paper down next to him and hit Pete Fanning's speed dial number.

"Yeah, Teddy, what's up?" The voice sounded short and impatient.

"Pete, you busy? Something I need to talk to you about."

"Not now, Teddy. I'm at Queens General Hospital. My friend, Mike Allen, got shot. He's in surgery right now. Let me get back to you, if not tonight, tomorrow. Will it hold?"

"Yes. Sure. I guess it can."

"Okay, then. We'll talk tomorrow."

Teddy picked up the newspaper and headed back down Twenty-third

Avenue. Astoria Park was a small community of modest one- and two-story homes. Originally, in the early twenties and thirties, Italian and Irish families had occupied it. During the last twenty years, the ethnic makeup had gradually changed. The second generation of Irish and Italian homeowners, enamored with the suburban lure of Long Island and Westchester, sold out and sank their huge profits into split-levels and ranch-style houses outside the borough of Queens. Gradually, the old neighborhood transformed into a Mid-Eastern ghetto.

He could see the long span of the sixty-six-year-old Triborough Bridge in front of him. It stretched out over the wide East River toward Wards Island, where, in the middle of the busy waterway, it split off in three different directions. He became overwhelmed with the vision of this imposing suspension bridge, always packed with bumper-to-bumper traffic to and from Queens, Manhattan and the Bronx, exploding and falling into the river below. He tried to shake the powerful image of this potential disaster. Not that farfetched, he thought. The destruction of the two World Trade Center towers was an unimaginable concept before 9/11. Why not a major bridge as the next al-Qaeda target?

Teddy thought again of the conversation in the mosque bathroom, albeit broken, scattered sentences, but words so lethal in content, they had to be a real concern to the Federal agents. In context of the growing fear of terrorism in this country, the mere mention of bomb-making elements should sound a loud alarm.

Overhearing the name of the Saudi prince, Faisal bin Abdullah, still puzzled him. What role could the nephew of Arabia's King Fahd be playing in all of this? He hoped the Feds had it figured out. Regardless, he felt good having come forward with the information.

He hoped the two FBI agents took him seriously. That troubled him. He prayed they would arrest the gravel-throated terrorist and his conspirators before they inflicted whatever damage they planned.

Although he was confident of Pete Fanning's sincerity to shield him and his family from harm, Jack Fields and Tony Condon were another matter. He was not convinced the agents cared much about his safety.

Fanning and Anne had reached the hospital at the same time, Fanning following the EMS ambulance out of Allen's driveway and Anne by taxi from their house. They watched the three EMS attendants filling in the doctor and nurses as they wheeled in his friend. Within minutes, they rushed him upstairs into surgery.

The waiting was torture. Four-thirty dragged on to five-thirty. Fanning kept checking the wall clock, then looking at his wristwatch as though he didn't trust the hospital's timepiece. Five-thirty became six-thirty, two hours since they wheeled Allen into the elevator. He peeked at his watch one more time before turning toward his wife. Anne's worried expression was the catalyst he needed. They rose together.

"Detective, we have nothing new to tell you," the RN said. "He's still in surgery. That's all we know now. I'm sorry."

Anne's quivering voice asked, "That's not good, is it?"

"Not necessarily," he said, trying to assure his wife. "It just means they're taking extra care. It's a good hospital, good medical staff, so don't start worrying now."

They returned to their seats, sidestepping a loose child flinging himself with abandon in their path. Fanning knew Anne looked to him for answers. He was the professional. His expertise was supposed to be guns and their consequences. He should know how to read the nurse's reply. The truth was he was in the dark. Fifteen years on the force, he had never taken a bullet, nor had any of his partners. They'd been lucky.

Any bullet could be life threatening. That much he knew. The bullet had entered Allen's shoulder area. He thought back to his police academy training. Some textbook he read said the shoulder was the part of the torso where a bullet caused the least damage—if attended to immediately. He prayed the author of that textbook was right.

A tall, young man in a white coat and dark blue trousers interrupted his musing. The man approached, striding across the floor in his Reebok sneakers. He looked young, had a razor thin frame, and a head of tangled, sandy-colored hair. His intense expression struck Fanning as out-of-character for so young a nurse's aide.

"Detective Fanning? I'm Doctor Whitson," he said, extending his hand.

Fanning was on his feet. Anne followed. He reached out and stammered, "Huh, oh, yeah, hi, Doctor." He examined the young physician with disbelief. Was someone pulling his leg?

"Sorry to keep you in the dark so long," Doctor Whitson began, "but we had to be sure we removed the largest of the bullet fragments. The shot went through the right side of Mr. Allen's back, entering below the scapula into the rib cage, striking a rib, puncturing the lung. Since he received emergency medical attention so quickly, his wounds are not life threatening."

Anne expelled a loud breath. "Oh, thank the good Lord. Thank you, thank you."

The surgeon produced a tiny grin.

"You said you removed the largest fragments?" Fanning asked. "Does that mean—"

"We couldn't get it all, just the largest."

Anne's jaw dropped. "Oh, God."

"It's nothing to worry about," the doctor assured her. "It's not uncommon. What's left is small. Those fragments will just sit there...not affect anything. Think of them like a calling card letting you know you've been shot."

"Oh, great," Fanning mumbled. "Mikey's going to love hearing that."

Doctor Whitson continued. "Mr. Allen's got powder burns. We treated them. We also had to put in a chest tube. There was some hemorrhaging.

We confirmed it on x-ray, but he's stable now. The tube is to inflate the lung that collapsed during the trauma."

Fanning's eyes widened. For all his experience on the force, this was becoming an education in ballistic damage that, somewhere along the line, he had missed.

"Considering he was shot at close range, he was a lucky man. No major blood vessels damaged or affected. The procedure went well. Mr. Allen is resting comfortably in recovery."

"How soon before we can see him?"

"He's just now coming out from the anesthesia. Not anytime tonight, I'm afraid. I will need to repeat chest x-rays regularly to check the chest tube. Why don't you wait until tomorrow?"

Walking through the hospital's parking lot toward the Taurus, Anne broke the silence. "He looked like he just got out of high school. I thought he was one of the orderlies."

"Who? Oh, you mean the doctor. Yeah, I was surprised, too. He looked too young to be a surgeon. You suppose that's because we're getting older?"

"Not me. Speak for yourself."

"Hey, we got kids coming into the department today that don't look much older than Luke."

"Well, it sounded like he knew his stuff," she said, adding, "at least, I hope he did."

Fanning opened the door for Anne before coming around to the driver's side.

"You playing the horses now?" she asked as he slid under the steering wheel.

He slipped the key in the ignition. "What?"

"That newspaper…the *Daily Racing Form*…there on the back seat."

He turned and saw the paper. "Oh, jeeze, I forgot it was there."

He was going to explain, but he realized he would have to relate in detail his visit to Seamus Slattery's safe house. Thinking quickly, he told her, "I picked it up the other day, out of curiosity. One of the guys down at the office mentioned a big race coming up next Saturday. The Belmont Stakes. A horse named Gallant Warrior is going for the Triple Crown. He's already won the Derby and the Preakness."

Anne reached back, picked up the paper and read aloud the headline bannered across the front page, *Gallant Warrior Ready to Wear the Crown.*

He looked over at her. "That's the story."

"So?"

"So I might pay a visit to the OTB on Queens Boulevard…bet a big ten dollars on the race."

She folded the paper and tossed it at her feet. "And if you win, you can take us out for a nice, fancy dinner."

"Sounds like a plan," he said, turning west onto Queens Boulevard.

Halfway home, she announced, "Speaking of dinner, I've nothing in the freezer for tonight. I never got around to doing any shopping before you called. Should we stop?"

"Forget it. We'll go out somewhere for a bite."

They pulled into the driveway and saw Luke standing at the back door.

"How's Mikey?" he asked the moment they emerged from the car.

"Looks like he's going to be okay," Anne said. "We didn't see him. He's still in recovery. Maybe tomorrow afternoon."

Luke's face relaxed. "Wow, that's great."

"Get washed up. Your father is taking us out to dinner with all the money he's going to win betting on Gallant Warrior."

"Who?"

"Never mind, it's just a joke," Fanning said.

"Where we gonna eat?" Luke wanted to know. "I vote for Chinese."

"Done," Anne answered.

"No vote for me?"

"Not necessary, Harry the Horse. It's two against one."

Teddy crawled into bed, setting the alarm for seven. He had a job interview in the morning, the first in two months. Kraft Guidance Systems, one of the few companies responding to his heavy resume mailings, was a technology company producing software for the government. Its location in an industrial park on Long Island meant a two-hour round trip commute if he got the job. He dismissed it from his mind. Negative thinking seeping into his unconscious might ruin his mindset during his meeting with the project manager.

His prospects looked good. The project manager seemed upbeat when he called, reciting the software language of Teddy's expertise that fit with the job description. They were offering a salary that matched the one at the job he had lost, so things were looking up.

Ellie snapped off the light in the bathroom and slipped in beside him. "What time is your meeting?" she asked, reaching for the bedside light switch.

"I'm on for ten."

"You set the alarm?"

"Took care of it."

"Nervous?"

"A little. It's the 9/11 syndrome that concerns me."

She fluffed up her pillow and edged closer to stroke his hair. "Maybe enough time has passed. Maybe things will be different now."

He lay there in the darkened bedroom, his mind a swirling eddy of thoughts of his interview. He remembered he needed to call Pete Fanning tomorrow.

CHAPTER 14

Monday, June 3

Fanning and Anne waited in the hall until the nurse came out of the room.

"It's okay, Detective, you can go in now. He is not able to sit up yet, and he'll probably tire quickly. So if you wouldn't mind, don't stay too long."

"We won't," Anne said.

They quietly entered the room, solemnly flanking each side of the bed like first-time visitors to the Sistine Chapel. They stared down at the figure before them, his eyelids shut tight, and his broad chest heaving with slow rhythmic breathing.

He was pale as the sheet that covered him. The intravenous drip hanging at the head of the bed was feeding steadily through the tube attached to his forearm. A second tube running from a large piece of equipment at the side of the bed was snaked under the sheets, pumping air into his lungs.

The sight overwhelmed Anne. "Oh, God," she gasped.

Fanning looked at Anne. Her face was expressionless except for a quivering upper lip. Certain she would start crying again, he moved around to offer her comfort when the sound of Allen's strained voice froze him where he stood.

"For Christ sake, stop mourning. I'm not dead yet," the man in the bed said. His eyes squeezed open, but his mouth had hardly moved.

"Oh, good Lord," Anne exclaimed. Fighting back tears, she bent over, preparing to embrace Mike's broad body when she suddenly caught herself. Instead, she reached for the chair next to the window and scraped it up to the side of the hospital bed.

Cradling the hand that had found its way out from under the sheet, she asked, "How are you feeling, you big boob?"

Before he could answer, Fanning jumped in. "Mikey, you dumb shit. Soon as you get out of here, I'm gonna whip your ass good. You tried hard to get yourself killed. You know that? Scared the crap out of me."

Anne glared at her husband. He stood at the foot of the bed, a grin forming on his face.

"Pete, for God's sake."

"Nah, he's right, Annie. I took on more than I could handle. But I waited ten years for that chance. I couldn't let it go." His voice was weak.

"Don't talk, sweetie. We're just so happy you're going to be okay."

Allen smiled up at her.

"Is there anything you want us to bring you?"

Allen shook his head.

Fanning pushed another chair up close to the bed and sat down. "Not now, Mikey, but later, when you're up to it. I can't wait to hear how this little adventure went down. I hope you took notes."

Allen gave up a small laugh. "Screwed up this time, didn't I?"

"That all depends on who we talk to. Don't worry about that right now. Just follow orders around here. Let them put you back together. We'll worry about the rest of it later."

They sat there quietly for another few minutes, watching their friend's chest rise and fall under the sheet that covered him. Soon Allen's eyes fluttered and then closed. He was fighting sleep. Anne noticed it.

"Maybe we should go?" she said.

"Yeah, you're probably right." Fanning stood. "Mikey, we'll check in with you tomorrow. Get some rest."

Anne slid her chair back against the window. "Luke sends his love. He said to tell you the Yanks took two out of three from the Indians this week. He said that should make you feel better."

There was no reaction. Mike had closed his eyes.

Before leaving the hospital, Fanning received assurance from Doctor Whitson that Allen would make a full recovery, but he required a few more days under his care. Thursday was the soonest he could be released.

Arriving home, Fanning made two telephone calls. The first was to Teddy.

"Okay, Teddy. What's up?"

"I'm on the Expressway heading back. Can we meet somewhere to talk?"

Fanning looked at his watch. One-forty five. He wasn't anxious to give Anne more reason to bitch about family neglect. "This important?"

"Something's got me worried. I need you to tell me if I'm imagining things. Okay?"

"Yeah, I guess I can meet you. But not at that kids' park again. How soon?"

"In forty-five minutes. Let's say three o'clock…play it safe. Traffic is light now but you never know."

"I don't want to be gone more than an hour, Teddy. Okay? Go to Budd's Tavern on Northern Boulevard and Eighty-first Street. I'll wait for you there. Bye, Teddy."

Fanning dialed again, this time to Casey Franks. Listening to the ringing, he wondered why he selected Budd's to meet with Teddy. Budd's was a special place, always the tavern of choice whenever he and Mike Allen met for a catch-up and a pitcher of beer. Had he grown fond of the Indian?

The ringing stopped. "Wanda, Pete Fanning. Is she in?"

"Hold a sec," she replied.

"Hey, Pete, where you been?"

"Tell me, did Fields and company find Seamus Slattery at the house in Woodside?"

"Are you kidding? The guy never came anywhere near the place. They have no idea where to start looking for him."

"No surprise."

"Oh, Pete, I heard from Jack Fields about Mike Allen. How is he?"

"Okay, so far. Doctor said he'd be fine once they pump his lung back up. He was lucky. A little more to the left, we'd be making funeral arrangements."

"Fields wants me to debrief him. When do you suppose he'll be up to answering questions?"

"Later in the week. He's still in intensive care. Wednesday, maybe."

"I'll call the hospital that morning to make sure," she said.

"You want me there? I'm dying to hear his story."

She hesitated. "I guess. Listen, Pete. I filled in Fields on our visit to Rory yesterday."

"You did?"

"Certainly."

"And...?"

"And he was pissed at me for not letting him know I was going out there."

"You're supposed to do that?"

"Of course. I'm not an investigator. I overstepped my responsibility and he was all over me for it."

"Wow, Casey, I'm sorry. I hope this doesn't get you in hot water downtown. I shouldn't have asked you to go."

"Don't sweat it, Pete. You didn't put a gun to my head. I should have known better. I needed to touch base with them first, that's all."

"Did you tell him it was my idea?"

"Yes."

Fanning snickered. "That must have frosted him."

"That's putting it mildly. I'm sure he's going to want to speak with you."

"Thanks for the heads-up. Listen, I gotta go, but I'll check in with you before Wednesday."

Fanning watched Teddy Vijay step through the door and hesitate. He looked out of place in this neighborhood bar where most of the regulars, Irish and Italians, were comfortable, as in their own living rooms. Teddy panned around until he saw Fanning waving to him.

The big man hustled to the table, pulled up a chair and sat down opposite Fanning. He was dressed in a grey, pin stripe, single-breasted suit. A dark blue, broadcloth shirt with a white collar peeked out from under the jacket that covered his broad chest. His red and white rep tie set off his neatly put together appearance. Fanning thought Teddy's sartorial transformation was amusing, a stark contrast with the hulk in the Mickey Mouse tee shirt he crashed into a week ago

"What's your pleasure? Want to split a pitcher?"

Teddy squeezed together his thick, black eyebrows and said, "My family strictly observed the Muslim prohibition against drinking. I was raised that way."

Fanning's cheeks warmed. "Hey, I didn't realize…then maybe a Coke or something."

Teddy chortled. "I didn't say I was religious about it. I just never acquired a taste for beer."

"Okay, so how about—"

"But I'll have one with you now. Just a bottle, though."

"You sure?"

"Yeah. Maybe it'll taste better this time…you know…as a celebration drink."

"Celebration? What are we celebrating?"

Teddy's eyes widened. "A new job."

"No shit? Is that where you were this morning?"

"An interview…Kraft Guidance Systems out on Long Island. It's not final yet, but the project manager looks hot to hire me. He has to run it past the division manager first."

"Well, that's just great, Teddy. Congratulations."

"Thanks."

Fanning stood. "Domestic beer okay?"

"Fine. I don't think I'd know the difference."

Fanning returned with two green bottles. "Heineken. I went for the good stuff. A Dutch brew, in your honor. You didn't want a glass, did you?"

Teddy shook his head.

"So, is this why you wanted to talk?" Fanning set down the bottles and dropped into his chair.

Teddy studied the label on the bottle as he raised it. *"Prosit,"* he said.

Fanning waited for Teddy to take a sip.

"Not bad," he said, lowering the bottle.

"Okay, now, what's bugging you?"

Teddy pulled down the knot of his tie and opened the top button of his shirt. His face became serious as he started to speak. "I saw one of the guys from that night in the mosque's bathroom. I ran into him in the parking lot after prayers this past Saturday night."

"How do you know it was him?"

"His voice…the raspy one. It had to be him."

Fanning edged his chair closer to the table. "Was he at the service with you?"

"No."

"What was he doing in the parking lot, then?"

"I was preparing to leave when this white panel truck pulled up to the back door of the mosque."

"Yeah. So?"

"The guy who got out was tall, had light-hair, definitely not a Muslim. The truck had lettering on the door panel. I was too far away to read it."

"Wait. I'm confused. You said the guy you heard, the one with the raspy voice, was Muslim?"

"That's right. The tall one wasn't the raspy voice."

"Who was he, then?"

"I don't know. I thought it might be the second of the two white guys the Feds spotted going in and out of the mosque."

"There are two? Not just one?"

Teddy took a long swallow of beer. "They know about the first guy. Fields asked me to be on the lookout for a second one…you know…try to get a description."

"What happened after you saw the tall one get out of the truck?"

Teddy squirmed. "I think he went into the mosque. I don't know for sure, because the Muslim with the raspy voice came up from behind. He surprised me. He got out of a pick-up truck parked ten yards away…a black one."

"What did he say?"

"He wanted to know if I had a problem. I said I was looking for my keys, that's all."

"And then what?"

"I got into my SUV and drove away. I saw him heading toward the mosque's rear door."

"Didn't you tell me on the phone you were worried you might be imagining something? What's that about?"

Teddy reached for the Heineken, his hand shaking. Without drinking, he set down the bottle. "It's Fields. He's not interested in hearing from me." The strain of frustration was obvious.

"Why would you say that?"

"He calls me Saturday afternoon. Asks if I'm going to the mosque that evening. I tell him yes. Then he asks me to keep a watch for anything that looks suspicious. For instance, like any non-Muslim that might be hanging around. He said he'd check with me Sunday."

"Okay. What's the problem?"

"He never called. I wanted to tell him what happened in the parking lot. I know damn well these bastards are up to something, something that could be as terrible as 9/11."

"Why didn't you call him, then?"

"Because he told me not to. He said he'd call me on Sunday."

"Well, maybe he was tied up. Maybe it slipped his mind."

Teddy pushed back in his chair and spread his open palms out to the side. "And maybe he isn't taking this threat seriously? Maybe he doesn't give a shit about me and my family?"

"Look, Teddy, Agent Fields may not be the sharpest pencil in the box, but he's quite serious when it comes to his responsibilities. I doubt he's treating this threat lightly."

"I hope you're right. I'd hate to think he was just trying to mollify me that day at their office. I'm worried what these crazy Muslim fanatics might do."

Fanning watched him pick up his beer and take a long pull. "Let me ask you something," he said when Teddy lowered the Heineken.

"What's that?"

"Are you Muslim by choice? I ask because I read somewhere that twenty percent of India is Muslim. The rest is Hindu. Is that right?"

"Yeah, that's pretty much the breakdown. I'm Muslim through a choice made three hundred years ago by the head of my family."

"Three hundred years ago?"

"Yeah. He migrated to a part of the Middle East that is now Pakistan after marrying a woman from that area. It was all Muslim."

"He was originally Hindu?"

"Right. When he arrived, he was given the three choices of Islamic law, according to the teachings of Muhammad and the *Quran.*"

"Three?"

"Yeah, you'll love this."

Fanning sensed the beer was taking effect, unwinding Teddy.

"Your first choice was to give up your beliefs and embrace Islam. If you chose not to, your second choice was to pay the *jizya*, a poll-tax on all non-Muslims."

"Like our IRS?"

"Worse. It was ongoing, quite stiff, and not based on your ability to pay. In addition to the tax, they treated you as inferior. You suffered constant humiliation. It's still practiced today in the heavy Muslim countries."

"What's the third option?" Fanning asked.

"You ready for this?"

Fanning held still. Teddy's face was animated.

"Death."

"You're pulling my leg?"

"No. My forefather must have loved his bride."

"To say nothing of his life."

"Today, moderate Muslims reject that dictate of the *Quran.* They're far more tolerant of other religions than Muhammad would have liked."

"But doesn't that seem like watering down Islam?"

"No, not at all. Moderate Muslims don't advocate violence in the name of their religion, even though the *Quran* is cited as the reason for *jihad* by Muslim fundamentalists."

Fanning heard the passion in Teddy's voice. "Why? Doesn't the moderate Muslim believe in the *Quran* and everything it preaches?"

"No. They're not *jihadists.* They don't subscribe to enforcing Islamic beliefs by violence."

"That's a break," Fanning said. "Considering the number of Muslims living in the U.S. these days, we'd be up to our asses in a civil war."

"Truth is, few Muslims, either jihadists or moderates, read the *Quran.* "

"Why is that?"

"It's written in classical Arabic, a difficult language. They memorize the words, then recite it by rote during Muslim prayers. No one has any clear idea of what they are saying."

"So, where do they learn about *jihad* and terrorist behavior if not from the Quran?"

"The preaching of fundamentalist sheikhs and imams. You remember Omar Abdel Rahman, the sheikh who conspired in the '93 World Trade Center attack? It's his kind that's the source of the terrorist problem in this country." Teddy sounded agitated. He grabbed for his Heineken. It was empty.

Fanning stood. "You ready?"

"Okay, one more, but let me buy."

"Not in my house. Be right back."

He returned to the table. Teddy had removed his jacket and placed it over the back of his chair. He had his chin tilted toward the ceiling and appeared to be deep in thought. Fanning slid the Heineken in front of him. Teddy looked down, startled.

"Didn't you want this?"

"Huh? Oh yeah. Sorry,"

Fanning sat down. "What's bothering you?"

"I was thinking of moderate Muslims in this country, like my family…the torment they must be going through."

"Like being whitewashed with blame for 9/11?"

"That too, but mostly how those terrorist bastards have destroyed our lives."

"So, you're not helpless. Do something."

"How can we? We hate them, but we can't speak."

Fanning screwed up his face. "Why the hell not?"

Teddy focused on his beer bottle. "What choice do we have? It's shut up or die."

"Look, you guys have flooded the states in the past twenty years. You come here for economic reasons, for freedoms you never had in your own Islamic countries. You're all over the place. Dearborn, Michigan, New York City, Chicago, Los Angeles."

"Something wrong with that?" Teddy asked. His dark eyes locked on Fanning's face.

"No, no, of course not, but once you settle somewhere, wherever it is you settle, you keep to yourselves."

"I didn't."

"You didn't because you're first generation American. The others, hey, they just want to cluster together and…"

"Like every ethnic group did for years. Like your own Irish relatives did."

"Yeah, but—"

"Doesn't every major city have a Chinatown or a Little Italy?"

"Okay, right, but those immigrants didn't become prey to fundamentalist sheikhs, those jihad fuckers who preach DEATH TO THE INFIDELS!" Fanning slammed down his bottle, splashing a spray

160

of beer onto the table.

Teddy's head jerked back. "And I guess the Italians in lower New York at the turn of the century weren't prey to the Mafia?"

"Sure they were. But over time they stopped protecting them. Besides, the Mafia's not political. They're self-serving gangsters, not religious fanatics looking to destroy America."

Teddy went silent.

Fanning continued. "That's my point. Christ, I've heard people say the Muslim migration is the religion's way of infiltrating a country, to bring it down from within. I know it sounds crazy but that's what a lot of people think is happening here."

Teddy took another swallow of beer. "You don't believe that, do you?"

"Tell me why I shouldn't."

Teddy shook his head and pushed his bottle to the middle of the table as if he'd had enough. He sat quietly, gazing at the green glass.

"Look, why don't moderate Muslims band together…you know…come out in the open and reject the bastards…not keep quiet? They know who the jihad terrorists are. Why don't they step up?"

"They're scared, afraid for their families."

Fanning nodded. "I realize that, but we can't do it alone."

"I did…step up, that is. Didn't I?"

"Yeah, you did. I wish there were thousands more like you."

Lifting his watch, Teddy said, "Shit, I gotta get going. It's five o'clock."

"You okay? Think you can manage driving?"

He rose, slipping his jacket from the back of his chair and tossing it over his shoulder. Fanning had moved to his side to take him by the elbow. Teddy shook it off. "I'm fine," he protested, standing erect as if to demonstrate his level of sobriety. "It's not the first beer I ever had."

"You're sure?"

"I'm fine."

Outside on the sidewalk, Teddy turned to Fanning. "What should I do about Jack Fields? Should I call him anyway?"

Fanning thought a moment. "Let me fill him in. If he needs any more, I'll get him to call you." Teddy made a face. Fanning continued. "Hey, pal, I hope I didn't say anything offensive or insulting in there. There's so much about your religion I don't understand."

Teddy grinned. "Don't worry, pal. You never laid a glove on me."

CHAPTER 15

The call from Jack Fields interrupted the Yankee half of the second inning. Pete had returned to the den with a Dewars when his cell phone sounded *Take Five*.

"Pete, can we meet somewhere?" Fields said it more as a command than a question.

"Right now? Tonight?"

"Yeah."

Fanning remembered the early warning Casey had given him. He decided not to further aggravate the agent by ignoring his invitation. If the Feds wanted to be hard assed, he knew they could make things hot for him with his Commander at Queens Narcotics, jeopardize a fifteen-year career on the NYPD.

"Sure, Jack. Where do we meet?"

He heard Fields speaking to someone before saying, "How about a cup of coffee at Starbucks in mid-town, the corner of Second Avenue and Forty-first Street? Figure an hour."

He looked at his watch. "See you at eight-fifteen," he said. He folded his phone and wondered why Fields had picked such a public place to tear his head off. Well, it just might work in his favor. How vocal could he get among the patrons of a crowded coffee shop?

❖

Fanning turned onto Second Avenue looking for a parking space, his mind spinning, full of worry. He now had Casey in trouble, maybe out of a job. On top of everything, the Feds could play rough with Mike Allen if they wanted. Maybe throw twenty-five years at him for unlawful abduction. Jesus, he thought, what a mess.

He entered Starbucks and looked around. Jack Fields and Tony Condon, sitting at a small round table in one corner, stood when he reached them. They shook hands like old friends and sat down, showing no appearance of being pissed. Then he remembered. They were trained Federal agents, always careful never to tip their hands.

Fields said, "Didn't pull you away from anything too important, I hope."

"No, not at all. A Yankees-Mariners game on the tube, that's all."

"Sorry about that."

"No problem."

"Let's go, then," he said, jumping to his feet. "We can't talk in here." He motioned to follow and turned toward the exit, hurrying out the door.

They reached the stairway on Forty-second Street leading up to the landmark residential area of Tudor City, a community of Tudor-style multi-storied apartment buildings. Fields started up the steps without waiting. Fanning hesitated at the base of the stairway, trying to figure out what was going on.

Coming up from behind, Condon said, "Keep going."

By the time he reached the top step, Fields was in the lead by twenty yards. His long strides took him down the lamp-lit sidewalk at a pace that was tough to match without breaking into a jog. Fanning drew quick, deep breaths, filling his lungs with the sticky humidity of the night.

Fields turned into one of Tudor City's small parks, a treed island of grass circled by a cluster of wooden benches. A warm, yellow glow flickering down from windows of the apartment buildings surrounding them, bathed the empty, dimly lit park. Between two residential structures of brick and intricate stonework just to the east, Fanning saw the shape of the United Nations building at the edge of the East River. He could hear the quiet hum of Manhattan's busy traffic flow as it moved below, unseen from this unique plateau of tranquility.

Fields came to a stop at one of the benches and sat down. "Sit here," he directed, patting the seat next to him. Condon remained standing, sentry-like, keeping alert.

Fanning sat down. Confused, he asked Fields, "What's going on?"

The agent took a moment to get his tall frame comfortable and stretched one arm over the back of the bench before he spoke. "I thought it might be a good time to air out a couple of things, things that are getting in the way of our efforts. See if we can't reach an understanding, one law-enforcement officer to another."

Fanning guessed what was coming. What fooled him was why Fields chose to handle it with this clandestine-like meet instead of a simple phone call. He nodded but said nothing.

"Let me begin by saying I wasn't happy when I learned you had entered that apartment in Woodside last week without authorization."

Fanning raised his chin to the canopy of tree limbs overhead. Nothing moved. The air was still, offering no relief from the muggy, warm temperature. He felt the sticky sweat in the armpits of his golf shirt and tried to ignore it.

"We knew about this safe house," Fields continued, "but we lacked the evidence that allowed for a search warrant. Good news, you gave us that evidence. Bad news, your illegal search flushed out the bad guys along with all the evidence and now—"

Fanning interrupted. "Can I say something?"

The agent lowered his head and raised his eyes, waiting.

"I'm sorry. Honest. It was a bonehead thing to do. I admit it."

"To say the least," Tony Condon injected with a sarcastic tone.

Fanning let the agent's comment pass.

"I had no idea you were involved in chasing down IRA dissidents at that time. My close friend, Mike Allen, disappeared after he told me he had spotted Slattery on the train and followed him home. You know that story."

The agent nodded.

"I was convinced either Mike did something irrational, or the Irishman got to him first. I had to find out. I was operating on pure emotion."

"I understand that," Fields said. "That's why we didn't come down on you." He pulled his arm from the back of the bench and bent forward, both forearms on his knees. "But when you and Casey took that trip out to Bay Shore to visit Rory McCauley, I was ready to go to your superiors, have you charged with interfering with an ongoing Federal investigation."

"But I had no idea—"

"We know that too," Fields said. "But Casey Franks did."

"Listen, Casey never said a word to me about your interest in this group. I just assumed she was helping me find Mike Allen, as a friend."

"That's why we're ready to let that slide too."

"I appreciate that." He wondered why the agent was cutting him so much slack.

Fields stood, stretched his arms, then lowered them to his sides. Fanning got to his feet, thinking they were done, ready to leave. He looked around at this quiet little escape, a true refuge from a hectic Manhattan. He understood now why they picked this location to conduct their reproach.

"Wait. We're not done yet," Jack Fields said, sitting down again.

"What next?" Fanning asked.

"I understand you're on administrative leave."

"That ended a week ago," he said, dropping back to the bench. "I'm on vacation now. I go back on The Job next Monday."

Condon took a seat on the next bench. Fanning saw him lean in toward Fields to listen. Now the real purpose of this get-together, Fanning thought.

No one spoke as an elderly couple hobbled past on their way to one of the apartment house entrances ahead.

Agent Fields broke the silence. "We know you're a good cop, Pete, with an outstanding fifteen-year record. You're someone with an excellent intuitive sense and outstanding investigative abilities."

Fanning stiffened. Those were the exact words used on his performance report during this year's annual review. He released his shoulder muscles and grinned. "Someone's been doing a little checking, I see."

"We have," Condon chimed in.

"That's right," Fields said. "And we've also spoken with your captain regarding an idea we have. We'd like to float it by you, see if you'd be willing to help us out. He's okay with it as long as it's on your time and doesn't put you in harm's way."

Fanning glanced at Fields, who looked at him, waiting for a reaction. "Let me have it," he said to the agent. "I'm sure it's an offer I can't refuse."

CHAPTER 16

Tuesday, June 4

Seamus Slattery had been pacing the back room of the shop since arriving Sunday night, drinking black coffee, complaining about *that feckin' tool* who snatched him, and how he blathered on and on about his wife's bad luck and *our feckin' Irish politics*. Pearse McCauley still had to wire together the explosive device, and Slattery felt anxious.

"When did Khalid say the urea-nitrate pellets would be here?" Slattery asked.

"Not 'til late tomorrow," Pearse answered.

"Jaysus, that doesn't give us a whole lot of time. What's the holdup?"

Pearse sat at a table under the barred window high above his head, chain smoking, trying to complete a crossword puzzle in the *New York Post*. "Don't know," he said without looking up. "He's upstairs sleeping. Go ask him," Pearse baited.

Slattery smiled. "Feck ya, sham."

Khalid bin Muhammad—The *Chemist*, he was called—made his home in the small apartment at the top of the iron spiral staircase in the corner at the west end of the building. Slattery had been up there once, at Khalid's invitation, to gather bedding when he and Pearse first arrived. It reeked of cooking smells foreign to him.

The room had one window, a double-pane opening that faced west. The vast excavation site running between that end of the building on Fifth Street and the East River several hundred yards away lent an unobstructed view of the Manhattan skyline, with the United Nations Plaza in the center of the picture. The large, lighted Pepsi Cola sign, visible just off to the left, loomed over the bottling plant at the water's edge on the Queens side of the river. The vista would disappear once they completed the planned luxury high-rise apartments on the excavated site. At one point after describing it to Pearse, Slattery had sneered, "Only the bloody privileged of New York City will monopolize that spectacular view."

Looking to Pearse at the table, he said, "Come on, you twat. Why is it taking so long?"

"Well, he said something about the '93 Trade Center bombing, that certain chemicals were tough to come by in large quantities. Might attract attention, ya know."

Slattery stopped moving. He planted both hands against one wall and pushed, stretching his back and hamstrings. His body still ached from spending two nights on a cement floor. The small cots supplied by Musab Yasin, the company owner, provided little more comfort.

"These feckin' things must be from the First World War," Slattery joked when he awoke Monday morning.

"Well, it better be here soon," Slattery said, switching from his right leg to his left. "He's got a lot of chemicals to mix."

Pearse continued to wrestle with the word puzzle. "We have all but the urea-nitrate."

Slattery let out a low, throaty guffaw. "Christ, this is going to be one feckin' potent bomb. Figured out yet what you're going to do with the triggering device, how we should wire it?"

"Uh-huh. I'll tell ya later," Pearse mumbled.

Slattery went to the storage closet behind the spiral staircase, to the mini-fridge Yasin had stocked for them the day before. He helped himself to a sweet roll and poured another cup of coffee. Watching Pearse working on the crossword puzzle, bent over the newspaper studying it, he thought he looked like an Irish schoolboy.

His partner's ability to wire the bomb didn't worry him. Devising the perfect ignition mechanism was child's play for Pearse. His specialty was intricate detonation systems.

"Seamus, what's a four letter word for seagull?"

Slattery ignored the question and walked out of the room into the machine shop. Canisters of chemicals—nitroglycerin, aluminum azide, magnesium azide, a half-gallon drum of sulfuric acid, and bottled hydrogen—lined the table on the back wall. He looked over the lethal collection, imagining the devastation it represented. If Khalid could work it in, he planned to add sodium cyanide to the mix, so the explosion emitted vapors going through the ventilation shafts and elevators of the structure.

When Slattery considered all that had gone into the planning, he had to acknowledge there was no way his small Real IRA group could have financed this size operation on their own. The al-Qaeda cell they hooked up with had sources with deep pockets. He remembered the World Trade Center bombing in '93 had cost at least ten times as much. That massive blast created a crater two hundred feet by one hundred feet wide in the Trade Center garage. If everything went as planned, Slattery expected their operation to achieve similar results. In that event, they had Khalid's word Arab sources would pipeline further financing into the coffers of the Real IRA.

❖

"Mr. Cannon's office," the soft voice said.

"Good morning. Is John available? This is Dectective-Sergeant Pete Fanning."

There was a short pause. He guessed his addressing the Chief as John had raised a red flag. Had it been Carmen, the well-preserved, sexy, long-time secretary of the former Chief of Detectives, she would have greeted him warmly. Carmen always had the hots for him.

"May I know the nature of your call?" the secretary asked politely.

"I'm an old friend of the chief, but my call is business related."

"Please hold," she replied, and the phone went to elevator music.

The familiar voice of John Cannon cut into the middle of "Leaving on a Jet Plane."

"Pete Fanning, how are you, old buddy?"

"Chief, I'm great. How've you been? How's retirement going?"

"Retirement? Hell, I'm working harder now than I did my last ten years on The Job."

"Yeah, but you get to go home after the last race."

"Not always. Around here, management likes to hold staff meetings in the evenings, so I seldom get home before I down the required minimum of three scotches."

Fanning heard someone in the background laugh.

"Hey, Chief, I know you're busy so I'll be quick."

"That's okay," Cannon said. "I'm in the middle of putting out another fire one of my able lieutenants couldn't handle alone. I don't know why I brought them along with me to this job. Nothing's changed since our days at One Police Plaza."

Again, Fanning heard a laugh in the background.

"Vince Bogan," Cannon said. "You remember him?"

"How ya doin', Pete?" the voice yelled.

"Hey, Vince."

"So what's up?" Cannon asked. "You looking for a retirement job?"

"No, no, Chief. Maybe in another ten years."

"Okay, then, what can I do for you?"

"Chief, I'm working on something…ah, something that might involve horse racing. I'd like to come out to Belmont and pick your brains."

He avoided telling him the *something* was not an official NYPD assignment, but a matter in which the Federal Bureau of Investigation was interested. Fields had instructed him not to send up any alarms until he had something solid to report.

"Sure," Cannon replied. "When?"

"Would tomorrow or Thursday work?"

"Hold a sec while I see what my calendar looks like. Got the big race coming up Saturday."

"So I've read. The Belmont Stakes."

The music resumed while Fanning waited.

The music stopped and Cannon returned. "Tomorrow's good. Come for lunch. I'll give you a tour of the track. Twelve-thirty okay?"

"Perfect."

"Clubhouse entrance. I'll leave your name at Will-Call. Ask them for directions to my office."

The ball hit the glove, a loud pop resounded in the air, and a meaty thumb jerked upward against a clear blue sky. The booming voice came from behind the mask of the squatting umpire in black. "Yer out," the thumb's owner declared.

The crowd's roar echoed throughout the packed stadium, but the sound of a lone female voice penetrated the din. "Mr. Allen, wake up."

Allen was confused, unable to understand how the speaker figured in the final game of the ALC playoff between his Yankees and the Boston Red Sox. He felt his one leg gently rocking.

"Mr. Allen, wake up. You have visitors."

Allen struggled to open his eyes. They seemed glued together. When they released, the first form that came into focus was a woman at the end of his bed

She smiled and spoke softly. "Hi, Mike."

Absorbing her face, he felt he knew her. It puzzled him. He struggled to sit up. The nurse moved to stabilize him with a second pillow and left the room.

"I'm Casey Franks," his visitor said. "I'm NYPD with the Joint Terrorism Task Force."

An image formed, a similar face, but when he searched for an English accent, he found none.

"Mikey, how you feeling?"

Allen blinked. Seeing Pete Fanning at the side of his bed, he remembered the phone call this morning from his friend. Was he up for an interview about his Seamus Slattery adventure? A rep from an official sounding agency wanted to ask him questions. He had forgotten about it.

"Hey, Pete," he said, rubbing his eyes with the heels of his hands. "Much better, thanks. Have a seat, will you?" he said to Casey, motioning to the chair at the side of his nightstand. "Pete, grab the one over there. That bed's empty."

Allen remained locked on the woman's face, but as she slid the chair around to sit, he noticed her dark-blue denim skirt covered her shapely rear end with an affectionate hug. She sat, placing her leather folder across her lap. A collarless, long sleeve white jersey covered her petite upper torso. She tilted to one side, her elbow on the chair arm, supporting her chin with her hand.

Allen looked at Fanning and then to Casey. "Am I in deep shit?"

"That depends on what you say happened," she answered.

Strands of blond hair had become loose and hung down, covering part of her wide forehead. Curling her lower lip over the upper, she blew a gust of air from one corner of her mouth. The bothersome strands returned to their place. Allen watched with guarded interest as she opened the leather folder and took out the ballpoint pen clipped to the inside cover.

"Where do you want me to begin?" he asked.

Before Casey could respond, Fanning leaped to his feet. "Wait. Don't start yet. Let me run to the john first. I've been holding this since lunch," he said, and pulled open the bathroom door.

Allen looked at Casey. A crooked smile formed. Her slate-gray eyes crinkled with amusement the way Kathy's did when he hit her funny bone with something outrageous.

"You should see him when he's drinking beer," Allen said. "He could wear out the carpet."

"You're right. I've seen him do that on a few occasions. Not much these days. Years ago at the academy, we used to meet…the whole group of us…at a place nearby. You know…burgers and pitchers of beer…that sort of thing."

Bingo! It came to him. Casey Franks was the recruit Fanning got involved with when the two were rookies. That explained why she looked familiar. He met her once, briefly, back when she and Fanning were dating. They had stopped by the restaurant for a quick drink on their way to a party in Manhattan. Obviously, he didn't make a lasting impression.

"So, you know him a long time?" Allen asked.

"Not as long as you do. You two go back a few years, I understand."

"High school. We're from the same neighborhood. I was born there," he said. He flashed back to Sunday and added, "Yeah, and nearly died there, too."

She wrinkled her small nose. "Lucky you."

The door to the bathroom swung open, and Fanning made straight for

174

his chair. "Okay, did I miss anything?" he asked, dropping into the seat. "You two didn't fall in love or cut a deal for clemency while I was out?"

Allen shot a look toward Casey and coughed several times while trying the catch his breath.

Fanning saw his pained expression and got to his feet. "You okay, pal?"

Tears ran down Allen's cheek. He pointed to the half-filled plastic tumbler on the nightstand. Casey leaped up and handed it to him. Lifting the straw to his mouth, he sucked up the liquid like a thirsty teenager, all the while keeping his eyes riveted on the woman.

"Jesus, Mikey, I'm sorry." Fanning looked at his friend still trying to catch his breath. "I was just kidding around. I didn't mean to upset you."

Allen's coughing quieted, and Casey took back the tumbler.

Fanning moved closer to Allen, and in a stage whisper said, "She didn't try to crawl in bed with you, did she?"

"No, you putz. You weren't gone long enough. Go take another pee." He cut to her face. "Sorry," he said to her, "but this guy triggers my saloon humor."

"Not to worry," she said. "I've heard worse. Now, before goofy here tires you out, let's start from the beginning. Tell me how you met up with Seamus Slattery and what happened."

"From the beginning?"

"Yes. I've heard some of it from Pete, but I would like to have it directly from you. Okay?" The open folder lay on her lap, the pen in her hand.

"Quite a tale," Casey said as they passed the reception desk in the marbled lobby.

"As the line goes, 'You can't make these things up.' He's spent the last ten years possessed by this Slattery guy, waiting for his chance to avenge his wife's death."

They paused on the sidewalk at the bottom of the hospital steps. "I'm surprised he didn't waste the Irishman while he had him."

"Mike's not a killer. He values life too much. He couldn't kill anyone unless it was in self-defense. Oh, I've seen him do heavy damage with his fists, but nothing more."

"Then why bother kidnapping the guy?"

Fanning grinned. "Like Mikey said up there, to ask him a few questions."

Casey turned serious. "You know, I think he had it in his head to kill him, but for whatever reason, he changed his mind."

Fanning remained silent, trying to avoid adding anything incriminating to her observation. They reached the Taurus in the parking lot. It was a few minutes before three o'clock.

"Where to?" he asked as he slid under the wheel.

"Drop me at the subway station. I need to go back to the office, make my report."

"You want me to drive you downtown?"

"No, no, that's all right. Thanks anyway."

Fanning slipped the key into the ignition and waited before turning on the engine. He glanced over to Casey as she buckled her seat belt.

"How hard do you think they'll go on him?" he asked.

"Tough to guess. It was clearly a kidnapping and—"

"Not if there's no one to bring charges. The guy's a wanted terrorist. What's he going to do, turn himself in so he can plead his case in court?"

"Well, there's still obstructing justice."

"What obstructing? Mike didn't know the guy was wanted. Neither did I until you told me."

"You should have warned him right away."

"By then it was too late. He'd already grabbed him. At that point, all he knew was the Irishman had received amnesty along with the rest of the IRA back in '98."

She released the seat belt, turned and pushed back against the car door. Her skirt hiked up, revealing a flash of thigh. Fanning noticed but tried not to be obvious.

"And suppose if Seamus hadn't gotten away, what do you think Mike would have done?"

He reached over and patted her exposed knee. "Take it from me…"

Casey pulled away quickly. She turned facing forward.

"Jesus, don't get so uptight. Mike would have come to me. I would have gotten in touch with you, not your knee," he said, laughing. "And guess what? Fields and Condon would be heroes." He caught her grinning, shaking her head.

"You're a piece of work, you are. You have all the answers." She re-buckled her seat belt and gazed though the windshield.

Dropping his voice, Fanning asked, "So what do you think?"

"I'll include your reasoning in my report. We'll see what happens."

He started the car. "No subway riding for my little collaborator. Not today." They pulled out onto Broadway and headed toward the Midtown Tunnel.

"That's not necessary. I can take the subway."

"Shush!" and that ended the protest.

They rode in silence during most of the trip. Fanning worried about the position the Feds might take concerning his friend. He decided not to continue lobbying her.

"By the way," Fanning said, reminded as they approached the tunnel entrance, "you get a chance to check on electric motor-repair companies located around here? Maybe Arab owned?"

Casey opened her folder and took out a slip of paper. "I found a couple of repair companies that did that type of work. Just one with Arab ownership." She held up the slip. "Arrow Electric. In business two years…owned by an Iraqi…Masab Yasin. Lives in Astoria, Queens."

"Know anything about him?"

"His family's been here over ten years. They settled in New Jersey. Their record is clean."

"Interesting. You let Fields know?"

"Of course."

"Good."

Teddy turned on the closet light. He mounted the small step stool and reached back toward several shoeboxes tucked in the corner of the top shelf, out of view. Opening the top box, he fingered the loose old pictures, sepia-tinted snapshots of his mother and father during their courting period in Delhi, India, at the university. Under them were photos documenting his development from birth to young child, a few in bathing attire during family vacations at the beach in Orissa on the Bay of Bengal, long before it became a crowded seaside resort.

He replaced the lid, swapping it for a second box of pictures, assorted shots of him and Ellie, taken at their wedding party in his parents' Brooklyn home, and snapshots of their time together before the children entered their lives. Thumbing through the photos, he traveled to that early period, working in the back office of Merrill Lynch on Wall Street during the day and attending NYU four nights a week, earning his degree in computer science. It was a time filled with feelings of well-being and hope, void of stress.

He slid the second box back onto the shelf and reached for the bottom container. It was heavier than the first two. He stopped to listen before taking it into his hand. Ellie had left the house with the children twenty minutes earlier, taking them to see *The Lion King* after dinner at the local movie house. He figured he had two hours alone. He heard no sound but his own heavy breathing when he stepped down off the ladder. He exited the kitchen door, walking to the garage at the rear of the house. He popped open the tail gate of the SUV and pulled the rubber matting off the spare tire compartment. Lifting the cover to the storage cavity, he set the shoebox on the spare and removed its content. The compact tire-well provided room enough for him to slip the 9-millimeter Walther PPK under one side of the spare. He replaced the matting and returned to the house with the empty shoebox.

CHAPTER 17

Fanning pulled the car into the driveway as the cell phone in his pocket sounded *Take Five.* He flipped it open and looked at the display, not recognizing the caller's number.

"Hello."

"Detective Fanning?" the voice asked.

"Yes. Who's this?"

Fanning heard muted voices against a noisy background. "That goes to table three," he heard the caller say to someone. "Oh, sorry, Detective. This is Rory McCauley. I hope you can spare a few moments."

"Sure, but it sounds like you're the busy one. What's up?"

"I thought of something yesterday. Might be of interest to you."

The phone's reception was poor, and the buzz of background conversations made it difficult to hear the restaurant owner.

Exiting the car, Fanning said, "Hold on a minute, Rory. I can't hear you."

He walked down the driveway, out onto the open sidewalk in front of the house.

"What was it you found?"

"Not found. Something I remembered, something that may be useful to you."

"We can use any help we can get."

"Well, I'm not sure just how it might fit, but there's a newsstand at the Sixty-first Street Station in Woodside, under the stairs on the uptown side."

"I know it," Fanning said. "I bought a *Racing Form* there last week."

"The news dealer…a tall, blond Irishman…name's Tommy Flynn."

Fanning recalled the man who had sold him the newspaper and had given him directions to the Queensboro Bridge. Unmistakably Irish and unquestionably affable.

"Yeah, I remember him."

"Hold on just a second. I'm walking back to my office so I won't be disturbed."

Or overheard, Fanning thought.

"Okay, now. I've closed the door," McCauley said.

"What about Tommy Flynn?"

"Yes, well, Tommy has had that newsstand since the late seventies. Remember when you asked me if I thought the Real IRA got financial support in the U.S.?"

"Yeah. You said you didn't know."

"That's so. But I do know Tommy Flynn and his twin bother, Colin, were local fundraisers for the IRA. For twenty years, everything they collected they funneled back to Ireland through accounts set up by Tommy's news business."

McCauley paused. Fanning heard him take in a quick breath.

"And you think he might be involved that way…here…now…with the Real IRA?"

"I've no proof of that, but as they say, in for a penny, in for a pound? As long as I knew them, the two Flynn brothers were strong lobbyists for

Home Rule, always preaching the gospel whenever they came by my pub." McCauley stopped. "Be out in a moment," he said to someone. "Like I said, I've no proof of anything, but I thought you just might find it interesting."

Fanning wondered what connection Seamus Slattery and Pearce McCauley might have had with the Flynns. "Rory, you ever see your brother or Seamus with Tommy Flynn?"

"Never. I don't know if they knew each other."

Curious, Fanning thought, recalling how, on the night Mike Allen trailed him home, Slattery dropped off the envelope he carried to the newsstand. Apparently, Tommy Flynn was their banker.

"Rory, this is good stuff."

"Maybe it's nothing at all, but I wanted to bounce it off you."

"I appreciate that," Fanning said. "You never know. Anything else?"

"No, that's it, Detective. Have to get back to business now."

"Bye, Rory, and thanks. Maybe we'll get out your way soon for another taste of that lobster."

"Hope so."

Fanning closed the phone and gazed up into the wispy clouds, visible through the failing light of early evening. Now, why would Rory McCauley want to hang the Flynns out to dry like that? He reopened the cell phone and punched in the direct-dial number to Jack Fields.

Fanning moved closer to Anne on the sofa in the living room, speaking softly—or so he thought—discussing Mike Allen's condition.

"The doctor said he could go home tomorrow, but I don't think he should be alone right away," Fanning said. "What would you think about him maybe staying here with us for the next few days?"

"He can have my room," Luke yelled from the kitchen.

"Finish the dishes," Anne called back.

Fanning smiled. "Well, that would solve the logistical problem of where to put him, that is, if you're okay with it. Luke can use the convertible in the den for a few days."

"I suppose it'll be all right," she said, "but hadn't you better ask Mike first? He may have other ideas."

"Like what? Checking into a hotel?"

"Well, you know how private he can be about some things. Besides, he may require nursing care for a while. Are you ready to help change his bandages?"

Fanning hesitated. "Hey, I can do that much. Remember, part of my police training back at the academy was administering emergency first aid."

"Okay, Nurse Fanning, you're on."

"Yes!" came the voice from the kitchen.

"They are down there, right now," Sheik Omar whispered into his cell phone. "I saw them go down five minutes ago while I was preparing for evening prayers. They slipped out of the room, but I watched them as they walked back to the stairs." His tense voice conveyed panic to Khalid bin Muhammad, The Chemist.

Khalid listened while signaling to Colin Flynn and Yousef Karim to drop what they were doing and get into his pickup truck. "Please calm down, Omar," Khalid said. "We'll be right there. Just keep watch on them."

The pickup sped out of the garage in Long Island City and pulled into the Astoria mosque's parking lot fifteen minutes later.

Khalid slowly descended the back stairs of the mosque. Flynn and Yousef followed closely at his heels. From behind and above, he could hear voices of the early arriving Muslim faithful, those who were answering the *adhan*, the call to *Isha* prayer, scheduled for 8:26 P.M. The bathroom was located halfway between the large prayer hall in the front of the mosque and the rear staircase. The chatter of those using the bathroom facility to complete their ritual ablution before the twenty-minute service filtered down. The Chemist silently cursed the bad timing of the imam's discovery. He now had to subdue the two FBI moles without attracting attention upstairs. Then he had to remove them quickly from the mosque's property to issue them their final disposition. His preference would have been to shoot them in place, but the arriving congregation had eliminated that option. His Beretta, left in the glove compartment of his pickup truck, was of little use at this moment; he had forgotten the suppressor back at the garage.

Khalid reached the bottom step, paused and looked ahead at the door to the storage room. He turned to Yousef, pointed to the locking unit, and mimed an unlocking motion. He stepped aside to allow his Muslim brother to pass while he placed a finger across his lips to emphasize the need for stealth. Khalid and Flynn flanked Yousef at the door while the Muslim eased in the key and gently twisted the knob. He held it until Khalid gave the signal to open the door slowly.

Silence greeted the three terrorists as they slipped into the storage area. The two Pakistanis, Abdul Basit and Rashid Alghamdi, were nowhere in sight. Khalid looked around and thought for one moment that Omar's alert had been a mistake. Then he remembered they had pushed all of the crates against the back wall, hidden beyond the elbow of the L-shaped alcove. He was certain they'd find the spies there.

Khalid pantomimed his plan of attack. He pointed to himself and held up one finger. They both nodded. Then he pointed two fingers towards Flynn and Yousef, indicating he wanted them to handle the second man together. Again, they nodded. When he covered his mouth with the flat of one hand to remind them he also wanted them gagged quickly, they acknowledged by patting the rags each carried in his waistband.

Khalid led the charge at the corner. He was like a predatory cat, pouncing on his unsuspecting prey. Abdul Basit was his mouse. Before the Pakistani could know he was under attack, Khalid was upon him, slamming the mole's head against the wall, watching him slide to the floor. Overpowered, Basit found Khalid's strong right arm wrapped around his neck, securing him with a vise-like chokehold. Khalid allowed him little opportunity to breathe or utter a sound while the man squirmed frantically to free himself.

Alghamdi had been bending over the opened crate of armament, watching his partner click off photos with the pen/camera. Before he could straighten up, Flynn and Yousef tackled him, throwing him face down to the cement floor. Yousef, the stronger of the two, leaped upon the man's body, pulling his head back by his hair, and placed him in a chokehold. Arms and legs kicked wildly until Flynn threw himself across the moving legs to keep them still. No sound came from the mole, his breathing cut short in Yousef's tight hold.

Flynn pulled a line of electric cable from his pocket and secured the man's ankles. Alghamdi continued to flail his arms while gasping for air. When Flynn had his arms under control, he jerked them behind the mole's back and secured his wrists with a second length of cable. Yousef pried open Alghamdi's mouth and Flynn shoved in the rag that Yousef yanked from his waistband. The sudden curtailment of oxygen caused Alghamdi's eyes to widen and bulge.

The arm Khalid had around Basit's neck was starting to go numb. He feared his grip might weaken. Cutting his eyes toward Flynn, he ordered, "Tie and gag him quickly. I can't hold him much longer." Basit was now trying to cry out, managing to emit a low gurgling noise. Flynn leaped to Basit's side, reached up and shoved a second rag into his mouth.

Yousef rolled Alghamdi onto his back and left him in that position.

He moved to the second Pakistani, Basit, and pinned his arms behind him so that Flynn could secure them with another length of cable. After he tied Basit's ankles in the same fashion, he dragged him next to Alghamdi so that the two moles lay motionless head to toe.

"We need to move them out of the mosque,"The Chemist said, looking at his watch. It was almost eight-fifteen. "Let's give it another twenty minutes. The Isha service will be well underway and we won't run the risk of being seen by anyone."

Flynn pointed to the two Pakistanis. "You still want to dump them where I suggested?"

"It's as good as any place I can think of."

"Well, I'm scheduled to work tonight. I go in at eleven, so I can't go with you. Can you and Yousef handle it without me?"

"What choice do we have? I don't want to call on anyone else. Besides, the fewer involved, the safer the secret of their disposition will be."

Flynn nodded. "After we load them in the truck, drive me back to the garage so I can get my car. You have to go that way anyway to pick up the Long Island Expressway. I have a map in my glove compartment. I can show you the exact route to the location."

"And I can pick up the damn suppressor for the Beretta."

Teddy pulled into the mosque's crowded parking lot and turned down a lane toward the south entrance. He was late again for service. Tonight he had to wait for Ellie to leave the house with the kids before he could retrieve the Walther PPK from the closet. That delayed him twenty minutes.

The black Chevy pickup truck heading toward him moved swiftly. Teddy hugged the right edge, giving room to the oncoming truck. It passed, but not before Teddy saw the face of the driver. The gravelly-voiced man. Two passengers sat next to him in the cab. One was speaking, looking in Teddy's direction as they passed. His face was sharp as a hatchet with a ruddy hue. His hair was a light color. Teddy saw the white letters stenciled on the door panel of the cab—*Arrow Electric.*

Teddy edged the SUV into a vacant space. He turned off his engine and sat motionless. His rapid breathing produced a pain in his chest. He wanted to follow the truck, but he remembered Jack Fields and his warning: "Just be another pair of eyes for us. Don't go beyond that." He walked to the front entrance of the mosque. What was their big hurry? he wondered.

Moonlight filtered through the trees, casting long shadows across the sandy surface. The uninhabited, protected Pine Barrens at the fork of Long Island's Suffolk County, sixty miles from the Astoria Park mosque, was a popular camping ground, used by the serious environmentalist. It was a vast area, over one hundred acres of recreational wetland preserve. Khalid bin Muhammad liked the irony of selecting this location, known for its diversity of rare earthly species, for the disposal of the two FBI moles.

Now that the moles had discovered the storehouse of guns and equipment in the basement of the mosque, he could not allow them to live knowing the cell's secret. Khalid was certain the FBI would act quickly once they discovered the two Pakistanis had gone missing.

After carrying Basit and Alghamdi through the rear entrance of the mosque, they'd loaded them on the folded-down rear seats of the Chevy quad-cab pick-up truck. Flynn's suggestion of the Pine Barrens was perfect. The location was desolate and remote. It would be a good while before anyone stumbled upon this burial spot.

Khalid and Yousef Karim, both dressed in black trousers and black turtlenecks, pulled the first man out of the truck and tossed him to the ground like a sack of flour. Khalid smiled, remembering the mole, Abdul

Basit, was a Baluch and a Sunni from western Pakistan. For that reason, he had come under the suspicious eye of the Astoria Park mosque's Mullah. His vigilance had paid off.

Khalid closed the door on the remaining mole, still prone across the seat of the rear compartment, while he and Yousef dragged Basit through the sandy underbrush for several yards. They turned back to the truck to get the second man.

The electrical wire around Basit's ankles had loosened and fallen away, unnoticed by Khalid in the dark. The mole leaped to his feet, and with hands still tied behind his back, darted into the night through a thicket of small trees.

"Yousef, get him!" Khalid shouted angrily as he sprinted after the fleeing Pakistani. They caught up with Basit immediately, jumped on him, beat him to the ground with their fists and kicked him into submission.

"Get the wire, Yousef," The Chemist ordered, wrapping his muscular arm under the man's chin and around his throat. Basit offered no resistance.

Yousef returned with the wire and retied Basit's ankles.

"The dumb ass," Khalid muttered, thinking of Colin Flynn's clumsiness. "This time, Yousef, make sure it doesn't come undone."

They removed the second mole from the truck in similar fashion. Khalid double-checked Alghamdi's bindings before placing him beside Basit.

The two moles hunkered on their knees, their heads encased in black wool hoods that came down below their chins. Muffled groans leaked out of Alghamdi's gagged mouth.

Basit's gag had pulled free when The Chemist put him in a chokehold. Khalid heard him praying quietly, certain that Basit's pathetic pleas to Allah were falling unheeded on the desolate, sandy surroundings. Lapping waves breaking on the shore of Peconic Bay a hundred yards away muted their desperate sounds.

A few feet in front of the two bound captives, Yousef shoveled out the sandy earth to create a hole large enough to serve as a grave. Khalid stood beside the kneeling men with a pistol hanging at his side, eager for Yousef to complete the digging.

"You almost done?" Khalid asked after fifteen minutes.

The sweating gravedigger paused to take a breath. He looked up at the speaker. "Khalid," he said, "Rashid is from my town in Pakistan. I knew his family."

"Shut up with your soft prattle, Yousef. They're our enemies, spies for the American government, traitors to Islam."

"But—"

"Yousef, unless you want to be buried along with them, finish. And no more talk."

The grave digging continued in silence for another ten minutes.

"That's deep enough," Khalid said. He removed the silencer from his pocket and screwed it onto the muzzle of the gun. "Stand up here and get ready to fill it in."

Khalid waited while Yousef obeyed. Without ceremony, he stepped behind the two kneeling men and raised the gun. Yousef turned away. Khalid placed the muzzle against the back of Basit's skull and pulled the trigger. A noise that sounded like the popping of a champagne cork broke the pristine silence of the nature sanctuary. Basit's body fell forward into the shallow grave.

Khalid swept the muzzle to the back of Alghamdi's head. A millisecond before he pulled the trigger, Alghamdi dropped his chin to his chest. The bullet pierced the right edge of his skull. This time the victim's body bolted sideways. The bullet's impact tore the hood off, sending it flying into the dark night.

Yousef stood riveted in stunned silence, watching Alghamdi's body twisting wildly in spasms on the ground near him. The Pakistani mole lay at the edge of the gravesite, his face exposed, part of his skull gone. His gagged voice wailed in muffled agony.

Khalid, angry with himself for botching the second kill, jumped over the writhing body and shouted, "Yousef, don't just stand there, you fool. Get a hold of his legs."

Basit complied swiftly, throwing himself across Alghamdi's legs and wrapping his arms around the man's jerking ankles. Khalid pressed his foot across Alghamdi's upper chest and throat to still his torso. Bending over, he placed the silencer's muzzle against the man's temple. A muffled pop sounded, and the body went limp. With a push from Khalid's foot, Alghamdi joined Basit in the sandy grave. He picked up the fallen hood and tossed it into the grave alongside Alghamdi.

"Cover them quickly, Yousef," he ordered.

Yousef filled in the grave then dragged broken tree limbs and leaves over the site to disguise the freshly dug hole.

Yousef nodded his approval. "Good enough. No one's going to wander in this deep any time soon."

He looked around at the ruts in the sandy trail made by the pickup. He knew by the time they were spotted and investigated, their al-Qaeda cell would have moved on.

"Put the shovel back in the truck, and let's go."

CHAPTER 18

Wednesday, June 5

"Yes, sir," the usher at the Will-Call entrance said, when Pete Fanning told him who he was there to see. "Straight ahead to the escalator. Second floor, turn left, walk toward the large rear window overlooking the paddock. The Paddock Restaurant is to the left of it, Mr. Cannon's to the right. It's an unmarked door, but that's Mr. Cannon's office, all right."

"Thanks for your help," Fanning said, and made his way to the moving staircase.

The middle-aged woman at the desk looked up as he entered the office. She was younger than Carmen, but not as sexy.

"Hi, I'm Pete Fanning. The Chief, ah, Mr. Cannon's expecting me."

She smiled "Mr. Fanning, hello. I'm Theresa."

"Theresa. Nice to meet you. I'm not too early, am I?"

She looked around at the closed door of the interior office behind her. "No, he's just finishing up with a long distance call. He'll be off in a minute, I'm sure. Have a seat," she said, motioning to the wing chair in the corner of the reception area. "Can I get you some coffee?"

"No thanks, I'm fine." Fanning dropped into the chair and picked up a magazine from the adjacent table. Flipping through several pages of the publication called, *The Blood-Horse,* he was relieved to see it wasn't advocating the slaughter of horses, but rather dedicated to the breeding of Thoroughbreds. Returning it to the pile, he sat back, wondering if his visit with the chief would prove to be productive to the Feds.

John Cannon emerged from his office and greeted Fanning, putting his arm around his shoulder. His snow-white hair formed a monk-like circle, and a red and green argyle vest showed prominently under his unbuttoned, light grey poplin suit jacket. The vest was a hallmark of Cannon's attire throughout his illustrious thirty-year career on the NYPD. Fanning remembered that when Cannon became Chief of Detectives, his associates at One Police Plaza had a daily betting pool on what color vest he'd be wearing when he showed up. It was anyone's guess because at least twenty-five of them, in various colors and patterns, hung in his closet.

"You hungry?" Cannon asked as he led Fanning across the clubhouse floor toward the trackside of the building.

"I was until I picked up that magazine in your office."

"Which one?"

"*The Blood-Horse.* Eeech!"

Laughing, Cannon said, "Oh, that one."

Cannon strode ahead through the milling crowd, certain of each step like an athlete, a relief pitcher entering the game in the eighth inning.

They approached two large wooden doors where an attendant in a blue uniform and a white cap turned to open one.

"Afternoon, Chief," he said.

"Eddie, how goes it?"

"Pretty good, today, Chief. Not terribly busy in there, but wait 'til

Saturday."

"You can say that again," Cannon said.

"Afternoon, sir," Eddie said to Fanning, nodding in polite recognition of the chief's guest.

They entered the dining room, were greeted by a tuxedoed maitre d', and followed him through the maze of tables to one in front of the wide picture-window. Tiered rows of private boxes overlooking the Belmont Park finish line filled the large glass panorama. A white linen cloth covered their table, and a bud vase with a fresh cut white carnation decorated the center. Fanning noticed a carnation adorned each table in the room.

"They do that every day?" he asked Cannon.

"Just this week," Cannon explained. "The carnation is the official flower of the Belmont Stakes. The Derby has the rose, the Preakness, the black-eyed Susan."

"Pretty elegant," Fanning said. The maitre d' handed him the leather menu folder.

"Yeah, well this room plays host to its share of elegant VIPs throughout the year. It's called the Trustees Room. Saturday it'll be packed with every big shot in the world of Thoroughbred racing, to say nothing of all the free-loading state politicians from the governor on down."

Fanning looked around at the numerous empty tables. "Not too busy today."

"Most of the time it's just a few board members, horse owners, and if they have a horse running in that day's featured race, their trainers too. And of course, NYRA executives," Cannon added, smiling.

"Nice perk," Fanning said.

"Part of the compensation package." He looked down at the opened menu in front of him. "See anything you like?"

Scanning the entrees, Fanning answered, "Everything."

The first two races on the program went off during lunch. Following the announcement of the second race results over the public address system, Fanning asked, "You ever bet, Chief?"

"No, I don't. Management frowns on it. They don't want to see executives at the mutuel windows. Makes it look like you're not doing your job."

"Well, I can understand that."

Cannon grinned. "But, if I get a good tip, I'll send Theresa out to the window to make the bet for me."

"You scamp, you."

"What is it you're looking for? Can you tell me? Is it something specific?"

"Chief, to be honest, I don't know what the hell I'm looking for. I'm hoping something will jump out at me, something that might make sense. You know, maybe a logical connection to a couple of bad guys who seem to have an interest in Thoroughbred racing."

Cannon nodded, with an expression that said, "Been there, done that."

Fanning wanted to answer Cannon without being dishonest, but he remembered the cautioning words of Fields. "We don't want to set off any alarms," Fields had told him, "what with that big race coming up this weekend. We think you can check it out under the radar. Make it sound like a local thing, like illegal bookmaking or race fixing. You know what I mean."

He understood why Fields and Condon had not wanted to cover this part of their investigation themselves. Instead, they asked him to pay his old friend a visit, explore the racetrack with him, see if he could tie in any significance to the stack of *Daily Racing Forms* found in Slattery's apartment. Fanning's own instincts were already edging him in that direction—a connection to the two Irish terrorists.

"Okay. Let's take a walk around," Cannon suggested. He unbuttoned his jacket as they exited the Trustees Room, releasing the argyle vest from the dining room's formality.

They circled the exterior wall of the restaurant to the open area of private boxes and took the steps down to the front row. Looking onto the track one level below, Fanning observed that the box section cantilevered over the rows of benches on the wide cement-apron that led out to the track railing fifty yards away. Today, there were a few patrons scattered below. On Saturday, however, the apron would be belly-to-belly with screaming racetrack fans.

"Great view," Fanning said. He looked across the track at the finish-line camera. "Sitting here, you don't have to guess who won."

"And on Saturday, this is where the starting gate for the big race will be positioned," Cannon said. "So you get to see a true mile and a half race, start to finish." He took off toward a flight of stairs at the corner of the box area. "Come on, follow me," he said over his shoulder. "We'll take a look at the jock's room, show you where they get suited up in their silks before a race."

Fanning and Cannon descended as the bugler's "Call-to-Post" sounded. They stopped at the foot of the stairs to watch the horses with their jockeys come through the tunnel for the third race post-parade. As the Thoroughbred contestants passed, Pete became aware of the intensive activity around this small, compressed area of the racetrack.

The horses cleared and Cannon hustled down the tunnel-path. Midway, he turned through a door, taking the stairs down to the jock's room. Fanning had to quickstep in order to keep up, amazed at the older man's energy level.

The jockeys' room buzzed with activity. Small men in tee shirts and spandex riding pants relaxed around the lounge area, talking, reading the *Racing Form*, snoozing, shooting pool, or just sitting on benches in front of their lockers, pulling on boots, readying for their next ride.

Racing-silks representing the various Thoroughbred stables packed a long metal rack lining one wall, creating a blaze of colors and patterns. At the door of the room, the track official responsible for weighing in jockeys before each race joked with a rider standing on the large floor scale, the jock's small saddle draped over his forearm.

Fanning stood to one side, taking in the scene. "So when the rider leaves this room, he goes up the stairs we just came down and walks the tunnel to the saddling area in the rear. Right?"

"That's what happens nine races a day."

Fanning thought about the routine. "If someone has a beef with one of these jocks, the little guy is a sitting duck when he enters the tunnel. That's scary."

"Well, so far, thank God, any attack on any jockey in recent times has been verbal. You should hear the insults hurled down at these poor riders by disgruntled track fans."

"I can imagine."

"Let's head out to the back stretch. Show you around the stable area."

Cannon proved to be an able tour guide, leading Fanning through several of the barns on the backside, introducing him to trainers and back stretch workers. Nothing Fanning observed or heard signaled any reason to be suspicious or concerned. The security in this part of the racetrack was tight. There were Pinkerton officers stationed around every grouping of stables, checking credentials to insure that only authorized personnel entered the barn area. He could not imagine Slattery—if he did turn out to be a bettor—having a serious enough gripe to want to threaten a horse or a trainer.

They returned in Cannon's car to the track, entering the building by driving down the ramp that led underneath the structure. The vehicle tunnel, which paralleled the track and ran the entire length of the building, measured twelve hundred feet long from the clubhouse end to the opposite grandstand end.

Cannon pulled up to the maintenance loading dock and turned off the ignition. "Let's take a walk through the maintenance area."

Fanning froze, staring at the white van parked alongside the chief's car. The New York Racing Association's logo decorated the vehicle's door panel: a blue outline forming the track's racing oval, with a silhouetted jockey riding a Thoroughbred in full stride on the top part of the oval, and the letters, N-Y-R-A, displayed in the center. He remembered seeing this logo on the track programs as he entered the clubhouse earlier, but he realized its familiarity did not begin there.

"Chief, who uses this van?"

Cannon turned to see what Fanning was talking about. "Oh, that. It's one of a fleet of six, used by the maintenance people around the property. Why?"

Fanning got out and stepped up to the van's window to look in. "Is it ever used off the property?"

"Sure. Sometimes to pick up supplies or run errands by one of the maintenance crew."

"For personal use, anytime? Like kept out overnight?"

"Not supposed to be, but you know, I wouldn't swear it hasn't happened."

Fanning walked to the rear of the vehicle and looked down the length of the long tunnel. He visualized a Hollywood-style car-chase.

"Where are we, in relation to what's above us, that is?"

Cannon looked up into the curved cement ceiling of the tunnel. "We're slightly to the rear of the clubhouse section, back from where the Trustees Room is located. Why?"

Fanning, aware his response had to be quick without revealing what he was thinking, said, "Oh, just that I was wondering if someone were to park a get-away car down here, could they access it from above to where we are now. That's all."

"If you're playing with the possibility of someone trying to knock over the mutuel department's money room, we're at the wrong end of the track. That room's at the other end."

"But they could get here from there, couldn't they?"

Cannon pointed to the maintenance loading dock. "Well, yeah, up there, behind the maintenance office, there's a passenger elevator and a freight elevator that go to all the floors of the track. Come. I'll show you."

They rode the passenger elevator to the first level. Fanning asked, "How many in your maintenance crew?"

"My guess is somewhere around thirty."

"Can I get a list of new hires within the last year?"

"No problem. Let's go to the personnel office. See how fast they can put one together for you. Anything else? Work schedules, employment records?"

"Not at the moment." They stepped off the elevator. "I assume everyone who gets hired has to have a level of security clearance, the NYRA being state-licensed."

"Yeah, sure, but you know how unreliable those things can be."

Fanning trailed Cannon toward a cluster of offices along one wall.

"I'm curious," Cannon said, before opening the door to the Personnel Office. "What's the connection of someone in the maintenance department with an attempt to rob the money room? That is, if that's what you're sniffing around about?"

"I don't know, for sure. No doubt he'd be valuable for his open access on and off the track."

"Hmmm," Cannon muttered and opened the door marked Personnel Department.

This time no one met him. The woman at the reception desk waved him by. Fanning had the impression they had just anointed him with an honorary membership into this elite society of FBI lawmen. He tried not to feel good.

He continued past the maze of cubicles into the middle of the twenty-third floor. He found the conference room, the same one as before. The door was ajar. He didn't bother to knock.

Jack Fields looked up from his yellow pad. "Come on in," he said. Agent Tony Condon sat to his left and Casey Franks sat two chairs away. He motioned to the opposite side of the round table. "Have a seat."

No one attempted to stand to shake hands when he entered, so he assumed the meeting would be business as usual, cold and formal. Casey offered a nod when he sat down.

"Before we start," Fields said, "let me thank you for coming all the way down here to brief us. I know we could have done it by phone, but I find in-person reports are always better."

"Absolutely," Fanning replied. He tried to sound like he meant it. The fate of Mike Allen still hung out there. He would do everything possible to improve his best friend's chances.

Fields looked pleased. "Your zone captain said we could have you for one day so we needed your briefing today. Sorry for the rush."

"No problem," Fanning answered. He opened the folder of notes he had set down on the table. "I haven't prepared a written report yet, but I'll have it for you tomorrow, the latest."

"Great," Fields said. "Why don't you begin?"

Forty minutes later, Fanning completed his briefing, going over in detail the ground he had covered around the racetrack, what he had observed, commenting on anything he felt was significant. He emphasized his reaction to the busy and vulnerable section that centered around the Trustees Room, the horse and rider tunnel that ran from the paddock area out onto the track, and the jockeys' quarters just below. He was unable to offer a particular motive for targeting the Belmont facility by al-Qaeda or any Irish terrorist group. He did, however, admit to a queasiness when picturing how crowded the track would become on Saturday for the big mile and a half race, a tempting target for anyone with mass devastation in mind.

"There seems to be widespread interest in this event," he told the agents, "but that happens anytime a horse is trying to win the third leg of the Triple Crown."

"What's at stake?" Condon asked.

"Only a million-dollar bonus," Casey volunteered.

The agents looked over at her

She laughed. "I read the sports pages, too."

Fanning assured the agents that John Cannon had cooperated and did so without forcing the question of what he was trying to ascertain.

"You sure you didn't sound any alarms?" Fields asked.

"Maybe a small one."

Fields looked up from his yellow pad.

"When I asked about the white maintenance van."

"Explain," Condon said.

Fanning closed the folder. "When Teddy described seeing a white van parked at the rear door of the Astoria Park mosque that night after prayer service, I never connected it to anything."

"Until now," Condon said. "The markings on the door panel...same as the one you saw?"

"I couldn't swear to it," Fanning replied. "Teddy didn't get a close enough look. But like he said, the man getting out of the van was tall and had light hair."

"Did Cannon suspect anything?" Fields asked.

"I think I covered it when I raised the robbery smoke screen...a get-away car using the track's long tunnel. He appeared unconcerned. He believes security around the track's money center is tight enough. Any plot to rip it off is unlikely to succeed, if not impossible to pull off."

Fanning reopened the folder and slipped out a computer printout. Sliding the paper over to the agents, he said, "This is a list of people the track's maintenance department hired during the past twelve months. Notice any familiar surnames?"

Both agents looked down the list of eight people, then up at Fanning. They showed no reaction.

"The call I got from Rory McCauley yesterday? I told you about it."

Fields held steady on Fanning, trying to remember. He looked down at the printout again. Without warning, he smacked his fist on the table. Casey bolted upright in her chair.

"Jesus, Pete, what a fantastic catch!" The agent leaped to his feet, spinning, waving the piece of paper, stopping to look at the names again and then continuing with his dance.

Good God, Fanning thought, the man is human after all.

CHAPTER 19

Mike Allen, still in his green hospital gown, sat in a chair reading the *New York Daily News* when Pete Fanning walked into the room. Allen held the newspaper with his one free hand while a sling supported his right arm. The empty breakfast tray remained on the serving table, waiting for an orderly to clear away.

"For Christ's sake, Mikey, you ain't dressed yet?"

Allen looked up. "You didn't expect me to put on that bloody shirt, did you?"

"Here, I brought you a change of clothes. This is all I could find in that messy closet of yours. You always throw your dirty laundry on the floor like that?"

"Pete, you gonna be a pain in the ass over my living habits, maybe I better stay here."

"And disappoint my son? Here, get dressed before the hospital throws you out."

Allen stood and looked at the clothes for several seconds. "You want to help me on with the shirt? I think I can manage the pants."

"Where's your shoes?"

"Over there, in that closet, on the shelf."

Pat Ryan pushed open the door to the room. Seeing Fanning bent over in front of the seated Allen, tying his shoelaces, the restaurateur asked, "What's this? You lose a bet, Pete?"

"Hell, no. This invalid bastard can't tie his own shoe laces so I gotta do it for him."

Allen looked up. "What the hell you doing here? You were here yesterday."

Ryan sat down on the edge of the bed. He unbuttoned the jacket of his three-piece suit. "Making sure you get out of here without wrecking the place and cause my health insurance carrier to jack up my rates."

Fanning stood and stretched out his hand. "How are you, pal?"

"Fine, Pete. Thought you could use a little help getting this big moose home. I want him back to work as soon as he's able to mix a cocktail."

"I think we got it handled," Fanning said.

The door opened, and a nurse backed a wheel chair into the room. Positioning the chair at the foot of the bed, she said, "Okay, Mike, your taxi's here. You ready?"

He slid into the chair and looked back at the nurse. "As I'll ever be."

The orderly, a burly black man, met them in the corridor and took Allen. They disappeared, rolling down the corridor toward the elevator.

"Listen, Pete," the restaurant owner said. He took him by the arm to slow him down. "I want to tell you something. That's why I came today."

"What's that, Pat?"

"Last night, two FBI agents came to the restaurant asking all kinds of questions about Mike."

"Fields and Condon?"

"That's right. You know them?"

"Pretty well, I'd say. What questions?"

"Work history, any personal problems, was he a loyal employee...that kind."

"Sounds harmless."

"They wanted to know his political affiliations. Was he ever an activist for any political cause? Did he have any political enemies?"

Fanning laughed. "I hope you told them he was a red-neck conservative, and the one and only political enemy he ever had was Clinton."

"I told them I had no idea. What was I going to say? That he wanted to take out the whole Middle East and every other country harboring terrorists?"

"Don't worry about it, Pat. They're going to look under every damn rock until they're satisfied that Mike's abduction of Seamus was nothing but a crazy, emotional act. Eventually, they'll see Mikey's dumb caper as just that. Trust me."

"But can they prosecute him for kidnapping?"

He put his arm around the restaurant owner's shoulder and started walking toward the elevator. "Too soon to know, honestly."

Fanning brought the Taurus around to the front of the hospital where Ryan helped Allen into the passenger seat. Closing the door, Ryan reached through the open window and squeezed the nape of his employee's neck. "Get some rest, Mike. And listen to your new nurse."

"If he doesn't," Fanning said, "I'll turn him over to the Feds."

They pulled out onto Broadway and turned toward Queens Boulevard. "You want me to stop by the house now to pick up more clothes, or do it later?" Fanning asked.

"Later."

"Okay."

They rode without speaking for several minutes until Allen asked, "Did you happen to put that *Daily News* I was reading in my bag with my things?"

"No. I left it on the chair. I thought you were through with it. Besides, it belongs to the hospital. Be stealing if I took it."

"Funny guy."

Driving east along Queens Boulevard, Fanning said, "There's a store on the corner where we turn. Want me to stop…pick up another?"

"Yeah, do that. There's a piece in the sports section, an article I read. I spotted something curious but never finished reading it."

"About the Yanks?"

"No. The Belmont Stakes."

"Jesus, the whole world seems to be interested in that race." He pulled the Taurus to the curb outside the stationery store and got out. Returning, he handed Allen a copy of the *New York Daily News* and a copy of the *Daily Racing Form*. "Here. If you're thinking of handicapping the race, you'll need a *Form*."

Allen broke into a laugh. "Shit, I don't know the first thing about handicapping. Something else caught my eye. You remember when I told Casey about the Irish politician, how Slattery went on about how much he hated his guts? Supposed to be representing Northern Ireland and the working class, but all he did was suck up to the British elite."

"Yeah, I think so. What about him?"

Allen wrestled with the tabloid to find the page he was looking for, attempting to open it with one hand. The paper came apart and fell to the floor at his feet.

"Oh, shit," he exclaimed.

"Stay put," Fanning said. He reached over Allen's knees to grab the pages and began reassembling them. He looked at Allen. "I guess I better get used to being your nursemaid for a while."

"I'll try not to be a burden," Allen said in a faux high-pitched voice.

"Okay, here's the sports section."

Fanning set it on his lap and Allen pointed to the story at the bottom of the page. "See this article?"

Fanning looked at the newspaper, to where Allen was pointing. "What?"

"It's him."

"Who?"

"The member of the Irish Parliament, Trevor McNeill. He'll be there at the Belmont Stakes."

Fanning steered the Taurus along the local street to a four-way stop sign. When the intersection cleared, he made a left turn into his street, continuing past a series of small, two-story Tudor homes until he reached the one he and Anne had purchased twenty months ago.

He pulled into the driveway. "What's so unusual?"

"His name jumped off the page at me. I thought it was a freaky coincidence, him being the nemesis of Seamus Slattery."

"Hey, the Irish are heavy into horse racing. They race over here all the time. No doubt he's involved in the sport back in Ireland."

"I guess."

Fanning turned off the Taurus. "Let's get you settled, and then we'll see what's for lunch."

Jack Fields sat behind his desk reading Pete Fanning's report of his Belmont Park visit, pleased by the professionalism of its presentation as well as by the numerous details and in-depth observations Fanning included in his write-up. Fanning's supervisor had spoken of the detective's outstanding investigative abilities, but this briefing document moved him well above the level Fields had been accustomed to seeing in the past from the NYPD. He was satisfied he had made the right call in asking for Fanning's help.

Tony Condon pushed open the door. "Jack, we have a major problem." He sounded out of breath as he pulled up the chair to the side of the desk.

Fields looked up. Condon's tone telegraphed he was going to reveal something serious.

"I didn't get my weekly briefing-call from Abdul this morning," Condon began, "I waited until noon before I called his cell on the secured line. No answer."

"You try reaching Rashid?"

"Yes. Same thing."

Fields stood, walked over to the window and gazed at the towers of glass and steel between Federal Plaza and the East River. "And you think something went wrong?"

"Here's the thing," Condon said. "I called his emergency number. The one Abdul filed with us, the one at his father's house over in Newark. The old man said Abdul's wife called him two nights ago. In a panic."

"What about?" Fields asked.

"Abdul never returned home from work. She hasn't had a word from him since. I called his brother, Hamed, at the store. Hasn't heard from him."

Fields moved from the window and looked at Condon. "Jesus, that's not good. Now I wish we had given Abdul's father a way into us, just for this reason. We might have known sooner."

"Should I try Rashid's emergency number?"

"Go ahead, but I'm thinking if you couldn't reach him on his cell, it's a good bet Rashid's gone missing too."

Ten minutes later, Condon returned. "Spoke with Rashid's brother. He lives next door to him in Astoria. Same thing. Rashid hasn't been home in two days."

Fields gestured to Condon to take a seat while he picked up the phone and punched in three numbers. "Sylvie, Fields here. See if Karl will see us, will you? We have an emergency."

❖

Ten minutes later, Slyvie ushered the two agents into the office of Karl Stevenson, the head agent of the FBI's New York City Field Office. Stevenson was at his large, dark mahogany desk, leaning back in a soft leather chair like someone ready to take an afternoon nap. The sixty-four-year-old Stevenson, dressed in a conservative three-button dark suit with narrow lapels that shouted *the seventies,* had been with the Bureau since the Cold War. He claimed to have known J. Edgar Hoover briefly when he joined the Bureau in 1970, a year before Hoover died, but to hear him speak of the former FBI chief, one would think they had been friends since childhood. Stevenson was a man with a gift of gab, guilty of hyperbole and prone to misquoting. Many in the Bureau felt he had bullshitted his way up the ranks through seven administrations.

"What have we got?" he asked.

Fields and Condon sat down. "The Astoria Park mosque," Fields said, without further explanation. He had kept Stevenson up to speed with this operation. "We think we lost our two contract people."

"Cover blown?" Stevenson asked.

"Worse. They've disappeared."

"How do you know that?"

Condon spoke up. "No contact at all in the last forty-eight hours. Checked with both emergency contact numbers on file. Their families reported them missing. Two days now."

Stevenson tilted back, stretched his arms overhead, clasping his fingers behind his head, a pose Fields had seen him take many times. It was supposed to mean he was in serious thought.

After several long beats, Stevenson responded. "So what are you recommending?"

Christ, Fields thought, just once I'd like to see him come up with his own original idea. He spun out his recommendation and Stevenson rubber-stamped it.

The two agents left to work out the details. They had to move fast, although Fields suspected it might already be too late. Acquiring a search warrant for the mosque would be tricky. He had all the probable cause he needed, but it was still an Islamic religious site. The Bureau would be sensitive to the political fallout in the Muslim community.

"If we come up empty on this raid," Condon reminded him, "the cell goes underground."

"If they've moved in on our two moles, I'd say they've already gone underground."

"Right," Condon said, "getting set to launch whatever they've been preparing for."

Fields paused for several moments, thinking. His ringing phone broke the silence.

"Detective Fanning on the line," the operator said.

The agent reached across his desk, picked up the briefing report he had finished reading earlier and turned on his speakerphone.

"Pete, how are you?"

"Great, Jack. Was the report okay?"

"Perfect," Fields said. "Thanks for dropping it off this morning. You must have gotten up at the crack of dawn."

"My usual time," Fanning said. "I had to be at Elmhurst Hospital late morning to pick up Mike Allen. I wanted to get it to you before I got involved with that chore."

"Well, thanks. It was an excellent job, and the Bureau appreciates it. How is Mr. Allen?"

"Mending, I'm happy to say. We're going to keep him at home with us for a few days, at least until he can manage a little better on his own."

"Have you spoken with Teddy Vijay in the last day or so?" Fields asked.

"Not since Monday afternoon. We had a couple of beers together to celebrate his new job. That's when he told me of the white van in the mosque parking lot, and I called you."

"I remember," Fields said. "No communication with him since?"

"No. None. I tried his cell phone earlier today. No answer. Why?"

Fields looked over at Condon, hesitating, while Condon shrugged in response. Fields answered the question. "Our two Pakistani contract agents at the Astoria Park mosque have fallen off the radar."

"My God. That's bad."

"We're not certain what happened, but I want to be sure Teddy is okay. I was going to call."

"If you reach him, let me know. I can call you back in ten minutes."

"Stay on the line. I'll put you on hold."

Fields scrolled the directory on his computer screen until he found Teddy's number. He waited through several rings, tapping a pencil against the telephone console, until Teddy's voice mail answered. Fields left a message to call him, leaving his direct-dial number.

"Didn't answer," he told Fanning. "I left a message on his cell. If I hear, I'll tell him to call you."

"Okay," Fanning said. "Thanks. Maybe I'll try his home number later. You mind?"

"No. If you reach him before I do, tell him to give me a call. Say nothing concerning the missing agents. I'll cover that with him."

"Of course."

"Anything else?" Fields asked. He felt edgy.

"Yeah, one more thing," Fanning said. "This morning before leaving the hospital, Mike Allen read something in the sports section of the *Daily News*…an Irish politician attending the Belmont Stakes on Saturday."

"What about it?" Fields asked.

"It just may be coincidental, but the politician is Trevor McNeill."

Fields knew the name, but his mind was preoccupied with his missing contract agent problem. "The name's familiar, but refresh me," he said.

"McNeill is a member of Ireland's government, one whose job is supposed to represent Ireland with the British Parliament."

"And...?"

"He's the same politician that Seamus Slattery ranted on and on about while Mike had him locked up in his basement."

"Oh yeah, now I recall." He remembered Casey Franks had put together a dossier on Trevor McNeill. He had it somewhere on his desk but hadn't reviewed it yet. "Pete, do me a favor."

"Sure, what?"

"Knock this around with Casey today. See what you can make of it. I believe she has a background folder on the guy. Right now, Tony and I need to jump on our missing contract agent problem. We're a bit stretched, so I'd appreciate the help."

"No problem."

"Tell her to advise me if she thinks there's anything to it beyond what we know."

"I'll do that. Hey, good luck."

"Thanks," Fields said. He hit the disconnect button and turned to Condon. "Okay, Tony, let's set up the raid on the mosque for tonight. I'll take care of the paperwork."

Teddy backed up the SUV, stopping a few feet short of the garage door. He lifted the vehicle's tailgate, preparing to unload the new GE Profile clothes dryer. Ellie had insisted on coming along with him to Home Depot even though she had already decided which brand and model she wanted. When they arrived with two reluctant children in tow, she studiously reviewed the large display of appliances, and in the process changed her mind several times before she finally went back to her original selection. It had been a frustrating three hours for Teddy and the kids. Ellie had refused to pay for delivery so he now had to unload the dryer and store it in the garage until he could recruit his neighbor to help him bring it into the house.

Teddy carefully slid the heavy carton down to the ground and, wrapping his arms around the box, began walking it, corner-to-corner, to the back of the garage. He heard the house phone ringing as he edged it closer to the wall.

"Teddy, it's for you," Ellie called from the back door.

"Who is it?" he asked impatiently.

"Pete Fanning," came her reply.

"Tell him I'll call him back in five minutes."

Giving the large appliance carton a final push against the back wall, he lifted the front of his New York University sweatshirt, bent over and blotted his forehead. The temperature was in the eighties, unseasonable for this time of year and easily the hottest day of the week. Leave it to Ellie, he thought, to choose this day to shop for the dryer.

He returned to the SUV, opened the storage compartment of the armrest and was surprised to find it empty. Puzzled, he suddenly remembered his cell phone was on top of his dresser in the bedroom. He had left it there earlier this morning when Ellie rushed him out of the house to make the trip to Home Depot.

He retrieved the phone and walked out the back door, unnoticed by his wife. The display showed he had two missed calls. The second number belonged to Pete Fanning, but he didn't recognize the first caller. He punched in the second number.

"Pete, hi. Teddy."

"Hey, pal, you sound out of breath. You okay?"

"Winded from my wrestling match with Ellie's new clothes dryer. That's all. She wouldn't let Home Depot deliver it so I won the job. I had to park it in the garage until I can get my neighbor to help me move it into the house."

"Is that where you've been all morning?" Pete asked. "I tried reaching you earlier on your cell. Got no answer and started to worry."

"I didn't have it with me."

"Oh."

"Why were you worried?" Teddy asked.

"Well, not really worried. Wrong word. Curious, is more like it. When I called your house, I got no answer there either. I wondered where you might be."

"Sorry. We were gone over three hours. Just got back fifteen minutes ago."

"No problem. I called to tell you Jack Fields was trying to reach you."

The other unanswered call, Teddy thought.

"He wants you to call him ASAP. You want his number?"

Teddy looked back at the house, remembering Ellie's reaction the last time Jack Fields called.

"No. I think I have it," Teddy said, and recited the number that appeared in his phone book display. "Is that it?"

"That's it."

"What's he need?" Teddy asked.

"Don't know, pal. Didn't say. Only that if I spoke with you, tell you to call him."

Teddy glanced around again at the house. "I will in a while. Can't call him from the house," he said, thinking he would wait until he left the house after dinner to attend daily prayer at the mosque later. "Is that why you called me?"

"Yeah. That and to see how you were doing."

"I'm doing fine but to tell the truth, Pete, I can't wait until I start the new job…if I get it."

"I hear you. I'm back to work Monday, thank God."

Ellie's face appeared in the kitchen window. "I better go, Pete, or I might stir up a new inquisition."

"Okay. Oh, hey, listen. If you need help with that dryer, I can come by sometime tomorrow if you like."

"Thanks for the offer, Pete, but my neighbor owes me one. I'm sure we'll manage."

CHAPTER 20

Seamus Slattery sat on a stool at the end of the workbench, chain-smoking, ignoring Khalid's constant warnings against smoking in the garage. He puffed away, defying The Chemist, still upstairs sleeping. Khalid had left word to wake him when Colin Flynn arrived.

Off to his left, Slattery watched Pearce McCauley, the sweating, lumpish man bent over the ignition device as he wired the last connection to the second bomb canister. The next step was to wrap and cushion them, get them ready for travel. The smallness of the package amazed him. Was it potent enough to produce the devastating impact he hoped for? Khalid had assured him the chemical formula he had concocted needed nothing larger. The bombs Slattery had utilized in Ireland and England were bigger and bulkier, he remembered, and his targets were not as massive. At this late stage, he would have to take The Chemist at his word.

It was a permanent twilight from inside the shop, even at midday. Little light filtered through the filth that coated the series of glass-block windows running the two hundred feet from one end of the brick building to the other. From the outside, the building looked more like a garage than a machine shop. It was a low one-story structure, except where Masab Yasin, Arrow Electric's proprietor, had framed-out the small apartment on top of the west end.

At twelve-thirty, the shrill scraping noise of metal against metal broke the concentration of Slattery. He looked up when he heard the electric motor labor, rolling open the metal door. Colin Flynn's green hatchback reflected the bright sun off its front windshield as he backed it into the garage. He got out and lifted the trunk. Slattery nodded, dropped the cigarette to the floor and mashed it with his shoe. It was time to wake up The Chemist.

"Help yourself to coffee," Casey said, "while I pull up the data we have on Trevor McNeill." She turned to the computer behind her. "How's Teddy doing, by the way? I understand Fields tried to reach him…worried since the disappearance of the two Pakistani moles."

"I talked with him earlier today. He's fine. He was out of the house for several hours when Jack called. Turned out he left his cell at home. He's okay."

"And Mike? How's he coming along?"

"Pretty good, considering," Fanning said. He dropped into a chair at the end of her cluttered desk. "He's staying with us for a few days, in Luke's room."

She looked up. "Good thing he has you."

"That's me. Pete Fanning. Nursing is my life."

"No, really. It's good of you and Anne to jump in like that."

"Well, we're all he has," he said, taking a sip of coffee. "There are no brothers or sisters."

She scrolled the cursor and hit the *print* button. "Parents alive?"

"No. Killed years ago in a horrible head-on crash on the Long Island Expressway. Then, to top it off, he loses his wife in that London bombing."

"Wow! No wonder he went nuts when he saw Seamus that night on the train."

She reached down toward the printer under the computer, causing the front of her open-collared blouse to billow out just enough for Fanning to catch a glimpse of the little cleavage that separated her two small breasts. Pages raced out of the printer. She scooped them up before Fanning could look away. He was certain she saw him.

He rolled his eyes toward the ceiling. "So what have you got on this Irish politician?"

Casey handed him the dossier. "Here, read it. I'll be right back." She disappeared out the door.

Fanning watched her leave and started to read:

Trevor McNeill, the oldest of three brothers, was born in 1960 in Dublin to Protestant parents. Members of his family had served in government in one capacity or another for the past eighty years, and during the last two decades, as active members of the Labour Party.

The McNeill family, rich landowners in the county of Kildare, had one of the largest Thoroughbred stud farms in the area. Trevor McNeill, educated in England at Cambridge, spent his early years on the McNeill Stud Farm learning the business of Thoroughbred breeding.

At twenty-four, he entered politics at the local level, coming under fire by his enemies and branded as a political dilettante and neophyte. This did not discourage him from running for election to the Dail four years later. He was successful in his bid, some say, through the family's influence with the Taoiseach. He distinguished himself in the Dail, serving the more centrist-leaning members of the Labour Party. In 1998, the newly formed British-Irish Parliamentary Body appointed him as a representative.

A year earlier, in 1997, the McNeill Stud Farm bred a Thoroughbred, which Trevor McNeill sold to Prince Faisal bin Abdullah of Saudi Arabia. The horse went on to win England's Epsom Derby. The Prince and Trevor McNeill were close in age and, thereafter, became good friends. They formed a business relationship that brought several more stakes winners into the Prince's racing stable.

The detail of the politician's background went on for several more pages. He finished reading and put down the report. McNeill's personal history was nothing out of the ordinary.

Casey returned, bouncing back into her chair and laying out a copy of the *Daily Racing Form* next to the report. "Any questions?"

"Yeah. What's a Dale, and what's a Ta-o-i- seach?" He tripped over the strange words.

She faced him, smirking. "I'm surprised at you, your ancestors being from the old sod."

Fanning scowled. "Well, Christ, I grew up speaking English, not Gaelic."

"Don't feel bad. I had to research it myself. Phonetically, you pronounce it, *Teeshock*. The Taoiseach is their Irish Prime Minister," she said. She got to her feet again and walked to the Mr. Coffee. She held up the pot and gave it a slight shake in his direction. "You ready?"

He shook his head and waited for her to sit down. He'd never seen her so wired. It was as if she had overdosed on caffeine that afternoon.

"Their House of Representatives is spelled, D-A-I-L, but it's pronounced *Dawl*.

He growled. "Who the hell would know that?"

Pointing to the report, she added, "And while it's not mentioned, their Senate is pronounced, *Shanod*, spelled, S-E-A-N-O-D." She looked at him and cocked her head to one side. "And that, my friend, is my Gaelic lesson for the day."

"Stop showing off."

"Anything else?" she asked.

"Well, I can't tell from this report why Seamus despises him so much. Taking a wild guess, I'd say McNeill does a piss poor job of representing the working class of his party."

"From what Seamus told Mike in his basement, it's logical to think that."

She was on her feet again, this time striding into the middle of the room. Fanning turned, his eyes following her. She stopped and twisted around as if she had forgotten something.

He noticed her skin tone had reddened. He had never seen her so animated. "Sit down, will you. You're making me nervous."

She ignored him. "But I researched it further. I found that Trevor McNeill was a key player in activities that led to the execution of four Real IRA dissidents captured in his district."

"How's that possible?"

"He was rather vocal when he lobbied for the death sentence. He had the presiding judge in his pocket, although no one had any proof of it."

"Why'd he do that?"

"He was looking to improve his image within his party as a hard liner on terrorism."

"Now I can see why that would piss off Seamus."

She returned to her chair. "Enough to target Trevor for assassination?" She looked at him as if she had just hinted at the secret of the universe.

"You think?"

"I think," she said. She sounded smug, enjoying the moment.

Fanning looked at the *Daily Racing Form* parked on her desk. "What's with the paper?" he asked.

She snapped forward and picked it up. "One of the guys down the hall. Frequents the OTB around the corner. He knew what I was working on so he showed me this article." She pointed to a column on the newspaper's front page.

Fanning took the paper. The headline read, *This Year's Belmont Ball at the Waldorf Astoria Plays Host to Royalty.* He looked back at her without reading the article. "And the royal is…?"

Her smirk grew larger. "Take a wild guess who owns the horse going for the Triple Crown in the Belmont."

Fanning could swear she licked her lips. "You mean, Gallant Warrior?"

"That's right."

She fidgeted in her leather seat, first sliding the chair forward, running her trouser-clad legs into the desk kneehole so that the center drawer pressed against her stomach, then pushing it back, banging the chair against the computer console behind her.

"I haven't the foggiest," Fanning admitted. He smiled as he watched her work herself up in a way he'd never seen before. "Some Arab, maybe?"

Her facial expression built with anticipation before she began to spoon-feed her revelation. "None other than Prince Faisal bin Abdullah…Trevor McNeill's buddy," purposely inserting a beat between the two names. Not done, she raised her voice to a higher pitch. "That was the name of the prince Teddy heard mentioned that day in the Astoria mosque. Remember?"

Fanning massaged the back of his neck, trying to process the information. His mind started to drift. The rising fervor in her demeanor was a turn on. He found himself wondering how her excitement might translate sexually.

Casey returned to her computer and patted several keys on the keyboard. "You know," she said, "the internet is a marvelous source for obscure information."

"Okay, lay it on me," he encouraged. "I know there's more. You're about to climax, so don't hold back." He enjoyed his sexual fantasy.

"The Prince is the nephew of Saudi Arabia's King Fahd. He is also the nephew of the powerful governor of Riyadh, who is the brother of Fahd.

The uncle turned Riyadh into a modern high-tech metropolis that boasts some of the ritziest malls in the Middle East."

"Okay. But that doesn't put a target on his back."

The door to the office opened. Wanda, her secretary, poked her head into the opening. "Casey, it's five o'clock. Will you need me to stay longer?"

Casey turned toward the door. "No, Wanda. That's okay. See you in the morning."

She turned back to Fanning, trying to recall where she left off. Fanning could see her eyes had lost a little of the passion that had been building. Coitus interruptus, he thought. "You were talking about the prince's uncle."

"That's right," she said. "Well, the prince's uncle used to be in the construction business with Osama bin Laden when they were building those malls."

Fanning sat upright. "And this is common knowledge?"

"Yep. Not just that. The uncle supported bin Laden's efforts during the Afghan war with the Soviets. They were very close, that is, until bin Laden began building his al-Qaeda organization and started creating havoc across the Middle East."

"You got all that off the internet?"

"Amazing, isn't it."

"Fascinating."

Her expression revealed she was going to deliver the *coup de grace*. Fanning imagined it was the way she looked when she was close to reaching a sexual climax.

"When bin Laden tried to set up shop with the al-Qaeda in Riyadh," she continued, "the governor summarily rejected him. The Saudi royal family ousted him from the country. That's when he moved his operation into Afghanistan."

"And built his al-Qaeda training camps there?"

"Right. And since that time, the uncle has become a bitter enemy of bin Laden."

"And a target for assassination."

"You got it, Dick Tracy. But not the uncle. The nephew."

CHAPTER 21

Teddy followed behind the black Chevy pick-up truck as it turned into the mosque's parking lot. He slowed to watch the vehicle dart ahead and race toward the rear entrance of the building. He made a quick right down a row partially filled with cars. It was still twenty minutes before the start of the seven-thirty evening prayers.

He circled around and pulled into a space under a tree, out of the glow of a nearby light pole. Angling the SUV so he could see the Chevy's lowered tailgate at the corner of the building, he watched. He had not seen the driver's face, but he knew it was the same truck. His pulse quickened. He remained motionless behind the wheel, wondering if he should call Jack Fields.

Three different men took turns loading boxes and large containers onto the bed of the truck. The fading light made it difficult to see, but Teddy was certain one of them was the Muslim he had encountered in the parking lot on Monday night. The second man, he realized, was the mosque's Sheikh Omar, dressed for evening prayers. The third man was a stranger, someone with a limp.

They loaded the truck in fifteen minutes. The driver switched on his headlights and aimed the vehicle in the direction of Teddy's SUV, heading toward the parking lot exit. Teddy dropped across the seat, making himself invisible until it passed. Sitting up, he spotted the truck turning onto the street. From behind him, filling his rear view mirror, Teddy saw a flood of headlights. A train of black cars pulled onto the property and stopped at the front entrance of the mosque. Something big was happening. He decided not to wait around to find out what it was.

He moved his SUV out of the parking lot and followed the pick-up after it had turned in the direction of the Triborough Bridge underpass. He stayed back at a distance, keeping the truck in sight. When it caught a red light at the first main intersection, he slowed and pulled to the curb. He waited for the light to change before pulling out again.

The street was a four-lane thoroughfare. Teddy knew this area well. The pick-up went through the Triborough Bridge underpass and remained on Twenty-first Street for several miles going south toward the Queensboro Bridge. He had no difficulty keeping up, but once they crossed under the Queensboro Bridge into the industrial district of Long Island City, he started to worry. This section ran parallel to the East River. It became a network of narrow streets and avenues. Many, he knew, led to dead ends. During the day, commercial traffic clogged these streets. Large and small service vehicles, delivery trucks making rounds to and from factories, small machine shops and huge warehouses often brought traffic to a standstill. At dusk, after employees vacated these businesses, the location became desolate.

The Chevy made a right turn at Forty-sixth Road and traveled west toward the river. Teddy stopped the SUV at the corner. The river was two blocks away. He turned off his headlights and waited until the truck reached the end of the street. When he saw the Chevy continue through the intersection into the next block, he pulled out to follow, edging into the intersection. He kept his headlights off. He slowed when he saw the

Chevy's brake lights glow red, stopping at the end of the next street. Seconds later, he watched the truck back up onto the sidewalk and melt into the building at the corner on the right side.

Teddy circled around, driving south for two streets before turning west. He arrived where the street dead-ended, parked and turned off the engine. Retrieving the Walther PPK from the tire well, he sat for several minutes, staring out across a wide span of rubble and dirt toward the skyline of Manhattan.

Looming above the soft drink bottling plant at the river's edge, a huge, fluorescent Pepsi Cola sign lit up the night's sky with its bright blue and red colors. He could see the green-tinted United Nations building on the Manhattan-side of the river, framed among the sparkling luminescence of the Big Apple's office buildings. It was a panoramic view Teddy always enjoyed whenever he drove across the Queensboro Bridge at night.

This was his city. He was born here. His family may not have arrived on the Mayflower, but they lived here as proud New Yorkers. Teddy grew up with the city's character as much an integral part of his personality as anyone he knew. "Teji," his father had told him many times, always using his Indian name, "never forget you are Indian and a Muslim by virtue of your birth, but a New Yorker by the benevolence of Allah."

Gazing at the Manhattan skyline pebbled with blinking lights, he felt a sudden surge of anger. He began to understand why he embarked on this risky and insane chase thirty minutes ago. These bastards, he thought, are scheming to destroy something in this city…my city. They're Muslims with a warped interpretation of Islamic principals and law. I will die first before I sit by and watch them drag down the image of my religion.

Teddy opened his cell phone and punched in the number for Jack Fields. The recorded voice told him no one was available at this time. He should leave a message. Frustrated, he dialed Pete Fanning.

❖

The Fannings rarely used their small, formal dining room, so when Pete called Anne earlier to say he had invited Casey Franks to dinner, she leaped at the opportunity to play hostess. He had decided it was time for the two women to meet, an opportunity to dispel Anne's growing suspicion every time he mentioned the detective's name.

Anne had placed Casey next to Allen at the table, unaware the two had met before in the hospital on Wednesday. "He looks pretty good," Anne said to Casey. "You'd never know he flirted with the Grim Reaper just a few days ago."

Allen chuckled. "And look where it got me…sitting next to the best looking cop on the NYPD."

Casey blushed, surprising Fanning. In the fifteen years he'd known her, this was the second time he had seen her react that way. The first was the other day in the hospital.

Following dinner, while Anne served dessert, Fanning's cell played *Take Five*.

"Excuse me," he said, stepping away into the kitchen.

The small talk at the table continued. Allen and Luke covered every aspect of the Yankee line up, while Anne had Casey's ear, plying her with questions on her career in law enforcement.

Fanning recognized Teddy's number on the display. "Teddy, what's up?"

"Pete…ah, I'm sorry. I tried to reach Fields…I mean…but he's got his phone off."

Teddy's speech sounded tight; he choked his words. An alarm went off in Fanning's head, and he moved further back into the kitchen.

"What's wrong? Where are you?"

Silence. Teddy's heavy breathing signaled he hadn't hung up.

"Teddy, what in hell's going on? Are you all right?" He tried to keep his words from traveling to the dining room.

"I'm in Long Island City," the shaky voice answered.

"Where?"

No response.

"Teddy!"

"You know, Pete, uh…maybe…maybe I should wait for Jack Fields."

"Teddy, damn it, what's going down? What are you doing in Long Island City?" Fanning could feel a level of angst rising in his chest.

Again, silence. This time Fanning shouted. "Teddy, for Christ's sake."

"It's the ones from the mosque."

Anne's voice reached him from the dining room. "Pete, what's wrong?" He ignored her. "What about them?"

In a whisper, Teddy related how he had spotted the terrorist truck, watched three men—one of them he identified as the mosque's imam—fill the vehicle with boxes and cartons before speeding out of the lot. He listened as Teddy described the swift arrival of a string of black Lincoln Town Cars at the mosque before he pulled out to follow the pick-up truck. Fanning knew it had to be an FBI raid, looking for their lost informers. That's why Teddy couldn't reach Fields.

Teddy continued. "I tailed them here to Long Island City. They pulled into a garage two blocks from where I'm parked."

Arrow Electric, Fanning thought. "Jesus, they see you following them?"

"I don't think so."

"Teddy, I want you to get out of there," he said. "Now!"

"Not yet. Not until Fields gets here, and I can show him where these guys are."

Fanning thought Teddy must have bumped his head on something. He wasn't grasping the level of danger he was in. If the terrorists discovered him, he was dead meat, for sure.

"Teddy, that's not necessary. Give me a description of the location. I'll call Fields myself."

"And what if they try to leave before Fields gets here?"

Christ, Fanning thought, he is not budging. "Will you get the hell out of there?"

"No, damn it!"

"Okay, then. Where, exactly, are you?" He reached for the pad and pencil on the counter.

"Pete, maybe I shouldn't get you involved."

"Teddy, I'm already involved, so just tell me. Where are you parked?"

"Wait a minute. It's too dark to read the street sign."

He heard Teddy open his SUV door and then close it. Several seconds later, Teddy announced, "The sign says Forty-seventh Road, but I can't see anything marking the street running north and south."

Fanning knew the general location. "What do you see looking west?"

"The river...Manhattan."

"Oh, okay, now I know where you are. That's Fifth Street in front of you. There's nothing between you and the river, right?"

"It's a beautiful view," Teddy said in a calm tone.

"Yeah, well you just get back in the car, sit there and enjoy it. Don't move, you hear me?"

This craziness was the last thing he expected from the Indian. Teddy had indicated a number of times the concern he had for his family's safety, but taking off like this on his own was insane. Then he remembered that Teddy had an enormous sense of justice, so why should he be surprised? He visualized Teddy Vijay and Mike Allen as a pair of matching bookends.

"Listen to me, you nut. I'm going to call the local precinct to send a car to your location."

"But, I can—"

"You can do nothing," Fanning shot back. "Just sit tight until the boys from the Forty-third get there. I'm calling Fields right now, so don't do anything stupid."

He returned to the dining room, and four heads turned toward him.

Mike Allen spoke first. "Problems?"

"Yeah, it never ends."

Fanning did not want to have to explain what happened in front of Anne and Luke. He knew they heard most of his conversation. They'd pump him later with questions.

"Teddy Vijay," he said, looking at Casey. Then he turned to Anne. "I hate to do this, but I gotta go pick him up."

"Where is he?" Casey asked.

"Over in Long Island City, somewhere near Arrow Electric." He knew she caught the significance of the name without having to go into detail. "It won't take me long."

Anne frowned. "Why do you have to pick him up? Doesn't he have his own car?"

"Yeah, but it's a long story."

Casey got to her feet. "Maybe I should go with you."

Anne cut her eyes toward her.

Fanning saw the look and started to wave Casey off, but he realized he might need backup. If he arrived at the scene before the Feds or a car from the Forty-third could get there, he'd be alone if the situation got hot.

He nodded to Casey. "Yeah, that might be a good idea. So we won't have to leave his car there," he said. It was the first reasonable excuse crossing his mind.

Casey moved out from the table. "I'm sorry," she said to Anne. "Really I am."

Allen pushed his chair from the table with one hand, struggling with his balance until Luke reached over to steady him. He turned to Casey. "Hey, I'm sorry too."

She took Allen's left hand and held it. "I hope we can do this again. It was fun."

Fanning watched the exchange and looked at Casey. "You ready?"

She grabbed her large purse containing her cosmetics and service weapon and followed him.

Two blocks north along Fifth Street, Teddy reached the southeast corner of Forty-sixth Road. He squinted through the shadows at the low brick building on the north side. The moon's position high in the black summer sky lit up the emptiness of the open construction site to his left. A street light at the building's corner shed a small puddle of illumination on the broken pavement below. Further up the street, Teddy could see two more lampposts, one lighted and one dark. The dark one, no doubt, made that way by a rock-throwing kid with a good aim.

The street was clear of vehicles except for two. The first was a mid-size panel truck, wheels half on the sidewalk and half in the street, parked under the lighted lamppost. Closer on the same side as the garage, under the damaged street light, Teddy could just make out the shape of a second—smaller—vehicle parked at the curb.

He examined the garage-like building. Its graffiti-covered, rolled-up metal doorway glinted eerily in the moonlight. The building looked like many of the one-story structures in that area. Except for its location, which he had given to Fanning, it would have been difficult to tell it apart from the other buildings surrounding it.

Along the front, a series of large glass-block windows lined the length of the brick two feet above shoulder height. Each window was secured with heavy metal bars creating a hatch-like design. Looking up, he wondered about the wooden framed, box-like structure erected on the roof at the west end. A short stretch of chain-link fence separated the east end of the building from the next building, a multi-storied warehouse.

Teddy crossed over and stood frozen for several seconds with his back to the wall, next to a small, solid metal door. The brick felt scratchy and warm as he fingered the pistol grip of the Walther PPK tucked in his belt.

To the right of the small doorway, the rolled-up vehicle entrance that had swallowed the pick-up truck remained shut tight. Teddy edged past the entrance to a window at the middle of the building. He placed his hands on the window ledge and pulled himself up on his toes. The opaque glass made it impossible to see inside. He quieted his breathing and cocked his head, trying to detect voices from within. The building yielded silence. Sensing the real danger of his situation, he turned around, looking for a safer place, a spot from where he could hide and watch for signs of movement.

The noise of a revving motor broke the stillness. Numbness climbed his spine. His heart struggled to leave his body as he jerked his head toward the sound. He saw the Chevy truck racing toward him out of the darkness. Headlights snapped on as the vehicle mounted the curb. Teddy reached for the Walther PPK and moved away from the building. Too late. He was a deer frozen in the high beams. The truck crashed into him and Teddy went to black.

CHAPTER 22

The trip from Forest Hills took less than fifteen minutes. During the drive, Casey reached Fields on her cell phone and filled him in on the situation. He mentioned that the raid on the Astoria Park mosque had yielded nothing.

"Now I know why," Fields told her. "We'll meet you at Teddy's location as soon as we wrap things up here."

They found Teddy's SUV parked where he had described. The locked doors told Fanning that the Indian had ignored his warning. "Son of a bitch," he muttered, "I told him to stay put."

"Do we wait for Fields?"

"No. Let's go," Fanning said. He realized that any delay could put Teddy deeper in jeopardy. When they reached the corner of Forty-sixth Road, they stopped. He peered around the corner, taking in the emptiness of the area, except for the parked panel truck up the street. "Cover me," he said. He started to cross.

Halfway into the street, a burst of gunfire flashed. It came from a doorway of the building on the side opposite the garage. Fanning dove forward to the base of the lamppost at the curb as bullets chipped into the brick ahead of him. Casey jumped out from the corner of the building. She raised her weapon with both hands and spotted the outline of the man firing. He had moved out from the doorway into the open. She took aim, squeezed off several shots and watched the large target go down like a bowling pin.

She edged toward the fallen shooter, shouting through the fading echo of gunshots, "You okay, Pete?"

"Okay," he yelled back. He got to his feet, brushing himself off.

He froze when he heard the low rumble. The garage's door rolled up. Kneeling over the fallen man, Casey heard it too. She dropped flat to the ground, taking shelter behind the large, inert body. The black Chevy pick-up truck roared out onto the street and turned left with tires screeching. The man on the passenger side fired into the darkness in her direction. Fanning returned fire without finding the target. He watched, helpless, as the truck fled up the one-way street and disappeared into the night.

Fanning raced to her side, adrenalin pumping harder and faster than he had ever experienced. He reached her, dropped to his knees and shoved the lookout's sprawled body toward the curb. She lay on her stomach, head to one side with her cheek against the sidewalk, eyes shut tight. He went cold with dread. He put his forehead against hers and could feel her warm breath seeping out from between her lips.

Her mouth parted. "Thank God for fat men."

"Holy shit, Casey. You scared the hell out of me. You okay?"

"I think so." She rolled up into a sitting position and motioned to the form of the dead man a few feet away. "That fat bastard saved my life. I felt his body recoil when two of the shots hit the sidewalk in front of him. If he hadn't been there, those ricochets had my name on them."

Fanning reached over, raising the limp arm of the fat man. He looked at his face for the first time and then felt for a pulse. After several seconds, he said, "Well, if your shots didn't get him, the two ricochets did. Looks like Pearse McCauley has passed his sell-by date."

He got to his feet and reached down for her. Looking across at the open garage door, he remembered the Indian. "Teddy," he said. "Did you see him in the truck?"

"I couldn't tell. I think there were just two of them, the driver and the guy shooting at me." She looked down at the dead Irishman. "But I couldn't be sure. It was too dark."

"Then he might still be in the building. Let's go."

He stepped out into the street with Casey right behind. Midway across, he reined up and extended his arms like a school-crossing monitor. She pulled up behind him.

"What's wrong?" she asked.

He grabbed her by the arm, pulling her. "Jesus, the place is wired. Run, God-damn it!" he screamed. He yanked her body in front of him and pushed her toward the corner of the building at the end of the street, running with the palm of his hand hard against the small of her back. They reached the corner just as the explosion rocked the night. The force of the blast lifted them off the ground and sent them sailing like paper airplanes to the sidewalk. Flying brick and glass rained down through the smoke-filled sky.

"Down this street," Fields directed. The convoy of Federal agents followed behind the agent's vehicle. Arriving at Teddy's parked SUV, he saw Fanning's empty Taurus behind it.

"The building is down two blocks...to the right...north corner," Condon reminded him. "How do you want to proceed?"

"Give it a minute. Let the others get into position. I want to come at this from every side."

"Base, this is Alpha-three," the voice in Jack Fields' bone-mic ear piece broke in. "Arrived at the top of Forty-sixth Road just after a black pick-up truck raced up the street. It turned north without stopping. Should we pursue or hold our position?"

"Damn! How many in the vehicle?" Fields asked.

"It made the turn before we got there. I couldn't tell. Too far away."

"Pursue," Fields commanded. "That's the suspect's truck. Alpha-five, go with them. Back 'em up and keep in touch. Alpha-four, move down to three's position and cover it."

Before he could say another word, an explosion lit up the night sky. The agent felt the car rock with the force of the blast. "Jesus H. Christ, what the hell happened?" he shouted to Condon.

"Base to Alpha-two," Condon called to the unit moving south on Fifth Street. "What happened? Can you see from your position?"

"Looks like the suspect building just exploded," the voice told him.

Condon looked at his partner, waiting for a response.

"Let's move in," Fields said. "Everyone, move with caution."

Condon pulled the car around the corner onto Fifth Street and parked on the river-side. The two agents, with weapons drawn, picked their way toward Forty-sixth Road.

Casey and Fanning were lying face down at the edge of the building across from the demolished garage. The air smelled acrid. Soot and debris from the blast covered them. Condon spotted the two prone figures through the swirling dust and rushed to their side.

Fields looked ahead at the unit coming south. "Alpha-two, hold up where you are."

Condon reached down and placed two fingers to the side of the detective's throat. "I have a strong pulse," he shouted. He moved to Casey, checked her and looked up, relieved. "Knocked unconscious," he said. Fields was now peering over his shoulder. "Don't know about internal injuries or broken bones. We'll have to wait for the paramedics."

A voice spoke in his ear. "Alpha-four to Base. Fire, paramedics, bomb squad on the way."

Straightening up, Fields looked through the choking dust at the demolished building. Where was Teddy Vijay? In the pick-up or left behind to go up with the building? If it was the latter…well, he knew it would take a major miracle for Teddy to survive a blast like that.

Several small fires burned along the remaining wall at the back of the building. The blast had been directed forward and upward, reducing to rubble most of the wall to the front and east. The walls at the Fifth Street side of the building were still standing, undamaged. The roof, ripped open to the sky, looked as if someone had taken a can opener to it. The lamppost on the corner had snapped like a soda straw and the metal garage door lay curled against the base of the building across the street, looking like the peel of an onion.

"Their bomb factory," Fields said.

"Arrow Electric. Don't they repair electric motors?" Condon said. "Yeah, my ass they do. We better pick up Masab Yasin, the owner, before he high-tails it out of the country."

Fields nodded. "Right now I'm worried about a possible second blast. I doubt that any of their bomb-making materials survived the explosion, but we'll wait here for the bomb squad."

"I hope the paramedics arrive soon," Condon said. "These two should get to a hospital fast."

"All units, hold your positions until the demo boys get here to check things out." Fields looked back to see an NYPD Blue and White. "Great, here comes the cavalry."

The cruiser pulled up to one side, and two young uniformed officers got out looking bewildered and unsure. Finding it difficult to hide his sarcasm, he said, "Agent Jack Fields, FBI. You're a bit late, the party's over."

The officers gaped with looks of disbelief at the war zone scene.

"Jack, he's coming around," Condon shouted. He placed his hands against Pete Fanning's shoulder blades to prevent him from moving too quickly. Fanning issued a low groan, attempting to lift his chin and turn his head. "Easy there, Pete. Stay still," the agent said. "The paramedics will be here any minute."

"Casey. Is she okay?" Fanning asked. The words rolled out the side of his mouth.

Condon looked over at Casey, her legs curled, an arm stretched above her head, the other reaching out in the direction of Fanning. She looked like she was sleeping. "She's alive," Condon said, "but still unconscious."

"Stay put a while longer," the EMS paramedic had told him. "Your system's still in shock. You need to let it calm down. From what I can tell, you didn't suffer a concussion."

Fanning sat up, propped against the building, still feeling a residual dizziness. His stomach felt nauseous, his temples throbbed. The ringing in his ears was not going away soon. He took in the chaotic scene: a scattering of a fleet of police cars, several fire trucks, a fire rescue vehicle, the bomb squad truck and the EMS ambulance, all clogging the area and contributing to the disorder. To his left, the peaceful, shimmering reflections of Manhattan's brightly lit skyline stood out on the river's surface in stark contrast to the upheaval in front of him. The fire truck's headlights and their mounted floodlights bathed the destroyed site with a manufactured daylight. He could see between the parked fire vehicles the shapes of several fire department and bomb disposal personnel passing back and forth while they combed the building's ruins.

The paramedic moved Casey into the ambulance so he could splint her broken left wrist. They had both survived the blast with scrapes received on their knees, legs and faces when they slid across the cement sidewalk. Fanning's bruised left hip hurt less than both hands, where minute cement fragments embedded themselves in the heel pads.

He could see Fields and Condon talking, standing over the dead body of Pearce McCauley. He thought of Rory. He tried to imagine his reaction. Would he be angry, sad or view it as the inevitable fate of his brother's terrorist career? He'd call him in the morning.

He watched two bomb-squad technicians emerge from the rubble and walk toward Fields and Condon. He guessed their slow, deliberate pace indicated the site was clear of further danger. He pushed himself erect, using the wall as support.

"Jack, the building? Can we get in now?"

The agent turned to one of the technicians, said something, and started toward him. "You feeling okay?"

"Yeah, sure, I'm fine. It's safe to go in there now, isn't it?"

"That's what the demo guys just said. You up for it?"

"Let's get going. If Teddy is in there under that rubble, every second counts."

Fields looked at him. "They've already searched most of the building. The walls on the west end weren't flattened by the blast. That's where they located Teddy…in the corner."

He felt a flash of hope and grabbed Fields by the arm. "Alive?"

"I don't think so, Pete."

"What do you mean?"

"They haven't been able to get close enough to confirm, is what I mean. They're waiting to get a piece of equipment to that corner of the building. They need to do some heavy lifting."

"Can we go in there?"

"Okay, if you're sure you want to."

Condon joined them as they picked their way across the piles of crushed mortar, broken bricks and splintered wooden beams. Fanning thought of the scene at the World Trade Center the day after 9/11, when he arrived to observe the devastation that took his brother's life. His throat felt dry. He found it hard to swallow the phlegm that had accumulated in his windpipe. The combination of dust residue and fear of what he might find made him wheeze as he tried to keep up with the two agents.

They arrived at the northwest corner. Fanning gasped. He stared through the heap of mortar and brick that covered the black metal, pipe-like structure. "Oh God, he's under there."

Khalid bin Muhammad, The Chemist, made a sharp left onto a street heading back in the direction of the river. Fifty yards further, he made another quick left, sweeping into a dark, narrow lane that ran between two six-story industrial buildings.

"Where the feck ya going?" Slattery shouted.

Khalid ignored him, navigating the truck with its headlights off through the small thoroughfare wide enough for a single car. Slattery turned around to see if the two vehicles were still behind after making the turn. Two pairs of headlights sped past the lane opening, continuing west still in pursuit. The federal agents' vehicles had fallen too far behind to catch sight of Khalid's sudden swing into the narrow street.

Reaching the end, the pick-up spilled out onto a street that ran perpendicular. Khalid made a left, speeding back toward the main road.

"Jaysus, that was a nifty piece of driving," Slattery shouted. "Do ya think we lost them?"

"We'll know in a few moments," Khalid said, steering the Chevy under the Queensboro Bridge and heading toward the wide four lanes of Jackson Avenue.

"How the hell did ya know about that street back there?"

Khalid offered no reply.

They rode in silence for several miles, keeping to the speed limit.

Slattery was relieved when Khalid said, "Nobody's following. I believe we lost them."

Slattery gazed out of the cab's window, thinking of Pearse. Leaving his partner back at the machine shop shamed him. He told himself he had no choice. When the garage door opened, he spotted his gunned down body on the sidewalk across from the shop. Someone bent over him. The charge was set to explode within minutes. They had to get out of there. He had screamed, "Go! Go!" at Khalid. Fueled by his anger, he began firing at the shadowed figure kneeling beside his partner.

Khalid made several turns before he pulled to the curb in front of a small, single-story house in a crowded residential area of Astoria. "We have to separate," he announced. "I'm going to stay here with Masab tonight. You take the truck." He held out the keys.

"And go where?"

Khalid put his hand on the cab's door handle, waiting for Slattery to take the keys. "Call Tommy Flynn. He'll get you a place. Get rid of the truck first, then have him pick you up."

Slattery looked at Khalid for several seconds, considering the al-Qaeda leader's suggestion. It sounded insane. He needed to get out of the city, away from what he knew would be going down soon. Tommy's brother Colin had the explosives in his car, prepared to move them to the target area tomorrow night. He would pull the trigger on Saturday. He and Pearse had completed their part of the job. It was time to get the hell out of the country. He took the keys.

"Remember," Khalid said, "our agreement has not yet been completed." He stepped out of the cab. "There will be no payment of the balance until then. *Allah akbah*," he said. He was smiling.

"Looks like he was in this corner, in a closet," the bomb disposal technician said. "When the ceiling collapsed, it brought down that steel spiral staircase with it."

The paramedic at Fanning's side spoke up. "It landed on top of him, hitting him in the head, fracturing his skull. I'm sure he died instantly, that is, if he wasn't already dead."

Fanning shot a look at the paramedic. "You think …" He swallowed the rest of the thought.

"That brutal impact to his left side was made by something other than the bomb explosion," the medic said. "An autopsy will tell us what happened."

Fanning stood wooden-like, staring down at Teddy's mangled form, still covered with debris. They had removed the steel staircase. The paramedics were getting ready to lift Teddy into a body bag. He felt his chest heaving; his open mouth began pumping breath like a fireplace bellows. Everything blurred through the watery haze that covered his eyes. The dam broke and he fell to his knees, cupping his hands over his face. Casey moved up from behind, placed her one good hand on his shoulder and gave it an empathetic squeeze.

The paramedics zipped up the body bag and rolled it onto a stretcher. No one spoke. Fanning got to his feet. He heard Jack Fields say, "I'm sorry."

"Thanks." He blotted his cheeks with his hand. "Funny how fast he grew on me."

"Well, he'll be remembered as a hero, a great example for every Muslim in America."

They walked out onto the street, following the stretcher to the EMS ambulance. Fanning remembered he hadn't spoken with Anne since he and Casey headed out together after dinner. He took out his cell phone and pressed the fast dial number.

"It's me," he said, trying to sound normal. "I'm sorry I didn't call sooner but—"

"For heaven's sake, Pete, are you all right?"

"Yes, I'm—"

"Oh, thank the Lord. Where the hell have you been?" she screeched into his ear.

"In Long Island City and—"

"My God, Pete, Mrs. Vijay called three hours ago looking for you. Teddy never returned home from prayer service. She's in a wild panic."

"Well, if you give me a chance to explain."

"She said she found your card on Teddy's dresser and—"

"Anne, for Christ's sake, stop talking. Teddy's dead."

The phone went silent.

"I have to call her now," he said. "I'm going over there, so don't wait up. Okay?"

CHAPTER 23

Friday, June 7

Fanning pulled into the driveway a few minutes past two AM. A light from the kitchen greeted him. He hoped Anne wasn't up waiting. Instead, he found Mike Allen at the kitchen table, drinking coffee. He entered, closed the screen door and stood facing his friend.

Allen raised his head. "You look like shit."

"Jesus, Mikey, what the hell did I get myself into?"

"Casey's okay?"

"Yeah, she's fine. Broke her wrist, though." Fanning looked at Allen's right arm in the sling, and shook his head. "You two are now a matched set."

"Grab a cup," Allen said. "There's still some left in the pot."

Fanning walked over to the counter. His head ached and his body filtered in the pain from his bruises, but nothing was broken. Despite escaping serious damage, he felt torn up physically and emotionally.

"How'd it go with Teddy's wife?" Allen asked.

Fanning sat down and lifted the mug with two hands. He took a sip, paused, and set it down like a priest returning the chalice to the altar surface. "Hardest thing I've ever done in my life."

"You must be wrecked."

He had examined his face in the rear view mirror of the Taurus. Bloodshot eyes spoke of exhaustion and pain. Placing his elbows on the table, he braced his heavy head with his hands. "The toughest part was convincing Ellie that Teddy's death wasn't in vain."

Allen creased his wide brow and lifted his bushy eyebrows. "Tough sell, I'm sure."

"If he hadn't told me about that conversation in the mosque…about these terrorists? At least now the Feds have a shot at stopping them."

Allen shook his head. "Sorry, Pete, I don't know what the hell you're talking about."

"Oh, that's right. I never said anything to you."

"Are you sure you want to now? I don't have to know."

"No, it's okay. I haven't told Anne anything either, but after tonight, I'm not going to be able to keep her in the dark much longer."

"Keep me in the dark about what?" the voice at the bottom of the stairs asked.

The two men turned to the doorway. Anne padded into the kitchen in her soft slippers with her bathrobe belted around her small waist. Her hair matted down during the few hours of stolen sleep, she looked angry and wild. Her tired face drooped with worry.

Fanning jumped up and took her into his arms. They hugged until she pulled back and looked into his face. "You're okay, right? Please tell me you're okay."

"I am," he said. "A little bruised but still in one piece."

She remained entwined in his arms, her face pressed against his chest, reluctant to let loose. When she released and stepped back, trails of tears streaked her cheeks.

"What a vacation," she said, struggling to stifle an all-out cry. "Next time, we leave…go somewhere…far from cop business." Her eyes pierced his. "Or damn it, Pete, I leave for good."

"I'm sorry, Anne, but this thing just blossomed into something I never expected."

"This thing," she hissed. "What exactly is this thing? Tell me."

"In the morning."

"No, now. I can't sleep anyway. That's why I got up. I heard you guys talking."

He looked back at Allen, still seated. "Better make another pot. This could be a long night."

Jack Fields sat listening to his voice mail. The digital clock blinked seven-forty-four. It felt like the middle of the night. Arriving at his midtown apartment before two AM, he had gotten three hours sleep before his alarm went off at six. This type of work schedule, he painfully recalled, had been responsible for the blowup of his thirteen-year marriage.

Tony Condon walked in holding a print-out. Fields noticed the agent's eyes were blood red from lack of sleep and his clothes rumpled from the previous twenty-four hours of wear.

"Casey's email yesterday," Condon said. "She thinks she found something interesting, something that might connect the al-Qaeda with the Real IRA. Maybe it'll give us a clue what their intended target is…or at least who the target is. She's coming over at ten."

Fields stretched overhead and yawned. "I wonder if it has anything to do with that Irish politician Fanning mentioned." He looked again at Condon's appearance. "My guess is you didn't go home last night."

"How could you tell?"

Condon lived with his wife and four children in Tenafly, a small town in northern New Jersey, a forty-five-minute commute when the traffic on the Palisades Parkway was not at peak volume. Fields knew he occasionally spent the night on the sofa in his office, and that he kept a change of clothes there.

"Why don't you hop down to the locker room and grab a shower and shave? That is, unless you intend to start a new dress-code trend for the Bureau."

"I'll do that," Condon said.

Fields walked to the window that looked down on City Hall a few blocks away. Before 2001, he could see the tops of the Twin Towers looming over the smaller buildings south of him. Now, just the southwest horizon appeared in his view.

Gazing out over lower Manhattan, he tried to assemble the events of the past several days. Progress on this investigation had become complicated with the introduction of an Irish terrorist connection. His two teams had struck out yesterday, losing the suspect truck in the labyrinth of Long Island City's streets. With it, Khalid bin Muhammad, the al-Qaeda key terrorist. That was bad enough, but now the elusive Seamus Slattery had slipped past a second time. Fields was pissed. The singular bright spot was nailing Pearse McCauley, but at a cost of losing Teddy Vijay. What a tragedy.

Fields watched several pigeons swoop down from above then disappear below, out of sight. The magician's line, *Now you see it, now you don't,* occurred to him. It reminded him of yesterday's events, an apt phrase to describe his present dilemma.

One of Condon's remarks jumped out at him, the one about Masab Yasin, Arrow Electric's proprietor, skipping the country. He walked to his desk and dialed Tony's number.

"Tony, you changed yet?"

"Five minutes," came the reply.

"Come on in, fast."

Tony Condon, leading four teams of field agents, arrived an hour later at Masab Yasin's house in Astoria. Two teams circled around back to cover the target house from the rear. The second two teams, with Condon in the lead car, traveled down the street, pulling up at the curb in front. The house sat on a small lot, sandwiched between two other look-alike houses. The way in or out was limited through the front door or the kitchen door in the rear.

"I want him alive," Jack Fields had instructed. "No unnecessary weapons fire."

The four agents exited their cars. Condon scanned the street. It was empty of traffic. Three of them moved to the front door. The fourth agent remained on the sidewalk to provide cover.

Condon spoke quietly. "Base to Alphas three and four, are you in position yet?"

"That's an affirmative."

"Okay, then. All units, on three. One…two…three, go!"

Battering rams hit their respective doors, exploding them on their hinges, getting no resistance. Simultaneously, the six agents rushed into the house with guns drawn. They fanned out, each team calling out to the other. The small kitchen yielded a flustered Masab Yasin standing in his skivvies at the stove, preparing breakfast. The second bedroom in the rear contained an unexpected prize.

Khalid bin Muhammad had lain down to sleep on the single bed in the back bedroom. The noise of the crashing agents woke him. Condon kicked open the bedroom door as Khalid reached for the weapon on the small nightstand next to the bed. He took aim at Condon, but the agent covering the rear of the house was at the open window and fired. The bullet hit The Chemist in the center of the back before he could get off his shot. The gun flew from the terrorist's hand, and he collapsed to the floor in a heap.

Condon rushed into the room. "Shit," he shouted. "Holster your weapons."

❖

"So, young lady," Karl Stevenson began, "how's your arm doing? Jack tells me you broke it."

"Yes, sir. More accurately, though, it's my wrist. It should mend like new in a month."

"That's good. So, if you're ready."

"Well, sir," Casey began, "you'll have to forgive me if some of the information is already known to you because I'm not sure how much—"

"Not to worry. I'm certain much of it bears repeating in the context of seeing the whole picture." He placed one arm across the back of the sofa, laying the other along the top of the rolled arm end, and pressed back into the soft upholstery. Fields sat at the other end.

She looked at Fields. "Well, if you remember, Seamus Slattery went on a tirade over a member of the Irish Parliament back when he was being held in Mike Allen's basement."

"I remember," Fields said.

"The MP's name is Trevor McNeill."

"No significance for me," Stevenson said.

She reached over and handed Fields the four pages. "Most of this information is off the internet."

Fields flipped through the document, giving it a cursory examination and offered it to Stevenson. "Why don't you give us a capsule summary for now?"

Casey Franks began. After several minutes, she noticed Stevenson started to show impatience. She talked faster. "...and the McNeill Stud Farm bred a Thoroughbred that Trevor McNeill sold to Prince Faisal bin Abdullah of Saudi Arabia. The horse went on to win England's Epsom Derby. Thereafter, they formed a business relationship that gave the prince several more stakes winners—"

"Very interesting," Stevenson said. "Now tell me, what's this dissident Irish group's connection with the al-Qaeda?"

"The Real IRA despises Trevor McNeill," she explained, "for not coming through on Northern Ireland's interests. He is their representative in the British Parliament." She paused to see if she still had Stevenson's attention. She did. "And the al-Qaeda is out for revenge on the prince's family. His uncle, the brother of King Fasil, had betrayed Osama bin Laden after years of being his close ally throughout the war in Afghanistan with the Russians."

Stevenson continued to stare.

"Tomorrow, at Belmont Park Racetrack, Gallant Warrior, a Thoroughbred owned by Prince Faisal bin Abdullah, will be trying to win the Belmont Stakes, the third leg of the Triple Crown."

"Okay. I think I read that in *Sports Illustrated*," Stevenson said.

"And tonight at the Waldorf Astoria, the Belmont Ball is to take place."

"And…?" Stevenson groaned.

"And the prince will have Trevor McNeill, his good friend and business partner, as his guest at the ball, as well as with him at the race on Saturday."

Casey watched Fields and Stevenson eye each other, waiting for the other to speak first, like children trying to guess the ending to a fairy tale. Neither man said anything until Stevenson sat upright. "Ah hah! Both in the same place, at the same time."

"That's it," she replied.

Stevenson jumped to his feet, excited. "A perfect opportunity. Wouldn't you say?"

Fields nodded in agreement.

The station chief strayed into the middle of the room. Coming to a stop, he shouted, "The Waldorf Astoria. We're going to need the full support of the NYPD on this."

"Are you sure? Fields asked. "Why wouldn't it be the racetrack on Saturday?"

"Why would they wait? The hotel is an easier target. Besides, how would they know where they'd be sitting at the track? The racetrack is enormous."

"They'd be in an assigned box seat in the clubhouse area. Surely you wouldn't expect them to be sitting in the grandstand?"

"No, Jack, trust me on this," he said. "Get the wheels in motion right away. There's not a lot of time to establish a plan. Start with the JTTF liaison guy, the NYPD and their intelligence division. Then get the hotel's security aboard. I want that hotel covered like a blanket."

Casey saw the frustration engulfing Fields. Stevenson was determined.

"Okay. I'll get the ball rolling out in Nassau County too," Fields said. "I'll get their police, fire and bomb squad prepped to cover Belmont Racetrack tomorrow, just in case."

"Good," Stevenson snapped, and bolted for the door. "Get back to me when everything's in place," he said.

The door closed and Fields looked at Casey. He shook his head. "Karl likes circuses, and this is going to turn into a big one."

Fields remained at his desk, thinking of the huge task before him. A bomb threat concerning a Saudi Prince and an Irish MP becomes a three-ring circus. It would require uniformed police to control pedestrian and vehicle traffic around the hotel. He would need the fire department and bomb squad on site, as well as the involvement of the NYPD Intelligence Division, the Secret Service and all levels of the JTTF.

He looked at his watch. He had less than seven hours to mobilize this army of diplomatic protection. A standing task force with an S.O.P. in place existed for just such alerts. The task force's liaison officer, whom Fields had already contacted, was ready to bring together the various representatives to formalize a security plan. Individual meetings followed, but given the short window of the threat at the hotel, there was time for one meeting.

His phone buzzed. He grabbed for it, listening without responding. After several seconds, he spoke. "Damn it, Tony! No, no, I understand how it happened. It just turns up the heat more, that's all." He lifted his head and closed his eyes. "Yeah, I know. He's the last one left. God knows where he is. We should interrogate the four from the mosque now. I'll send Ferguson and Harris over to Metropolitan Corrections, see what they can drag out of them. No, not you. I need you here, right now. We've got a show to put on."

CHAPTER 24

Fanning woke to the smell of bacon crisping in the fry pan. Rolling onto his back, he stretched his legs. He felt a rifle shot of pain from his thighs to his buttocks and into his lower back. Daylight seeped through the slats of the blinds. He brought his wristwatch up to his face. The sudden raising of his arm sent a stabbing pain to his shoulder.

He squinted at the dial. He thought he'd stay in bed—until he saw the time. It was nine forty-five. Kicking off the covers, he eased to his feet and stumbled into the bathroom.

The hot, pulsing shower felt therapeutic.

The table was set when he walked into the kitchen. It was a warm June morning. Streaming sunlight passing through the window made the room extra inviting. The small radio at the far end of the counter, tuned into his favorite jazz station, hosted Miles Davis finishing the closing notes of a cut from his CD, *Kind of Blue*.

He found Mike Allen at the counter next to the stove. He had a metal bowl of egg yolks in front of him, the bowl sliding from side to side, as he attempted to whip the eggs using one good hand. The metal vessel kept eluding him until he had it cornered between the backsplash and the stove. Allen turned his head, working the whisk like a handicapped short order cook.

"How you feeling?"

Fanning grinned. "You know the old gag about, *did you get the license of the truck that hit me?*"

"You get enough sleep?" Allen asked. He checked the bagels in the toaster.

"Yeah, I think so. Anne go out?"

"Shopping for tonight. She made breakfast and left. Pour yourself a cup. It's a fresh pot."

Fanning filled a mug before he sat down at the table. He watched Allen making his way around the breakfast preparations with one hand still in a sling. His handicapped friend was doing fine. "You're gonna make somebody a good wife some day. Need any help?"

"I got it." He fed the whipped eggs from the bowl into the heated frying pan. With a wooden fork, he raked the liquid eggs toward the middle of the pan. "I think the bacon's done. Wrap them in a paper towel, will you? These won't take long."

They ate in silence. Over their third cup of coffee, Allen asked about the explosion in Long Island City.

"Scary as hell. I thought Casey had taken a hit. When I got to her on the sidewalk lying behind the big body of Pearse, my heart was in my mouth."

"Lucky it was dark," Allen said.

"Not that dark. The moon was straight up. When they pulled out of the building, the shooter could see Pearse on the ground and Casey bent over him."

"The shooter. That being Seamus?"

"I think so. The truck belongs to the Arrow Electric. I'm sure the Muslim was driving."

"How close to the building were you when it blew?"

Fanning took a gulp of coffee and set the mug down. He pressed his finger on a loose sesame seed and lifted it to his tongue. His hand shook when he reached for the mug again. "We were half way into the street when I realized the building was primed to blow."

"And…?"

"I shoved Casey back across the street to the corner of the building as fast as I could."

"It blew before you got there?"

"The force picked us up, sent us flying. We landed face down."

"Wow!" Allen said, sitting back, studying his friend.

"I went out the second I hit the sidewalk. Casey, too."

"Wow!" Allen said again.

"Yeah. Wow, is right."

"How the hell did you know it was going to explode?"

Fanning laughed. "Remember how I used to doze off in class in high school?"

"Uh, huh."

"When I was at Fort Benning, they made us attend a two-day seminar on explosives and detonating devices. Some guy from the FBI's Bomb Data Center droned on and on how illegal bombs were constructed and exploded."

"I sat through something like that in England," Allen said. "But mine was just two hours."

"Well, this was the one classroom situation where I had to stay awake." He swallowed a mouthful of coffee, collecting his thoughts. "Believe it or not, the single thing I remembered from those two days was the part about the Stope Timer."

"The Stope Timer?" Allen parroted.

"Yeah. A time-delay detonating device, so simple, that's why I remembered it."

"And that's what they used in the garage?"

"Lucky for us. If they had rigged a more sophisticated timer, Casey and I would be gone."

Allen laughed. "Thank you, Mr. Stope."

"That's not why it's called that. Gold miners in South Africa use Stope Timers to set off small charges when they blast through the rock face of the tunnel wall. The face is called the stope."

"But you said the blast took out the whole building. That wasn't a small charge."

"I know, but you can also use it with larger explosives…that is, if you can run fast enough. The Stope has a built-in red light that glows in the dark two minutes before the charge is timed to go off, a warning to the miners to get the hell out of range."

"You saw the red light?"

"For a split second. At first I didn't know what it was. Then I remembered the seminar."

Allen sat staring at his friend. "What a lucky break."

"That makes three of us. Casey, you and me. Don't forget, a little more to the left, the bullet you took would have put you away for good."

Allen's expression pained. "Don't think that hasn't crossed my mind."

"Something I can't figure. Rory told me Seamus was an expert shooter. But for Pearse's fat body, he might have nailed Casey. On the other hand, with you—"

"Maybe he got shaky…you know…too much in a hurry to get out of the basement?" Allen laughed. "Or maybe he's a terrorist with a heart?"

"I doubt that, Mikey. The guy's a killer. Then again, you could have tweaked something in Seamus…something like remorse…Kathy dying in that London bombing, and all that."

Fanning remembered the picture he found at the apartment in

Woodside, Slattery posed with a young woman, looking like it was their wedding photo. Perhaps that crossed his mind before he aimed the gun at Mike.

"We'll never know for sure," he said, "unless the Feds grab him before he gets out of the country. We could ask him then."

"Nah, I don't think so. It was close. Just wasn't my time." Allen stood. Using one hand, he began stacking the plates on the table. "I think I should be getting out of your hair, go back to my house. I can get around well enough now."

"You sure? Are you strong enough? You just got out of the hospital."

"Yeah, I'm okay. Besides, I still have to get my car out of Tony's. He's probably got a FOR SALE sign on it by now."

"Let's wait for Anne to get back. I'll drive you home whenever you're ready."

Returning to the house, Fanning heard the muffled beep from his cell phone. The display read: *one unanswered message.* His instinct said it was a call he would regret.

Waiting at a red light, he dialed in his voice mail. The caller failed to identify himself but he recognized the voice of Rory McCauley. The message was short, delivered low and slow. "A person of interest is visiting. Call me at this number."

The number had a Suffolk County prefix. It didn't match the number he had for The Lobster Shack. That puzzled him. He replayed the message. It was Rory, all right, using his cell phone. He pulled the Taurus to the curb a block from the house. The call from McCauley was not a social one. He was certain of that.

He sat for several minutes, thinking of the events of the past week. How much more tension could his psyche absorb? How much abuse could his body withstand? The week had taken a toll on him, as well as on Anne, pushing her mental state and patience to the limit.

He pressed back into the headrest, shutting his eyes. An image of a Mickey Mouse tee shirt formed. Above it, he could see Teddy's large, round face and dark, soft eyes looking out at him, the Indian's bewildered expression filled with questions.

The apparition dissolved into the shape of a large pile of rubble. He could make out an arm stretched through the crushed plaster and stone, part of a torn sneaker-covered foot visible at the base of the pile.

The sound of a horn from a passing car brought him upright and back to the moment. A wave of anger shot through him. He hesitated before dialing the number, thinking of Anne and Luke. He should not get further involved. He knew that. Then he remembered that Monday he'd be back chasing drug dealers, putting his life on the line with every bust. Could this be any worse?

It rang once. "Detective Fanning," the voice said, "is this a secure line?"

"As secure as a cell phone can be."

"Good. Are you alone?"

"Uh huh, in my car. This Rory?"

"Yes, and I need to see you. Today. Can you come out to Bay Shore?"

"Can't we cover it on the phone?"

McCauley paused before answering. "Detective Fanning, we need to talk, and you need to be here when we do. It's a matter of extreme concern for both of us."

"Your visiting person of interest?"

"Yes, and you need to come alone."

An alarm sounded. "I'm not sure I'm comfortable with that," he said. "Will you—"

"Detective, you have little to fear. However, I do. I'll explain why when you get here."

Fanning hesitated. His indecisiveness bothered him. If this were an official assignment, he'd have back-up. But alone? He was no Rambo, but he worried that these past few days had dampened his willingness to take risks. If so, he'd be applying for a desk job when he got back to Creedmore.

"When and where?"

"After dark, seven, seven-fifteen, The Seahorse Boat-tel. It's at the end of Cottage Avenue on the bay front in Bay Shore. Take Sunrise out to Clinton Avenue, and then take a right on—"

"I'll find it," he said.

"Remember," McCauley said, "come alone." His voice was firm.

Casey Franks looked at her watch. "Mike, I can't. I have to be in a meeting at three-thirty. Can we do it another night?"

"No problem. I just thought—"

"Dinner sounds great, honest. As soon as my schedule gets back to normal, okay?"

"I'll give you a call next week."

"I'd like that." She wanted to explain why the meeting was so important, but the need for secrecy was paramount.

She put the phone down and looked again at her watch. The JTTF liaison officer had set up the planning meeting in the FBI's main conference room. Representatives from every agency and service, from the federal level down to the local police and fire units were convening with speed and efficiency that always amazed her.

Her phone buzzed before she had a chance to gather the folders on her desk. She needed Wanda to make multiple copies of several documents for the meeting. She picked up the phone. "Wanda, give me five minutes."

"All right, but Detective Fanning is on the phone."

"Oh? Okay. I'll buzz you when I have the papers together."

Wanda put the call through, and Casey looked again at her watch. "Pete, I'm short of time. I'm trying to get to a three-thirty meeting at Federal Plaza. What's up?"

"I won't keep you, but you should know where I'm going later today. Just in case."

"In case of what?"

"In case it turns out to be not what it's supposed to be."

She laughed. "Sounds like a riddle. Where are you going?"

"Rory McCauley called me a while ago. He wants me to come out to meet with him. He says he has a person of interest visiting."

"Seamus?"

"Sounds like it to me."

"Christ, Pete, did you call Jack Fields?"

"That's the rub. I can't. Rory wants me to come out alone."

"That's crazy. This could be a set up. Maybe Seamus has a gun to his head."

"Seamus doesn't know me from a hole in the ground. Why would Rory want to set me up?"

"No doubt Seamus told him his brother was killed. Maybe he wants revenge?"

"Nah, I don't think so."

"Well then, why do you think he wants you to come alone? Did he say?"

"No, but he made a point of saying I had nothing to fear. In fact, he said he was the one that had something to fear, and he'd explain that when I got there."

"You trust him?"

"I guess so. Be nice to have a little insurance, though. Maybe some back-up...like at arm's distance. You know anybody with the Suffolk County PD?"

She thought a moment. "They're a strange lot. They haven't been terribly collegial lately. Even the Feds have a problem with them."

"No one you can call? Someone who owes you…maybe willing to provide a little cover?"

"I do know a lieutenant in their Narcotics Division. Let me give you his name and number. Call him." She pulled up her computer data base and scrolled down.

"Great, I appreciate it."

"I'd call for you, but I'm leaving in ten minutes. Tell him I told you to call. Be sure to tell him of your connection with Jack Fields." She recited his name and direct telephone number. "He's a good guy."

"I'll tell him you said that."

"Pete, what if you find Seamus there?"

"Take him into custody, of course, that is if it doesn't become a shoot-out. But I don't think it will if Rory is leveling with me."

"You realize Seamus and Colin Flynn are our last hope to get any information on the intended target?"

"I do. That's why I'm going."

"Well, don't try to take him alone. You sure you don't want me to alert Fields now?"

"No. Anyway, I have a good feeling about this."

"Listen, Pete, what time and where are you meeting him?"

"He said around seven at the Seahorse Boat-tel at the end of Cottage Avenue in Bay Shore. Sounds like it's right on the bay."

"I'll be at the Waldorf by then, but call me on my cell when you can. You know I'll have to cover it with Fields when I see him, don't you?"

"Absolutely."

"He'll go through the roof, but he has to know. I'm sure he'll be calling you. Keep your cell on you. By the way, what are you going to tell Anne…you know…where you're going?"

"I don't know yet. I'll think of something."

"Gotta go," she said. "Stay in touch. And Pete, for God's sake, don't take any chances."

❖

After Pete Fanning's visit to the track on Wednesday, Chief Cannon had instructed his Pinkerton officers to keep a close watch on the six white maintenance vans. He wanted them accounted for at the end of each race day, parked at the loading dock in the tunnel where they were supposed to be.

The call earlier today from Captain Frank Shields of the Nassau County Police Department didn't come as a surprise. He had guessed Pete Fanning's walk-through on Wednesday had more substance to it than just a vague suspicion of a money-room robbery. As the NYPD's Chief of Detectives for many years, John Cannon had been involved with numerous bomb threats. He knew the chaos they could create at a crowded facility—like a racetrack.

Vince Bogan sat across from the chief when the call came in. Captain Shields did most of the talking while Cannon acknowledged with a nodding head. He hung up, looking drained.

"What's the matter, John?" Bogan asked.

"Jesus, we don't need this. It'll be one big nightmare. I pray it turns out to be a hoax."

"What is it?"

"A bomb threat…tomorrow. They think the target is Gallant Warrior's owner, the prince."

"No shit! Who? The Arabs?"

"They think so. Maybe al-Qaeda."

"Why target him? He's a businessman. He's not political."

"Who the hell knows? But the JTTF is meeting today to roll out the troops."

"For today or tomorrow?"

"Tomorrow…here. They're setting up first at the Waldorf for tonight's Belmont Ball. I'd forgotten the prince was attending with his buddy, the Irish MP, what's his name?"

"McNeill. Trevor McNeill."

Cannon remembered they had booked for lunch tomorrow in the Trustees Room but changed their minds. Instead, they were coming out to the track by helicopter around three to avoid the anticipated traffic jam on the Cross Island Parkway. He had a vision of the helicopter being shot out of the air with a surface-to-air missile over the backstretch landing pad.

He thought of the possibility of canceling the race, but he knew the Board of the New York Racing Association would consider it only if the federal government insisted. Of course, they could always tell the prince to stay away, but once the word got out—a sure bet knowing the press—the eighty-thousand people expected to attend would stay away as well. At that rate, they might as well cancel the whole day.

"As soon as the JTTF meeting breaks up later," Cannon said, "Shields and his task force rep will be out here to brief us."

"What time? Did he say?"

"He didn't, but alert everyone to plan for a late night."

Bogan turned to leave and stopped at the door. "Just security personnel?"

"No. I want every Pinkerton, security officer and department head to attend this briefing in the Trustees Room. I'll let management know what's going on so they can be there too."

CHAPTER 25

F anning explained the situation to Lieutenant Armand Dingillo of Suffolk County's Narcotics Division. "How many men you think you'll need?" he asked. "I've got two teams working undercover in that area right now. I think I can spare them for a few hours."

"Just one team is fine, Lieutenant. As I said, I don't think it will come to anything, but I'll feel a hell of a lot better knowing a couple of your guys are off in the wings watching."

"One team? You're sure, Detective?"

"Yes sir, two men will be just fine."

"You got 'em. Terry Dorgan and Gary Lewis. Do you want to stop by and pick up a radio?"

"No sir, I don't think I'll have time. Can I communicate with the team using a cell phone?"

"Yeah, that'll work. Take down this number."

Dingillo recited the number. "I'll have them parked at the end of Cottage Avenue, down from the boat-tel before seven. Okay?"

"Perfect. And I appreciate the favor." Fanning looked at his watch. He needed at least two hours to get out to Bay Shore, and it was nearing three-thirty.

"Well, Casey's done us a few favors in the past. She's a good egg, and we're happy to accommodate the JTTF."

"I'll tell her that," he replied.

"Say hi to Jack Fields for me. He's a straight-up guy. Best the Feds have in this region."

"I will, Lieutenant, and thanks again."

Anne was upstairs in Luke's room changing the linens on the bed. He walked through the door and yelled up the staircase, "Yo, kiddo, I'm back."

"He get settled okay?" she called down.

"Yeah." He took a soft drink from the refrigerator and went into the den.

Anne appeared at the doorway. "Was the house a mess?"

"I helped him straighten things. He needs a cleaning person in to do a more thorough job."

She grinned. "You get the feeling he's taken a shine to Casey?"

He looked up and laughed. "I love it when you use those old fashioned expressions."

"What? What's old fashioned?"

"'Shine? What you mean to say is does Mike have the hots for Casey?"

"Oh, for God's sake, Pete. I just thought I saw a little spark in him last night. Something we haven't seen since Kathy died."

"Yeah, I suppose there might be an interest there. It's still too early to pull out my tux."

"Oh, you're such a downer," she said. "You're not jealous of him, are you?"

He thought of the question. He was jealous, he conceded, but not as Anne had implied. More, he thought, in the fashion that a person might feel if his best friend began showing more attention to another person.

"You're right," he admitted. "But I'm jealous of both of them."

Anne looked back and grinned. She caught his meaning.

"What do you want for dinner?" she asked. "I bought some great looking veal chops, enough to feed an army. I didn't know Mike was going home. Or I could make a meat loaf."

"I've got to go out to Bay Shore to see Rory McCauley," he said. He watched her face, "So I won't be having dinner with you."

"Why?" she asked. "Why do you have to go out there again?"

"I wanted to tell him about his brother on the phone, but considering who killed him…you know…Casey shooting him, I decided I owed him a face-to-face explanation."

"Oh, Good Lord, Pete, tomorrow's Saturday. Can't you do it then?"

"No. Look, he has information on Seamus Slattery that Jack Fields needs right away, so I can accomplish both purposes by going out tonight."

She continued to press. "So why doesn't Jack Fields—"

"Stop it, Anne. When all this is over, I'll explain everything. Right now, I can't."

Tears formed at the corners of her eyes as she turned away and stormed off to the kitchen. Her angry voice floated back. "What time are you leaving?"

"In an hour."

Fanning turned off Sunrise Highway onto Clinton Avenue and drove to the end, missing the Cottage Avenue turn. He retraced his route. Cottage Avenue was a short jog off Clinton, dead-ending at the water's edge of the Great South Bay. To his left, he could see the ferry traffic leaving their slips off Maple Avenue, heading out to different towns on Fire Island.

A number of small cottage-style houses dotted each side, separated by clusters of shrubbery and fronted by scrubbed-white gravel driveways hosting parked vehicles and boat trailers. The Seahorse Boat-tel at the end of the street sat adjacent to a wide wooden dock extending out over the water. Fanning could see boats of various sizes tied up in their slips.

He turned into the Boat-tel's small parking lot. The sun had set, leaving traces of red and yellow rays braided along the horizon line. The darkening sky silhouetted shapes around him. Lights from the small craft and water-taxis out on the bay sparkled like tiny diamonds as they motored along the calm inlet. It was a serene picture. He could understand the appeal of this popular location.

It was six-fifty. He walked through the motionless air to the corner of the building, toward the Seahorse's front entrance, wondering if Dorgan and Lewis had arrived. The sound of footsteps startled him. A man appeared out of the shadows. Fanning reached inside his windbreaker.

"Detective Fanning, thanks for coming," Rory McCauley announced.

The greeting seemed a few decibels louder than necessary. He could feel his tension mushroom. He looked around before he realized the stillness that surrounded them amplified all sound. He relaxed his shoulders.

McCauley extended his hand and Fanning met it with a strong grasp. "How was traffic coming out?"

"Not bad, once out of the city limits."

Holding his hand, McCauley placed his free one on Fanning's shoulder, squeezing it slightly. "I think you're gonna find the trip worthwhile. And I appreciate your trusting me."

"I gave it serious thought, but I couldn't come up with a reason not to."

McCauley let go and laughed. "Detective, you need to take care in your business. That's for certain." He turned his head and looked to the dock, toward the line-up of boats. "I've a thirty-three-foot cabin cruiser down there," he said, pointing. "Let's go aboard. We'll be more comfortable talking there."

Without waiting, McCauley moved off. Fanning hesitated, thinking of Dorgan and Lewis. Could they follow without revealing themselves? His mind raced through the various scenarios he might face by going aboard the boat with McCauley. He slid his hand under his windbreaker again, making certain the holster snap was open.

He trailed the big Irishman down the ramp onto the dock. They headed toward the Chris Craft tied up two-thirds of the way out. Their shoes clacked over the ramp's wooden surface. The two men walked side-by side without speaking while Fanning recalled the question Casey had asked. Was McCauley setting him up? As they neared the cruiser, he realized he faced two choices: walk away or trust the man. He thought of the quote the Irishman had used the other day. *In for a penny, in for a pound.*

McCauley tugged on the line, pulling the stern of the boat closer. Bumpers down the side of the hull cushioned its impact as it bounced against the dock's hard edge. He reached out, grabbing the stainless steel handrail, holding it while Fanning stepped aboard onto the teakwood deck.

McCauley pointed to the door of the cabin. "Let's sit inside, at the table."

Fanning glanced through the narrow doorway opening with two steps leading down to the interior, a small room with one way in or out. He turned around. Waving his hand toward the three deck chairs at the bow, he said, "Why don't we sit there?"

McCauley stopped and looked to where Fanning had gestured. He laughed. "Still not sure, are you?"

"Well...ah...I'd feel more comfortable out in the open."

"That'd be fine except for the foot traffic of other boat owners. When you hear why I invited you, you'll understand. No, let's go below, if you don't mind."

Fanning shrugged. "In for a penny," he recited aloud and went through the cabin door.

McCauley laughed. "Atta boy, Detective. Trust old Rory."

Fanning sat down facing out on one of the two padded bench seats at the small table in the galley area. He looked around, surprised by how much of the interior was wood. "I'm no boat person, but aren't these things always made of fiberglass?"

"They are indeed. Today, that is. This is a wooden hull, 1953 Chris Craft Futura, restored ten years ago."

"You restore it?"

"No, no. I bought it this way soon after I moved out here."

McCauley set down two coffee cups. "Cream and sugar, Detective?"

"No, black is fine."

Fanning was amazed at the compactness of the interior. The polished mahogany paneling on the cabin walls reflected the interior lights like mirrors. Mahogany panels covered the cabinets above and around the small sink and stove. The flooring was teakwood throughout. He noticed the proud look on McCauley's face as the Irishman eyed him.

"Sleeps two. When they built it, they advertised it as the *Jaguar of the Cruisers*. Last winter, I had twin 350 Crusader rebuilt engines installed."

"Sounds like a dream."

"It is."

Fanning felt himself relaxing the more McCauley talked about the boat. It was difficult to think of him jeopardizing so much of what he loved—the restaurant, the cabin cruiser, the good life—by throwing in with the likes of the Real IRA, fighting for a dead cause. He looked at his watch. It was time to get to the purpose of his visit.

McCauley sensed it too. He looked over. "To begin, let me set the record straight." He paused, as though trying to decide where to start.

Fanning waited for him to continue.

"Honest, I never knew what Pearse and Seamus were up to. I figured it was something to do with getting money for the organization in Ireland. That's why I tipped you off to the Flynn brothers."

"You mean, like knocking off a bank or a racetrack?"

"That had occurred to me. I wasn't sure. I figured law enforcement would handle it."

"Were you in touch with Pearse all along?"

"No, not for six months. I had no idea he had thrown in with the al-Qaeda. I'd have said something to you that day you came to the restaurant."

"You know now he was? How?"

The Irishman took a breath. "Seamus."

"He's here?"

"Wait. Before we deal with that, let me finish what I have to say."

Fanning watched him wiggle in his seat. He tried to guess what was coming.

McCauley hesitated while the tapping sound of footsteps on the wooden dock passed. Fanning could see out the doorway, to the walker in a Jets jersey going by. Dorgan or Lewis, he hoped.

"Whatever you do, the results of this conversation cannot be connected to me in any way. You didn't get any information from me, and no association with me is to be made public."

Fanning listened, wondering what McCauley had in mind with these demands.

"I will leave it to your invention to create how things came about here and how they went down, but they must not involve me."

Fanning nodded. "Okay, you have my word. Now tell me why."

"Detective, I still have a younger brother in Belfast with a wife and four kiddies. He is not at all politically involved. He's a career postal worker and a good man."

Fanning was beginning to see where McCauley was going.

"If something tragic happened to him or his family…"

McCauley's face was solemn, no doubt concerned about possible retribution. Fanning remembered hearing how vicious the members of the original IRA were to various factions within their own organization. Revenge killings were commonplace. McCauley's worry was real.

"I understand," Fanning said.

McCauley sat without moving, staring down into his coffee cup, his wide girth pressing against the table's edge.

"Rory, are you aware how Pearse died?" He was certain that Slattery had already delivered the bad news about his brother.

"Yes I am. I hate to sound heartless, but I'm glad it's over for him. Bound to happen…sooner or later…only a matter of time, it was."

Fanning thought of telling him about the shootout at the garage, that he and Casey were involved, but he decided the less said the better. McCauley knew Pearse was dead. He didn't have to know who put the bullet in him.

"Aren't you worried about your own safety here," he asked, "that someone might find out?"

"No, but that brings me to my next concern. I'd hate to see Seamus extradited back to Belfast instead of jailed here in the States."

"I don't know enough international law. I can't promise you that wouldn't happen."

"Well, then, perhaps you can arrange to put a bullet in his skull."

Fanning's mouth dropped. "You're kidding, aren't you?"

"Yes, I am," McCauley said, forcing a grin. "But it wouldn't sadden me to know he was dead."

"Where is he?"

"I'll tell you, but first there are a few other things you'll want to know."

"Like what?"

"To start, when Seamus showed up at the restaurant yesterday, he was looking for a place to hide until he could get on a plane to Boston."

"Why Boston?"

"More coffee, Detective?" McCauley asked, rising up to reach for the pot.

Fanning heard his stomach growl with a hunger spasm. "Yeah, please."

His host filled both cups and sat down. "There was a group in Boston that used to provide fake passports and IDs to members of the IRA before the amnesty agreement."

Chattering voices passing outside the cabin again halted the narration. When the sound drifted off into the night, McCauley continued. "Seamus wanted me to call them, fix him up with a passport as well as provide him with an airline ticket to Belfast."

"And he needed you to get him to Boston?"

"Correct. But he's in no condition to travel."

"Would you like to explain why?"

"I will, but first let me finish. This is the part that I'm sure will interest you the most."

Fanning pressed against the table. He felt McCauley was stringing out the story. He wanted him to speed it up.

"I learned what they were up to, about their collaboration with al-Qaeda."

"He told you?"

"Yes. Not all of it voluntarily, you understand."

CHAPTER 26

Casey Franks and Jack Fields watched from the middle of Park Avenue. She could not believe there was an annual black-tie affair going on in the Waldorf's main ballroom, the *Who's Who in the Racing Industry*, oblivious to what was happening outside. In fifteen years with the NYPD, she had never seen an emergency operation of this size. The logistics were enormous.

The Waldorf-Astoria, one of New York City's premier hotels, was a huge structure, spanning an entire city block between Forty-ninth and Fiftieth Streets, and from Lexington to Park Avenues. Police barriers, placed at both ends of Forty-ninth and Fiftieth Streets, closed off access to all but official vehicles. Several squad cars flanked the hotel's front and rear entrances, monitoring those entering or leaving.

An emergency fire vehicle parked on an angle at the corner of Forty-ninth Street added to the chaos. Traffic on Park Avenue snaked by as uniformed police directed the flow. They had parked the Command Center trailer at the curb in front of the entrance to St. Bartholomew's Church. It was from within the trailer that they orchestrated the complicated operation.

Sirens screaming in the background made it difficult to hear. Casey couldn't tell if Fields was getting all that she was relating to him. She scrutinized his face, watching for a reaction as her words spilled out, describing Rory McCauley's telephone conversation with Pete Fanning.

"Jesus Christ, doesn't that guy ever learn?" Fields shouted back when she finished. It was clear he was frustrated, but he didn't appear angry. He shook his head. "Do you know if he was able to get back-up from Suffolk County?"

"I do not," she said, "but it was Lieutenant Dingillo's number that I gave him."

"Narcotics, right?"

"That's him."

Fields shook his head again.

"Pete said he'll call us when he has something to report," she added. She hoped it would soften the breach of procedure.

Fields reached out and latched onto her arm, pulling her out of the way of a police emergency van, its siren hooting, its lights flashing.

"Let's get up on the sidewalk before we get flattened," he said.

Another bomb squad vehicle followed a police emergency van into Fiftieth Street. The first bomb squad truck arriving on the scene earlier had now blocked off the entrance to the hotel's garage. The hotel's main ballroom was directly over it, three stories up.

When the bomb squad and emergency vehicles had cleared the intersection, Fields shouted to her, "Let's get the hell out of the way."

He started across Fiftieth Street toward the Command Center with Casey close behind. He stopped short at the trailer door, twisting his upper body to look back. Her momentum carried her into him, banging her damaged left wrist against his arm. She winced with pain.

He reached out to steady her. "Jesus, I'm sorry. You all right?"

"Yeah, fine."

"I'm sorry," he repeated. "I didn't realize you were right behind me. I stopped because I wanted to say something to you, something that I didn't want to say inside."

Casey waited.

"I was going to say, I think this whole operation is going to turn out to be a waste of the taxpayer's money. That's all."

❖

"Come on, Rory," Fanning said, "are you telling me Seamus opened up to you about their bomb plot? Why seek you out to do that?"

"Seamus said there was no one left, no one he could rely on to get him out of the country. He thought I could put him together with the Boston people. He had no other way to reach them."

Fanning leaned back into the cushion, trying to shake the growing stiffness. The residual soreness from the bomb blast yesterday had begun to creep back into his body. He raised his arms, clasping his fingers together behind his head. "Were you going to help him?"

"Detective, let's go up on deck where you'll be more comfortable. I think most of my neighbors have left by now."

Fanning slid off the bench seat, getting to his feet. He paused to allow the wave of dizziness to pass and followed McCauley out onto the deck.

"I couldn't have helped him if I wanted to," McCauley said. He dropped into one of the three canvas chairs at the bow. "Those people are no longer in business."

Fanning glanced back toward the boat-tel. A shadow moved through the spilled glow from the light stanchion at the dock's entrance.

"Because of the Peace Accord?" he asked. He stretched his arms again, breathing in the night's salty air, before sitting down. He felt better being outside again.

"In years past, I did occasionally help a few lads on the run, steering them in the Boston direction. That ended with the '98 amnesty; however,

Seamus didn't know that."

"No kidding?"

A grin appeared on the big man's face. "Before we discussed anything, he had to hand over his weapon. He did. Told him he needed to tell me what devious mischief he and Pearse were up to before I'd do anything. I held out the offer like a carrot on a stick." McCauley angled closer to Fanning. "The carrot worked, along with this," he added. He held up his meaty clenched fist.

"You beat it out of him?"

"Aye, whenever his tongue became tied. One of my specialties back when I was an active player in Belfast, you know." He chuckled. "Always the interrogator and I haven't lost a step." His head rocked back as his chuckle reformed into a rapid fire of guffaws, the outbursts rising into the silence of the evening like a series of small explosions.

Fanning watched, imagining Rory McCauley in his prime, a fierce revolutionary with little patience for anyone attempting to block his way. He guessed the former IRA soldier had been a feared brawler, perhaps someone who enjoyed the physical side of his job. Beating up on Slattery was no doubt therapeutic for the man after hearing of his brother's death.

McCauley stopped laughing.

"You ready now to tell me what's going down?" Fanning asked.

The Irishman stared for several seconds as though he was trying to shake the effect of his reverie. "Oh, sorry, lad," he said. "Yes, of course."

Fanning glanced at his watch. He had been there over forty-five minutes. Casey was waiting to hear from him. He was getting anxious to end this. "Well, what is it?" he asked, making no effort to hide his impatience.

"They've planned a bombing, all right. No surprise, I'm sure."

"That much I already guessed. Did he said where? When?"

"Belmont Park Racetrack, tomorrow. They're targeting the Irish MP,

Trevor McNeill and some Saudi prince. I don't know his name."

"Does Seamus have the bomb with him?"

"Jaysus, I hope not. No, heavens no. It's with Colin Flynn."

"The brother of the news dealer?"

"Same man."

"Didn't you tell me you thought Pearse and Seamus didn't know the Flynns?"

"Apparently I was wrong."

Colin Flynn was the name on the personnel roster of Belmont Park's maintenance department. It made sense to Fanning now. Flynn had open access anywhere on the track property. Bringing the explosive device with him when he reported for work was the easy part.

"He tell you any details about the bomb, like when Colin was bringing it in, where on the track he was going to plant it?"

McCauley lowered his chin, staring down at the deck. When he looked up, he rolled his eyes. The dim glow from the cabin lights revealed a small grin. "Afraid I didn't get that far."

"Why?"

The Irishman brought up his clenched fist again and shook it. "When the bastard told me he didn't know, I lost it."

"What did you do?" Fanning asked.

"I lamped him out of it." McCauley said, punching the air in front of him. "I had all I could do to keep from tearing his head off. But I knew that wouldn't be productive."

"You figured I would get the rest of the information from him? That's why you called me?"

"You're right, Detective. When he came to, he was gone in the head. He started spewing a load of garbage about Trevor McNeill and the prince. I told him to shut his face and keep low until I could get in touch with the Boston people. I left him. Came here to call you."

"His gun. Where is it?"

McCauley stood, making his way back down into the cabin. Fanning could see him pull down the lid of a bulkhead compartment just beyond the table. He retraced his steps and handed over the weapon. "Here," he said

Fanning recognized Mike Allen's Colt .45. "This the only one he had?"

"Yeah, unless he had another stashed in the truck. To be honest, I never checked."

Fanning rose to his feet and stuffed the barrel of the gun down the front of his waistband. He thought of the possibility of a second weapon.

"I grabbed his truck keys when he was out cold," McCauley explained. "Even if he tried legging it, he wouldn't get far."

"Where is he, then?" Fanning asked.

"In my cottage. You passed it. A small place. Most of the time, I have it rented out over the summer."

"What's the layout?"

"Living room, bedroom, a Pullman kitchen. Not too many places to hide."

"Can I get in?"

"It's open. The door locks from the outside. I have the key."

"Well then, I guess it's show time. You gonna stay here, of course."

"Surely you don't need my help, Detective. He's yours for the taking. I told you it was going to be easy, nothing to fear."

"Thanks," Fanning said, taking McCauley's hand. "And the story will be local police spotted his truck when he drove to the restaurant. They followed him here. Okay?"

"Sounds good."

Fanning reached the Taurus in the boat-tel parking lot and locked Mike's .45 in the glove compartment. He dialed the number he had for

the two narcotics detectives located somewhere out there in the darkness.

"Dorgan," the quiet voice answered.

"Detective…Fanning here. My subject is in a cottage up the street, number 22, on the left side."

"Is he armed?" Dorgan asked.

"Negative."

"Are you going in for him now?"

"In five minutes."

"Do you want us with you?"

Fanning thought for a moment. The less involved they were, the easier to make good on his promise to McCauley for anonymity. "No thanks. I'm sure I can handle it."

"Okay. We'll be in the driveway just across the street."

Fanning punched in the number for Casey.

"Franks," she answered on the second ring.

"Casey, Pete."

"Hold on, Pete. Let me get outside where the reception is better." After several seconds, she asked, "What's happening?"

Fanning gave her an abridged account of his meeting with McCauley. "I'll bring Seamus to Metropolitan Corrections when I get into the city. Tell Jack Fields he can expect me there in three hours."

"Boy, is he going to be happy to hear the target is Belmont Racetrack."

"Why?"

"He guessed right. Based on your visit there, he felt everything pointed that way. His boss couldn't see it. That's why we've got a three-ring circus going on here at the Waldorf."

"Well, he's going to have twelve hours, give or take, to nail Colin Flynn once I get Seamus to him. I think he'll want to ask the shit-for-brains a few questions of his own."

"Okay, I'll brief him. You sure you don't want your back-ups to go in with you?"

"No. Rory says he's softened him up for me. Besides, he's unarmed."

"Hope you're right. Just be careful."

"I will. See you soon."

Fanning took the handcuffs lying on the seat next to him and slipped them into his windbreaker pocket. He checked his holster again. Running his fingers over the freed up pistol grip, he sucked in several deep breaths. Each time, he filled his cheeks like small balloons, popping the air between his compressed lips. He wiped the sweat from his palms on the sides of his pant legs and felt his racing heartbeat begin to slow.

The street was dark, heavily treed on both sides with full-leafed branches blocking the moon, allowing intermittent slivers of light to penetrate. He made his way into the spackled darkness, over the gravel-covered pathway toward the screened-in porch. The black Chevy quad-cab pick-up parked in the driveway was a painful reminder of his experience at the garage in Long Island City that took his friend's life. He reached inside his jacket, gripped the butt of his 9 mm and removed it from the shoulder holster. The thick shrubbery between cottages provided a serenade of crickets and the sweet aroma of lilac.

Fanning slipped through the screened porch. A card table and three metal chairs occupied one end. The smell of cigarettes hung heavy in the air. Pushing open the front door, he edged into the main room, hesitating in the darkness until objects came into focus. It was a small square-box of a room with two standard-size windows on each side. He could make out the scattered outlines of summer cottage-type wicker furniture. The Pullman kitchen took up most of the left wall. A ribbon of light squeezed out at the base of the closed bedroom door at the right corner of the room.

He inched down the left side, past the efficiency kitchen where the wall recessed back to a small bathroom. The door stood ajar. He stopped to listen. Sounds from the noisemakers in the shrubs outside leaked through the open windows. He moved along the rear wall toward the splash of light on the floor. Pausing before the doorway, he raised the Glock with his finger resting on the trigger.

Before his hand found the doorknob, a heavy force slammed across his back, sending him to the floor. He landed on his chest, his arms splayed out in front of him, and the butt end of the weapon banged against the wooden floor surface. His trigger finger jerked closed. The Glock discharged, sending a loud report echoing into the night. For a moment, the crickets stopped singing.

Fanning lay spread-eagled on the floor, the folded metal chair next to him. Beneath his closed lids, white and black lights flashed like a strobe, while the pain from his previous injuries revisited his body. When his head cleared, he rolled over in time to see the form of a man dashing out through the screened door. He remembered the pick-up truck parked in the driveway, but relaxed when he remembered that McCauley had taken the keys.

"Stop! Police!" The voice came from across the street.

Fanning struggled to his feet. Making his way to the front door, he heard the sound of running steps followed by the repeated command.

"Stop! Police!"

This time a volley of gunshots broke the silence.

Fanning froze in the doorway. "Wait, hold your fire," he called. "I need him alive."

A tall figure raced up the path toward the cottage. "Holy shit!" he shouted. "We heard a shot. We thought he'd taken you down." It was one of the narcotics detectives.

The voice of the second detective reached them from up the street. "I have him, Dorgan. He's down. He's been hit."

"Jesus," Fanning exclaimed. He started in their direction with Dorgan running at his side. "Is he alive?" he shouted, nearing the second undercover crouched over the downed man.

"I think so." Lewis sounded relieved.

One of Lewis's bullets had hit the man, spinning him around so that he landed on his back. Fanning knelt down to get a look at his face. He ran his hand under his nose and felt air. But something didn't compute. The man's appearance; he had light hair, a long body—over six feet—dressed in a pair of trousers that hiked mid-way up to his shins. In the hospital on Tuesday, Mike Allen had described Seamus Slattery in detail. This was not Slattery.

A quick phone call to McCauley provided the answer. "Your description sounds like Colin Flynn, one of the two Flynn brothers. By God, when I left Seamus, he was alone in the cottage. That's the truth. Colin must have slipped in later."

It was apparent to Fanning that Slattery had fled, taking Flynn's car, leaving the Muslim's pickup truck and switching clothes with Flynn. It didn't take long to realize where Slattery was heading when he left Bay Shore.

The EMS ambulance from the local Southside Hospital arrived ten minutes after Dorgan put in the call. Flynn was still unconscious when they drove off. The EMS attendant explained to Fanning that one of the detective's bullets had caught Flynn in the lower torso area. A second one had glanced off the right side of his skull.

CHAPTER 27

The Pinkerton officer on the gate peered through the overhead pool of halogen lights at the decal on the hatchback's windshield. His focus traveled to the driver's side window. Slattery had his gaze fixed on the road ahead, but he could see the Pinkerton trying to get a look at his profile. He kept his head still so that the half-closed right eye that McCauley's fists had pummeled would not be visible. The officer hesitated, then stepped inside the gatehouse without speaking. Slattery watched to see if he was going to the phone. Instead, the Pinkerton picked up a clipboard, made a notation, and returned outside. He waved to Slattery, and the terrorist, wearing Flynn's work coveralls with the letters NYRA on the left breast, passed through the Plainfield Avenue entrance onto the Belmont Park property.

Flynn had told him it was rare they stopped anyone to produce identification. Track employees used this gate daily, and their cars became familiar to the officers on duty. He guessed the officer on duty this night was new.

Following Flynn's directions, Slattery drove through the racetrack's backstretch, past the endless rows of stables and barns that housed the large population of expensive Thoroughbreds. Some of the Belmont Stakes contestants, he read, had been purchased as untested two-year-olds for several millions of dollars. What a waste of good money, he thought.

He kept to the fifteen-mile-per-hour speed limit as he threaded the hatchback to the clubhouse corner of the building and entered the tunnel. Flynn had described the loading dock and where to find the maintenance vans parked in their usual spots. He pulled alongside and popped his hatchback's lock. He saw a light in the maintenance office, but the room was empty. The surrounding area was quiet. According to Flynn, the maintenance staff would be off working throughout various sections of the building, preparing it for the big race day.

Slattery pushed open the hatchback. He reached in for a large canvas tool bag and a small folded stepladder. With the bag in one hand and the ladder in the other, he swung around the end van and climbed the six steps to the large deck of the loading dock. Limping past the window of the empty office, he made his way down the wide hallway toward the two elevators at the rear. The floor indicator of the passenger elevator showed it idle at the third level of the clubhouse. He entered the opened door of the freight elevator and placed the ladder against the wall. Pulling down on the lever, he closed the heavy doors and looked up at the car's ceiling. He placed the ladder under the square panel that allowed access to the top of the elevator.

After several minutes, Slattery returned to the hatchback, laid the stepladder in the back and placed the tool bag beside it. He slipped in behind the wheel and drove out of the tunnel.

Slattery maneuvered the vehicle over the narrow roads of the backstretch. He eased past sleeping Thoroughbreds to an empty barn at the northeastern corner of the property. He would wait there—like the twelve Belmont Stakes entries in other barns scattered about—until tomorrow's eighth race.

❖

Fanning was surprised she answered on the first ring. "Hello," she said. She sounded sleepy.

"Anne, I'm sorry I didn't call you earlier but things got a little complicated."

Her voice became animated. "Pete, for Christ's sake, you okay?"

"Yeah, I'm fine. It just took longer than I expected."

"Where are you? It's eleven o'clock."

He hesitated. Saying *South Side Hospital* would guarantee she'd become alarmed. "I'm still out in Bay Shore." He hoped she would assume he was with Rory McCauley at his restaurant.

"Well, when are you coming home?"

"Not right away. I got another hour here," he said. He remembered they might expect him to fill out a report at the local Bay Shore Precinct.

He could hear Anne's irregular breathing. He knew she was fighting back tears of frustration. "I'm okay, Anne, honest," he said.

"Aah, Pete, we can't go on like this."

"Yeah, I know. I'm sorry, sweetheart. How's Luke?"

"Fine. Sound asleep, like I hope I can be again after I hang up."

"That's right, hon. Go back to sleep. I'll be home soon. Okay? Gotta go. See you in the morning. Bye." He closed the cell phone before she could respond.

Looking at the drawn curtain covering the hospital operating area, he remembered he had to call Jack Fields. He punched in his cell number. Fields answered immediately. After filling him in on the switch, Fanning told him he was sure Slattery had taken off for Belmont.

"Stay with Flynn until we can transport him back to the city," Fields instructed. "I'm sending an ambulance and two federal agents to take him into custody whenever the hospital says he can travel. They should get there sometime around one this morning."

Damn, Fanning thought. I should have told Anne it was going to be more like late morning.

"Until then," Fields told him, "see what information you can get out of the Irish bastard. Maybe get some more specifics on what the hell they're planning, what Seamus is up to."

Fanning sat in the lounge area across from the two undercover detectives. He didn't want to consider how pissed Anne would be when he arrived home. He had poured gas on the fire, but he couldn't help himself. He had to finish this.

Dorgan and Lewis had their attention locked on the television set hanging in the bracket above his head. They had waited for him while he retrieved the Taurus from the boat-tel parking lot and followed them to the hospital.

Terry Dorgan, the taller of the two men and the older member of the team, wore a short-sleeved, open-neck shirt under a lightweight windbreaker, with khaki slacks and sneakers. He had a mop of hair the color of wheat and a disheveled moustache under his long nose.

Gary Lewis was a muscular, short man with dark eyes that blinked when he spoke. His ragtag jeans covered the tops of his heavy-duty work shoes. He wore a New York Jets jersey, the jersey Fanning remembered seeing as Lewis passed McCauley's boat earlier. He thought the jersey was a great touch, appropriate for the role of an undercover working in this area.

Dorgan mentioned they had been partners for the past five years. He confessed, sounding apologetic, that neither had ever shot someone in the line of duty.

The ER doctor in charge, wearing fresh green scrubs, booties and cap, came out from behind the drawn curtain surrounding the emergency operating area and looked around. Fanning spotted him and got up from his chair in the lounge.

"Hi, Doctor, I'm Detective Fanning. How's my guy doing?"

"Doctor Stern," he said, taking Fanning's outstretched hand.

Dorgan and Lewis jumped up from their chairs and hurried to join Fanning.

"We removed the bullet in his left hip and stemmed the bleeding for now." He delivered the information in a slow monotone, as if he was ordering medical supplies over the phone. He continued with his phone-order delivery. "Lucky for him his head wound was superficial."

Fanning's look of surprise provoked an answer before he could ask it.

"The bullet grazed his right ear, taking off part of the upper edge as it skimmed past the skull," Stern explained. "We've got him stabilized. It doesn't appear to be life threatening."

Fanning heard the two narcotics detectives expel a unified sigh of relief. He offered them a look of understanding. Their lives over the next few weeks just became simplified. Had Lewis been more on target, they would be facing an administrative nightmare.

"Well, the Feds will be happy to hear that. They're sending transportation for him."

"Is he conscious?" Dorgan asked.

"Yes, but he's sedated," the doctor replied.

"When can I question him?" Fanning asked.

"Give it an hour."

"I don't have much more than an hour," he shot back. "There's a bomb ticking somewhere. I need to get some answers from him."

Dorgan and Lewis looked at each other, wide eyed. Turning to Fanning, Lewis asked, "Who the fuck is this guy?"

"An international terrorist."

The ER doctor stepped over to a nearby counter and picked up a clipboard. "We're going to move him now to a room in the ICU," he said. He turned and walked away.

"You want an officer posted at the door?" Dorgan asked.

Fanning nodded. "Might be a good idea."

Dorgan looked at his partner. "Call it in, Gary. Ask the precinct commander for two uniforms. Let's not take any chances with this mother."

Lewis hesitated. His face showed concern.

"What? What's the matter?" Dorgan asked.

"This is going to cost the county some dough. Lieutenant Dingillo…he's gonna be pissed."

"Tough shit. Go call it in," Dorgan replied. "Tell them to rush it."

Fanning looked at the clock over the doorway. An hour should put it a little after midnight, he thought. Turning to Dorgan, he asked, "Any place nearby I can get a fast bite? I'm starved."

"Yeah, sure," he said. "There's a Mickey D's out on Montauk Highway that's open until two on Friday night. Wait until the uniforms get here, and we'll take you. I could do with a cup of coffee and a Big Mac."

"Close the door, Vince," Chief Cannon said. He removed his suit jacket and dropped down into his desk chair. Leaning back with his hands clasped across his belly, he shut his eyes.

"Tired, Chief?" Vince Bogan asked.

"Exhausted. Did you get anything to eat before the meeting?"

"Just those sandwiches the chef set out for us on the buffet table. I had enough."

John Cannon opened his eyes and watched Bogan settle into the wing chair. Cannon thought back over the years he'd known this man. They'd first met twenty-five years ago when Bogan, as a rookie detective, came under Cannon's command to become a part of the squad he led in the Bronx. He remembered with pride how the young detective had excelled within a short period to become an outstanding investigator. Over time, a close working relationship formed.

Cannon closed his eyes again and began running the task-force briefing details through his mind. He suddenly got to his feet. "What time is the county's bomb squad supposed to be here in the morning?"

"Before six. Five-thirty, maybe. Gates open at ten-thirty. If we don't get a clean bill by nine-thirty, we're gonna be forced to scratch the whole day."

The chief thought of the consequences of canceling this historic sporting event. It would mean a huge loss of revenue for the NYRA, an incredible wasted expense on the part of all the participating stables, to say nothing of the disruption of the racing calendar. Then, too, the chance for a Triple Crown winner would go by the wayside, as well as the indescribable loss of purse and bonus money to Gallant Warrior's owner-connections.

"Christ, canceling would be catastrophic."

"Chief, let's not worry about it until we have to. We still have time to ferret it out."

Cannon continued as though he hadn't heard Bogan "Then there's the historic effect. This race has been going on since 1867. It missed running only twice—1911 and 1912, the two years New York state outlawed racing. That's an incredible record of consistency."

"Incredible," Bogan echoed.

Cannon visualized the logistics involved during the next hours. "I hope Nassau County Police emergency vehicles can be kept out of sight until we need them."

"Not to worry about the police cars parked at the entrances," Bogan reminded him. "Happens anytime a major political figure or foreign dignitary shows up for a big race."

"On the other hand," Cannon added, "a vehicle identified as the Nassau County Bomb Squad would hardly go unnoticed. Have all the maintenance vans been accounted for?"

"Yes. We checked that earlier, Chief, before the briefing,"

"Okay, but I want them checked again every hour until we close off access in the morning. Is Colin Flynn working today?"

"He doesn't come in until eleven o'clock. He's scheduled on the night crew."

"When he steps foot on the property, take him into custody. Alert the Pinkertons on the Plainfield Avenue gate. We don't know yet if he's involved with this bomb threat, but we're not taking any chances. Understood?"

"Yes, Chief."

"Before you leave, get a hold of MacAfee. Have him get a security crew together and go over every inch of the Trustees Room." He expelled an exhausted yawn. "Then make certain the place is locked up tight until morning."

Bogan nodded. "Not to worry, Chief. I'm here for the night. Why don't you go on home? Catch a little sleep. We'll take care of everything."

"Good idea." He got up and buttoned his vest. "I'll be back by five."

"See you then, Chief." Bogan said.

Minutes later John Cannon took the escalator to the first level and headed to his car in the executive parking area. It was a fifteen-minute drive to his house in Garden City. He was sure he could get in at least four hours of sleep. "Damn!" he said aloud, recalling how, during his years as Chief of Detectives, these kinds of emergencies always created mass confusion beyond imagining. He prayed the JTTF and the Feds were better at it these days than the NYPD was back then, before 9/11.

Cannon unlocked the car and hesitated, thinking he had forgotten to remind Bogan to post a security man on the Trustees Room trackside door. He rewound his thoughts, going back through all of his instructions. Yes, he had mentioned it. He climbed in behind the wheel and looked out through the windshield, overcome with an unsettling notion of dread. This was going to be a Belmont Stakes Day to remember.

CHAPTER 28

Saturday, June 8

The clock over the doorway of the ER examining room showed twenty after twelve when Fanning walked in, followed by Dorgan and Lewis carrying McDonald's coffee cups.

The duty nurse behind the counter looked up. "Hey, Terry."

"Hi, Lenora. Just come on?"

"Yeah, twelve to eight tonight. What's up?"

"We got a gunshot victim in 2214. Is the doc around? Detective Fanning here needs to ask the vic a few questions."

"The guy being guarded?" she asked.

"That's the one. Can we go up?"

Lenora stood up on her toes and bent over the counter to see down the hallway. "I don't think he's on this floor right now. Let me page him. Find out if it's okay."

The page went out over the P.A. Stern answered right away and told her they could go up.

When they entered the hospital room, Dorgan and Lewis moved to the window and stood looking out into the darkness. Fanning pulled his chair to the side of the lone bed. He sat without moving, examining Colin Flynn's face. The large gauze patch on the right side of the Irishman's head, held in place by a bandage wrap, was the only visible sign of his recent near-death encounter. The terrorist's eyes were open, staring at the ceiling, his chest rising and falling normally. He showed no outward signs of discomfort. Fanning thought of Teddy and fought off the urge to kick the bed.

He wondered how much more information Flynn would give up. Rory McCauley, he remembered, had to use his fist on Slattery and the promise of safe passage back to Ireland. Fanning held no such ace with Flynn. He wondered how the two undercover narcs would react if he decided to get physical.

Fanning walked to the two detectives standing at the window. Lowering his voice, he said, "Guys, would you mind waiting downstairs while I see what I can get out of this bird?"

"Huh? Oh, sure," Dorgan said. "We didn't mean—"

Fanning waved a hand in dismissal. "It's just that the Feds will be here any moment, and you know how they are about their cases."

"Yeah, sure, no problem." Dorgan motioned to Lewis, and they started for the door.

Before the two men reached it, Fanning called to them. "Hold it a second." He moved close and whispered, "Can one of you leave your cuffs with me?"

Dorgan's puzzled expression turned into a grin. His mustache twitched as he reached inside his jacket pocket. "Here's the key. We'll be downstairs if you need us."

"Thanks. Oh, and tell the officers outside that if they hear any loud shouting, pay it no mind."

"Right," Dorgan said. The two undercovers disappeared out the door.

Fanning looked at Colin Flynn. He had closed his eyes and pressed his arms against his sides, his palms resting on his thighs, not moving.

Fanning returned to his chair at the side of the bed. He dragged it closer and leaned in toward the bandaged ear of the Irishman. "How's the bullet in the ass feel?"

There was no response.

"You were lucky."

"Who the hell are you?" Flynn asked, keeping his eyes closed.

"We never met before you flattened me with that chair. But I met two of your friends a couple of nights ago in Long Island City."

"What two friends? Where?"

"At the garage they blew up. I'm sure they told you about that."

He stared at Fanning for several seconds. "You the one ..." He stopped and turned away.

"Got the plate number of the pickup before it disappeared," Fanning lied.

Flynn said nothing.

"It was spotted out here by the local police," Fanning said, continuing his lie.

"It's not my truck," the terrorist fired back. It was as though denying ownership removed him from any connection with the bombing.

"We know that. The guy who owns it wants it back." He was guessing the man in the bed was still in the dark about the capture of Masab Yasin and wouldn't know of The Chemist's shootout at the house. "Let's get down to business," Fanning said. "We know what you're up to, your plan to bomb Belmont Park sometime today."

"What the hell you talking about?" Flynn blurted.

"I'm talking about the bomb plot Khalid bin Muhammad told us about," Fanning said, electing to use the full name of The Chemist.

The Irishman snapped back. "I don't know a fuckin' thing about it."

Fanning pushed closer. "Okay, let's stop jerkin' my chain. Because if you don't help me out here, I promise, you'll burn for it along with Seamus Slattery and bin Muhammad." He let a few beats go by, and then added, "If I don't kill you first."

"Look, all I know is the Muslim wanted someone at the racetrack dead. I was never told who or why. They paid me to provide some of the chemicals for the explosives. That's all I know."

Fanning stood and walked around the foot of the bed to the window. Off in the distance, headlights on Montauk Highway flitted like fireflies through the trees that flanked the busy road. He pressed his forehead against the cool glass, struggling to get his rising anger under control. A jumble of images raced in his head, primarily a large racetrack of dead people.

He heard his stomach gurgle from the greasy Big Mac. He pulled his head back and rolled it around, stretching the ache at the base of his neck. When he looked out again, instead of seeing his own reflection, he saw a fuzzy aura forming of his brother Gerry. And his friend Teddy.

Fanning reached in his pocket. Slipping out the set of cuffs he took from Dorgan, he walked to the side of the bed. Flynn had shut his eyes, appearing as though he might have dozed off.

With speed, Fanning slapped one end of the cuffs onto the left wrist of the Irishman. He yanked the arm above Flynn's head and locked the other end of the cuffs to the post of the metal headboard behind. Flynn pulled away, rolling side to side, until he rolled on top of the bullet wound in his hip. He screamed.

Fanning raced to the other side of the bed. While Flynn writhed in pain, he locked his own set of cuffs on the Irishman's right wrist, then to that side of the headboard.

The helpless terrorist shrieked. "You fuckin' can of piss, what are you doin'? Take these things off me, you asshole. I ain't goin' nowhere."

"You're damn right, you're not," Fanning shouted back, hoping the two officers at the door were ignoring the noise.

He stood watching the man—legs kicking, head rocking, hands and fingers twisting in the cuffs. In his furor to free himself, Flynn tossed his head too far to the right and landed on his damaged ear. He gave out another cry of pain.

Fanning allowed him to struggle until Flynn tired himself. He had kicked the blanket half way down. His hospital gown had come loose, working its way up, exposing the bandage around his waist. His testicles hung free. Flynn peered down at his revealed privates and groaned.

Fanning took hold of the blanket end and pulled it up. "We don't want you catching cold before you finish answering my questions, now do we?"

"Shove it!"

No surprise. Flynn was uncooperative. Fanning knew it would come down to using physical threats. He was prepared to go that far. So be it, he thought, but I had better do it before the federal agents arrive to transport the man. They might not approve of my methods.

Fanning stood at the head of the bed. "Okay, here's what you're going to tell me, my friend."

The terrorist spit out his words. "Don't be a moron. I have nothing to tell you."

Fanning remained calm. Flynn's expression, still flushed from his tussle with the handcuffs, hardened.

"Listen to me carefully. You don't want to test me. I'm prepared to kill you right here, so you better think about it."

The terrorist's defiance softened. His eyes widened, showing more white than cornea. The threat had reached his understanding.

"This is what I want to know. Are you listening?" Fanning paused, and then in rapid fire, he reeled off the questions. "Who's involved? Who's their target? How do they plan to get the explosive onto the track?

Where will they plant it? How and when will they detonate it?"

Flynn turned away. "I don't know any of that."

"Let's start with who's involved besides Seamus Slattery."

"I already told you. The only one I know is the Muslim."

"Okay, Khalid told us Belmont Park was the target. Look at me, shithead. That true?"

Flynn turned back. "Yeah, if that's what he said."

"Yeah, that's what he said. But why the racetrack?"

"To kill lots of people, I guess. I don't know. He never told me."

"You said before that Khalid wanted to kill someone there. Who is it?"

"Ask him. I don't know."

"And you don't know how they're getting the explosive onto the track either?"

"Haven't the foggiest."

Fanning's anger began to rise, not so much from the Irishman's denials. Most of it he already knew. It was more the arrogance in the man's tone that pissed him off. He thought Flynn had reconsidered the seriousness of his threat to kill him, and he decided to play with him now.

It was twelve-fifty. The Feds would be arriving soon. Fanning had to act fast. The trip to the city would cost them several hours before Fields could question the terrorist.

Fanning turned, walked to the window, this time to open his cell phone and pretend to make a call. After a moment, he spoke in a voice loud enough for Flynn to hear. "It's me. No. Nothing. Yeah, I know. So what? He's no good to us now. Don't worry, I got that covered. No witnesses. Okay. Bye."

Fanning waited, looking through the window. He heard Flynn jerk his legs around under the blanket. He returned to the head of the bed and remained standing. Looking down at his captive, he said, "Let's try a few more questions, see if you get a sudden memory rush."

The man's breathing quickened, faster than before the bogus phone conversation. His eyes darted around. As they slowed, they rested on Fanning, showing an expression of concern.

"How was the bomb supposed to get onto the track property?" Fanning shouted. "You? You work there, don't you?"

"How the hell do I know? I supplied some of the chemicals. That's all."

"You fucking liar," Fanning screamed.

Without warning, he flung himself across the bed and landed on the man's chest. Flynn released a loud gust of breath. The Irishman squeezed his eyes together and grimaced when the force of Fanning's body came down on him.

Spinning his torso around like a top, Fanning pushed himself up and knelt on the man's thighs, pinning them to the mattress with his knees. Flynn struggled, trying to catch his breath. Before he could, Fanning reached up and yanked the pillow from under his head. Grasping both ends, he forced it down onto the face of the squirming man and held it there with his weight on his forearms. Flynn's feet kicked furiously beneath the blanket.

Fanning held him under the pillow while the man tried to force his head up and to the sides with little success. He fought the best way he could, emitting muffled sounds as he choked for air. Overhead, his hands danced like marionettes within the locked cuffs. He was losing the battle. When the movement of his feet started to slow, Fanning released the pillow. He placed it behind him.

The sudden return to the open air produced rapid gasping and coughing as the struggling Irishman fought to retake the breath of life. His face was crimson with strain. His eyes teared as though he had sprung a leak. His chest heaved under the weight of Fanning's body.

Fanning remained astride, watching. After a few moments, the man's breathing quieted. He held the pillow out to one side and looked down at the panicked face.

"I told you not to test me. You're fooling with the wrong guy. I just got the go ahead to snuff you. I can't tell you how much I'd love to do that."

"You're outta your bloody head, you are." He struggled to get the words out.

Fanning laughed. "That I am, and don't you forget it. Now, you have a choice. Answer my questions or go back under?" He lifted the pillow for him to view. "What's it gonna be?"

Flynn took in a deep gulp of air. His voice was still weak. "I can tell you only what I know."

"That's fine, so long as it's the truth. No bullshitting. Understand?"

He nodded.

"Who's carrying the explosive onto the track?"

"I did."

"You did? When? Today? Before coming out here?"

"No. Yesterday. When I went to work in the morning." He pulled several times at the handcuffs on his wrists. Shutting his eyes in obvious discomfort, he said, "Can't you take these damn things off? They're killing my wrists."

"Not until you tell me everything you know."

"Well then, at least get the fuck off me."

Fanning remained kneeling. "What did you do with it?"

"With what?"

Fanning reached back for the pillow. "The bomb, you God-damn piece of shit. Where did you plant it?" He bent over and placed his face inches away from Flynn while he brought the pillow to one side. "Where on the track did you plant the bomb?"

The man turned away. "In the clubhouse," he said, the pitch of his voice rising.

"Where in the clubhouse?" Fanning shouted. He dragged the pillow across the man's face again. "Tell me, you son of a bitch, or you're going to take your last breath on this earth."

"Wait...wait...Jesus Christ," Flynn pleaded with muffled words of panic.

Fanning lifted the pillow a few inches. "Okay, tell me, but no more bullshit."

The frightened Irishman's head twisted as if on a swivel. "It's wired to the undercarriage...the van...the maintenance van."

"And where is the van now?" Fanning raised the pillow again.

"I don't know."

"What do you mean, you don't know?"

"I'm not the only one that uses it."

"Where is it going to be parked today, during the race?"

Flynn hesitated, until he saw Fanning lowering the pillow. "It'll be somewhere in the clubhouse, the area where Trevor McNeill and the Arab prince were going to have lunch."

The Trustees Room, Fanning thought. He remembered the six maintenance vans parked overnight at the loading dock in the tunnel, under the room. "You know how they wired the bomb, what kind of detonator they used?"

Flynn blurted the answer. "A timer...I mean a radio controlled transmitter."

"So which is it? A timer or transmitter?"

"Transmitter."

"So it could be triggered from anywhere on the track? Right?"

"That's right."

"What range?"

"Two miles."

Fanning thought back to his tour around the backstretch with John Cannon. He tried to picture the view from that area. It meant that someone could be sitting anywhere on the backstretch, across the mile-and-a-half racing oval, out of range of the blast when he triggers the bomb.

"That's where Seamus will be?"

"Yes," Flynn said.

Fanning pitched himself off the man's chest, tossing the pillow to the floor. A red stain had saturated the bed sheet; the swatch of blood was just under the left hip of the terrorist. He had aggravated the gunshot wound when he climbed on. He'd mention it to Lenora, the duty nurse, before he left the hospital, but now he needed to make a call. He was convinced Flynn had told him all he knew. He had to get the information to Jack Fields right away. Flynn could bleed to death for all he cared.

The spent Irishman stared at the ceiling while Fanning unlocked the cuffs from the bedposts. "What's going to happen to me?" he asked. His earlier arrogance had disappeared.

"What do you think? Nobody here is going to throw you a party."

"Well, can I ask you, what would you be charging me with? I never killed anyone."

"I guess you forgot. You and your gang set off the charge that blew up the garage in Long Island City. The explosion killed a good person."

"No. That was the Muslim's doing. I wasn't there."

"Well, you're guilty by association. Too bad Teddy's not around to argue with you."

"I didn't have a say—"

"Bullshit! Like the bombings at the train stations in London ten years ago, killing six innocent people, including my friend's wife. That wasn't your group's doing, either?"

The terrorist furrowed his brow. "That fella a friend of yours?" he asked after piecing the information together.

"My best friend. Slattery came within inches of ending his life too."

Flynn went silent, thinking. "Seamus said he put one in his shoulder to keep him down. That's all. Stayed away from his vitals. He didn't kill him. Could have, you know."

"I'll have Mike send him a thank-you note."

Fanning turned when he heard voices outside the door. He pocketed both sets of handcuffs. The Feds had arrived and were speaking with the two uniformed police officers. He turned back to Flynn. "Looks like your ride is here."

CHAPTER 29

Jack Fields and Tony Condon arrived at their Federal Plaza office at one-forty-five. Festivities at the Belmont Ball had ended at midnight. The police removed the emergency vehicles and personnel from around the Waldorf-Astoria Hotel, reopening the streets on either side to traffic. It had been an exercise in futility, Fields decided, since in the end the Irish MP and the prince turned out to be no-shows.

Alone in his office at his desk, Fields mulled over how the racetrack was to be the next possible target. They needed to repeat the whole scene in the morning, this time with Nassau County law enforcement.

His direct phone line lit up. "Fields."

"Jack, Pete here."

"Where the hell are you?"

"Still at the hospital. Your guys just left with Colin Flynn. Should be in there in two hours."

"You get anything from—"

"Yeah."

"What?"

"It's definitely Belmont Park."

"Today?"

"Right."

"Did he say where they planned to put the explosive?"

"Yeah. He planted it yesterday under the floorboard of one of the six maintenance vans parked in the tunnel at the clubhouse end."

"Christ, I find that hard to believe. How the hell could he do that without being seen?"

"Belmont's a big place, over four-hundred and thirty acres. He could have driven the van to any out-of-the-way spot on the track."

"And you think he leveled with you?"

"I do. Considering how I got the information from him."

"I'd ask you to explain that, but later, maybe. Did he say where Slattery was heading?"

"Belmont, sometime today. According to Flynn, he's carrying the detonator. My guess it'll be from somewhere on the backstretch."

"Son-of-a-bitchin' cell phones," Fields mumbled. He looked at his watch. It was two in the morning. "Listen, Pete. You think I can reach John Cannon at the track now?"

"Probably, but just in case, take down his cell phone."

Fields scribbled the number. "I'm calling him and the Nassau County Bomb Squad right now. Get them on those six vans as soon as possible. Then they need to do a thorough sweep of that whole clubhouse section pronto, in the event he planted more than one bomb and forgot to tell you. Anything else I need to know?"

"That's it. If I come up with anything, I'll call you."

"Why don't you meet us there, unless you're too tired?"

"I can be there in an hour. I'll meet you in the chief's office."

Fields dialed John Cannon's home number. When no one picked up, he dialed the cell phone. The groggy voice of NYRA's head of security answered.

"Mr. Cannon," Fields said, "Mr. Cannon, this is Agent Jack Fields, FBI. Did I wake you?"

"Ah, yeah. That's okay. Just catching a few hours before I go back. What's up?"

"We've received confirmation that the track is the target."

"So the JTTF briefing told us," the chief said.

"Yeah, but now we've got it from one of the terrorists we're holding."

"Oh, Christ."

"Chief, we think we know where the bomb is, but we need to do a complete search of the entire clubhouse area. We can't take the chance they didn't plant more than one. We'll meet you in your office within the hour. I'm calling in the Nassau County Bomb Squad. Can they get through the main gate?"

"It's locked right now," Cannon said. "Every gate is locked with the exception of Plainfield Avenue. I'll get my security out to the main gate right away."

"What time do you open to the public?" Fields heard Cannon sigh into the phone.

"Ten-thirty."

"Not sooner?"

"No, not on Belmont Stakes Day. On other days we allow the public in at seven for the Breakfast at Belmont program."

"What's that?" Fields asked.

"It's where fans can have breakfast at trackside while they watch the horses during their morning workouts on the main track," Cannon explained. "But we sweep them out at nine."

"But not this morning, right?"

"Right."

"You have a training track, don't you?"

"Yes."

"The horses can work out there…on the training track, that is, instead of the main track?"

Cannon hesitated. "Yeah. Of course. I'll get the word out to the trainers."

"Chief, we don't want anyone in the vicinity of the clubhouse until we locate that bomb, disarm it and sweep the area."

"Makes sense."

"Good. See you in an hour, Chief. Your office."

"Okay, Agent Fields. If my office is still there."

At the Plainfield Avenue gate, Fanning identified himself to the man in the Nassau County Police Department uniform. A second police officer stood at the side of the Pinkerton on duty inside the gatehouse. Fanning was happy to see the security back-up. Jack Fields had gotten the ball rolling with the neighboring Fifth Precinct in Elmont. Seamus could not get through now, unless on foot, or, unless he had entered earlier before they sounded the alarm…or, unless he could fly.

He followed the Pinkerton's directions over the backstretch roads. His drive through the maze of barns and stable areas reminded him of the difficulty they faced. If Slattery made it onto the property, it would take an army of security to comb all of the places he could be hiding.

He entered the building and headed for the escalator. Before he stepped on, he heard Vince Bogan's voice. He looked up. The security lieutenant rode down and stepped off.

"How are you, Vince?"

"Pete, hi. You alone?"

"Yeah. Came in from Bay Shore. The Feds not here yet?"

"No, but the Fifth Precinct arrived with a dozen men to shore up the gate security."

"I met two coming in. Chief Cannon upstairs?"

Bogan's eyes widened. "No. He's in Hempstead Hospital."

"Jesus, what happened?"

"It's awful. He…I mean…he called me a little over an hour ago." Bogan shook. "He said he was coming to meet the Feds in his office."

"And…?"

"Then a half hour ago, Mrs. Cannon called." Bogan looked away, upset.

"Vince, for God's sake, calm down. Tell me what happened." Fanning grasped his arm. Leading him toward a nearby bench, he forced him to sit.

"The chief never made it to his car." Bogan bent over, his head in his hands.

"What…what's wrong? Is he okay?"

"His heart. He's had this problem…eight years ago just before he left The Job. It must have hit him again. He collapsed, leaving the house."

"I'm sure he'll be okay."

Bogan looked up. "Damn it, Pete. The man is seventy-five. He's like my father."

"Hey, they got to him right away. I'm sure he'll be fine."

"God, I hope so. I think the pressure of this bomb threat was too much for his heart."

"You might be right," Fanning said. "We all have our limits."

By five-thirty, everyone had arrived for the bomb squad briefing. They relocated the gathering to a small TV viewing room at the grandstand end of the track, out of harm's way.

As Fanning surveyed the room, his gaze landed on Bogan's determined face. He stood in front of the giant TV screen next to the bomb squad leader, Detective Lieutenant Matt Hannon. Bogan was in charge of track security now. Fanning thought he was up to the challenge. During Bogan's active years on The Job, the NYPD held him in high regard.

Jack Fields and Tony Condon sat in the front row. Fanning and several members of the bomb squad sat in the row behind. Three NYRA security officers occupied chairs in the back.

Hannon, the bomb squad leader, was speaking. "In the movies, the terrorist or criminal uses some form of timing device instead of a radio activated trigger to detonate explosives."

"Why is that?" Fields asked.

"It gives the film director an opportunity to build an edge-of-the-seat suspense before the good guys find and defuse it. Always at the eleventh hour, of course. But realistically, timers can be undependable unless they're the sophisticated kind."

Fanning listened, hoping to hear something encouraging.

The squad leader continued. "Our guy obviously doesn't want to risk a timer failure, so he's opted to go with a radio detonator. That way he can be several miles away from the bomb and still control when it explodes. Like an electrical switch."

"Same with a cell phone," Fanning said.

"True, but their reliability can be risky, too. No, I think this guy's not taking any chances. My question is the cost. Dependable radio detonators of this type are pricey."

"Well, this group appears to have deep pockets," Fields said. "To say nothing of employing experienced bombers."

Condon spoke next. "What worries me is the possibility of someone inadvertently setting it off. There's plenty of electronic equipment around here, what with all the video cameras around the perimeter of the track and—"

Bogan cut in. "Yeah, and how about our closed-circuit television operation throughout?"

"Not to worry," Hannon said. "One of the special features of these expensive detonators is their high level of protection against unintentional initiation."

"Like what things?" Fields asked.

"Things like extreme stray or induced currents, radio or radar waves, static electricity or atmosphere discharges. That sort of thing. That's why they're expensive."

"Aren't they the type of detonator used for blasting in construction projects?" Fanning asked.

"Exactly," Hannon said. "That's why these guys chose this type. They sure as hell don't want something to initiate the explosion before they're ready."

"Which won't be until their targets arrive on the property," Condon said.

Bogan stood and peered at his watch. "That's between the first and second races...by helicopter. We don't have that long to find the bomb and disarm it."

All heads turned his way.

He threw up his hands. "We're scheduled to open the gates at ten-thirty."

"Not if we don't find and disarm the bomb before that time," Fields said.

Fanning waited for Bogan to voice an objection, but none came.

Fire and emergency vehicles crowded into the parking circle at the main entrance to the clubhouse, their teams hustling, preparing to go to work the moment disaster struck. Police cars from the Fifth Precinct clustered in front of the track's main gate with uniformed men posted along the fence perimeter.

Fanning stood next to the bomb technician, his back against the white box-like bomb squad trailer. The trailer, parked on the blacktop apron near the track railing and positioned fifty yards away from the doors to the clubhouse lobby, served as the control center. He listened while the technician explained to him what they could expect to happen once they located the van with the bomb.

"Forget the image of a bomb tech with sweat beading down his face, standing before an elaborate combination of timers, explosives and multi-colored wires," he was saying. "You know that scene? As the music swells, he cuts the red one…"

Fanning laughed.

"That's Hollywood. Reality is never so simple."

Fanning nodded, watching the shadowed figures dressed in Kevlar bomb suits. They guided two bomb-sniffing canines down the ramp of the tunnel toward the parked maintenance vans. Above, throughout the floodlit second level, he could see federal agents and bomb squad personnel, with several more canines, combing the rows of tiered box seats in the clubhouse section. They had already completed a pass-through of the Trustees Room.

Looking up into the building, he asked, "I suppose you guys think there might be more than one bomb?"

"Always a possibility," the technician answered. "We can't afford to take chances."

"Well, when the dogs find which van has the bomb, what happens first?"

The technician turned and pointed to the bomb-disposal robot at the rear of the trailer. "Billy-The-Kid, there, goes to work. He operates by remote control from inside."

"Man! High tech."

"Oh yeah," the technician said. He patted the side of the trailer. "This baby here is state-of-the-art. Billy has four cameras that feed back what he sees to the television monitor inside."

"Fantastic," Fanning said.

"The robot is amazing, so incredibly navigable," the technician added. "A body frame made from high grade aluminum, runs on twin tracks and weighs around 800 pounds."

Take Five from the cell phone in Fanning's pocket interrupted. Removing it, he looked at the caller ID display and saw his home number. He flipped it open, forgetting he had left it on speakerphone.

"Good morning, Miss Sunshine."

"Son of a bitch."

"Excuse me, will you?" he said to the technician. He walked to a bench nearby. "Now, Anne—"

"No! You said you were coming right home. You don't expect me to be happy, do you?"

"This is a bad time to have this conversation, Anne. I'm sorry. We're trying to find a…" He caught himself. "I mean, I can't…that is…oh, shit, Anne, I'm all right, for Christ's sake. I'll be home as soon as I can. You have to stop worrying. It's driving me nuts."

"Promise you'll ask for a transfer to another division. No more narcotics, no more erratic work hours, or I swear I'll leave you."

"We'll talk when I get home." His weariness prevented him from mounting any reasonable argument at this time. She was asking that he give up something he loved doing, despite the dangers involved. His work helping to clean up the narcotics problem in New York City was not a gratuitous or meaningless job.

"Your obligation to your family comes first," she demanded.

Still hung up on her father's tragic death on The Job, he thought. She'll never get past it.

"Pete, let me ask…I mean, how long do you think I can put up with you living on the edge?"

"Come on, Anne. It's not always this way. Cut me some slack, will you?"

"My father—"

"That's what this is about, isn't it?"

"He asked my mother to do the same—"

Her tone was a combination of anger and hurt. He wished he hadn't answered the phone. "And he died in the line of duty. I know. But he died doing the thing he loved best."

"He had a family. You have a family, damn it! It doesn't seem to matter."

Fanning looked up again at the shadowed movements in the lighted box-seat section. He knew they hadn't yet started a search for Slattery hiding somewhere on the racetrack. "Let's deal with the bomb first," Jack Fields had said. "Then we'll deal with Slattery."

"Anne, your father was a cop. I'm a cop. It's what I do for a living…fighting bad guys. Should I quit? Become a bank teller?"

It occurred to him he'd never before expressed that to Anne. When he joined the NYPD fifteen years ago, it was for that reason: to rid society of criminals. It gave him a purpose that he liked. Many cops he knew came on the force to find a safe, comfortable niche for twenty years, riding it out for the pension and benefits. That wasn't his motivation.

He thought of Teddy Vijay, dying at the hands of terrorists, trying to right a wrong he couldn't believe in, and Mike Allen flirting with losing his life in an attempt to understand the wrong that took his wife. And there were Detectives Dorgan and Lewis, laying it on the line each time they went undercover. Same with Jack Fields and Tony Condon. All with the same goal in mind: to make a difference for society.

"No, I don't want you to quit," Anne replied, "but…but it isn't enough you risk your life on The Job. You need to stick your nose into a situation that was none of your business."

He realized she was right. "That was unintentional. You know that. If Mike hadn't—"

"You could have let the FBI handle it."

"Did you want Mike to face obstruction-of-justice charges? Maybe kidnapping?"

"Yes…I mean, no."

"Once Mike got involved, it became my business. Mike is family, isn't he? Look, I'm scheduled to take the exam for lieutenant next month. If I pass it, and I see no reason why I wouldn't, things will change for the better."

"How so?" she asked. He heard her blow her nose.

"For one thing, regular hours. Except in emergencies, of course." He was trying not to paint it as a nine-to-five job. "For another, less street involvement, less personal exposure."

Anne was silent.

"I'm sorry about this past week. Maybe I got carried away. I'll be home when this is over, as soon as I can. Okay?"

"Okay, I guess. What choice do I have?"

"Look, I gotta go. I love you." He closed the cell phone and walked back to the trailer where the technician was standing.

"You know what bugs me?" the man said when Fanning returned. "The internet. It's made our job so much more difficult."

"How do you figure?" Fanning asked, struggling to dismiss the upset he felt from his conversation with Anne.

"It's this so-called age of information. Too much of it out there, that's what. You want to blow up your school? Hey, just go on line. A quick search on Google will give you a step-by-step primer on how to build a bomb."

"You're right. I'm knocked out by what this country allows in the name of free speech."

"And you know what else is making our job harder? Cell phones. Yeah, cell phones."

Fanning fingered the instrument in his pocket. Mine too, he thought.

"The detonator of choice for terrorists. A simple alarm clock or a digital watch with an alarm can become a timing device to explode a bomb. You know there are sites on the internet that tell you, in detail, how to wire one up?"

"Incredible," Fanning said.

The chirping radio clipped to the technician's hip chased him back into the trailer, cutting Fanning off. Within minutes, he heard excited shouts from several bomb squad men racing out of the tunnel heading toward him. The bomb-sniffing dogs had located the wired van among the six parked at the maintenance dock. The men rushed the robot down the ramp toward the vehicle.

CHAPTER 30

Shortly before six-fifteen, the backstretch kitchen bustled with activity. Loud, hurried conversations filled the eatery in both English and Spanish. The smell of burnt toast and overcooked eggs permeated the air. Grooms and hot walkers occupied the linoleum-top tables, gulping black coffee and wolfing down buttered rolls between expressive hand gestures.

Rudy Sanchez sat across from Lefty, his exercise rider, at a table in one corner of the kitchen, blowing steadily into his hot coffee. The assistant trainer had the *Racing Form* spread out, studying the past performance chart of the fifth race.

When Sanchez looked up, Lefty said, "So how do you figure it?"

"Figure what?" Sanchez asked.

"Why the car was parked in the shed row?"

"I dunno, man. Maybe some groom got homeless, had to sleep in his car."

Lefty shook his head. "Naah, I don't think so. He'd have parked outside the barn, not under the shed row. Too risky. He'd know it's a serious fire hazard."

"Yeah, you're right. Must be one dumb fucker." Sanchez lowered his head to study the newspaper but looked up again. "Where did you say you saw it?"

Lefty sqinted. "I think it was that barn that's never used...you know the one...over on Calumet Way."

"Back where the road leads to the gap at the top of the turn?"

"Yeah. That's the way I took Huggable Tom to the training track."

Sanchez glared. "You're not supposed to use that gap to get on the track. You know that."

"Ah, man, the main gap is such a long way from our barn."

"Better not let Dwayne know. He'll fire your ass in a minute."

Lefty continued. "That's why I spotted the car parked at the end of the rear shed row. I was going by the barn. Sun was just coming up. I saw the reflection off the windshield as I rode past."

"Don't worry," Sanchez said. "I'll call security when we get back to the barn."

The bomb squad was busy at work down in the tunnel. Fanning started to tap on the trailer door to ask if he could watch Billy-The-Kid in action when he saw Vince Bogan running toward him. He was out of breath when he arrived from the paddock area behind the building where he and two of his security people searched the saddling stalls.

"Pete, where's Jack Fields?" he asked, his complexion flushed with excitement.

"Down in the tunnel with Tony. They found the bomb."

"Jesus, my duty officer...I mean...he just got a call from one of our trainers," Bogan said. Out of breath, he placed his hand on the side of the trailer, steadying himself. "The rider," he said, "I mean, his exercise rider...he spotted a vehicle parked in a barn on the backstretch. It was under the shed row...not two hours ago."

Fanning looked back, puzzled. "So?"

314

"That's strictly forbidden."

"It is?"

"Yeah. The biggest fire hazard we have. All that hay and straw."

"Maybe someone was unloading—"

"No. Anyone who works on the backstretch would know better."

It took seconds for it to register. He felt his pulse quicken. Slattery would be unaware of the prohibition against bringing vehicles under a barn's shed row. "Did the trainer mention the make of the vehicle?" Fanning asked.

"No. He couldn't tell. It was still too dark."

"What's Colin Flynn drive?"

"According to our records, a 1996 green Dodge hatchback."

Fanning called Fields on his cell phone. "Jack, where are you?"

"We're in the tunnel. What's going on?"

"Vince has something. Can you come up now? It's hot."

He heard him say something to someone. "Where are you?" Fields asked.

"By the trailer."

"Okay, be right there."

He closed his phone and looked back at Bogan. "Did the trainer say which barn?"

"Over on Calumet Way. It's the last street on that corner of the property. The training track is just behind it."

"Are there Thoroughbreds in the barn?"

"No. It's been vacant for a while."

"How come?"

"It needs some heavy repairs. No stable will occupy it until it's done."

"That's a break." He turned when he heard Fields approaching.

"What have you got?" Fields asked. Tony Condon was with him.

Bogan briefed the two agents.

"How do we get there?" Fields asked. "What's the best way to go?"

"Roads leading to either end of the barn. There's a road in front. Calumet Way. Nothing but a foot path behind because it backs up to the training track."

"What about the barn. Anything unique?"

"No," Bogan replied. "Enclosed shed rows down both sides, paths at each end, and a cross-over pathway in the center."

"Okay, here's what we do," Fields said. "We don't know that it's Slattery, but if it is, we don't want to spook him with his finger on the button. So let's keep it small, stealth-like." He turned to Condon. "Tony, I should stay here until they've disarmed the bomb and complete the sweep of this section of the building. I'll send Meyers with you. Take him and Vince, go check it out."

"Okay if I go along?" Fanning asked.

Jack Fields looked at him. He shook his head. "Haven't had enough?"

"Hey, I've come this far."

"Up to you," Fields said. "And Tony, let me know right away what you find. Okay?"

Condon nodded, and Fields walked back toward the tunnel opening.

Agent Gil Meyers appeared. "Let's go," Condon said. "We'll take two cars. Vince, you lead the way."

"I'll ride with Vince," Fanning said.

"Okay. Pull up before you get there, a couple hundred yards away. We need to decide how we're gonna proceed."

Fanning slid into the passenger seat. Before Bogan started the car, Condon appeared at the driver's side and motioned to him to roll down his window.

"Vince, you carrying?" he asked the lieutenant.

Bogan hesitated. Pulling the key from the ignition, he reached over, unlocked the glove compartment and removed his holstered .38. "I am now, I guess."

"Good."

"Jesus, Tony…I mean…that is…I hope we won't have to fire our weapons." Bogan's face twisted with worry. "I mean…you know…there's still barns of Thoroughbreds in that area. A firefight is certain to create chaos for those animals."

Fanning watched as Condon put his face up to the open window. "Don't worry," he said. "We need Slattery alive. No shooting unless…unless he makes a move toward the detonator." Condon winked.

The two cars headed out toward the backstretch with Bogan leading the way. He drove without speaking. Fanning said nothing, leaving the quiet moment to the many thoughts he knew whirled through the lieutenant's worried mind. Now, with Chief Cannon out of the picture, all the weight of responsibility had fallen on his shoulders.

Bogan stopped the car at an intersection with barns at the four corners and along each side of the road. The car with the two agents pulled up behind. The area was alive with activity: hot walkers, grooms and assistant trainers tending to their morning chores. Fanning exited and looked around. He hoped Bogan was right, that the barn was vacant.

The four men huddled between cars. "How far is it?" Condon asked.

Pointing ahead, Bogan said, "We're two roads back. It's on Calumet Way."

"How do we come up on it?" the agent asked.

"I suggest we hit it from both ends. It has two rows of back-to-back stalls running parallel down both sides. It's divided in the middle by a pass-through, like the letter H."

"No exits at the rear?"

"Only at the ends. The shed rows here at Belmont and Aqueduct are enclosed. The winter weather, you know."

While the two men talked, Fanning watched a groom removing the tack from a Thoroughbred outside one of the barns. A hot walker held the animal's reins. When the groom finished, he coupled the brass connector of a hose to a spigot on the side of the barn and ran a soft stream over the length of the horse.

Taking in the early morning backstretch scene, Fanning understood Bogan's reaction when Condon mentioned guns. The dilemma they faced was dangerous if not short of impossible. Slattery sat in a barn two roads away with his finger on a detonator. They could clear the area around the barn before going in after him; however, to do so would spook the terrorist.

Condon had the same thought. "We need to get the jump on him before he can react."

Fanning looked at his watch. It was a little after eight. "Why don't you guys leave your jackets and ties in the car? Let your shirts hang out over your pants. Keep your piece in your belt, hidden underneath."

Condon twisted, looking back at him. Fanning was sure he was going to ask, "Are you out of your mind?" Instead, he laughed. "You mean we look out of place?"

They removed their jackets and ties. Condon paired Bogan with Meyers, instructing them to make their way to the barn's west end. "Pete, you go with me."

"Okay, but if he's parked at our end, maybe Vince and Gil should enter the front shed row at their end and cross over to the rear in the center. You know…a zig and a zag."

"Good. That makes sense," Condon replied. "That way we limit him to a quarter of the barn area. Gil, give me a short beep when you're in place."

"At what point do we go in?" Bogan asked.

"When you get to Calumet Way, wait there. I'll give the high sign to move across."

Staying against the sides of the barns, Fanning and Condon reached the corner of Calumet Way and stopped. The barn with Slattery was ahead of them. To the right, a shoulder-high line of thick hedges bordered a low-roofed building. Bogan had said it was a storage facility for harrows and other track-grading equipment.

Between buildings, Fanning caught glimpses of galloping Thoroughbreds as they rounded the top of the turn at that end of the training track. He remembered from his earlier backstretch tour with the chief that training ordinarily ended by eight each morning, leaving the track idle by this time. Not this morning.

Condon looked down the road to his left. Bogan and Meyers were already at the intersection. "You ready?" Fanning nodded. The agent raised his arm and dropped it. The four men hurried across Calumet Way.

Fanning and Condon lay flat against the front corner of the vacant barn for several seconds. Both held their weapons at the ready. Fanning glanced behind, relieved to see no backstretch activity around them. The horses and exercise riders on the training track, however, were still a serious concern.

Condon crouched, listening for signs of movement from within the barn. Fanning bent over behind him, straining to hear. The sounds he heard were the rhythmic slap of horse's hooves on the track's dirt surface and the low, guttural noises that came from their riders as they urged their mounts to keep to the pace.

Condon's radio gave off a faint beep. Meyers and Bogan were in position at the back corner of the pass-through. Condon motioned to Fanning, bringing his weapon behind his ear. He rose and darted around the building corner to the opening of the rear-shed row. Fanning was on his heels.

The green Dodge hatchback, parked twenty yards up the shed row, faced out toward them. They turned into the opening and could see no one in the vehicle. Was Slattery down on the seat, perhaps sleeping? Or crouched under the dash, waiting to spring?

Meyers and Bogan raced down the shed row from behind. Footing was a problem. Bogan stumbled, his street shoes slipping with each stride on the slick, packed-down dirt surface.

Condon inched toward the car, reaching it first. "FBI. Don't move!" he shouted. He stuck his weapon through the open window on the driver's side. Fanning went to the other side. After several seconds, Condon yelled, "Damn! He's not here."

They found the back of the rear seat pushed forward and locked down. A folded metal stepladder lay across the floor, next to a canvas tool bag. The ignition key was still in place. Condon reached in to remove it then walked to the back of the car and pulled up the hatchback. Cautiously, he slid the tool bag toward him, spread it open and looked in. It was empty except for a small cardboard box. He looked back at Fanning and tapped the side of the bag. "This is how he carried in the bomb." Reaching, he picked up the cardboard box to examine it. Something inside slid to one side when he tipped it. He opened the flaps, looked in, and spilled out a small cell phone onto the carpeted deck. "So much for the sophisticated radio controlled detonator-theory."

Fanning noticed lettering on the box label, obscured in part by the packing tape wrapped around the four sides. The circular logo of *GE* was still visible on one end.

"Why the ladder?" Fanning wondered aloud.

Condon tossed the box back into the tool bag after pocketing the cell phone. "Never mind that," he said. He looked up and down the shed row. "Let's find where the fucker went."

Bogan busied himself checking each stall of the rear-shed row, one by one, while Meyers did the same on the front row. Fanning had turned from the hatchback, looking out of the opened end of the barn. Movement behind the hedges across the road caught his attention.

"Tony," he shouted, "there he is."

Hearing Fanning's call, Bogan pushed the half-door of the stall that had started to close behind him. It slammed against the wall of the barn, creating a noise that sounded like a gunshot. Fanning and Condon flinched and reached for their weapons.

Slattery burst through a narrow separation in the hedge line, holding a weapon, and turned toward Calumet Way to make his escape. Fanning, the closest to him, took off running. "Stop! Police!" He had raised his Glock ready to fire, but lowered it when he saw Meyers step from the front shed-row, cutting off the terrorist's flight.

With his escape route blocked, Slattery stopped in the middle of the road. Looking in both directions, he saw Fanning and Condon coming toward him. He turned in the opposite direction and started toward the training track. He reached the gap opening—moving with amazing speed despite his limp—and dashed onto the track's sandy surface.

Condon reached the end of the barn and raised his weapon. "Stop right there or I'll fire."

Fanning heard the warning as he neared the gap opening in pursuit of Slattery. He prayed the agent was bluffing. Slattery continued to flee, limping, moving with the curve of the railing at the top of the oval, struggling to gain speed in the deep, soft dirt.

It happened in a flash. A roan-colored Thoroughbred, galloping to the outside of the track near the rail, came up from behind. His rider, surprised by the sudden appearance of a human form, tried to pull the mount to the inside to avoid a collision. It was too late. Fanning stopped at the rail opening. He watched as the horse veered, his hindquarters and legs swinging around, clipping Slattery. It sent him airborne, upside down like a rag doll, his head and leg banging the railing as he soared over it.

The rider pulled up his mount and leaped off. He held onto the reins, cooing softly to the fractious animal, trying to calm him with soothing pats on the side of his sweaty neck and shoulder. Exercise riders approaching the top of the turn steered their Thoroughbreds to the inside, giving the dismounted horse and rider a wide berth.

Fanning scrambled down the outside of the rail and made his way toward the stretched-out body of Slattery. He found him face down in the tall grass, motionless. Fanning placed his hand under the Irishman's nose and felt light breathing. Agents Condon and Meyers arrived and found Teddy Vijay's Walther PPK in the sand at the edge of the railing.

Bogan jumped onto the track, took charge, and directed riders and horses away from the area. The rider, too shaken to continue the workout, led the roan Thoroughbred off the track and walked him back to his barn.

Condon knelt over the body of Slattery, his radio in his hand. "What's his condition?" Fields was asking.

"Unconscious," Condon said. "Pulse still strong. His right shinbone is showing through the skin. Must have clipped the railing going over and landed on his head."

"I'll get an ambulance to you. Bring him here. I hope the paramedics can revive him fast. We need some questions answered. We're running short of time. Did you find a detonator?"

"Yes," he answered looking back at the vehicle. "A fucking cell phone."

CHAPTER 31

Fanning and Bogan remained in the barn to complete a stall-by-stall search of the two shed rows. Finding nothing, they returned to the hatchback to go over it top-to-bottom as Condon had requested. Together, they examined under the hood, the engine well and every corner of the interior. They removed the carpeting on the rear deck and looked in the spare tire compartment.

While Fanning replaced the deck carpeting, he noticed, for the first time, a strong oil smell. A transmission leak, he thought. Except he hadn't seen signs of a leak earlier when he looked under the car. He rubbed his hand over the carpeting and felt traces of an oily coating located in the area where the canvas tool bag had been sitting. Lifting the bag by the handles, he ran his hand underneath. A heavy film covered the canvas bottom.

"Look at this," he said.

Bogan approached. "What did you find?" he asked.

"This bag's been sitting in a sticky substance. Feel it."

Bogan reached under. "You're right. Feels tacky. A little like grease. I guess he wasn't careful where he set it down."

After completing the search of the barn, Fanning followed Bogan back to the clubhouse, driving the Dodge hatchback. He parked the vehicle in the executive parking lot and left it for the Nassau County DMV to pick up. Then he delivered the tool bag to Condon's vehicle.

It was ten-fifteen when the army of federal agents, NYRA security and Nassau County Bomb Squad personnel concluded their sweep of the entire four floors of the clubhouse. Earlier, they moved the bomb squad's control trailer into the tunnel, out of sight. Fire and emergency vehicles remained in position on the apron in front of the building, packing up to leave. Gates opened in fifteen minutes, allowing entry to a flood of eager racing fans ready to fill every corner of the racetrack, staking out their viewing positions for the day's racing program.

Fanning and Bogan sat in the Paddock Restaurant on the second floor, looking out onto the walking ring and saddling stalls. The statue of Triple Crown winner Secretariat glistened at the center of the ring. The kitchen had prepared them a hot breakfast.

Fanning looked across the table at Bogan's tired face. There was an absence of tension for the first time since he met him in the clubhouse lobby five hours before. "Well, I guess the chief will be happy to get the news," he told the security lieutenant.

"I called the hospital as soon as the bomb squad gave us the green light. Mrs. Cannon told me the chief was still asleep, but the bypass operation went smoothly."

"That's great news."

Condon and Fields had remained with the bomb squad leader, Matt Hannon, to tie up loose ends. Fields was unsuccessful in getting more information from Slattery, except to confirm the existence of the bomb under the van. They dispatched the terrorist by ambulance to Manhattan to share temporary incarceration with Colin Flynn in the medical ward of the Metropolitan Correction Center.

"I'm sorry, after all this, you can't stay for the race," Bogan said.

"Christ, that would be the last phone call to my wife I'd ever get to make."

"Well, the race doesn't go off until around six. Eighth one on the card. You could be back later with her before the post parade."

"Pal, when I get home, first she's going to wallop me upside the head. Then I'm gonna pass out in bed. I can watch it on CBS. But how about you? You look exhausted."

"I am. I'll catch an hour or two in my office later on."

"And you thought you had it tough when you were on The Job."

Bogan managed a weak smile, too tired to laugh. "By the way, I've been meaning to ask, how the hell did you ever get involved with this whole thing? You're in Narcotics, aren't you?"

Fanning stared out the window, at the paddock scene below. His thoughts raced back over the details of the past two weeks. "Doing a favor for a friend. Next thing I knew, I was up to my ass in this adventure."

Bogan waited.

"My closest friend, Mike Allen, lost his wife...ten years ago in England...an IRA bombing at a London rail station."

"Wait. Don't tell me. Seamus Slattery was involved?"

"You got it. In fact, it was two rail stations...simultaneous explosions...across town from each other. The IRA liked to pull off double hits that way. She was in one of them."

"Sad." Bogan said.

Fanning turned his eyes up toward the TV monitor on the wall behind Bogan's head. After flickering to life, it began showing a race in progress—a replay of last year's Belmont Stakes.

"That's what's been bothering me."

"What do you mean?" Bogan asked.

"They planted one bomb here, according to Colin Flynn. He and Seamus were IRA. One bomb is uncharacteristic. My gut tells me he gave up the one in the van too easily."

Bogan's eyes widened.

Pete shook his head as though trying to jog together pieces of a puzzle. "You know, I remember now. Colin misspoke in the hospital when I asked him what type of detonator they used. At first he said, *timer.* Then he had second thoughts and changed it to *radio controlled transmitter.* I didn't think anything of it then."

"But it turned out to be a cell phone," Bogan reminded him.

"Right. For the one in the van."

"You think—"

"Jesus, I don't know. I wish I didn't have this uneasy feeling."

Jack Fields arrived at the table with Tony Condon trailing him. "What's good to eat in this place?" he asked.

"We both had omelets," Bogan said, "but the chef will make anything you want." He raised an arm to get a waiter's attention.

"Everything wrapped up?" Fanning asked.

Fields took a chair next to Bogan. "Yep," he said. He looked around. "They're pouring in like spooked cattle. Somebody could get run over in this stampede."

"What's the capacity of this place?" Condon asked.

"We seat around thirty-three thousand," Bogan answered, "but we've had over a hundred thousand for a few past Belmont Stakes."

The restaurant began to fill, those serious punters arriving early to capture tables in close proximity to the television monitors spotted around the large dining room. Fanning was sure the racetrack would be at capacity before noon.

"Vince, what did you do with the tool bag?" Fields asked. "You didn't leave it in the car, did you?"

"No, of course not. Pete put it in Tony's car, in the back on the floor."

"Good. Thanks. We're going to need it as evidence."

Bogan turned to Condon. "When you leave, don't put it on the seat. There's grease on the bottom of it."

"I left the ladder though," Fanning said. You didn't want that, did you?"

The waiter had placed a menu in front of Fields. He had it opened, studying it. He looked up. "Ladder? Oh, right. There was one in the car, wasn't there?"

At his own mention of the ladder, something clicked in Fanning's head. He remained statue-like, processing several factors with the speed of a computer, while his stomach churned furiously: *the grease on the bottom of the bag, the presence of the ladder in the car, the arrival last night of Slattery wearing work coveralls belonging to Colin Flynn, the small box found in the bag, the IRA's preference for simultaneous explosions.* In a flash, all the elements came together; the pieces of the puzzle he struggled with gelled. He looked across to Bogan. His eyes had narrowed, and his forehead wrinkled.

"You thinking what I am?" Fanning asked. His felt his pulse quicken when he asked it.

"Elevator?"

"That's where my money is," Fanning said. He spun around in his chair to face the agent. "Jack, did the search cover the two elevators in the rear of the maintenance area?"

"Yes, certainly. Both were clean. Why?"

"Did they check the roofs of the cars?"

Fields hesitated and then looked over at Tony Condon.

"To be honest, I don't recall. I know the dogs didn't pick up anything suspicious."

Fanning looked alarmed. "Jesus, I just realized. If there was anything on top of the elevator car, the dogs couldn't have sniffed it because of the updraft in the elevator shaft." He stood, looking toward the restaurant door. "I hope the guys from bomb squad haven't left. I'm willing to bet there's a bomb with a timer on top of one of those two elevators."

"What makes you so sure?" Condon asked.

"The grease on the bottom of the bag. Slattery used that ladder to get up to the elevator's roof. That small box we found in the bag? I have a feeling it once contained a type of alarm clock."

"My God," Bogan gasped. "What are we going to do about all the people already here?"

Fields leaped up. "Get them the hell out, that's what."

Jack Fields reached Matt Hannon by phone as the bomb squad trailer had just exited through the gate. The trailer made a fast U-turn in the middle of Hempstead Avenue and retraced its route. The Fifth Precinct and the Elmont fire department acted with haste after receiving calls made by Hannon. Within fifteen minutes, all emergency vehicles were back on the track property. The bomb squad was once again in position on the apron opposite the clubhouse entrance.

Shortly after eleven, they locked down and cordoned off the entire clubhouse end of the building. The public address system announced there was an emergency in the clubhouse, without spelling it out. They herded out those several thousand fans that had arrived in this section earlier, like an old-fashioned cattle drive. Every Pinkerton, FBI agent and NYRA security personnel assisted the uniformed police from the Nassau County Fifth Precinct. They led the migration down through the vast grandstand to the other end of the racetrack.

Fanning and Bogan moved in among the crowd of FBI agents and police that milled around the main track, on the infield, lined up against the inside railing. Some of the group sat on the grass as though they were waiting for the delivery of a picnic lunch. The search of the two elevators was underway.

Fanning looked up into the building. He could see no movement on the upper tiers of the clubhouse. "They get all the early arrivals out?" he asked.

Bogan shook his head in disbelief. "Amazing. Everyone stayed calm. They only bitched about the inconvenience of losing their favorite viewing positions. They couldn't give a shit about the bomb. Typical of hardcore racing fans."

Fanning turned his attention back to the bomb squad trailer and saw Jack Fields step out the door. He waved to them.

They reached the agent and asked, "What's up?"

"We found it. Damn, we found it…like you thought…on the roof of the freight elevator. Now the robot's ready to go. Come in, come in. Watch it on the monitor."

The technician seated at the control console worked his dials and levers. Fanning, Bogan, Fields, Condon and Lieutenant Hannon crowded around. After navigating Billy-The-Kid to the rear of the maintenance area, the technician positioned the robot in front of the freight elevator.

The monitor displayed a split screen of four images. In one picture, Fanning saw into the top half of the opened freight elevator door through the point-of-view of one of the robot's four cameras. They had lowered the car to the base of the elevator pit. A second camera displayed, close-up, the roof of the car at eye level, showing the wrapped bomb package secured to one of the cables. The camera sent back pictures as it rotated 180 degrees to either side of the bomb. It was clear where Slattery had wired up the timer, a small digital clock.

"I'm pissed I missed those signs," Fields whispered to Fanning. "Fact is, I'm embarrassed."

"Hey, you know what they say? Two heads and all that."

"Yeah, well anyway, we owe a large thanks to you and Vince."

Fanning watched in awe as Billy's camera moved around the bomb. "How the hell did they get it up the stairs of the loading dock?"

The bomb technician at the console turned around. "This baby can climb stairs, too," he announced. "Just like a Slinky."

All eyes locked on the four scenes displayed on the monitor.

"Everyone stay still," the technician cautioned as he switched the monitor to full screen.

They watched in silence while he extended the disruptor arm to within six feet of the bomb package. Everyone's breathing slowed. When he was satisfied with Billy's aim, the technician released a powerful stream of water that hit the bomb package with explosive force and pinpoint accuracy. The bomb's circuitry blew apart before their eyes.

No one spoke until the technician shouted, "Bulls-eye. Done!"

TWO WEEKS LATER

Saturday, June 22

"Where did Anne and Casey go?" Fanning asked when he returned to his seat with a tray of hotdogs. He handed one to Mike Allen, who nursed a beer in a tall plastic cup.

"The ladies room," Allen said. "Don't you know they invented the seventh inning stretch for people with weak bladders?"

Fanning looked around at the packed stadium of devoted baseball fans, many wearing Yankee caps and jerseys. Most stood, gesturing, sipping beer and munching hotdogs, chattering about the second inning homers hit by Derek Jeter and Jason Giambi, and the over-the-shoulder catch by Bernie Williams in the sixth.

"Peanuts," the vendor at the end of their aisle shouted. He tossed a package over their heads to a fan standing ten yards away. The fan caught it with one hand, to the cheers of his pals. Money passed down to Fanning and Allen and ended up in the hands of the waiting vendor.

"Is that Luke down there?" Fanning pointed his hotdog to the right of the Yankee's dugout.

"Yeah. He spotted Derek Jeter and ran down to get his program autographed."

Fanning smiled. "And I thought I was his hero."

"Oh, you are, after today. How the hell did you score these box seats for this weekend series with Boston?"

"Compliments of the Feds. After the presentation of my citation at Federal Plaza on Wednesday, they gave me these five tickets. I'm sure that was Jack Fields' handiwork. Good touch, don't you think?"

"Nice. Who was there…at the presentation, I mean?"

"My zone captain, Casey, Jack Fields, Tony Condon and their boss, Karl Stevenson, the head of the FBI's New York office."

"No Anne and Luke?"

"Yeah, of course."

"She must have felt pretty proud, don't you think?"

Fanning laughed. "She wanted to know just one thing. Would it grease my career track toward becoming a lieutenant?"

"You need to pass the exam first, right?"

"Right. Then wait for an opening and a recommendation."

"Hey, after getting that citation, the easiest part has to be the recommendation."

"How's it going at the restaurant? You back to normal?"

"Uh huh, but now Pat wants me to take over as the daytime manager."

"Great. That should mean a nice boost in pay."

"Yeah, but I'll miss bartending. Remember, I'm a social kind of guy."

Luke came running up the steps, taking them two at a time, waving his program like a flag. "I got it. I got it," he shouted.

Luke slipped past and fell into his seat. Fanning said, "Here, take one of these hotdogs before I drop them. You want a soda?" He looked around for the vendor. "There he goes, back there." He handed his son a five-dollar bill.

Luke left to chase after his soda, and Allen asked, "What are they gonna do with Seamus?"

"Extradition as soon as he can travel. He faces multiple murder charges in Ireland. They have first call on him."

"Is that the way it works?"

"Yeah, afraid so. But the Feds have the rest of those mutts from the Astoria Park mosque in custody, including that Sheik Omar. They're looking at ten to twenty for conspiracy. The guy who aided Khalid in killing the two moles, he faces a murder rap. They recovered their remains last week and returned them to their families for a proper burial." Fanning shook his head. "Sad. Their contract provided for a generous compensation to their families, but it's still sad."

"Tragic," Allen said. "And how about the Flynns?"

"Colin's going away for a long, long time, and Tommy faces five to ten."

"By the way," Allen said, "the prince must have been destroyed when Gallant Warrior didn't win. 93,000 fans showed up for nothing."

"True, if we hadn't found the bomb in time."

"I read it wasn't a record crowd."

"Nope, not even close. But speaking of records, get this," Fanning added. "The long-shot horse that won returned the highest two-dollar payoff in Belmont Stakes history. His half-length win paid a nifty $152.50."

"Where did Gallant Warrior finish?"

"He stumbled out of the gate, lost heart and finished eighth."

Allen laughed. "Well, I guess that's horseracing."

Pete nodded. "Yeah, and if you don't watch out, life can be that way too."

EPILOGUE

Wednesday, June 25

Mike Allen and Casey Franks traveled the marble corridor looking for the room number they had been given. As they made the turn toward the west end of the Metropolitan Correction Center's medical ward, they spotted the uniformed police officer sitting outside the door.

"Looks like that's it," Allen said. "You sure the FBI is okay with this?"

"Yes. Stop worrying. Jack Fields said just fine as long as we watch what we say."

"Fields knows why I wanted to speak with him?"

"I told him. He just laughed."

Allen made a face.

"Well, come on, Mike. He's a cop, not a psychiatrist. He thinks you should be grateful he missed you…that you should let it go at that."

Allen stopped walking. "Do you think I should?"

Casey pulled up to his side and, reaching out, took him by the arm. "No, Mike, no. That's why I arranged this visit. I understand what's bothering you."

Fanning had told Allen of the Irishman's reputation as an expert shooter. It made him wonder. Had Slattery intentionally spared him? Had the terrorist found contrition for causing the death of Kathy? Allen wanted to believe that.

The uniformed officer stood up. "Can I help you?" he asked.

They approached the officer. Casey held out the letter of approval Jack Fields wrote. "I'm Detective-Sergeant Casey Franks. We have FBI permission to visit the suspect, Seamus Slattery. Agent Jack Fields set it up."

The officer took the letter, scanned it and handed it back to her. He shot a quick look through the small window in the door. He nodded his head. "Okay," he said. "I think he's awake." He reached over with the key, unlocked the door and pushed it open. "Go on in."

Casey entered first, holding the door for Allen. When the door closed behind them, Allen heard the audible click of the lock. It was a small, antiseptic room with space enough for a single hospital bed and nightstand. One metal chair occupied a spot next to the rolling food-serving cart. A sliver of bright sunlight, squeezing through the room's narrow and barred single window, augmented the recessed neon ceiling lights. Allen had the feeling he had walked into a monk's cubicle in some far off monastery.

Slattery opened his eyes when they entered. The head of the bed was partially raised, just enough to allow him to view his visitors without straining. He remained motionless, his fractured right leg covered up to his knee in a cast and suspended over the bed in a trapeze. The bandage that covered the upper half of his skull revealed the only other visible damage.

No one spoke for several seconds. Slattery stared at the ceiling. When he broke the silence, he let out a noise between his lips that sounded like released air from an over-inflated tire. In a voice filled with anger, he said,

"So what would ya be wanting of me now?"

Allen turned to Casey, wondering if she would make a formal introduction. When she hesitated, he said to the man in the bed, "I guess you don't remember."

Slattery shook his head as though he was going to explode with impatience. "For Jaysus sake, how many times ya need me to go over this?"

Casey stepped to the foot of the bed. "Mr. Slattery, we're not FBI. Our visit is unofficial. Mr. Allen, here, wants to ask you a few questions."

Slattery squeezed his eyes, his flat nose flattened even more. He pushed out another breath of air between his clenched teeth. "Well then, who the hell are the two of ya?"

"I'm Detective Franks. Mr. Allen is the man who played host to you...two weeks ago for a couple of days...in the basement of his home."

Slattery's eyes continued to stare at the ceiling. Allen was certain he was digesting the information, trying to decide how to react. He looked ten years older, worn and bloodless.

"I don't know what ya talkin' about."

Casey looked at Allen and nodded her head toward the Irishman. She stepped back against the wall and took a seat.

Allen moved in closer. "Oh, I think you do."

"Hump off, sham. I don't know ya from a pot of piss."

Allen felt a twinge of anger. He folded his arms, waiting to continue. "The last time we saw each other...in a cubicle not much smaller than this hospital room. Remember? We did a lot of talking."

"Ya way off the mark, fella. Ya have the wrong person."

"We talked about Ireland...about Ireland's history...about how the IRA's battles with the English cost my wife her life...in that London railway station bombing...ten years ago."

Slattery rolled his head away from Allen, putting pressure on his bandaged ear. The pain caused him to retreat from that position. Instead, he shut his eyes, attempting to block out his annoying questioner.

"You put a bullet in my back."

The words echoed with impact. Slattery's eyes flashed open and closed. Allen might have missed it if he hadn't been scrutinizing the man's face.

Slattery looked up. "Said ya wanted to ask some questions. Ask them, for God's sake. Then maybe you'll be leaving me alone."

Allen shot a look over at Casey, who had tilted forward in the chair, her elbows on her knees. Her face was unreadable, but he knew she was taking it all in. His mind raced, thinking of a way to pose the questions to Slattery without provoking dishonest answers.

"Did anything we spoke of reach you...get you thinking?"

"Feck, no," Slattery responded.

Allen looked down at him. He remembered the photo in the *New York Times* article. The terrorist's arrogant expression was gone.

"Okay, then. How is it you didn't kill me?"

The question hung in the air for some time before he heard Slattery mumble, "I have a wife."

Allen turned to Casey. "Okay. Let's go."

END

ACKNOWLEDGMENTS

Early in my advertising career, I showed the start of my first short story to the agency's proofreader who was also a published writer. She handed it back to me the next day, saying, "Keep writing, kid." So I did. Thanks, Anna Santoro, wherever you are.

I also owe a big thanks to the following people:

Ellen Feldman, novelist and my first workshop leader at Marymount College, for providing the encouragement to complete my first group of short stories.

James Robison, novelist, short story writer and professor of English for his incredible inspiration and encouragement, as well as his expert critiquing and initial editing of this novel.

Don Wilson, Linda Bilodeau, and Pina Olson, members of my critique group, who could always be counted on for invaluable feedback and support while writing this novel.

Frank Shields, retired NYPD Homicide Detective Sergeant, for his vetting of my police jargon and procedures, making me sound like I knew what I was doing.

Richard Vincent, nephew and Plantation, Florida PD Sergeant, for setting me technically straight with the novel's opening scenes.

Michael O'Donoghue, for being my authority on everything Irish—from Irish history to Irish accents to Irish swear words.

Donald Shelton, for his critical attention as proofreader of the first draft.

Carole Greene, whose deft editorial touch, patience and sharp eye, made countless improvements in shaping this novel.

Jeff Schlesinger, publisher, for his acceptance, patience and continuing support throughout the publishing process.

CPSIA information can be obtained at www.ICGtesting.com
Printed in the USA
LVOW08s0119221213

366372LV00002B/574/P